*The A*

*V*

Fifty Years ... Asimov

# THE ASIMOV CHRONICLES
# Volume Two

Edited by
Martin H. Greenberg

CENTURY
A LEGEND BOOK
LONDON SYDNEY AUCKLAND JOHANNESBURG

First published in Great Britain in 1991 by
Legend, an imprint of Random Century Group
20 Vauxhall Bridge Rd,
London SW1V 2SA

Century Hutchinson South Africa (Pty) Ltd
PO Box 337, Bergvlei 2012
South Africa

Random Century Australia Pty Ltd
20 Alfred St, Milsons Point, Sydney, NSW 0261
Australia

Random Century New Zealand Ltd
PO Box 40–086, Glenfield, Auckland 10
New Zealand

British Library Cataloguing in Publication Data
Asimov, Isaac
The Asimov chronicles: Vol 2. – (Legend books)
I. Title II. Series
813[F]

ISBN 0–7126–4970–8

Printed and bound in Great Britain by
Mackays of Chatham PLC, Chatham, Kent

*Table of Contents*

*Acknowledgements*

The Publishers would like to express their gratitude to the following people. Thank you: Dawn Austin, Kathy Jo Camacho, Stan and Phyllis Mikol, Wayne Sommers, Dr Stan Gurnick PhD, Tony Hodes, Bertha Curl, Kurt Scharrer, Gary Fronk, Linda Solar, Ken Morris, the people of the All American Print Center, Dick Spelman, Maureen Austin, Luis Trevino, Raymond, Teresa and Mark Stadalsky, Tom Pas, Ken and Lynda Fotos, and Ann Cameron Williams.

And, of course, special thanks go to: Martin H. Greenberg, Isaac Asimov, Ron Lindahn and Val Lakey Lindahn.

# Author! Author!

It occurred to Graham Dorn, and not for the first time, either, that there was one serious disadvantage in swearing you'll go through fire and water for a girl, however beloved. Sometimes she takes you at your miserable word.

This is one way of saying that he had been waylaid, shanghaied and dragooned by his fiancée into speaking at her maiden aunt's Literary Society. Don't laugh! It's not funny from the speaker's rostrum. Some of the faces you have to look at!

To race through the details, Graham Dorn had been jerked onto a platform and forced upright. He had read a speech on "The Place of the Mystery Novel in American Literature" in an appalled tone. Not even the fact that his own eternally precious June had written it (part of the bribe to get him to speak in the first place) could mask the fact that it was essentially tripe.

And then when he was weltering, figuratively speaking, in his own mental gore, the harpies closed in, for lo, it was time for the informal discussion and assorted feminine gush.

—Oh, Mr. Dorn, do you work from inspiration? I mean, do you just sit down and then an idea strikes you—all at once? And you must sit up all night and drink black coffee to keep you awake till you get it down?

—Oh, yes. Certainly. (His working hours were two to four in the afternoon every other day, and he drank milk.)

Oh, Mr. Dorn, you must do the most awful research to get all those bizarre murders. About how much must you do before you can write a story?

—About six months, usually. (The only reference books he ever used were a six-volume encyclopedia and year-before-last's World Almanac.)

—Oh, Mr. Dorn, did you make up your Reginald de Meister from a real character? You must have. He's oh, so convincing in his every detail.

—He's modeled after a very dear boyhood chum of mine. (Dorn had never known *anyone* like de Meister. He lived in continual fear of meeting someone like him. He had even a cunningly fashioned ring containing a subtle Oriental poison for use just in case he did. So much for de Meister.)

Somewhat past the knot of women, June Billings sat in her seat and smiled with sickening and proprietary pride.

Graham passed a finger over his throat and went through the pantomime of choking to death as unobtrusively as possible. June smiled, nodded, threw him a delicate kiss, and did nothing.

Graham decided to pass a stern, lonely, woman-less life and to have nothing but villainnesses in his stories forever after.

He was answering in monosyllables, alternating yesses and noes. Yes, he did take cocaine on occasion. He found it helped the creative urge. No, he didn't think he could allow Hollywood to take over de Meister. He thought movies weren't true expressions of real Art. Besides, they were just a passing fad. Yes, he would read Miss Crum's manuscripts if she brought them. Only too glad to. Reading amateur manuscripts was such fun, and editors are really such brutes.

And then refreshments were announced, and there was a sudden vacuum. It took a split-second for Graham's head to clear. The mass of femininity had coalesced into a single specimen. She was four feet ten and about eighty-five pounds in weight. Graham was six-two and two hundred ten worth of brawn. He could probably have handled her without difficulty, especially since both her arms were occupied with a pachyderm of a purse. Still, he felt a little delicate, to say nothing of queasy, about knocking her down. It didn't seem quite the thing to do.

She was advancing, with admiration and fervor disgustingly clear in her eyes, and Graham felt the wall behind him. There was no doorway within armreach on either side.

"Oh, Mr. de Meister—do, do please let me call you Mr. de Meister. Your creation is so real to me, that I can't think of you as simply Graham Dorn. You don't mind, do you?"

"No, no, of course not," gargled Graham, as well as he could through thirty-two teeth simultaneously set on edge. "I often think of myself as Reginald in my more frivolous moments."

"Thank you. You can have no idea, *dear* Mr. de Meister, how I have looked *forward* to meeting you. I have read *all* your works, and I think they are wonderful."

"I'm glad you think so." He went automatically into the modesty routine. "Really nothing, you know. Ha, ha, ha! Like to please the readers, but lots of room for improvement. Ha, ha, ha!"

"But you really are, you know." This was said with intense earnestness. "I mean good, *really* good. I think it is wonderful to be an author like you. It must be almost like being God."

Graham stared blankly. "Not to editors, sister."

Sister didn't get the whisper. She continued, "To be able to create living characters out of nothing; to unfold souls to all the world; to put thoughts into words; to build pictures and create worlds. I have often thought that an author was the most gloriously gifted person in creation. Better as inspired author starving in a garret than a king upon his throne. Don't you think so?"

"Definitely," lied Graham.

"What are the crass material goods of the world to the wonders of weaving emotions and deeds into a little world of its own?"

"What, indeed?"

"And posterity, think of posterity!"

"Yes, yes. I often do."

She seized his hand. "There's only one little request. You might," she blushed faintly, "you might give poor Reginald—if you will allow me to call him that just once—a chance to marry Letitia Reynolds. You make her just a little too cruel to him. I'm sure I weep over it for hours together sometimes. But then he is too, too real to me."

And from somewhere, a lacy frill of handkerchief made its appearance, and went to her eyes. She removed it, smiled bravely, and scurried away. Graham Dorn inhaled, closed his eyes, and gently collapsed into June's arms.

His eyes opened with a jerk. "You may consider," he said severely, "our engagement frazzled to the breaking point. Only my consideration for your poor, aged parents prevents your being known henceforward as the ex-fiancée of Graham Dorn."

"Darling, you are so noble." She massaged his sleeve with her cheek. "Come, I'll take you home and bathe your poor wounds."

"All right, but you'll have to carry me. Has your precious, loveable aunt got an axe?"

"But why?"

"For one thing, she had the gall to introduce me as the brain-father, God help me, of the famous Reginald de Meister."

"And aren't you?"

"Let's get out of this creep-joint. And get this. I'm no relative by brain or otherwise, of that character. I disown him. I cast him into the darkness. I spit upon him. I declare him an illegitimate son, a foul degenerate, and the offspring of a hound, and I'll be damned if he ever pokes his lousy patrician nose into my typewriter again."

They were in the taxi, and June straightened his tie. "All right, Sonny, let's see the letter."

"What letter?"

She held out her hand. "The one from the publishers."

Graham snarled and flipped it out of his jacket pocket. "I've thought of inviting myself to his house for tea, the damned flintheart. He's got a rendezvous with a pinch of strychnine."

"You may rave later. What does he say? Hmm—uh-huh—'doesn't quite come up to what is expected—feel that de Meister isn't in his usual form—a little revision perhaps towards—feel sure the novel can be adjusted—are returning under separate cover—' "

She tossed it aside. "I told you you shouldn't have killed off Sancha Rodriguez. She was what you needed. You're getting skimpy on the love interest."

"*You* write it! I'm through with de Meister. It's getting so clubwomen call me Mr. de Meister, and my picture is printed in newspapers with the caption Mr. de Meister. I have no individuality. No one ever heard of Graham Dorn. I'm always: Dorn, Dorn, you know, the guy who writes the de Meister stuff, *you* know."

June squealed, "Silly! You're jealous of your own detective."

"I am not jealous of my own character. Listen! I hate detective stories. I never read them after I got into the two-syllable words. I wrote the first as a clever, trenchant, biting satire. It was to blast the entire false school of mystery writers. That's why I invented this de Meister. He was the detective to end all detectives. The Compleat Ass, by Graham Dorn.

"So the public, along with snakes, vipers, and ungrateful children takes this filth to its bosom. I wrote mystery after mystery trying to convert the public—"

Graham Dorn drooped a little at the futility of it all.

"Oh, well." He smiled wanly, and the great soul rose above adversity. "Don't you see? I've got to write other things. I can't waste my life. But who's going to read a serious novel by Graham Dorn, now that I'm so thoroughly identified with de Meister?"

"You can use a pseudonym."

"I will not use a pseudonym. I'm proud of my name."

"But you can't drop de Meister. Be sensible, dear."

"A normal fiancée," Graham said bitterly, "would want her future husband to write something really worthwhile and become a great name in literature."

"Well, I do want you to, Graham. But just a little de Meister once in a while to pay the bills that accumulate."

"Ha!" Graham knocked his hat over his eyes to hide the sufferings of a strong spirit in agony. "Now you say that I can't reach prominence unles I prostitute my art to that unmentionable. Here's your place. Get out. I'm going home and write a good scorching letter on asbestos to our senile Mr. MacDunlap."

"Do exactly as you want to, cookie," soothed June. "And tomorrow when you feel better, you'll come and cry on my shoulder, and we'll plan a revision of *Death on the Third Deck* together, shall we?"

"The engagement," said Graham, loftily, "is broken."

"Yes, dear. I'll be home tomorrow at eight."

"That is of no possible interest to me. Good-bye!"

* * *

Publishers and editors are untouchables, of course. Theirs is a heritage of the outstretched hand and the well-toothed smile; the nod of the head and the slap of the back.

But perhaps somewhere, in the privacy of the holes to which authors scurry when the night falls, a private revenge is taken. There, phrases may be uttered where no one can overhear, and letters may be written that need not be mailed, and perhaps a picture of an editor, smiling pensively, is enshrined above the typewriter to act the part of bullseye in an occasional game of darts.

Such a picture of MacDunlap, so used, enlightened Graham Dorn's room. And Graham Dorn himself, in his usual writing costume (streetclothes and typewriter), scowled at the fifth sheet of paper in his typewriter. The other four were draped over the edge of the wastebasket, condemned for their milk-and-watery mildness.

He began:

"Dear Sir—" and added slowly and viciously, "or Madam, as the case may be."

He typed furiously as the inspiration caught him, disregarding the faint wisp of smoke curling upward from the overheated keys:

"You say you don't think much of de Meister in this story. Well, I don't think much of de Meister, period. You can handcuff your slimy carcass to his and jump off the Brooklyn Bridge. And I hope they drain the East River just before you jump.

"From now on, my works will be aimed higher than your scurvy press. And the day will come when I can look back on this period of my career with the loathing that is its just—"

Someone had been tapping Graham on the shoulder during the last paragraph. Graham twitched it angrily and ineffectively at intervals.

Now he stopped, turned around, and addressed the stranger in his room courteously: "Who the devilish damnation are you? And you can leave without bothering to answer. I won't think you rude."

The newcomer smiled graciously. His nod wafted the delicate aroma of some unobtrusive hair-oil toward Graham. His lean, hard-bitten jaw stood out keenly, and he said in a well-modulated voice:

"De Meister is the name. Reginald de Meister."

Graham rocked to his mental foundations and heard them creak.

"Glub," he said.

"Pardon?"

Graham recovered. "I said, 'glub,' a little code word meaning *which* de Meister."

"*The* de Meister," explained de Meister, kindly.

"My character? My detective?"

De Meister helped himself to a seat, and his finely-chiseled features assumed that air of well-bred boredom so admired in the best circles. He lit a Turkish cigarette, which Graham at once recognized as his detective's favorite brand, tapping it slowly and carefully against the back of his hand first, a mannerism equally characteristic.

"Really, old man," said de Meister. "This is really excruciatin'ly funny. I suppose I am your character, y'know, but let's not work on that basis. It would be so devastatin'ly awkward."

"Glub," said Graham again, by way of rejoinder.

His mind was feverishly setting up alternatives. He didn't drink, more, at the moment, was the pity, so he wasn't drunk. He had a chrome-steel digestion and he wasn't overheated, so it wasn't a hallucination. He never dreamed, and his imagination—as befitted a paying commodity—was under strict control. And since, like all authors, he was widely considered more than half a screwball, insanity was out of the question.

Which left de Meister simply an impossibility, and Graham felt relieved. It's a very poor author indeed who hasn't learned the fine art of ignoring impossibilities in writing a book.

He said smoothly, "I have here a volume of my latest work. Do you mind naming your page and crawling back into it. I'm a busy man and God knows I have enough of you in the tripe I write."

"But I'm here on business, old chap. I've got to come to a friendly arrangement with you first. Things are deucedly uncomfortable as they are."

"Look, do you know you're bothering me? I'm not in the habit of talking to mythical characters. As a general thing, I don't pal around with them. Besides which, it's time your mother told you that you really don't exist."

"My dear fellow, I always existed. Existence is such a subjective thing. What a mind thinks exists, *does* exist. I existed in your mind, for instance, ever since you first thought of me."

Graham shuddered. "But the question is, what are you doing *out* of my mind? Getting a little narrow for you? Want elbow room?"

"Not at all. Rather satisfact'ry mind in its way, but I achieved a more concrete existence only this afternoon, and so I seize the opportunity to engage you face to face in the aforementioned business conversation. You see, that thin, sentimental lady of your society—"

"What society?" questioned Graham hollowly. It was all awfully clear to him now.

"The one at which you made a speech—" de Meister shuddered in his turn—"on the detective novel. She believed in my existence, so naturally, I exist."

He finished his cigarette and flicked it out with a negligent twist of the wrist.

"The logic," declared Graham, "is inescapable. Now, what do you want and the answer is no."

"Do you realize, old man, that if you stop writing de Meister stories, my existence will become that dull, wraithlike one of all superannuated fictional detectives. I'd have to gibber through the gray mists of Limbo with Holmes, Lecocq, and Dupin."

"A very fascinating thought, I think. A very fitting fate."

Reginald de Meister's eyes turned icy, and Graham suddenly remembered the passage on page 123 of *The Case of the Broken Ashtray*:

*His eyes, hitherto lazy and unattentive, hardened into twin pools of blue ice and transfixed the butler, who staggered back, a stifled cry on his lips.*

Evidently, de Meister lost none of his characteristics out of the novels he adorned.

Graham staggered back, a stifled cry on his lips.

De Meister said menacingly, "It would be better for you if the de Meister mysteries continue. Do you understand?"

Graham recovered and summoned a feeble indignation. "Now, wait a while. You're getting out of hand. Remember: in a way, I'm your father. That's right. Your mental father. You can't hand me ultimatums or make threats. It isn't filial. It's lacking in the proper respect and love."

"And another thing," said de Meister, unmoved. "We've got to straighten out this business of Letitia Reynolds. It's gettin' deucedly borin', y'know."

"Now you're getting silly. My love scenes have been widely heralded as miracles of tenderness and sentiment not found in one murder mystery out of a thousand. —Wait, I'll get you a few reviews. I don't mind your attempts to dictate my actions so much, but I'm damned if you'll criticize my writing."

"Forget the reviews. Tenderness and all that rot is what I don't want. I've been driftin' after the fair lady for five volumes now, and behavin' the most insufferable ass. This has got to stop."

"In what way?"

"I've got to marry her in your present story. Either that, or make her a good, respectable mistress. And you'll have to stop making me so damned Victorian and gentlemanly towards ladies. I'm only human, old man."

"Impossible!" said Graham, "and that includes your last remark."

De Meister grew severe. "Really, old chap, for an author, you display the most appallin' lack of concern for the well-bein' of a character who has supported you for a good many years."

Graham choked eloquently. "Supported me? In other words, you think I couldn't sell real novels, hey? Well, I'll show you. I wouldn't write another de Meister story for a million dollars. Not even for a fifty percent royalty and all television rights. How's that?"

De Meister frowned and uttered those words that had been the sound of doom to so many criminals: "We shall see, but you are not yet done with me."

With firmly jutting jaw, he vanished.

Graham's twisted face straightened out, and slowly—very slowly —he brought his hands up to his cranium and felt carefully.

For the first time in a long and reasonably ribald mental life, he felt that his enemies were right and that a good dry cleaning would not hurt his mind at all.

The *things* that existed in it!

* * *

Graham Dorn shoved the doorbell with his elbow a second time. He distinctly remembered her saying she would be home at eight.

The peep-hole shoved open. "Hello!"

"Hello!"

Silence!

Graham said plaintively, "It's raining outside. Can't I come in to dry?"

"I don't know. Are we engaged, Mr. Dorn?"

"If I'm not," was the stiff reply, "then I've been turning down the frenzied advances of a hundred passion-stricken girls—beautiful ones, all of them—for no apparent reason."

"Yesterday, you said—"

"Ah, but who listens to what I say? I'm just quaint that way. Look, I brought you posies." He flourished roses before the peep-hole.

June opened the door. "Roses! How plebeian. Come in, cookie, and sully the sofa. Whoa, whoa, before you move a step, what have you got under the other arm? Not the manuscript of *Death on the Third Deck?*"

"Correct. Not that excrescence of a manuscript. This is something different."

June's tone chilled. "That isn't your precious novel, is it?"

Graham flung his head up, "How did you know about it?"

"You slobbered the plot all over me at MacDunlap's silver anniversary party."

"I did not. I couldn't unless I were drunk."

"Oh, but you were. Stinking is the term. And on two cocktails too."

"Well, if I was drunk, I couldn't have told you the right plot."

"Is the setting a coal-mine district?"

"—Uh—yes."

"And are the people concerned real, earthy, unartificial, down-to-earth characters, speaking and thinking just like you and me? Is it a story of basic economic forces? Are the human characters lifted up and thrown down and whirled around, all at the mercy of the coal mine and mechanized industry of today?"

"—Uh—yes."

She nodded her head retrospectively. "I remember distinctly. First, you got drunk and were sick. Then you got better, and told me the first few chapters. Then I got sick."

She approached the glowering author. "Graham." She leant her golden head upon his shoulder and cooed softly. "Why don't you continue with the de Meister stories? You get such pretty checks out of them."

Graham writhed out of her grasp. "You are a mercenary wretch, incapable of understanding an author's soul. You may consider our engagement broken."

He sat down hard on the sofa, and folded his arms. "Unless you will consent to read the script of my novel and give me the usual story analysis."

"May I give you my analysis of *Death on the Third Deck* first?"

"No."

"Good! In the first place, your love interest is becoming sickening."

"It is not." Graham pointed his finger indignantly. "It breathes a sweet and sentimental fragrance, as of an older day. I've got the review here that says it." He fumbled in his wallet.

"Oh, bullfeathers. Are you going to start quoting that guy in the Pillsboro (Okla.) Clarion? He's probably your second cousin. You know that your last two novels were completely below par in royalties. And *Third Deck* isn't even being sold."

"So much the better—Ow!" He rubbed his head violently. "What did you do that for?"

"Because the only place I could hit as hard as I wanted to, without disabling you, was your head. Listen! The public is tired of your corny Letitia Reynolds. Why don't you let her soak her 'gleaming golden crown of hair' in kerosene and get familiar with a match?"

"But June, that character is drawn from life. From you!"

"Graham Dorn! I am not here to listen to insults. The mystery market today is swinging towards action and hot, honest love and you're still in the sweet, sentimental stickiness of five years ago."

"But that's Reginald de Meister's character."

"Well, change his character. Listen! You introduce Sancha Rodriguez. That's fine. I approve of her. She's Mexican, flaming, passionate, sultry, and in love with him. So what do you do? First he behaves the impeccable gentleman, and then you kill her off in the middle of the story."

"Hmm, I see— You really think it would improve things to have de Meister forget himself. A kiss or so—"

June clenched her lovely teeth and her lovely fists. "Oh, darling, how glad I am love is blind! If it ever peeked one tiny little bit, I couldn't stand it. Look, you squirrel's blue plate special, you're going to have de Meister and Rodriguez fall in love. They're going to have an affair through the entire book and you can put your horrible Letitia into a nunnery. She'll probably be happier there from the way you make her sound."

"That's all *you* know about it, my sweet. It so happens that Reginald de Meister is in love with Letitia Reynolds and wants *her*, not this Rodriguez person."

"And what makes you think that?"

"He told me so."

"Who told you so?"

"Reginald de Meister."

"*My* Reginald de Meister."

"What do you mean, your Reginald de Meister?"

"My *character*, Reginald de Meister."

June got up, indulged in some deep-breathing and then said in a very calm voice, "Let's start all over."

She disappeared for a moment and returned with an aspirin. "Your Reginald de Meister, from your books, told you, in person, he was in love with Letitia Reynolds?"

"That's right."

June swallowed the aspirin.

"Well, I'll explain, June, the way he explained it to me. All characters really exist—at least, in the minds of the authors. But when people really begin to believe in them, they begin to exist in reality, because what people believe in, is, so far as they're concerned, and what is existence anyway?"

June's lip trembled. "Oh, Gramie, please don't. Mother will never let me marry you if they put you in an asylum."

"Don't call me Gramie, June, for God's sake. I tell you he was there, trying to tell me what to write and how to write it. He was almost as bad as you. Aw, come on, Baby, don't cry."

"I can't help it. I always thought you were crazy, but I never thought you were *crazy!*"

"All right, what's the difference? Let's not talk about it, any more. I'm never going to write another mystery novel. After all—" (he indulged in a bit of indignation)—"when it gets so that my own character—my *own* character—tries to tell me what to do, it's going too far."

June looked over her handkerchief. "How do you know it was really de Meister?"

"Oh, golly. As soon as he tapped his Turkish cigarette on the back of his hand and started dropping g's like snowflakes in a blizzard, I knew the worst had come."

The telephone rang. Jane leaped up. "Don't answer, Graham. It's probably from the asylum. I'll tell them you're not here. Hello. Hello. Oh, Mr. MacDunlap." She heaved a sigh of relief, then covered the mouthpiece and whispered hoarsely, "It might be a trap."

"Hello, Mr. MacDunlap! . . . No, he's not here. . . . Yes, I think I can get in touch with him. . . . At Martin's tomorrow, noon. . . . I'll tell him . . . With who? . . . With who???" She hung up suddenly.

"Graham, you're to lunch with MacDunlap tomorrow."

"At his expense! Only at his expense!"

Her great blue eyes got greater and bluer. "And Reginald de Meister is to dine with you."

"What Reginald de Meister?"

"Your Reginald de Meister."

"*My* Reg—"

"Oh, Gramie, *don't.*" Her eyes misted, "Don't you see, Gramie, now they'll put us both in an insane asylum—and Mr. MacDunlap, too. And they'll probably put us all in the same padded cell. Oh, Gramie, three is such a dreadful crowd."

And her face crumpled into tears.

* * *

Grew S. MacDunlap (that the S. stands for "Some" is a vile untruth spread by his enemies) was alone at the table when Graham Dorn entered. Out of this fact, Graham extracted a few fleeting drops of pleasure.

It was not so much, you understand, the presence of MacDunlap that did it, as the absence of de Meister.

MacDunlap looked at him over his spectacles and swallowed a liver pill, his favorite sweetmeat.

"Aha. You're here. What is this corny joke you're putting over on me? You had no right to mix me up with a person like de Meister without warning me he was real. I might have taken precautions. I could have hired a bodyguard. I could have bought a revolver."

"He's *not* real. God damn it! Half of him was *your* idea."

"That," returned MacDunlap with heat, "is libel. And what do you mean, he's not real? When he introduced himself, I took three liver pills at once and he didn't disappear. Do you know what three pills are? Three pills, the kind I've got (the doctor should only drop dead), could make an elephant disappear—if he weren't real. I *know.*"

Graham said wearily, "Just the same, he exists only in my mind."

"In your mind, I know he exists. Your mind should be investigated by the Pure Food and Drugs Act."

The several polite rejoinders that occurred simultaneously to Graham were dismissed almost immediately as containing too great a proportion of pithy Anglo-Saxon expletives. After all—ha, ha—a publisher is a publisher however Anglo-Saxony he may be.

Graham said, "The question arises, then, how we're to get rid of de Meister."

"Get rid of de Meister?" MacDunlap jerked the glasses off his nose in his sudden start, and caught them in one hand. His voice thickened with emotion. "Who wants to get rid of him?"

"Do you want him around?"

"God forbid," MacDunlap said between shudders. "Next to him, my brother-in-law is an angel."

"He has no business outside my books."

"For my part, he has no business inside them. Since I started reading your manuscripts, my doctor added kidney pills and cough syrups to my medicines." He looked at his watch, and took a kidney pill. "My worst enemy should be a book publisher only once a year."

"Then why," asked Graham patiently, "Don't you want to get rid of de Meister?"

"Because he is publicity."

Graham stared blankly.

"Look! What other writer has a real detective? All the others are fictional. Everyone knows that. But yours—*yours* is real. We can let him solve cases and have big newspaper writeups. He'll make the Police Department look silly. He'll make—"

"That," interrupted Graham, categorically, "is by all odds the most obscene proposal I have ever had my ears manured with."

"It will make money."

"Money isn't everything."

"Name one thing it isn't . . . Shh!" He kicked a near-fracture into Graham's left ankle and rose to his feet with a convulsive smile, "Mr. de Meister!"

"Sorry, old dear," came a lethargic voice. "Couldn't quite make it, you know. Loads of engagements. Must have been most borin' for you."

Graham Dorn's ears quivered spasmodically. He looked over his shoulder and reeled backward as far as a person could reel while in a sitting position. Reginald de Meister had sprouted a monocle since his last visitation, and his monocular glance was calculated to freeze blood.

De Meister's greeting was casual. "My dear Watson! So glad to meet you. Overjoyed deucedly."

"Why don't you go to hell?" Graham asked curiously.

"My dear fellow. Oh, my dear fellow."

MacDunlap cackled, "That's what I like. Jokes! Fun! Makes everything pleasant to start with. Now shall we get down to business?"

"Certainly. The dinner is on the way, I trust? Then I'll just order a bottle of wine. The usual, Henry." The waiter ceased hovering, flew away, and skimmed back with a bottle that opened and gurgled into a glass.

De Meister sipped delicately, "So nice of you, old chap, to make me a habitué of this place in your stories. It holds true even now, and it is most convenient. The waiters all know me. Mr. MacDunlap, I take it you have convinced Mr. Dorn of the necessity of continuing the de Meister stories."

"Yes," said MacDunlap.

"No," said Graham.

"Don't mind him," said MacDunlap. "He's temperamental. You know these authors."

"Don't mind him," said Graham. "He's microcephalic. You know these publishers."

"Look, old chappie. I take it MacDunlap hasn't pointed out to you the unpleasanter side of acting stubborn."

"For instance what, old stinkie?" asked Graham, courteously.

"Well, have you ever been haunted?"

"Like coming behind me and saying, Boo!"

"My dear fellow, I say. I'm much more subtle than that. I can really haunt one in modern, up-to-date methods. For instance, have you ever had your individuality submerged?"

He snickered.

There was something familiar about that snicker. Graham suddenly remembered. It was on page 103 of *Murder Rides the Range:*

*His lazy eyelids flicked down and up. He laughed lightly and melodiously, and though he said not a word, Hank Marslowe cowered. There was hidden menace and hidden power in that light laugh, and somehow the burly rancher did not dare reach for his guns.*

To Graham it still sounded like a nasty snicker, but he cowered, and did not dare reach for his guns.

MacDunlap plunged through the hole the momentary silence had created.

"You see, Graham. Why play around with ghosts? Ghosts aren't reasonable things. They're not *human!* If it's more royalties, you want—"

Graham fired up. "Will you refrain from speaking of money? From now on, I write only great novels of tearing human emotions."

MacDunlap's flushed face changed suddenly.

"No," he said.

"In fact, to change the subject just a moment—" and Graham's tone became surpassingly sweet, as the words got all sticky with maple syrup—"I have a manuscript here for you to look at."

He grasped the perspiring MacDunlap by the lapel firmly. "It is a novel that is the work of five years. A novel that will grip you with its intensity. A novel that will shake you to the core of your being. A novel that will open a new world. A novel that will—"

"No," said MacDunlap.

"A novel that will blast the falseness of this world. A novel that pierces to the truth. A novel—"

MacDunlap, being able to stretch his hand no higher, took the manuscript.

"No," he said.

"Why the bloody hell don't you read it?" inquired Graham.

"Now?"

"Well, start it."

"Look, supposing I read it tomorrow, or even the next day. I have to take my cough syrup now."

"You haven't coughed once since I got here."

"I'll let you know immediately—"

"This," said Graham, "is the first page. Why don't you begin it? It will grip you instantly."

MacDunlap read two paragraphs and said, "Is this laid in a coal-mining town?"

"Yes."

"Then I can't read it. I'm allergic to coal dust."

"But it's not real coal dust. MacIdiot."

"That," pointed out MacDunlap, "is what you said about de Meister."

Reginald de Meister tapped a cigarette carefully on the back of his hand in a subtle manner which Graham immediately recog-nized as betokening a sudden decision.

"That is all devastatin'ly borin', you know. Not quite gettin' to the point, you might say. Go ahead, MacDunlap, this is no time for half measures."

MacDunlap girded his spiritual loins and said, "All right Mister Dorn, with you it's no use being nice. Instead of de Meister, I'm getting coal dust. Instead of the best publicity in fifty years, I'm getting social significance. All right, Mister Smartaleck Dorn, if in one week you don't come to terms with me, *good* terms, you will be blacklisted in every reputable publishing firm in the United States and foreign parts." He shook his finger and added in a shout, "Including Scandinavian."

Graham Dorn laughed lightly, "Pish," he said, "tush. I happen to be an officer of the Author's Union, and if you try to push me around I'll have *you* blacklisted. How do you like that?"

"I like it fine. Because supposing I can prove you're a plagiarist."

"Me," gasped Graham, recovering narrowly from merry suffocation. "Me, the most original writer of the decade."

"Is that so? And maybe you don't remember that in each case you write up, you casually mention de Meister's notebooks on previous cases."

"So what?"

"So he has them. Reginald, my boy, show Mister Dorn your notebook of your last case.—You see that. That's *Mystery of the Milestones* and it has, in detail, every incident in your book—and dated the year before the book was published. Very authentic."

"Again so what?"

"Have you maybe got the right to copy his notebook and call it an original murder mystery?"

"Why, you case of mental pliomyelitis, that notebook is my invention."

"Who says so? It's in de Meister's handwriting, as any expert can prove. And maybe you have a piece of paper, some little contract or agreement, you know, that gives you the right to use his notebooks?"

"How can I have an agreement with a mythical personage?"

"What mythical personage?"

"You and I know de Meister doesn't exist."

"Ah, but does the jury know? When I testify that I took three strong liver pills and he didn't disappear, what twelve men will say he doesn't exist?"

"This is blackmail."

"Certainly. I'll give you a week. Or in other words, seven days."

Graham Dorn turned desperately to de Meister. "You're in on this, too. In my books I give you the keenest sense of honor. Is this honorable?"

De Meister shrugged. "My dear fellow. All this—and haunting, too."

Graham rose.

"Where are you going?"

"Home to write you a letter." Graham's brows beetled defiantly. "And this time I'll mail it. I'm not giving in. I'll fight to the last ditch. And, de Meister, you let loose with one single little haunt and I'll rip your head out of its socket and spurt the blood all over MacDunlap's new suit."

He stalked out, and as he disappeared through the door, de Meister disappeared through nothing at all.

MacDunlap let out a soft yelp and then took a liver pill, a kidney pill, and a tablespoon of cough syrup in rapid succession.

* * *

Graham Dorn sat in June's front parlor, and having long since consumed his fingernails, was starting on the first knuckles.

June, at the moment, was not present, and this, Graham felt, was just as well. A dear girl; in fact, a dear, sweet girl. But his mind was not on her.

It was concerned instead with a miasmic series of flashbacks over the preceding six days:

—Say, Graham, I met your side-kick at the club yesterday. You know, de Meister. Got an awful shock. I always had the idea he was a sort of Sherlock Holmes that didn't exist. That's one on me, boy. Didn't know— Hey, where are you going?

—Hey, Dorn, I hear your boss de Meister is back in town. Ought to have material for more stories soon. You're lucky you've got someone to grind out your plots readymade— Huh? Well, good-bye."

—Why, Graham, darling, wherever were you last night? Ann's affair didn't get *anywhere* without you; or at least, it wouldn't have, if it hadn't been for Reggie de Meister. He asked after you; but then, I guess he felt lost without his Watson. It must feel wonderful to Watson for such— *Mister* Dorn! And the same to you, sir!

—You put one over on me. I thought you made up those wild things. Well, truth is stranger than fiction, ha, ha!

—Police officials deny that the famous amateur criminologist Reginald de Meister has interested himself in this case. Mr. de Meister himself could not be reached by our reporters for comment. Mr. de Meister is best known to the public for his brilliant solutions to over a dozen crimes, as chronicled in fiction form by his so-called "Watson," Mr. Grayle Doone.

Graham quivered and his arms trembled in an awful desire for blood. De Meister was haunting him—but good. He was losing his individuality, exactly as had been threatened.

It gradually dawned upon Graham that the monotonous ringing noise he heard was not in his head, but, on the contrary, from the front door.

Such seemed likewise the opinion of Miss June Billings, whose piercing call shot down the stairs and biffed Graham a sharp uppercut to the ear-drums.

"Hey, dope, see who's at the front door, before the vibration tears the house down. I'll be down in half an hour."

"Yes, dear!"

Graham shuffled his way to the front door and opened it.

"Ah, there. Greetin's," said de Meister, and brushed past.

Graham's dull eyes stared, and then fired high, as an animal snarl burst from his lips. He took up that gorilla posture, so comforting to red-blooded American males at moments like this, and circled the slightly-confused detective.

"My dear fellow, are you ill?"

"I," explained Graham, "an not ill, but you will soon be past all interest in that, for I am going to bathe my hands in your heart's reddest blood."

"But I say, you'll only have to wash them afterwards. It would be such an obvious clue, wouldn't it?"

"Enough of this gay banter. Have you any last words?"

"Not particularly."

"It's just as well. I'm not interested in your last words."

He thundered into action, bearing down upon the unfortunate de Meister like a bull elephant. De Meister faded to the left, shot out an arm and a foot, and Graham described a parabolic arc that ended in the total destruction of an end table, a vase of flowers, a fish-bowl, and a five-foot section of wall.

Graham blinked, and brushed away a curious goldfish from his left eyebrow.

"My dear fellow," murmured de Meister, "oh, my dear fellow."

Too late, Graham remembered that passage in *Pistol Parade:*

*De Meister's arms were whipcord lightning, as with sure, rapid thrusts, he rendered the two thugs helpless. Not by brute force, but by his expert knowledge of judo, he defeated them easily without hastening his breath. The thugs groaned in pain.*

Graham groaned in pain.

He lifted his right thigh an inch or so to let his femur slip back into place.

"Hadn't you better get up, old chap?"

"I will stay here," said Graham with dignity, "and contemplate the floor in profile view, until such time as it suits me or until such time as I find myself capable of moving a muscle. I don't care which. And now, before I proceed to take further measures with you, what the hell do you want?"

Reginald de Meister adjusted his monocle to a nicety. "You know, I suppose, that MacDunlap's ultimatum expires tomorrow?"

"And you and he with it, I trust."

"You will not reconsider."

"Ha!"

"Really," he Meister sighed, "this is borin' no end. You have made things comfortable for me in this world. After all, in your books you've made me well-known in all the clubs and better restaurants, the bosom friend, y'know, of the mayor and the commissioner of police, the owner of a Park Avenue penthouse and a magnificent art collection. And it all lingers over, old chap. Really quite affectin'."

"It is remarkable," mused Graham, "the intensity with which I am not listening and the distinctness with which I do not hear a word you say."

"Still," said de Meister, "there is no denyin' my book world suits me better. It is somehow more fascinatin', freer from dull logic, more apart from the necessities of the world. In short, I must go back, and to active participation. You have till tomorrow!"

Graham hummed a gay little tune with flat little notes.

"Is this a new threat, de Meister?"

"It is the old threat intensified. I'm going to rob you of every vestige of your personality. And eventually public opinion will force you to write as, to paraphrase you, de Meister's Compleat Stooge. Did you see the name the newspaper chappies pinned on you today, old man?"

"Yes, Mr. Filthy de Meister, and did you read a half-column item on page ten in the same paper. I'll read it *for* you: 'Noted Criminologist in 1-A. Will be inducted shortly draft board says."

For a moment, de Meister said and did nothing. And then one, after another, he did the following things: removed his monocle slowly, sat down heavily, rubbed his chin abstractedly, and lit a cigarette after long and careful tamping. Each of these Graham Dorn's trained authorial eye recognized as singly representing perturbation and distress on the part of his character.

And never, in any of his books, did Graham remember a time when de Meister had gone through all four consecutively.

Finally, de Meister spoke. "Why you had to bring up draft registrations in your last book, I really don't know. This urge to be topical; this fiendish desire to be up to the minute with the news is the curse of the mystery novel. A true mystery is timeless; should have no relation to current events; should—"

"There is one way," said Graham, "to escape induction—"

"You might at least have mentioned a deferred classification on some vital ground."

"There is one way," said Graham, "to escape induction—"

"Criminal negligence," said de Meister.

"Look! Go back to the books and you'll never be filled with lead."

"Write them and I'll do it."

"Think of the war."

"Think of your ego."

Two strong men stood face to face (or would have, if Graham weren't still horizontal) and neither flinched.

Impasse!

And the sweet, feminine voice of June Billings interrupted and snapped the tension:

"May I ask, Graham Dorn, what you are doing on the floor. It's been swept today and you're not complimenting me by attempting to improve the job."

"I am not sweeping the floor. If you looked carefully," replied Graham gently, "you would see that your own adored fiancé is lying here a mass of bruises and a hotbed of pains and aches."

"You've ruined my end table!"

"I've broken my leg."

"And my best lamp."

"And two ribs."

"And my fishbowl."

"And my Adam's apple."

"And you haven't introduced your friend."

"And my cervical verte—What friend?"

"This friend."

"Friend! Ha!" And a mist came over his eyes. She was so young, so fragile to come into contact with hard, brutal facts of life. "This," he muttered brokenly, "is Reginald de Meister."

De Meister at this point broke a cigarette sharply in two, a gesture pregnant with the deepest emotion.

June said slowly, "Why—why, you're different from what I had thought."

"How had you expected me to look?" asked de Meister, in soft, thrilling tones.

"I don't know. Differently than you do,—from the stories I heard."

"You remind me, somehow, Miss Billings, of Letitia Reynolds."

"I think so. Graham said he drew her from me."

"A very poor imitation, Miss Billings. Devastatin'ly poor."

They were six inches apart now, eyes fixed with a mutual glue, and Graham yelled sharply. He sprang upright as memory smote him a nasty smite on the forehead.

A passage from *Case of the Muddy Overshoe* occurred to him. Likewise one from *The Primrose Murders*. Also one from *The Tragedy of Hartley*

*Manor*, *Death of a Hunter*, *White Scorpion* and, to put it in a small nutshell, from every one of the others.

The passage read:

*There was a certain fascination about de Meister that appealed irresistibly to women*

And June Billings was—as it had often, in Graham's idler moments, occurred to him—a woman.

And fascination simply gooed out of her ears and coated the floor six inches deep.

"Get out of this room, June," he ordered.

"I will not."

"There is something I must discuss with Mr. de Meister, man to man. I demand that you leave this room."

"Please go, Miss Billings," said de Meister.

June hesitated, and in a very small voice said, "Very well."

"Hold on," shouted Graham. "Don't let him order you about. I demand that you stay."

She closed the door very gently behind her.

The two men faced each other. There was that in either pair of eyes that indicated a strong man brought to bay. There was stubborn, undying antagonism; no quarter; no compromise. It was exactly the sort of situation Graham Dorn always presented his readers with, when two strong men fought for one hand, one heart, one girl.

The two said simultaneously, "Let's make a deal!"

Graham said, "You have convinced me, Reggie. Our public needs us. Tomorrow I shall begin another de Meister story. Let us shake hands and forget the past."

De Meister struggled with his emotion. He laid his hand on Graham's lapel. "My dear fellow, it is I who have been convinced by your logic. I can't allow you to sacrifice yourself for me. There are great things in you that must be brought out. Write your coal-mining novels. They count, not I."

"I couldn't, old chap. Not after all you've done for me, and all you've meant to me. Tomorrow we start anew."

"Graham, my—my spiritual father, I couldn't allow it. Do you think I have no feelings, *filial* feelings—in a spiritual sort of way."

"But the war, think of the war. Mangled limbs. Blood. All that."

"I must stay. My country needs me."

"But if I stop writing, eventually you will stop existing. I can't allow that."

"Oh, that!" De Meister laughed with a careless elegance. "Things have changed since. So many people believe in my existence now that my grip upon actual existence has become too firm to be broken. I don't have to worry about Limbo any more."

"Oh." Graham clenched his teeth and spoke in searing sibilants: "So that's you scheme, you snake. Do you suppose I don't see you're stuck on June?"

"Look here, old chap," said de Meister haughtily. "I can't permit you to speak slightingly of a true and honest love. I love June and she loves me—I know it. And if you're going to be stuffy and Victorian about it, you can swallow some nitro-glycerine and tap yourself with a hammer."

"I'll nitro-glycerine you! Because I'm going home tonight and beginning another de Meister story. You'll be part of it and you'll get back into it, and what do you think of that?"

"Nothing, because you can't write another de Meister story. I'm too real now, and you can't control me just like *that*. And what do you think of that?"

It took Graham Dorn a week to make up his mind what to think of that, and then his thoughts were completely and startingly unprintable.

In fact, it was impossible to write.

That is, startling ideas occurred to him for great novels, emotional dramas, epic poems, brilliant essays—but he couldn't write anything about Reginald de Meister.

The typewriter was simply fresh out of Capital R's.

Graham wept, cursed, tore his hair, and anointed his finger tips with liniment. He tried typewriter, pen, pencil, crayon, charcoal, and blood.

He could not write.

The doorbell rang, and Graham threw it open.

MacDunlap stumbled in, falling over the first drifts of torn paper directly into Graham's arms.

Graham let him drop. "Hah!" he said, with frozen dignity.

"My heart!" said MacDunlap, and fumbled for his liver pills.

"Don't die there," suggested Graham, courteously. "The management won't permit me to drop human flesh into the incinerator."

"Graham, my boy," MacDunlap said, emotionally, "no more ultimatums! No more threats! I come now to appeal to your finer feelings, Graham—" he went through a slight choking interlude—"I love you like a son. This skunk de Meister must disappear. You must write more de Meister stories for my sake. Graham—I will tell you something in private. My wife is in love with this detective. She tells me I am not romantic. I! Not romantic! Can you understand it?"

"I can," was the tragic response. "He fascinates all women."

"With that face? With that monocle?"

"It says so in all my books."

MacDunlay stiffened. "Ah ha. You again. Dope! If only you ever stopped long enough to let your mind know what your typewriter was saying."

"You insisted. Feminine trade." Graham didn't care any more. Women! He snickered bitterly. Nothing wrong with any of them that a block-buster wouldn't fix.

MacDunlap hemmed. "Well, feminine trade. Very necessary.—But Graham, what shall I do? It's not only my wife. She owns fifty shares in MacDunlap, Inc. in her own name. If she leaves me, I lost control. Think of it, Graham. The catastrophe to the publishing world."

"Grew, old chap," Graham sighed a sigh so deep, his toenails quivered sympathetically. "I might as well tell you. June, my fiancée, you know, loves this worm. And he loves her because she is the prototype of Letitia Reynolds."

"The what of Letitia?" ased MacDunlap, vaguely suspecting an insult.

"Never mind. My life is ruined." He smiled bravely and choked back the unmanly tears, after the first two had dripped off the end of his nose.

"My poor boy!" The two gripped hands convulsively.

"Caught in a vise by this foul monster," said Graham.

"Trapped like a German in Russia," said MacDunlap.

"Victim of an inhuman fiend," said Graham.

"Exactly," said MacDunlap. He wrung Graham's hand as if he were milking a cow. "You've got to write de Meister stories and get him back where, next to Hell, he most belongs. Right?"

"Right! But there's one little catch."

"What?"

"I can't write. He's so real now, I *can't* put him into a book."

MacDunlap caught the significance of the massed drifts of used paper on the floor. He held his head and groaned, "My corporation! My wife!"

"There's always the Army," said Graham.

MacDunlap looked up. "What about *Death on the Third Deck*, the novel I rejected three weeks ago?"

"That doesn't count. It's past history. It's already affected him."

"Without being published?"

"Sure. That's the story I mentioned his draft board in. The one that put him in 1-A."

"I could think of better places to put him."

"MacDunlap!" Graham Dorn jumped up, and grappled MacDunlap's lapel. "Maybe it can be revised."

MacDunlap coughed hackingly, and stiffled out a dim grunt.

"We can put anything we want into it."

MacDunlap choked a bit.

"We can fix things up."

MacDunlap turned blue in the face.

Graham shook the lapel and everything thereto attached. "Say something, won't you?"

MacDunlap wrenched away and took a tablespoon of cough syrup. He held his hand over his heart and patted it a bit. He shook his head and gestured with his eyebrows.

Graham shrugged. "Well, if you just want to be sullen, go ahead. I'll revise it without you."

He located the manuscript and tried his fingers gingerly on the typewriter. They went smoothly, with practically no creaking at the joints. He put on speed, more speed, and then went into his usual race, with the portable jouncing along merrily under the accustomed head of steam.

"It's working," he shouted. "I can't write new stories, but I can revise old, unpublished ones."

MacDunlap watched over his shoulder. He breathed only at odd moments.

* * *

"Faster," said MacDunlap, "faster!"

"Faster than thirty-five?" said Graham, sternly. "OPA* forbid! Five more minutes."

"Will he be there?"

"He's always there. He's been at her house every evening this week." He spat out the fine ivory dust into which he had ground the last inch of his incisors. "But God help you if your secretary falls down on the job."

* The Office of Price Administration was in charge of gasoline rationing at this period. Remember "A" stickers? D.R.B.

"My boy, on my secretary you can depend."

"She's got to read that revision by nine."

"If she doesn't drop dead."

"With my luck, she will. Will she believe it?"

"Every word. She's seen de Meister. She *knows* he exists."

Brakes screeched, and Graham's soul cringed in sympathy with every molecule of rubber frictioned off the tires.

He bounded up the stairs, MacDunlap hobbling after.

He rang the bell and burst in at the door. Reginald de Meister standing directly inside received the full impact of a pointing finger, and only a rapid backward movement of the head kept him from becoming a one-eyed mythical character.

June Billings stood aside, silent and uncomfortable.

"Reginald de Meister," growled Graham, in sinister tones, "prepare to meet your doom."

"Oh, boy," said MacDunlap, "are you going to get it."

"And to what," asked de Meister, "am I indebted for your dramatic but unilluminatin' statement? Confusin', don't you know." He lit a cigarette with a fine gesture and smiled.

"Hello, Gramie," said June, tearfully.

"Scram, vile woman."

June sniffed. She felt like a heroine out of a book, torn by her own emotions. Naturally, she was having the time of her life.

So she let the tears dribble and looked forlorn.

"To return to the subject, what is this all about?" asked de Meister, wearily.

"I have rewritten *Death on the Third Deck*."

"Well?"

"The revision," continued Graham, "is at present in the hands of MacDunlap's secretary, a girl on the style of Miss Billings, my fianceé that was. That is, she is a girl who aspires to the status of a moron, but has not yet quite attained it. She'll believe every word."

"Well?"

Graham's voice grew ominous, "You remember, perhaps, Sancha Rodriguez?"

For the first time, Reginald de Meister shuddered. He caught his cigarette as it dropped. "She was killed by Sam Blake in the sixth chapter. She was in love with me. Really, old fellow, what messes you get me into."

"Not half the mess you're in now, old chap. Sancha Rodriguez did *not* die in the revision."

"Die!" came a sharp, but clear female voice, "I'll show him if I died. And where have *you* been this last month, you two-crosser?"

De Meister did not catch his cigarette this time. He didn't even try. He recognized the apparition. To an unprejudiced observer, it might have been merely a svelte Latin girl equipped with dark, flashing eyes, and long, glittering fingernails, but to de Meister, it was Sancha Rodriguez—*undead!*

MacDunlap's secretary had read and believed.

"Miss Rodriguez," throbbed de Meister, charmingly, "how fascinatin' to see you."

'Mrs. de Meister to you, you double-timer, you two-crosser, you scum of the ground, you scorpion of the grass. And who is this woman?"

June retreated with dignity behind the nearest chair.

"*Mrs.* de Meister," said Reginald pleadingly, and turned helplessly to Graham Dorn.

"Oh, you have forgotten, have you, you smooth talker, you low dog. I'll show you what it means to deceive a weak woman. I'll make you mince-meat with my fingernails."

De Meister back-pedaled furiously. "But darling—"

"Don't you make sweet talk. What are you doing with this woman?"

"But, darling—"

"Don't give me any explanation. What are you doing with this woman?"

"But darling—"

"Shut up! What are you doing with this woman?"

Reginald de Meister was up in a corner, and Mrs. de Meister shook her fists at him. "Answer me!"

De Meister disappeared.

Mrs. de Meister disappeared right after him.

June Billings collapsed into real tears.

Graham Dorn folded his arms and looked sternly at her.

MacDunlap rubbed his hands and took a kidney pill.

"It wasn't my fault, Gramie," said June. "You said in your books he fascinated all women, so I couldn't help it. Deep inside, I hated him all along. You believe me, don't you?"

"A likely story!" said Graham, sitting down next to her on the sofa. "A likely story. But I forgive you, maybe."

MacDunlap said tremulously, "My boy, you have saved my stocks. Also, my wife, of course. And remember—you promised me one de Meister story each year."

Graham gritted, "Just one, and I'll henpeck him to death, and keep one unpublished story forever on hand, just in case. And you're publishing my novel, aren't you, Grew, old boy?"

"Glug," said MacDunlap.

"Aren't you?"

"Yes, Graham. Of course, Graham. Definitely, Graham. Positively, Graham."

"Then leave us now. There are matters of importance I must discuss with my fiancée."

MacDunlap smiled and tiptoed out the door.

Ah, love, love, he mused, as he took a liver pill and followed it up by a cough-syrup chaser.

# Eyes Do More Than See

After hundreds of billions or years, he suddenly thought of himself as Ames. Not the wavelength combination which, though all the universe was now the equivalent of Ames—but the sound itself. A faint memory came back of the sound waves he no longer heard and no longer could hear.

The new project was sharpening his memory for so many more of the old, old, eons-old things. He flattened the energy vortex that made up the total of his individuality and its lines of force stretched beyond the stars.

Brock's answering signal came.

Surely, Ames thought, he could tell Brock. Surely he could tell somebody.

Brock's shifting energy pattern communed. "Aren't you coming, Ames?"

"Of course."

"Will you take part in the contest?'

"Yes!" Ames's lines of force pulsed erratically. "Most certainly. I have thought of a whole new art-form. Something really unusual."

"What a waste of effort! How can you think a new variation can be thought of after two hundred billion years. There can be nothing new."

For a moment Brock shifted out of phase and out of communion, so that Ames had to hurry to adjust his lines of force. He caught the drift of other-thoughts as he did so, the view of the powdered galaxies against the velvet of nothingness, and the lines of force pulsing in endless multitudes of energy-life, lying between the galaxies.

Ames said, "Please absorb my thoughts, Brock. Don't close out. I've thought of manipulating Matter. Imagine! A symphony of Matter. Why bother with Energy. Of course, there's nothing new in Energy; how can there be? Doesn't that show we must deal with Matter?"

"Matter!"

Ames interpreted Brock's energy-vibrations as those of disgust.

He said, "Why not? We were once Matter ourselves back—back—Oh, a trillion years ago anyway! Why not build up objects in a Matter medium, or abstract forms or—listen, Brock—why not build up an imitation of ourselves in Matter, ourselves as we used to be?"

Brock said, "I don't remember how that was. No one does."

"I do," said Ames with energy, "I've been thinking of nothing else and I am beginning to remember. Brock, let me show you. Tell me if I'm right. Tell me."

"No. This is silly. It's—repulsive."

"Let me try, Brock. We've been friends; we've pulsed energy together from the beginning—from the moment we became what we are. Brock, please!"

"Then, quickly."

Ames had not felt such a tremor along his own lines of force in—well, in how long? If he tried it now for Brock and it worked he could dare manipulate Matter before the assembled Energy-beings who had so drearily waited over the eons for something new.

The Matter was thin out there between the galaxies, but Ames gathered it, scraping it together over the cubic light-years, choosing the atoms, achieving a clayey consistency and forcing matter into an ovoid form that spread out below.

"Don't you remember, Brock?" he asked softly. "Wasn't it something like this?"

Brock's vortex trembled in phase. "Don't make me remember. I don't remember."

"That was the head. They called it the head. I remember it so clearly, I want to say it. I mean with sound." He waited, then said "Look, do you remember that?"

On the upper front of the ovoid appeared HEAD.

"What is that?" asked Brock.

"That's the word for head. The symbols that meant the word in sound. Tell me you remember, Brock!"

"There was something," said Brock hesitantly, "something in the middle." A vertical bulge formed.

Ames said, "Yes! Nose, that's it!" And NOSE appeared upon it. "And those are eyes on either side," LEFT EYE—RIGHT EYE.

Ames regarded what he had formed, his lines of force pulsing slowly. Was he sure he liked this?

"Mouth," he said, in small quiverings, "and chin and Adam's apple, and the collar-bones. How the words come back to me." They appeared on the form.

Brock said, "I haven't thought of them for hundreds of billions of years. Why have you reminded me? Why?"

Ames was momentarily lost in his thoughts, "Something else. Organs to hear with; something for the sound waves. Ears! Where do they go? I don't remember where to put them!"

Brock cried out, "Leave it alone! Ears and all else! Don't remember!"

Ames said, uncertainly, "What is wrong with remembering?"

"Because the outside wasn't rough and cold like that but smooth and warm. Because the eyes were tender and alive and the lips of the mouth trembled and were soft on mine." Brock's lines of force beat and wavered, beat and wavered.

Ames said, "I'm sorry! I'm sorry!"

"You're reminding me that once I was a woman and knew love; that eyes do more than see and I have none to do it for me."

With violence, she added matter to the rough-hewn head and said, "Then let *them* do it" and turned and fled.

And Ames saw and remembered, too, that once he had been a man. The force of his vortex split the head in two and he fled back across the galaxies on the energy-track of Brock—back to the endless doom of life.

And the eyes of the shattered head of Matter still glistened with the moisture that Brock had placed there to represent tears. The head of Matter did that which the energy-beings could do no longer and it wept for all humanity, and for the fragile beauty of the bodies they had once given up, a trillion years ago.

# The Key

Karl Jennings knew he was going to die. He had a matter of hours to live and much to do.

There was no reprieve from the death sentence, not here on the Moon, not with no communications in operation.

Even on Earth there were a few fugitive patches where, without radio handy, a man might die without the hand of his fellow man to help him, without the heart of his fellow man to pity him, without even the eye of his fellow man to discover the corpse. Here on the Moon, there were few spots that were otherwise.

Earthmen knew he was on the Moon, of course. He had been part of a geological expedition—no, selenological expedition! Odd, how his Earth-centered mind insisted on the "geo-."

Wearily he drove himself to think, even as he worked. Dying though he was, he still felt that artificially imposed clarity of thought. Anxiously he looked about. There was nothing to see. He was in the dark of the eternal shadow of the northern interior of the wall of the crater, a blackness relieved only by the intermittent blink of his flash. He kept that intermittent, partly because he dared not consume its power source before he was through and partly because he dared not take more than the minimum chance that it be seen.

On his left hand, toward the south along the nearby horizon of the Moon, was a crescent of bright white Sunlight. Beyond the horizon, and invisible, was the opposite lip of the crater. The Sun never peered high enough over the lip of his own edge of the crater to illuminate the floor immediately beneath his feet. He was safe from radiation—from that at least.

He dug carefully but clumsily, swathed as he was in his spacesuit. His side ached abominably.

The dust and broken rock did not take up the "fairy castle" appearance characteristic of those portions of the Moon's surface exposed to the alternation of light and dark, heat and cold. Here, in eternal cold, the slow crumbling of the crater wall had simply piled fine rubble in a heterogeneous mass. It would not be easy to tell there had been digging going on.

He misjudged the unevenness of the dark surface for a moment and spilled a cupped handful of dusty fragments. The particles dropped with the slowness characteristic of the Moon and yet with the appearance of a blinding speed, for there was no air resistance to slow them further still and spread them out into a dusty haze.

Jennings' flash brightened for a moment, and he kicked a jagged rock out of the way.

He hadn't much time. He dug deeper into the dust.

A little deeper and he could push the Device into the depression and begin covering it. Strauss must not find it.

Strauss!

The other member of the team. Half-share in the discovery. Half-share in the renown.

If it were merely the whole share of the credit that Strauss had wanted, Jennings might have allowed it. The discovery was more important than any individual credit that might go with it. But what Strauss wanted was something far more, something Jennings would fight to prevent.

One of the few things Jennings was willing to die to prevent.

And he was dying.

They had found it together. Actually, Strauss had found the ship; or, better, the remains of the ship; or, better still, what just conceivably might have been the remains of something analogous to a ship.

"Metal," said Strauss, as he picked up something ragged and nearly amorphous. His eyes and face could just barely be seen through the thick lead glass of the visor, but his rather harsh voice sounded clearly enough through the suit radio.

Jennings came drifting over from his own position half a mile away. He said, "Odd! There is no free metal on the Moon."

"There shouldn't be. But you know well enough they haven't explored more than one per cent of the Moon's surface. Who knows what can be found on it?"

Jennings grunted assent and reached out his gauntlet to take the object.

It was true enough that almost anything might be found on the Moon for all anyone really knew. Theirs was the first privately financed selenographic expedition ever to land on the Moon. Till then, there had been only government-conducted shotgun affairs, with half a dozen ends in view. It was a sign of the advancing space age that the Geological Society could afford to send two men to the Moon for selenological studies only.

Strauss said, "It looks as though it once had a polished surface."

"You're right," said Jennings.

"Maybe there's more about."

They found three more pieces, two of trifling size and one a jagged object that showed traces of a seam.

"Let's take them to the ship," said Strauss.

They took the small skim boat back to the mother ship. They shucked their suits once on board, something Jennings at least was always glad to do. He scratched vigorously at his ribs and rubbed his cheeks till his light skin reddened into welts.

Strauss eschewed such weakness and got to work. The laser beam pock-marked the metal and the vapor recorded itself on the spectrograph. Titanium-steel, essentially, with a hint of cobalt and molybdenum.

"That's artificial, all right," said Strauss. His broad-boned face was as dour and as hard as ever. He showed no elation, although Jennings could feel his own heart begin to race.

It may have been the excitement that trapped Jennings into beginning, "This is a development against which we must steel ourselves—" with a faint stress on "steel" to indicate the play on words.

Strauss, however, looked at Jennings with an icy distaste, and the attempted set of puns was choked off.

Jennings sighed. He could never swing it, somehow. Never could! He remembered at the University—Well, never mind. The discovery they had made was worth a far better pun than any he could construct for all Strauss's calmness.

Jennings wondered if Strauss could possibly miss the significance.

He knew very little about Strauss, as a matter of fact, except by selenological reputation. That is, he had read Strauss's papers and he presumed Strauss had read his. Although their ships might well have passed by night in their University days, they had never happened to meet until after both had volunteered for this expedition and had been accepted.

In the week's voyage, Jennings had grown uncomfortably aware of the other's stocky figure, his sandy hair and china-blue eyes and the way the muscles over his prominent jawbones worked when he ate. Jennings, himself, much slighter in build, also blue-eyed, but with darker hair, tended to withdraw automatically from the heavy exudation of the other's power and drive.

Jennings said, "There's no record of any ship ever having landed on this part of the Moon. Certainly none has crashed."

"If it were part of a ship," said Strauss, "it should be smooth and polished. This is eroded and, without an atmosphere here, that means exposure to micrometeor bombardment over many years."

Then he *did* see the significance. Jennings said, with an almost savage jubilation, "It's a non-human artifact. Creatures not of Earth once visited the Moon. Who knows how long ago?"

"Who knows?" agreed Strauss dryly.

"In the report—"

"Wait," said Strauss imperiously. "Time enough to report when we have something to report. If it was a ship, there will be more to it than what we now have."

But there was no point in looking further just then. They had been at it for hours, and the next meal and sleep were overdue. Better to tackle the whole job fresh and spend hours at it. They seemed to agree on that without speaking.

The Earth was low on the eastern horizon, almost full in phase, bright and blue-streaked. Jennings looked at it while they ate and experienced, as he always did, a sharp homesickness.

"It looks peaceful enough," he said, "but there are six billion people busy on it."

Strauss looked up from some deep inner life of his own and said, "Six billion people ruining it!"

Jennings frowned. "You're not an Ultra, are you?"

Strauss said, "What the hell are you talking about?"

Jennings felt himself flush. A flush always showed against his fair skin, turning it pink at the slightest upset of the even tenor of his emotions. He found it intensely embarrassing.

He turned back to his food, without saying anything.

For a whole generation now, the Earth's population had held steady. No further increase could be afforded. Everyone admitted that. There was those, in fact, who said that "no higher" wasn't enough; the population had to drop. Jennings himself sympathized with that point of view. The globe of the Earth was being eaten alive by its heavy freight of humanity.

But *how* was the population to be made to drop? Randomly, by encouraging the people to lower the birth rate still further, as and how they wished? Lately there had been the slow rise of a distant rumble which wanted not only a population drop but a selected drop—the survival of the fittest, with the self-declared fit choosing the criteria of fitness.

Jennings thought: I've insulted him, I suppose.

Later, when he was almost asleep, it suddenly occurred to him that he knew virtually nothing of Strauss's character. What if it were his intention to go out now on a foraging expedition of his own so that he might get sole credit for—?

He raised himself on his elbow in alarm, but Strauss was breathing heavily, and even as Jennings listened, the breathing grew into the characteristic burr of a snore.

* * *

They spent the next three days in a single-minded search for additional pieces. They found some. They found more than that. They found an area glowing with the tiny phosphorescence of Lunar bacteria. Such bacteria were common enough, but nowhere previously had their occurrence been reported in concentration so great as to cause a visible glow.

Strauss said, "An organic being, or his remains, may have been here once. He died, but the micro-organisms within him did not. In the end they consumed him."

"And spread perhaps," added Jennings. "That may be the source of Lunar bacteria generally. They may not be native at all but may be the result of contamination instead—eons ago."

"It works the other way, too," said Strauss. "Since the bacteria are completely different in very fundamental ways from any Earthly form of micro-organism, the creatures they parasitized—assuming this was their source—must have been fundamentally different too. Another indication of extraterrestrial origin."

The trail ended in the wall of a small crater.

"It's a major digging job," said Jennings, his heart sinking. "We had better report this and get help."

"No," said Struss somberly. "There may be nothing to get help for. The crater might have formed a million years after the ship had crashlanded."

"And vaporized most of it, you mean, and left only what we've found?"

Strauss nodded.

Jennings said, "Let's try anyway. We can dig a bit. If we draw a line through the finds we've made so far and just keep on . . ."

Strauss was reluctant and worked halfheartedly, so that it was Jennings who made the real find. Surely that counted! Even though Strauss had found the first piece of metal, Jennings had found the artifact itself.

It *was* an artifact—cradled three feet underground under the irregular shape of a boulder which had fallen in such a way that it left a hollow in its contact with the Moon's surface. In that hollow lay the artifact, protected from everything for a million years or more; protected from radiation, from micrometeors, from temperature change, so that it remained fresh and new forever.

Jennings labeled it at once the Device. It looked not remotely similar to any instrument either had ever seen, but then, as Jennings said, why should it?

"There are no rough edges that I can see," he said. "It may not be broken."

"There may be missing parts, though."

"Maybe," said Jennings, "but there seems to be nothing movable. It's all once piece and certainly oddly uneven." He noted his own play on words, then went on with a not-altogether-successful attempt at self-control. "*This* is what we need. A piece of worn metal or an area rich in bacteria is only material for deduction and dispute. But this is the real thing—a Device that is clearly of extraterrestrial manufacture."

It was on the table between them now, and both regarded it gravely.

Jennings said, "Let's put through a preliminary report, now."

"No!" said Strauss, in sharp and strenuous dissent. "Hell, no!"

"Why not?"

"Because if we do, it becomes a Society project. They'll swarm all over it and we won't be as much as a footnote when all is done. No!" Strauss looked almost sly. "Let's do all we can with it and get as much out of it as possible before the harpies descend."

Jennings thought about it. He couldn't deny that he too wanted to make certain that no credit was lost. But still—

He said, "I don't know that I like to take the chance, Strauss." For the first time he had an impulse to use the man's first name, but fought it off. "Look, Strauss," he said, "it's not right to wait. If this is of extraterrestrial origin, then it must be from some other planetary system. There isn't a place in the Solar System, outside the Earth, that can possibly support an advanced life form."

"Not proven, really," grunted Strauss, "but what if you're right?"

"Then it would mean that the creatures of the ship had interstellar travel and therefore had to be far in advance, technologically, of ourselves. Who knows what the Device can tell us about their advanced technology. It might be the key to—who knows what. It might be the clue to an unimaginable scientific revolution."

"That's romantic nonsense. If this is the product of a technology far advanced over ours, we'll learn nothing from it. Bring Einstein back to life and show him a micro-protowarp and what would he make of it?"

"We can't be certain that we won't learn."

"So what, even so? What if there's a small delay? What if we assure credit for ourselves? What if we make sure that we ourselves go along with this, that we don't let go of it?"

"But Strauss"—Jennings felt himself moved almost to tears in his anxiety to get across his sense of the importance of the Device—"What if we crash with it? What if we don't make it back to Earth? We can't risk this thing." He tapped it then, almost as though he were in love with it. "We should report it now and have them send ships out here to get it. It's too precious to—"

At the peak of his emotional intensity, the Device seemed to grow warm under his hand. A portion of its surface, half-hidden under a flap of metal, glowed phosphorescently.

Jennings jerked his hand away in a spasmodic gesture and the Device darkened. But it was enough; the moment had been infinitely revealing.

He said, almost choking, "It was like a window opening into your skull. I could see into your mind."

"I read yours," said Strauss, "or experienced it, or entered into it, or whatever you choose." He touched the Device in his cold, withdrawn way, but nothing happened.

"You're an Ultra," said Jennings angrily. "When I touched this"—And he did so. "It's happening again. I see it. Are you a madman? Can you honestly believe it is humanly decent to condemn almost all the human race to extinction and destroy the versatility and variety of the species?"

His hand dropped away from the Device again, in repugnance at the glimpses revealed, and it grew dark again. Once more, Strauss touched it gingerly and again nothing happened.

Strauss said, "Let's not start a discussion, for God's sake. This thing is an aid to communication—a telepathic amplifier. Why not? The brain cells have each their electric potentials. Thought can be viewed as a wavering electromagnetic field of micro-intensities—"

Jennings turned away. He didn't want to speak to Strauss. He said, "We'll report it now. I don't give a damn about credit. Take it all. I just want it out of our hands."

For a moment Strauss remained in a brown study. Then he said, "It's more than a communicator. It responds to emotion and it amplifies emotion."

"What are you talking about?"

"Twice it started at your touch just now, although you'd been handling it all day with no effect. It still has no effect when I touch it."

"Well?"

"It reacted to you when you were in a state of high emotional tension. That's the requirement for activation, I suppose. And when you raved about the Ultras while you were holding it just now, I felt as you did, for just a moment."

"So you should."

"But listen to me. Are you sure *you're* so right. There isn't a thinking man on Earth that doesn't know the planet would be better off with a population of one billion rather than six billion. If we used automation to the full—as now the hordes won't allow us to do—we could probably have a completely efficient and viable Earth with a population of no more than, say, five million. Listen to me, Jennings. Don't turn away, man."

The harshness in Strauss's voice almost vanished in his effort to be reasonably winning. "But we can't reduce the population democratically. You know that. It isn't the sex urge, because uterine inserts solved the birth control problem long ago; you know that. It's a matter of nationalism. Each ethnic group wants other groups to reduce themselves in population first, and I agree with them. I want my ethnic group, *our* ethnic group, to prevail. I want the Earth to be inherited by the elite, which means by men like ourselves. We're the true men, and the horde of half-apes who hold us down are destroying us all. They're doomed to death anyway; why not save ourselves?"

"No," said Jennings strenuously. "No one group has a monopoly on humanity. Your five million, trapped in a humanity robbed of its variety and versatility, would die of boredom—and serve them right."

"Emotional nonsense, Jennings. You don't believe that. You've just been trained to believe it by our damn-fool equalitarians. Look, this Device is just what we need. Even if we can't build any others or understand how this one works, this one Device might do. If we could control or influence the minds of key men, then little by little we can superimpose our views on the world. We already have an organization. You must know that if you've seen my mind. It's better motivated and better designed than any other organization on Earth. The brains of mankind flock to us daily. Why not you too? This instrument is a key, as you see, but not just a key to a bit more knowledge. It is a key to the final solution of men's problems. Join us! Join us!" He had reached an earnestness that Jennings had never heard in him.

Strauss's hand fell on the Device, which flickered a second or two and went out.

Jennings smiled humorlessly. He saw the significance of that. Strauss had been deliberately trying to work himself into an emotional state intense enough to activate the Device and had failed.

"You can't work it," said Jennings. "You're too darned supermannishly self-controlled and can't break down, can you?" He took up the Device with hands that were trembling, and it phosphoresced at once.

"Then *you* work it. Get the credit for saving humanity."

"Not in a hundred million years," said Jennings, gasping and barely able to breathe in the intensity of his emotion. "I'm going to report this now."

"No," said Strauss. He picked up one of the table knives. "It's pointed enough, sharp enough."

"You needn't work so hard to make your point," said Jennings, even under the stress of the moment conscious of the pun. "I can see your plans. With the Device you can convince anyone that I never existed. You can bring about an Ultra victory."

Strauss nodded. "You read my mind perfectly."

"But you won't," gasped Jennings. "Not while I hold this." He was smiling Strauss into immobility.

Strauss moved raggedly and subsided. He held the knife out stiffly and his arm trembled, but he did not advance.

Both were perspiring freely.

Strauss said between clenched teeth, "You can't keep it—up all—day."

The sensation was clear, but Jennings wasn't sure he had the words to describe it. It was, in physical terms, like holding a slippery animal of vast strength, one that wriggled incessantly. Jennings had to concentrate on the feeling of immobility.

He wasn't familiar with the Device. He didn't know how to use it skillfully. One might as well expect someone who had never seen a sword to pick one up and wield it with the grace of a musketeer.

"Exactly," said Strauss, following Jennings' train of thought. He took a fumbling step forward.

Jennings knew himself to be no match for Strauss's mad determination. They both knew that. But there was the skim boat. Jennings had to get away. With the Device.

But Jennings had no secrets. Strauss saw his thought and tried to step between the other and the skim boat.

Jennings redoubled his efforts. Not immobility, but unconsciousness. Sleep, Strauss, he thought desperately. Sleep!

Strauss slipped to his knees, heavy-lidded eyes closing.

Heart pounding, Jennings rushed forward. If he could strike him with something, snatch the knife—

But his thoughts had deviated from their all-important concentration on sleep, so that Strauss's hand was on his ankle, pulling downward with raw strength.

Strauss did not hesitate. As Jennings tumbled, the hand that held the knife rose and fell. Jennings felt the sharp pain and his mind reddened with fear and despair.

It was the very access of emotion that raised the flicker of the Device to a blaze. Strauss's hold relaxed as Jennings silently and incoherently screamed fear and rage from his own mind to the other.

Strauss rolled over, face distorted.

Jennings rose unsteadily to his feet and backed away. He dared do nothing but concentrate on keeping the other unconscious. Any attempt at violent action would block out too much of his own mind force, whatever it was; too much of his unskilled bumbling mind force that could not lend itself to really effective use.

He backed toward the skim boat. There would be a suit on board—bandages—

* * *

The skim boat was not really meant for long-distance runs. Nor was Jennings, any longer. His right side was slick with blood despite the bandages. The interior of his suit was caked with it.

There was no sign of the ship itself on his tail, but surely it would come sooner or later. Its power was many times his own; it had detectors that would pick up the cloud of charge concentration left behind by his ion-drive reactors.

Desperately Jennings had tried to reach Luna Station on his radio, but there was still no answer, and he stopped in despair. His signals would merely aid Strauss in pursuit.

He might reach Luna Station bodily, but he did not think he could make it. He would be picked off first. He would die and crash first. He wouldn't make it. He would have to hide the Device, put it away in a safe place, *then* make for Luna Station.

The Device . . .

He was not sure he was right. It might ruin the human race, but it was infinitely valuable. Should he destroy it altogether? It was the only remnant of non-human intelligent life. It held the secrets of an advanced technology; it was an instrument of an advanced science of the mind. Whatever the danger, consider the value—the potential value—

No, he must hide it so that it could be found again—but only by the enlightened Moderates of the government. Never by the Ultras . . .

The skim boat flickered down along the northern inner rim of the crater. He knew which one it was, and the Device could be buried here. If he could not reach Luna Station thereafter, either in person or by radio, he would have to at least get away from the hiding spot; well away, so that his own person would not give it away. And he would have to leave *some* key to its location.

He was thinking with an unearthly clarity, it seemed to him. Was it the influence of the Device he was holding? Did it stimulate his thinking and guide him to the perfect message? Or was it the hallucination of the dying, and would none of it make any sense to anyone? He didn't know, but he had no choice. He had to try.

For Karl Jennings knew he was going to die. He had a matter of hours to live and much to do.

* * *

H. Seton Davenport of the American Division of the Terrestrial Bureau of Investigation rubbed the star-shaped scar on his left cheek absently. "I'm aware, sir, that the Ultras are dangerous."

The Division Head, M. T. Ashley, looked at Davenport narrowly. His gaunt cheeks were set in disapproving lines. Since he had sworn off smoking once again, he forced his groping fingers to close upon a stick of chewing gum, which he shelled, crumpled, and shoved into his mouth morosely. He was getting old, and bitter, too, and his short iron-gray mustache rasped when he rubbed his knuckles against it.

He said, "You don't know how dangerous. I wonder if anyone does. They are small in numbers, but strong among the powerful who, after all, are perfectly ready to consider themselves the elite. No one knows for certain who they are or how many."

"Not even the Bureau?"

"The Bureau is held back. We ourselves aren't free of the taint, for that matter. Are you?"

Davenport frowned. "I'm not an Ultra."

"I didn't say you were," said Ashley. "I asked if you were free of the taint. Have your considered what's been happening to the Earth in the last two centuries? Has it never occurred to you that a moderate decline in population would be a good thing? Have you never felt that it would be wonderful to get rid of the unintelligent, the incapable, the insensitive, and leave the rest. *I* have, damn it."

"I'm guilty of thinking that sometimes, yes. But considering something as a wish-fulfillment idea is one thing, but planning it as a practical scheme of action to be Hitlerized through is something else."

"The distance from wish to action isn't as great as you think. Convince yourself that the end is important enough, that the danger is great enough, and the means will grow increasingly less objectionable. Anyway, now that the Istanbul matter is take care of, let me bring you up to date on this matter. Istanbul was of no importance in comparison. Do you know Agent Ferrant?"

"The one who's disappeared? Not personally."

"Well, two months ago, a stranded ship was located on the Moon's surface. It had been conducting a privately financed selenographic survey. The Russo-American Geological Society, which had sponsored the flight, reported the ship's failure to report. A routine search located it without much trouble within a reasonable distance of the site from which it had made its last report.

"The ship was not damaged but its skim boat was gone and with it one member of the crew. Name—Karl Jennings. The other man, James Strauss, was alive but in delirium. There was no sign of physical damage to Strauss, but he was quite insane. He still is, and that's important."

"Why?" put in Davenport.

"Because the medical team that investigated him reported neurochemical and neuroelectrical abnormalities of unprecedented nature. They'd never seen a case like it. Nothing human could have brought it about."

A flicker of a smile crossed Davenport's solemn face. "You suspect extraterrestrial invaders?"

"Maybe," said the other, with no smile at all. "But let me continue. A routine search in the neighborhood of the stranded ship revealed no signs of the skim boat. Then Luna station reported receipt of weak signals of uncertain origin. They had been tabbed as coming from the western rim of Mare Imbrium, but it was uncertain whether they were of human origin or not, and no vessel was believed to be in the vicinity. The signals had been ignored. With the skim boat in mind, however, the search party headed out for Imbrium and located it. Jennings was aboard, dead. Knife wound in one side. It's rather surprising he had lived as long as he did.

"Meanwhile the medicos were becoming increasingly disturbed at the nature of Strauss's babbling. They contacted the Bureau and our two men on the Moon—one of them happened to be Ferrant—arrived at the ship.

"Ferrant studied the tape recordings of the babblings. There was no point in asking questions, for there was, and is, no way of reaching Strauss. There is a high wall between the universe and himself —

probably a permanent one. However, the talk in delirium, although heavily repetitious and disjointed, can be made to make sense. Ferrant put it together like a jigsaw puzzle.

"Apparently Strauss and Jennings had come across an object of some sort which they took to be of ancient and non-human manufacture, an artifact of some ship wrecked eons ago. Apparently it could somehow be made to twist the human mind."

Davenport interrupted. "And it twisted Strauss's mind? Is that it?"

"That's exactly it. Strauss was an Ultra—we can say 'was' for he's only technically alive—and Jennings did not wish to surrender the object. Quite right, too. Strauss babbled of using it to bring about the self-liquidation, as he called it, of the undesirable. He wanted a final, ideal population of five million. There was a fight in which only Jennings, apparently, could handle the mind-thing, but in which Strauss had a knife. When Jennings left, he was knifed, but Strauss's mind had been destroyed."

"And where was the mind-thing?"

"Agent Ferrant acted decisively. He searched the ship and the surroundings again. There was no sign of anything that was neither a natural Lunar formation nor an obvious product of human technology. There was nothing that could be the mind-thing. He then searched the skim boat and its surroundings. Again nothing."

"Could the first search team, the ones who suspected nothing — could they have carried something off?"

"They swore they did not, and there is no reason to suspect them of lying. Then Ferrant's partner—"

"Who was he?"

"Gorbansky," said the District Head.

"I know him. We've worked together."

"I know you have. What do you think of him?"

"Capable and honest."

"All right. Gorbansky found something. Not an alien artifact. Rather, something most routinely human indeed. It was an ordinary white three-by-five card with writing on it, spindled, and in the middle finger of the right gauntlet. Presumably Jennings had written it before his death and, also presumably, it represented the key to where he had hidden the object."

"What reason is there to think he had hidden it?"

"I said we had found it nowhere."

"I mean, what if he had destroyed it, as something too dangerous to leave intact?"

"That's highly doubtful. If we accept the conversation as

reconstructed from Strauss's ravings—and Ferrant built up what seems a tight word-for-word record of it—Jennings thought the mind-thing to be of key importance to humanity. He called it 'the clue to an unimaginable scientific revolution.' He wouldn't destroy something like that. He would merely hide it from the Ultras and try to report its whereabouts to the government. Else why leave a clue to its whereabouts?"

Davenport shook his head, "You're arguing in a circle, chief. You say he left a clue because you think there is a hidden object, and you think there is a hidden object because he left a clue."

"I admit that. Everything is dubious. Is Strauss's delirium meaningful? Is Ferrant's reconstruction valid? Is Jennings' clue really a clue? Is there a mind-thing, or a Device, as Jennings called it, or isn't there? There's no use asking such questions. Right now, we must act on the assumption that there is such a Device and that it must be found."

"Because Ferrant disappeared?"

"Exactly."

"Kidnapped by the Ultras?"

"Not at all. The card disappeared with him."

"Oh—I see."

"Ferrant has been under suspicion for a long time as a secret Ultra. He's not the only one in the Bureau under suspicion either. The evidence didn't warrant open action; we can't simply lay about on pure suspicion, you know, or we'll gut the Bureau from top to bottom. He was under surveillance."

"By whom?"

"By Gorbansky, of course. Fortunately Gorbansky had filmed the card and sent the reproduction to the headquarters on Earth, but he admits he considered it as nothing more than a puzzling object and included it in the information sent to Earth only out of a desire to be routinely complete. Ferrant—the better mind of the two, I suppose–did see the significance and took action. He did so at great cost, for he has given himself away and has destroyed his future usefulness to the Ultras, but there is a chance that there will be no need for future usefulness. If the Ultras control the Device—"

"Perhaps Ferrant has the Device already."

"He was under surveillance, remember. Gorbansky swears the Device did not turn up anywhere."

"Gorbansky did not manage to stop Ferrant from leaving with the card. Perhaps he did not manage to stop him from obtaining the Device unnoticed either."

Ashley tapped his fingers on the desk between them in an uneasy and uneven rhythm. He said at last, "I don't want to think that. If we find Ferrant we may mind out how much damage he's done. Till then, we must search for the Device. If Jennings hid it, he must have tried to get away from the hiding place. Else why leave a clue? It wouldn't be found in the vicinity."

"He might not have lived long enough to get away."

Again Ashley tapped, "The skim boat showed signs of having engaged in a long speedy flight and had all but crashed at the end. That is consistent with the view that Jennings was trying to place as much space as possible between himself and some hiding place."

"Can you tell from what direction he came?"

"Yes, but that's not likely to help. From the condition of the side vents, he had been deliberately tacking and veering."

Davenport sighed, "I suppose you have a copy of the card with you."

"I do. Here it is." He flipped a three-by-five replica toward Davenport. Davenport studied it for a few moments. It looked like this:

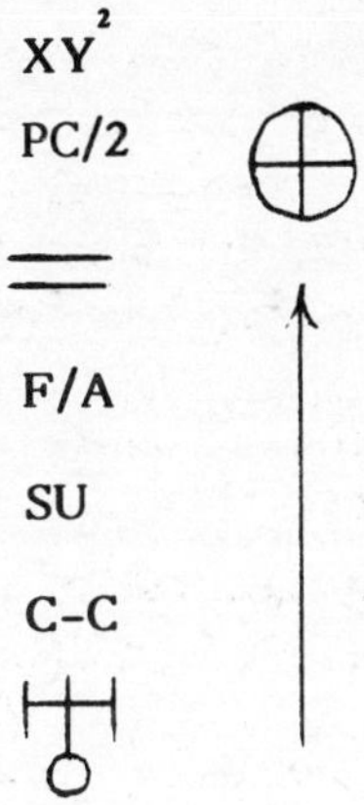


Davenport said, "I don't see any significance here."

"Neither did I, at first, nor did those I first consulted. But consider. Jennings must have thought that Strauss was in pursuit; he might not have known that Strauss had been put out of action, at least, not permanently. He was deadly afraid, then, that an Ultra would find him before a Moderate would. He dared not leave a clue too open. This"—and the Division Head tapped the reproduction—"must represent a clue that is opaque on the surface but clear enough to anyone sufficiently ingenious."

"Can we rely on that?" asked Davenport doubtfully. "After all, he was dying, frightened man, who might have been subjected to this mind-altering object himself. He need not have been thinking clearly, or even humanly. For instance, why didn't he make an effort to reach Luna Station? He ended half a circumference away almost. Was he too twisted to think clearly? Too paranoid to trust even the Station? Yet he must have tried to reach them at first since they picked up signals. What I'm saying is that this card, which looks as though it is covered with gibberish, *is* covered with gibberish."

Ashley shook his head solemnly from side to side, like a tolling bell. "He was in panic, yes. And I suppose he lacked the presence of mind to try to reach Luna Station. Only the need to run and escape possessed him. Even so this can't be gibberish. It hangs together too well. Every notation on the card can be made to make sense, and the whole can be made to hang together."

"Where's the sense, then?" asked Davenport.

"You'll notice that there are seven items on the left side and two on the right. Consider the left hand side first. The third one down looks like an equals sign. Does an equals sign mean anything to you, anything in particular?"

"An algebraic equation."

"That's general. Anything particular?"

"No."

"Suppose you consider it as a pair of parallel lines?"

"Euclid's fifth postulate?" suggested Davenport, groping.

"Good! There is a crater called Euclides on the Moon—the Greek name of the mathematician we call Euclid."

Davenport nodded. "I see your drift. As for F/A, that's force divided by acceleration, the definition of mass by Newton's second law of motion—"

"Yes, and there is a crater called Newton on the Moon also."

"Yes, but wait awhile, the lowermost item is the astronomic symbol for the planet Uranus, and there is certainly no crater—or any other lunar object, so far as I know—that is named Uranus."

"You're right there. But Uranus was discovered by William Herschel, and the H that makes up part of the astronomic symbol is the initial of his name. As it happens, there is a crater named Herschel on the Moon—three of them, in fact, since one is named for Caroline Herschel, his sister, and another for John Herschel, his son."

Davenport thought awhile, then said, "PC/2—Pressure times half the speed of light. I'm not familiar with that equation."

"Try craters. Try P for Ptolemaeus and C for Copernicus."

"And strike an average? Would that signify a spot exactly between Ptolemaeus and Copernicus?"

"I'm disappointed, Davenport," said Ashley sardonically. "I thought you knew your history of astronomy better than that. Ptolemy, or Ptolemaeus in Latin, presented a geocentric picture of the Solar System with the Earth at the center, while Copernicus presented a heliocentric one with the Sun at the center. One astronomer attempted a compromise, a picture halfway between that of Ptolemy and Copernicus—"

"Tycho Brahe!" said Davenport.

"Right. And the crater Tycho is the most conspicuous feature on the Moon's surface."

"All right. Let's take the rest. The C-C is a common way of writing a common type of chemical bond, and I think there is a crater named Bond."

"Yes, named for an American astonomer, W. C. Bond."

"The item on top, $XY^2$. Hmm. XYY. An X and two Y's. Wait! Alfonso X. He was the royal astronomer in medieval Spain who was called Alfonso the Wise. X the wise. XYY. The Crater Alphonsus."

"Very good. What's SU?"

"That stumps me, chief."

"I'll tell you one theory. It stands for Soviet Union, the old name for the Russian Region. It was the Soviet Union that first mapped the other side of the Moon, and maybe it's a crater there. Tsiolkovsky, for instance. You see, then, the symbols on the left can each be interpreted as standing for a crater: Alphonsus, Tycho, Euclides, Newton, Tsiolkovsky, Bond, Herschel."

"What about the symbols on the right-hand side?"

"That's perfectly transparent. The quartered circle is the astronomic symbol for the Earth. An arrow pointing to it indicates that Earth must be directly overhead."

"Ah," said Davenport, "the Sinus Medii—the Middle Bay—over which the Earth is perpetually at zenith. That's not a crater, so it's on the right-hand side, away from the other symbols."

"All right, so there's at least a good chance that this isn't gibberish and that it is trying to tell us something. But what? So far we've got seven craters and a non-crater mentioned and what does that mean? Presumably, the Device can only be in one place."

"Well," said Davenport heavily, "a crater can be a huge place to search. Even if we assume he hugged the shadow to avoid Solar radiation, there can be dozens of miles to examine in each case. Suppose the arrow pointing to the symbol for the Earth defines the crater where he hid the Device, the place from which the Earth can be seen nearest the zenith."

"That's been thought of, old man. It cuts out one place and leaves us with seven pinpointed craters, the southernmost extremity of those north of the Lunar equator and the northernmost extremity of those south. But which of the seven?"

Davenport was frowning. So far, he hadn't thought of anything that hadn't already been thought of. "Search them all," he said brusquely.

Ashley crackled into brief laughter. "In the weeks since this has all come up, we've done exactly that."

"And what have you found."

"Nothing. We haven't found a thing. We're still looking, though."

"Obviously one of the symbols isn't interpreted correctly."

"Obviously!"

"You said yourself there were three craters named Herschel. The symbol SU, if it means the Soviet Union and therefore the other side of the Moon, can stand for any crater on the other side: Lomonosov, Jules Verne, Joliot-Curie, any of them. For that matter, the symbol of the Earth might stand for the crater Atlas, since he is pictured as supporting the Earth in some versions of the myth. The arrow might stand for the Straight Wall."

"There's no argument there, Davenport. But even if we get the right interpretation for the right symbol, how do we recognize it from among all the wrong interpretations, or from among the right interpretations of the wrong symbols? Somehow there's got to be something that leaps up at us from this card and gives us so clear a piece of information that we can tell it at once as the real thing from among all the red herrings. We've all failed and we need a fresh mind, Davenport. What do you see here?"

"I'll tell you one thing we could do," said Davenport reluctantly. "We can consult someone I—Oh, my God!" He half-rose.

Ashley was all controlled excitement at once. "What do you see?"

Davenport could feel his hand trembling. He hoped his lips weren't. He said, "Tell me, have you checked on Jennings' past life?"

"Of course."

"Where did he go to college?"

"Eastern University."

A pang of joy shot through Davenport, but he held on. That was not enough. "Did he take a course in extraterrology?"

"Of course, he did. That's routine for a geology major."

"All right, then, don't you know who teaches extraterrology at Eastern University?"

Ashley snapped his fingers. "That oddball. What's-his-name — Wendell Urth."

"Exactly, an oddball who is a brilliant man in his way. An oddball who's acted as a consultant for the Bureau on several occasions and given perfect satisfaction every time. An oddball I was going to suggest we consult this time and then noticed that this card was *telling* us to do so. An arrow pointing to the symbol for the Earth. A rebus that couldn't mean more clearly 'Go to Urth,' written by a man who was once a student of Urth and would know him."

Ashley stared at the card, "By God, it's possible. But what could Urth tell us about the card that we can't see for ourselves?"

Davenport said, with polite patience, "I suggest we ask him, sir."

* * *

Ashley looked about curiously, half-wincing as he turned from one direction to another. He felt as though he had found himself in some arcane curiosity shop, darkened and dangerous, from which at any moment some demon might hurtle forth squealing.

The lighting was poor and the shadows many. The walls seemed distant, and dismally alive with book-films from floor to ceiling. There was a Galactic Lens in soft three-dimensionality in one corner and behind it were star charts that could dimly be made out. A map of the Moon in another corner might, however, possibly be a map of Mars.

Only the desk in the center of the room was brilliantly lit by a tightbeamed lamp. It was littered with papers and opened printed books. A small viewer was threaded with film, and a clock with an old-fashioned round-faced dial hummed with subdued merriment.

Ashley found himself unable to recall that it was late afternoon outside and that the sun was quite definitely in the sky. Here, within, was a place of eternal night. There was no sign of any window, and the clear presence of circulating air did not spare him a claustrophobic sensation.

He found himself moving closer to Davenport, who seemed insensible to the unpleasantness of the situation.

Davenport said in a low voice, "He'll be here in a moment, sir."

"Is it always like this?" asked Ashley.

"Always. He never leaves this place, as far as I know, except to trot across the campus and attend his classes."

"Gentlemen! Gentlemen!" came a reedy tenor voice, "I am so glad to see you. It is good of you to come."

A round figure of a man bustled in from another room, shedding shadow and emerging into the light.

He beamed at them, adjusting round, thick-lensed glasses upward so that he might look through them. As his fingers moved away, the glasses slipped downward at once to a precarious perch upon the round nubbin of his snub nose. "I am Wendell Urth," he said.

The scraggly gray Van Dyke on his pudgy, round chin did not in the least add to the dignity which the smiling face and the stubby ellipsoidal torso so noticeably lacked.

"Gentlemen! It is good of you to come," Urthe repeated, as he jerked himself backward into a chair from which his legs dangled with the toes of his shoes a full inch above the floor. "Mr. Davenport remembers, perhaps, that it is a matter of—uh—some importance to me to remain here. I do not like to travel, except to walk, of course, and a walk across the campus is quite enough for me."

Ashley looked baffled as he remained standing, and Urth stared at him with a growing bafflement of his own. He pulled a handkerchief out and wiped his glasses, then replaced them, and said, "Oh, I see the difficulty. You want chairs. Yes. Well, just take some. If there are things on them, just push them off. Push them off. Sit down, please."

Davenport removed the books from one chair and placed them carefully on the floor. He pushed the chair toward Ashley. Then he took a human skull off a second chair and placed the skull even more carefully on Urth's desk. Its mandible, insecurely wired, unhinged as he transferred it, and it sat there with jaw askew.

"Never mind," said Urth, affably, "it will not hurt. Now tell me what is on your mind, gentlemen?"

Davenport waited a moment for Ashley to speak, then, rather gladly, took over. "Dr. Urth, do you remember a student of yours named Jennings? Karl Jennings?"

Urth's smile vanished momentarily with the effort of recall. His somewhat protuberant eyes blinked. "No," he said at last. "Not at the moment."

"A geology major. He took your extraterrology course some years ago. I have his photograph here, if that will help."

Urth studied the photograph handed him with nearsighted concentration, but still looked doubtful.

Davenport drove on. "He left a cryptic message which is the key to a matter of great importance. We have so far failed to interpret it satisfactorily, but this much we see—it indicates we are to come to you."

"Indeed? How interesting! For what purpose are you to come to me?"

"Presumably for your advice on interpreting the message."

"May I see it?"

Silently Ashley passed the slip of paper to Wendell Urth. The extraterrologist looked at it casually, turned it over, and stared for a moment at the blank back. He said, "Where does it say to ask me?"

Ashley looked startled, but Davenport forestalled him by saying, "The arrow pointing to the symbol of the Earth. It seems clear."

"It was found on the Moon, Dr. Urth, and it could, I suppose, mean that. However, the reference to you seemed clear once we realized that Jennings had been a student of yours."

"He took a course in extraterrology here at the University?"

"That's right."

"In what year, Mr. Davenport?"

"In '18."

"Ah. The puzzle is solved."

"You mean the significance of the message?" said Davenport.

"No, no. The message has no meaning to me. I mean the puzzle of why it is that I did not remember him, for I remember him now. He was a very quiet fellow, anxious, shy, self-effacing—not at all the sort of person anyone would remember. Without this"—and he tapped the message—"I might never have remembered him."

"Why does the card change things?" asked Davenport.

"The reference to me is a play on words. Earth—Urth. Not very subtle, of course, but that is Jennings. His unattainable delight was the pun. My only clear memory of him is his occasional attempts to perpetrate puns. I enjoy puns, I adore puns, but Jennings—yes, I remember him well now—was atrocious at it. Either that, or distressingly obvious at it, as in this case. He lacked all talent for puns, yet craved them so much—"

Ashley suddenly broke in. "This message consists entirely of a kind of wordplay, Dr. Urth. At least, we believe so, and that fits in with what you say."

"Ah!" Urth adjusted his glasses and peered through them once more at the card and the symbols it carried. He pursed his plump lips, then said cheerfully, "I make nothing of it."

"In that case—" began Ashley, his hands balling into fists.

"But if you tell me what it's all about," Urth went on, "then perhaps it might mean something."

Davenport said quickly, "May I, sir? I am confident that this man can be relied on—and it may help."

"Go ahead," muttered Ashley. "At this point, what can it hurt?"

Davenport condensed the tale, giving it in crisp, telegraphic sentences, while Urth listened carefully, moving his stubby fingers over the shining milk-white desktop as though he were sweeping up invisible cigar ashes. Toward the end of the recital he hitched up his legs and sat with them crossed like an amiable Buddha.

When Davenport was done, Urth thought a moment, then said, "Do you happen to have a transcript of the conversation reconstructed by Ferrant?"

"We do," said Davenport. "Would you like to see it?"

"Please."

Urth placed the strip of microfilm in a scanner and worked his way rapidly through it, his lips moving unintelligibly at some points. Then he tapped the reproduction of the cryptic message. "And this, you say, is the key to the entire matter? The crucial clue?"

"We think it is, Dr. Urth."

"But it is not the original. It is a reproduction."

"That is correct."

"The original has gone with this man, Ferrant, and you believe it to be in the hands of the Ultras."

"Quite possibly."

Urth shook his head and looked troubled. "Everyone knows my sympathies are not with the Ultras. I would fight them by all means, so I don't want to seem to be hanging back, but—what is there to say that this mind-affecting object exists at all? You have only the ravings of a psychotic and your dubious deductions from the reproduction of a mysterious set of marks that may mean nothing at all."

"Yes, Dr. Urth, but we can't take chances."

"How certain are you that this copy is accurate? What if the original has something on it that this lacks, something that makes the message quite clear, something without which the message must remain impenetrable?"

"We are certain the copy is accurate."

"What about the reverse side? There is nothing on the back of this reproduction. What about the reverse of the original?"

"The agent who made the reproduction tells us that the back of the original was blank."

"Men can make mistakes."

"We have no reason to think he did, and we must work on the assumption that he didn't. At least until such time as the original is regained."

"Then you assure me," said Urth, "that any interpretation to be made of this message must be made on the basis of exactly what one sees here."

"We think so. We are virtually certain," said Davenport with a sense of ebbing confidence.

Urth continued to look troubled. He said, "Why not leave the instrument where it is? If neither group finds it, so much the better. I disapprove of any tampering with minds and would not contribute to making it possible."

Davenport placed a restraining hand on Ashley's arm, sensing the other was about to speak. Davenport said, "Let me put it to you, Dr. Urth, that the mind-tampering aspect is not the whole of the Device. Suppose an Earth expedition to a distant primitive planet had dropped an old-fashioned radio there, and suppose the native population had discovered electric current but had not yet developed the vacuum tube.

"The population might discover that if the radio was hooked up to a current, certain glass objects within it would grow warm and would glow, but of course they would receive no intelligible sound, merely, at best some buzzes and crackles. However, if they dropped the radio into a bathtub while it was plugged in, a person in that tub might be electrocuted. Should the people of this hypothetical planet therefore conclude that the device they were studying was designed solely for the purpose of killing people?"

"I see your analogy," said Urth. "You think that the mind-tampering property is merely an incidental function of the Device?"

"I'm sure of it," said Davenport earnestly. "If we can puzzle out its real purpose, earthly technology may leap ahead centuries."

"Then you agree with Jennings when he said"—here Urth consulted the micro-film—" 'It might be the key to—who knows what? It might be the clue to an unimaginable scientific revolution.' "

"Exactly!"

"And yet the mind-tampering aspect is there and is infinitely dangerous. Whatever the radio's purpose, it *does* electrocute."

"Which is why we can't let the Ultras get it."

"Or the government either, perhaps?"

"But I must point out that there is a reasonable limit to caution. Consider that men have always held danger in their hands. The first flint knife in the old Stone Age; the first wooden club before that could kill. They could be used to bend weaker men to the will of stronger ones under threat of force and that, too, is a form of mind-tampering. What counts, Dr. Urth, is not the Device itself, however dangerous it may be in the abstract, but the intentions of the men who make use of the Device. The Ultras have the declared intention of killing off more than 99.9 per cent of humanity. The government, whatever the faults of the men composing it, would have no such intention."

"What *would* the government intend?"

"A scientific study of the Device. Even the mind-tampering aspect itself could yield infinite good. Put to enlightened use, it could educate us concerning the physical basis of mental function. We might learn to correct mental disorders or cure the Ultras. Mankind might learn to develop greater intelligence generally."

"How can I believe that such idealism will be put into practice?"

"*I* believe so. Consider that you face a possible turn to evil by the government if you help us, but you risk the certain and declared evil purpose of the Ultras if you don't."

Urth nodded thoughtfully. "Perhaps you're right. And yet I have a favor to ask of you. I have a niece who is, I believe, quite fond of me. She is constantly upset over the fact that I steadfastly refuse to indulge in the lunacy of travel. She states that she will not rest content until someday I accompany her to Europe or North Carolina or some other outlandish place—"

Ashley leaned forwardly earnestly, brushing Davenport's restraining gesture to one side. "Dr. Urth, if you help us find the Device and if it can be made to work, then I assure you that we will be glad to help you free yourself of your phobia against travel and make it possible for you to go with your niece anywhere you wish."

Urth's bulging eyes widened and he seemed to shrink within himself. For a moment he looked wildly about as though he were already trapped. "*No!*" he gasped. "Not at all! Never!"

His voice dropped to an earnest, hoarse whisper. "Let me explain the nature of my fee. If I help you, if you retrieve the Device and learn its use, if the fact of my help becomes public, then my niece will be on the government like a fury. She is a terribly headstrong and shrill-voiced woman who will raise public subscriptions and organize demonstrations. She will stop at nothing. And yet you must not give in to her. You must *not!* You must resist all pressures. I wish to be left alone exactly as I am now. That is my absolute and minimum fee."

Ashley flushed. "Yes, of course, since that is your wish."

"I have your word?"

"You have my word."

"Please remember. I rely on you too, Mr. Davenport."

"It will be as you wish," soothed Davenport. "And now, I presume, you can interpret the items?"

"The items?" asked Urth, seeming to focus his attention with difficulty on the card. "You mean these markings, $XY^2$ and so on?"

"Yes. What do they mean?"

"I don't know. Your interpretations are as good as any, I suppose."

Ashley exploded. "Do you mean that all this talk about helping us is nonsense? What is this maundering about a fee, then?"

Wendell Urth looked confused and taken aback. "I would like to help you."

"But you don't know what these items mean."

"I—I don't. But I know what this message means."

"You do?" cried Davenport.

"Of course. Its meaning is transparent. I suspected it halfway through your story. And I was sure of it once I read the reconstruction of the conversations between Strauss and Jennings. You would understand it yourself, gentlemen, if you would only stop to think."

"See here," said Ashley in exasperation, "you said you don't know what the items mean."

"I don't. I said I know what the *message* means."

"What is the message if it is not the items? Is it the paper, for Heaven's sake?"

"Yes, in a way."

"You mean invisible ink or something like that?"

"No! Why is it so hard for you to understand, when you yourself stand on the brink?"

Davenport leaned toward Ashley and said in a low voice, "Sir, will you let me handle it, please?"

Ashley snorted, then said in a stifled manner, "Go ahead."

"Dr. Urth," said Davenport, "will you give us your analysis?"

"Ah! Well, all right." The little extraterrologist settled back in his chair and mopped his damp forehead on his sleeve. "Let's consider the message. If you accept the quartered circle and the arrow as directing you to me, that leaves seven items. If these indeed refer to seven craters, six of them, at least, must be designed merely to distract, since the Device surely cannot be in more than one place. It contained no movable or detachable parts—it was all one piece.

"Then, too, none of the items are straightforward. SU might, by your interpretation, mean any place on the other side of the Moon, which is an area the size of South America. Again PC/2 can mean 'Tycho,' as Mr. Ashley says, or it can mean 'halfway between Ptolemaeus and Copernicus,' as Mr. Davenport thought, or for that matter 'halfway between Plato and Cassini.' To be sure, $XY^2$ could mean 'Alfonsus'—very ingenious interpretation, that—but it could refer to some co-ordinate system in which the Y co-ordinate was the square of the X co-ordinate. Similarly C-C would mean 'Bond' or it could mean 'halfway between Cassini and Copernicus.' F/A could mean 'Newton' or it could mean 'between Fabricius and Archimedes.'

"In short, the items have so many meanings that they are meaningless. Even if one of them had meaning, it could not be selected from among the others, so that it is only sensible to suppose that all the items are merely red herrings.

"It is necessary, then, to determine what about the message is completely unambiguous, what is perfectly clear. The answer to that can only be that it *is* a message, that it *is* a clue to a hiding place. That is the one thing we are certain about, isn't it?"

Davenport nodded, then said cautiously, "At least, we think we are certain of it."

"Well, you have referred to this message as the key to the whole matter. You have acted as though it were the crucial clue. Jennings himself referred to the Device as a key or a clue. If we combine this serious view of the matter with Jennings' penchant for puns, a penchant which may have been heightened by the mind-tampering Device he was carrying—So let me tell you a story.

"In the last half of the sixteenth century, there lived a German Jesuit in Rome. He was a mathematician and astonomer of note and helped Pope Gregory XIII reform the calendar in 1582, performing all the enormous calculations required. This astonomer admired Copernicus but he did not accept the heliocentric view of the Solar System. He clung to the older belief that the Earth was the center of the Universe.

"In 1650, nearly forty years after the death of this mathematician, the Moon was mapped by another Jesuit, the Italian astonomer, Giovanni Battista Riccioli. He named the craters after astronomers of the past and since he too rejected Copernicus, he selected the largest and most spectacular craters for those who placed the Earth at the center of the Universe—for Ptolemy, Hipparchus, Alfonso X, Tycho Brahe. The biggest crater Riccioli could find he reserved for his German Jesuit predecessor.

"This crater is actually only the second largest of the craters visible from Earth. The only larger crater is Bailly, which is right on the Moon's limb and is therefore very difficult to see from the Earth. Riccioli ignored it, and it was named for an astronomer who lived a century after his time and who was guillotined during the French Revolution."

Ashley was listening to all this restlessly. "But what has this to do with the message?"

"Why, everything," said Urth, with some surprise. "Did you not call this message the key to the whole business? Isn't it the crucial clue?"

"Yes, of course."

"Is there any doubt that we are dealing with something that is a clue or key to something else?"

"No, there isn't," said Ashley.

"Well, then—The name of the German Jesuit I have been speaking of is Christoph Klau—pronounced 'klow.' Don't you see the pun? Klau—clue?"

Ashley's entire body seemed to grow flabby with disappointment. "Farfetched," he muttered.

Davenport said anxiously, "Dr. Urth, there is no feature on the Moon named Klau as far as I know."

"Of course not," said Urth excitedly. "That is the whole point. At this period of history, the last half of the sixteenth century, European scholars were Latinizing their names. Klau did so. In place of the German 'u', he made use of the equivalent letter, the Latin 'v'. He then added an 'ius' ending typical of Latin names and Christoph Klau became Christopher Clavius, and I suppose you are all aware of the giant crater we call Clavius."

"But—" began Davenport.

"Don't 'but' me," said Urth. "Just let me point out that the Latin word 'clavis' means 'key'. Now do you see the double and bilingual pun? Klau, clue, Clavius—clavis—key. In his whole life, Jennings could never have made a double, bilingual pun, without the Device. Now he could, and I wonder if death might not have been almost triumphant under the circumstances. And he directed you to me because he knew I would remember his penchant for puns and because he knew I loved them too."

The two men of the Bureau were looking at him wide-eyed.

Urth said solemnly, "I would suggest you search the shaded rim of Clavius, at that point where the Earth is nearest the zenith."

Ashley rose. "Where is your videophone?"

"In the next room."

Ashley dashed. Davenport lingered behind. "Are you sure, Dr. Urth?"

"Quite sure. But even if I am wrong, I suspect it doesn't matter."

"What doesn't matter?"

"Whether you find it or not. For if the Ultras find the Device, they will probably be unable to use it."

"Why do you say that?"

"You asked me if Jennings had ever been a student of mine, but you never asked me about Strauss, who was also a geologist. He was a student of mine a year or so after Jennings. I remember him well."

"Oh?"

"An unpleasant man. Very cold. It is the hallmark of the Ultras, I think. They are all very cold, very rigid, very sure of themselves. They can't empathize, or they wouldn't speak of killing off billions of human beings. What emotions they possess are icy ones, self-absorbed ones, feelings incapable of spanning the distance between two human beings."

"I think I see."

"I'm sure you do. The conversation reconstructed from Strauss's ravings showed us he could not manipulate the Device. He lacked the emotional intensity, or the type of necessary emotion. I imagine all Ultras would. Jennings, who was not an Ultra, could manipulate it. Anyone who could use the Device would, I suspect, be incapable of deliberate cold-blooded cruelty. He might strike out of panic fear as Jennings struck at Strauss, but never out of calculation, as Strauss tried to strike at Jennings. In short, to put it tritely, I think the Device can be actuated by love, but never by hate, and the Ultras are nothing if not haters."

Davenport nodded. "I hope you're right. But then—why were you so suspicious of the government's motives if you felt the wrong men could not manipulate the Device?"

Urth shrugged. "I wanted to make sure you could bluff and rationalize on your feet and make yourself convincingly persuasive at a moment's notice. After all, you may have to face my niece."

# The Billiard Ball

James Priss—I suppose I ought to say Professor James Priss, though everyone is sure to know whom I mean even without the title—always spoke slowly.

I know. I interviewed him often enough. He had the greatest mind since Einstein, but it didn't work quickly. He admitted his slowness often. Maybe it was *because* he had so great a mind that it didn't work quickly.

He would say something in slow abstraction, then he would think, and then he would say something more. Even over trivial matters, his giant mind would hover uncertainly, adding a touch here and then another there.

*Would* the Sun rise tomorrow, I can imagine him wondering. What do we mean by "rise"? Can we be certain that tomorrow will come? Is the term "Sun" completely unambiguous in this connection?

Add to this habit of speech a bland countenance, rather pale, with no expression except for a general look of uncertainty; gray hair, rather thin, neatly combed; business suits of an invariably conservative cut; and you have what Professor James Priss was—a retiring person, completely lacking in magnetism.

That's why nobody in the world, except myself, could possibly suspect him of being a murderer. And even I am not sure. After all, he *was* slow-thinking; he was *always* slow-thinking. Is it conceivable that at one crucial moment he managed to think quickly and act at once?

It doesn't matter. Even if he murdered, he got away with it. It is far too late now to try to reverse matters and I wouldn't succeed in doing so even if I decided to let this be published.

* * *

Edward Bloom was Priss's classmate in college, and an associate, through circumstance, for a generation afterward. They were equal in age and in their propensity for the bachelor life, but opposites in everything else that mattered.

Bloom was a living a flash of light; colorful, tall, broad, loud, brash, and self-confident. He had a mind that resembled a meteor strike in the sudden and unexpected way it could seize the essential. He was no theoretician, as Priss was; Bloom had neither the patience for it, nor the capacity to concentrate intense thought upon a single abstract point. He admitted that; he boasted of it.

What he did have was an uncanny way of seeing the application of a theory; of seeing the manner in which it could be put to use. In the cold marble block of abstract structure, he could see, without apparent difficulty, the intricate design of a marvelous device. The block would fall apart at his touch and leave the device.

It is a well-known story, and not too badly exaggerated, that nothing Bloom ever built had failed to work, or to be patentable, or to be profitable. By the time he was forty-five, he was one of the richest men on Earth.

And if Bloom the Technician were adapted to one particular matter more than anything else, it was to the way of thought of Priss the Theoretician. Bloom's greatest gadgets were built upon Priss's greatest thoughts, and as Bloom grew wealthy and famous, Priss gained phenomenal respect among his colleagues.

Naturally it was to be expected that when Priss advanced his Two-Field Theory, Bloom would set about at once to build the first practical anti-gravity device.

* * *

My job was to find human interest in the Two-Field Theory for the subscribers to *Tele-News Press*, and you get that by trying to deal with human beings and not with abstract ideas. Since my interviewee was Professor Priss, that wasn't easy.

Naturally, I was going to ask about the possibilities of anti-gravity, which interested everyone; and not about the Two-Field Theory, which no one could understand.

"Anti-gravity?" Priss compressed his pale lips and considered. "I'm not entirely sure that is possible, or ever will be. I haven't—uh—worked the matter out to my satisfaction. I don't entirely see whether the Two-Field equations would have a finite solution, which they would have to have, of course, if—" And then he went off into a brown study.

I prodded him. "Bloom says he thinks such a device can be built."

Priss nodded. "Well, yes, but I wonder. Ed Bloom has had an

amazing knack at seeing the unobvious in the past. He has an unusual mind. It's certainly made him rich enough."

We were sitting in Priss's apartment. Ordinary middle-class. I couldn't help a quick glance this way and that. Priss was not wealthy.

I don't think he read my mind. He saw me look. And I think it was on *his* mind. He said, "Wealth isn't the usual reward for the pure scientist. Or even a particularly desirable one."

Maybe so, at that, I thought. Priss certainly had his own kind of reward. He was the third person in history to win two Nobel Prizes, and the first to have both of them in the sciences and both of them unshared. You can't complain about that. And if he wasn't rich, neither was he poor.

But he didn't sound like a contented man. Maybe it wasn't Bloom's wealth alone that irked Priss; maybe it was Bloom's fame among the people of Earth generally; maybe it was the fact that Bloom was a celebrity wherever he went, whereas Priss, outside scientific conventions and faculty clubs, was largely anonymous.

I can't say how much of all this was in my eyes or in the way I wrinkled the creases in my forehead, but Priss went on to say, "But we're friends, you know. We play billiards once or twice a week. I beat him regularly."

(I never published that statement. I checked it with Bloom, who made a long counterstatement that began: "He beats *me* at billiards. That jackass—" and grew increasingly personal thereafter. As a matter of fact, neither one was a novice at billiards. I watched them play once for a short while, after the statement and counterstatement, and both handled the cue with professional aplomb. What's more, both played for blood, and there was no friendship in the game that I could see.)

I said, "Would you care to predict whether Bloom will manage to build an anti-gravity device?"

"You mean would I commit myself to anything? Hmm. Well, let's consider, young man. Just what do we mean by anti-gravity? Our conception of gravity is built around Einstein's General Theory of Relativity, which is now a century and a half old but which, within its limits, remains firm. We can picture it—"

I listened politely. I'd heard Priss on the subject before, but if I was to get anything out of him—which wasn't certain—I'd have to let him work his way through in his own way.

"We can picture it," he said, "by imagining the Universe to be a flat, thin, super-flexible sheet of untearable rubber. If we picture mass as being associated with weight, as it is on the surface of the Earth, then we would expect a mass, resting upon the rubber sheet, to make an indentation. The greater the mass, the deeper the indentation.

"In the actual Universe," he went on, "all sorts of masses exist, and so our rubber sheet must be pictured as riddled with indentations. Any object rolling along the sheet would dip into and out of indentations it passed, veering and changing direction as it did so. It is this veer and change of direction that we interpret as demonstrating the existence of a force of gravity. If the moving object comes close enough to the center of the indentation and is moving slowly enough, it gets trapped and whirls round and round that indentation. In the absence of friction, it keeps up that whirl forever. In other words, what Isaac Newton interpreted as a force, Albert Einstein interpreted as geometrical distortion."

He paused at this point. He had been speaking fairly fluently—for him—since he was saying something he had said often before. But now he began to pick his way.

He said, "So in trying to produce anti-gravity, we are trying to alter the geometry of the Universe. If we carry on our metaphor, we are trying to straighten out the indented rubber sheet. We could imagine ourselves getting under the indenting mass and lifting it upward, supporting it so as to prevent it from making an indentation. If we make the rubber sheet flat in that way, then we create a Universe—or at least a portion of the Universe—in which gravity doesn't exist. A rolling body would pass the non-indenting mass without altering its direction of travel a bit, and we could interpret this as meaning that the mass was exerting no gravitational force. In order to accomplish this feat, however, we need a mass equivalent to the indenting mass. To produce anti-gravity on Earth in this way, we would have to make use of a mass equal to that of Earth and poise it above our heads, so to speak."

I interrupted him. "But your Two-Field Theory—"

"Exactly. General Relativity does not explain both the gravitational field and the electromagnetic fields in a single set of equations. Einstein spent half his life searching for that single set—for a Unified Field Theory—and failed. All who followed Einstein also failed. I, however, began with the assumption that there were two fields that could not be unified and followed the consequences, which I can explain, in part, in terms of the 'rubber sheet' metaphor."

Now we came to something I wasn't sure I had ever heard before. "How does that go?" I asked.

"Suppose that, instead of trying to lift the indenting mass, we try to stiffen the sheet itself, make it less indentable. It would contract, at least over a small area, and become flatter. Gravity would weaken, and so would mass for the two are essentially the same phenomenon in terms of the indented Universe. If we could make the rubber sheet completely flat, both gravity and mass would disappear altogether.

"Under the proper conditions, the electromagnetic field could be made to counter the gravitational field, and serve to stiffen the indented fabric of the Universe. The electromagnetic field is tremendously stronger than the gravitational field, so the former could be made to overcome the latter."

I said uncertainly, "But you say 'under the proper conditions.' Can those proper conditions you speak of be achieved, Professor?"

"That is what I don't know," said Priss thoughtfully and slowly. "If the Universe were really a rubber sheet, its stiffness would have to reach an infinite value before it could be expected to remain completely flat under an indenting mass. If that is also so in the real Universe, then an infinitely intense electromagnetic field would be required and that would mean anti-gravity would be impossible."

"But Bloom says—"

"Yes, I imagine Bloom thinks a finite field will do, if it can be properly applied. Still, however, ingenious he is," and Priss smiled narrowly, "we needn't take him to be infallible. His grasp on theory is quite faulty. He—he never earned his college degree, did you know that?"

I was about to say that I knew that. After all, everyone did. But there was a touch of eagerness in Priss's voice as he said it and I looked up in time to catch animation in his eye, as thought he were delighted to spread that piece of news. So I nodded my head as if I were filing it for future reference.

"Then you would say, Professor Priss," I prodded again, "that Bloom is probably wrong and that anti-gravity is impossible?"

And finally Priss nodded and said, "The gravitational field can be awakened, of course, but if by anti-gravity we mean a true zero-gravity field—no gravity at all over a significant volume of space—then I suspect anti-gravity may turn out to be impossible, despite Bloom."

And I had, after a fashion, what I wanted.

* * *

I wasn't able to see Bloom for nearly three months after that, and when I did see him he was in an angry mood.

He had grown angry at once, of course, when the news first broke concerning Priss's statement. He let it be known that Priss would be invited to the eventual display of the anti-gravity device as soon as it was constructed, and would even be asked to participate in the demonstration. Some reporter—not I, unfortunately—caught him between appointments and asked him to elaborate on that and he said:

"I'll have the device eventually; soon, maybe. And you can be there, and so can anyone else the press would care to have there. And Professor James Priss can be there. He can represent Theoretical Science and after I have demonstrated anti-gravity, he can adjust his theory to explain it. I'm sure he will know how to make his adjustments in masterly fashion and show exactly why I couldn't possibly have failed. He might do it now and save time, but I suppose he won't."

It was all said very politely, but you could hear the snarl under the rapid flow of words.

Yet he continued his occasional game of billiards with Priss and when the two met they behaved with complete propriety. One could tell the progress Bloom was making by their respective attitudes to the press. Bloom grew curt and even snappish, while Priss developed an increasing good humor.

When my umpteenth request for an interview with Bloom was finally accepted, I wondered if perhaps that meant a break in Bloom's quest. I had a little daydream of him announcing final success to *me*.

It didn't work out that way. He met me in his office at Bloom Enterprises in upstate New York. It was a wonderful setting, well away from any populated area, elaborately landscaped, and covering as much ground as a rather large industrial establishment. Edison at his height, two centuries ago, had never been as phenomenally successful as Bloom.

But Bloom was not in a good humor. He came striding in ten minutes late and went snarling past his secretary's desk with the barest nod in my direction. He was wearing a lab coat, unbuttoned.

He threw himself into his chair and said, "I'm sorry if I've kept you waiting, but I didn't have as much time as I had hoped." Bloom was a born showman and knew better than to antagonize the press, but I had the feeling he was having a great deal of difficulty at that moment in adhering to this principle.

I made the obvious guess. "I am given to understand, sir, that your recent tests have been unsuccessful."

"Who told you that?"

"I would say it was general knowledge, Mr. Bloom."

"No, it isn't. Don't say that, young man. There is no general knowledge about what goes on in my laboratories and workshops. You're stating the Professor's opinions, aren't you? Priss's, I mean."

"No, I'm—"

"Of course you are. Aren't you the one to whom he made that statement—that anti-gravity is impossible?"

"He didn't make the statement that flatly."

"He never says anything flatly, but it was flat enough for him, and not as flat as I'll have his damned rubber-sheet Universe before I'm finished."

"Then does that mean you're making progress, Mr. Bloom?"

"You know I am," he said with a snap. "Or you should know. Weren't you at the demonstration last week?"

"Yes, I was."

I judged Bloom to be in trouble or he wouldn't be mentioning that demonstration. It worked but it was not a world beater. Between the two poles of a magnet a region of lessened gravity was produced.

It was done very cleverly. A Mössbauer-Effect Balance was used to probe the space between the poles. If you've never seen an M-E Balance in action, it consists primarily of a tight monochromatic beam of gamma rays shot down the low-gravity field. The gamma rays change wavelength slightly but measurably under the influence of the gravitational field and if anything happens to alter the intensity of the field, the wave length-change shifts correspondingly. It is an extremely delicate method for probing a gravitational field and it worked like a charm. There was no question but that Bloom had lowered gravity.

The trouble was that it had been done before by others. Bloom, to be sure, had made use of circuits that greatly increased the ease with which such an effect had been achieved—his system was typically ingenious and had been duly patented—and he maintained that it was by this method that anti-gravity would become not merely a scientific curiosity but a practical affair with industrial applications.

Perhaps. But it was an incomplete job and he didn't usually make a fuss over incompleteness. He wouldn't have done so this time if he weren't desperate to display *something*.

I said, "It's my impression that what you accomplished at that preliminary demonstration was 0.8 *g*, and better than that was achieved in Brazil last spring."

"That so? Well, calculate the energy input in Brazil and here, and then tell me the difference in gravity decrease per kilowatt-hour. You'll be surprised."

"But the point is, can you reach 0 *g*—zero-gravity? That's what Professor Priss thinks may be impossible. Everyone agrees that merely lessening the intensity of the field is no great feat."

Bloom's fist clenched. I had the feeling that a key experiment had gone wrong that day and he was annoyed almost past endurance. Bloom hated to be balked by the Universe.

He said, "Theoreticians make me sick." He said it in a low, controlled voice, as though he were finally tired of not saying it, and he was going to speak his mind and be damned. "Priss has won two Nobel Prizes for sloshing around a few equations, but what has he done with it? Nothing! I *have* done something with it and I'm going to do more with it, whether Priss likes it or not."

"*I'm* the one people will remember. *I'm* the one who gets the credit. He can keep his damned title and his Prizes and his kudos from the scholars. Listen, I'll tell you what gripes him. Plain old-fashioned jealousy. It kills him that I get what I get for doing. He wants it for *thinking*.

"I said to him once—we play billiards together, you know—"

It was at this point that I quoted Priss's statement about billiards and got Bloom's counterstatement. I never published either. That was just trivia.

"We play billiards," said Bloom, when he had cooled down, "and I've won my share of games. We keep things friendly though. What the hell—college chums and all that—though how he got through I'll never know. He made it in physics, of course, and in math, but he got a bare pass—out of pity, I think—in every humanities course he ever took."

"You did not get your degree, did you, Mr. Bloom?" That was sheer mischief on my part. I was enjoying his eruption.

"I quit to go into business, damn it. My academic average, over the three years I attended, was a strong B. Don't imagine anything else, you hear? Hell, by the time Priss got his Ph.D., I was working on my second million."

He went on, clearly irritated, "Anyway, we were playing billiards and I said to him, 'Jim, the average man will never understand why you get the Nobel Prize when I'm the one who gets the results. Why do you need two? Give me one!' He stood there, chalking up his cue, and then he said in his soft namby-pamby way, 'You have two billions, Ed. Give me one.' So you see, he wants the money."

I said, "I take it you don't mind his getting the honor?"

For a minute I thought he was going to order me out, but he didn't. He laughed instead, waved his hand in front of him, as though he were erasing something from an invisible blackboard in front of him. He said, "Oh, well, forget it. All that is off the record. Listen, do you want a statement? Okay. Things didn't go right today and I blew my top a bit, but it will clear up. I think I know what's wrong. And if I don't, I'm going to know.

"Look, you can say that I say that we *don't* need infinite electromagnetic intensity; we *will* flatten out the rubber sheet; we *will* have zero gravity. And when we get it, I'll have the damndest demonstration you ever saw, exclusively for the press and for Priss, and you'll be invited. And you can say it won't be long. Okay?"

Okay!

* * *

I had time after that to see each man once or twice more. I even saw them together when I was present at one of their billiard games. As I said before, both of them were *good*.

But the call to the demonstration did not come as quickly as all that. It arrived six weeks less than a year after Bloom gave me his statement. And at that, perhaps it was unfair to expect quicker work.

I had a special engraved invitation, with the assurance of a cocktail hour first. Bloom never did things by halves and he was planning to have a pleased and satisfied group of reporters on hand. There was an arrangement for trimensional TV, too. Bloom felt competely confident, obviously; confident enough to be willing to trust the demonstration in every living room on the planet.

I called up Professor Priss, to make sure he was invited too. He was.

"Do you plan to attend, sir?"

There was a pause and the professor's face on the screen was a study in uncertain reluctance. "A demonstration of this sort is most unsuitable where a serious scientific matter is in question. I do not like to encourage such things."

I was afraid he would beg off, and the dramatics of the situation would be greatly lessened if he were not there. But then, perhaps, he decided he dared not play the chicken before the world. With obvious distaste he said, "Of course, Ed Bloom is not really a scientist and he must have his day in the sun. I'll be there."

"Do you think Mr. Bloom can produce zero gravity, sir?"

"Uh . . . Mr. Bloom sent me a copy of the design of his device and . . . and I'm not certain. Perhaps he can do it, if . . . uh . . . he says he can do it. Of course"—he paused again for quite a long time—"I think I would like to see it."

So would I, and so would many others.

The staging was impeccable. A whole floor of the main building at Bloom Enterprises—the one on the hilltop—was cleared. There were the promised cocktails and a splendid array of hors d'oeuvres, soft music and lighting, and a carefully dressed and thoroughly jovial Edward Bloom playing the perfect host, while a number of polite and unobtrusive menials fetched and carried. All was geniality and amazing confidence.

James Priss was late and I caught Bloom watching the corners of the crowd and beginning to grow a little grim about the edges. Then Priss arrived, dragging a volume of colorlessness in with him, a drabness that was unaffected by the noise and the absolute splendor (no other word would describe it—or else it was the two martinis glowing inside me) that filled the room.

Bloom saw him and his face was illuminated at once. He bounced across the floor, seized the smaller man's hand and dragged him to the bar.

"Jim! Glad to see you! What'll you have? Hell, man, I'd have called it off if you hadn't showed. Can't have this thing without the star, you know." He wrung Priss's hand. "It's your theory, you know. We poor mortals can't do a thing without you few, you damned *few* few, pointing the way."

He was being ebullient, handing out the flattery, because he could afford to do so now. He was fattening Priss for the kill.

Priss tried to refuse a drink, with some sort of mutter, but a glass was pressed into his hand and Bloom raised his voice to a bull roar.

"Gentlemen! A moment's quiet, please. To Professor Priss, the greatest mind since Einstein, two-time Nobel Laureate, father of the Two-Field Theory, and inspirer of the demonstration we are about to see—even if he didn't think it would work, and had the guts to say so publicly."

There was a distinct titter of laughter that qickly faded out and Priss looked as grim as his face could manage.

"But now that Professor Priss is here," said Bloom, "and we've had our toast, let's get on with it. Follow me, gentlemen!"

The demonstration was in a much more elaborate place than had housed the earlier one. This time it was on the top floor of the building. Different magnets were involved—smaller ones, by heaven—but as nearly as I could tell, the same M-E Balance was in place.

One thing was new, however, and it staggered everyone, drawing much more attention than anything else in the room. It was a billiard table, resting under one pole of the magnet. Beneath it was the companion Pole. A round hole, about a foot across, was stamped out of the very center of the table and it was obvious that the zero-gravity field, if it was to be produced, would be produced through that hole in the center of the billiard table.

It was as though the whole demonstration had been designed, surrealist fashion, to point up the victory of Bloom over Priss. This was to be another version of their everlasting billiards competition and Bloom was going to win.

I don't know if the other newsmen took matters in that fashion, but

I think Priss did. I turned to look at him and saw that he was still holding the drink that had been forced into his hand. He rarely drank, I knew, but now he lifted the glass to his lips and emptied it in two swallows. He stared at that billiard ball and I needed no gift of ESP to realize that he took it as a deliberate snap of fingers under his nose.

Bloom led us to the twenty seats that surrounded three sides of the table, leaving the fourth free as a working area. Priss was carefully escorted to the seat commanding the most convenient view. Priss glanced quickly at the trimensional cameras which were now working. I wondered if he were thinking of leaving but deciding that he couldn't in the full glare of the eyes of the world.

Essentially, the demonstration was simple; it was the production that counted. There were dials in plain view that measured the energy expenditure. There were others that transferred the M-E Balance readings into a position and size that were visible to all. Everything was arranged for easy trimensional viewing.

Bloom explained each step in a genial way, with one or two pauses in which he turned to Priss for a confirmation that had to come. He didn't do it often enough to make it obvious, but just enough to turn Priss upon the spit of his own torment. From where I sat I could look across the table and see Priss on the other side.

He had the look of a man in Hell.

As we know, Bloom succeeded. The M-E Balance showed the gravitational intensity to be sinking steadily as the electromaganetic field was intensified. There were cheers when it dropped below the 0.52 *g* mark. A red line indicated that on the dial.

"The 0.52 *g* mark, as you know," said Bloom confidently, "represents the previous record low in gravitational intensity. We are now lower than that at a cost in electricity that is less than ten per ent what it cost at the time that mark was set. And we will go lower still."

Bloom—I think deliberately, for the sake of the suspense—slowed the drop toward the end, letting the trimensional cameras switch back and forth between the gap in the billiard table and the dial on which the M-E Balance reading was lowering.

Bloom said suddenly, "Gentlemen, you will find dark goggles in the pouch on the side of each chair. Please put them on now. The zero-gravity field will soon be established and it will radiate a light rich in ultraviolet."

He put goggles on himself, and there was a momentary rustle as others went on too.

I think no one breathed during the last minute, when the dial reading dropped to zero and held fast. And just as that happened a cylinder of light sprang into existence from pole to pole through the hole in the billiard table.

There was a ghost of twenty sighs at that. Someone called out, "Mr. Bloom, what is the reason for the light?"

"It's characteristic of the zero-gravity field," said Bloom smoothly, which was no answer, of course.

Reporters were standing up now, crowding about the edge of the table. Bloom waved them back. "Please, gentlemen, stand clear!"

Only Priss remained sitting. He seemed lost in thought and I have been certain ever since that it was the goggles that obscured the possible significance of everything that followed. I didn't see his eyes. I couldn't. And that meant neither I nor anyone else could even begin to make a guess as to what was going on behind those eyes. Well, maybe we couldn't have made such a guess, even if the goggles hadn't been there, but who can say?

Bloom was raising his voice again. "Please! The demonstration is not yet over. So far, we've only repeated what I have done before. I have now produced a zero-gravity field and I have shown it can be done practically. But I want to demonstrate something of what such a field can do. What we are going to see next will be something that has never been seen, not even by myself. I have not experimented in this direction, much as I would have liked to, because I have felt that Professor Priss deserved the honor of—"

Priss looked up sharply. "What—what—"

"Professor Priss," said Bloom, smiling broadly, "I would like you to perform the first experiment involving the interaction of a solid object with a zero-gravity field. Notice that the field has been formed in the center of a billiard table. The world knows your phenomenal skill in billiards, Professor, a talent second only to your amazing aptitude in theoretical physics. Won't you send a billiard ball into the zero-gravity volume?"

Eagerly he was handing a ball and cue to the professor. Priss, his eyes hidden by the goggles, stared at them and only very slowly, very uncertainly, reached out to take them.

I wonder what his eyes were showing. I wonder, too, how much of the decision to have Priss play billiards at the demonstration was due to Bloom's anger at Priss's remark about their periodic game, the remark I had quoted. Had I been, in my way, responsible for what followed?

"Come, stand up, Professor," said Bloom, "and let *me* have your seat. The show is yours from now on. Go ahead!"

Bloom seated himself, and still talked, in a voice that grew more organlike with each moment. "Once Professor Priss sends the ball into the volume of zero gravity, it will no longer be affected by Earth's gravitational field. It will remain truly motionless while the Earth rotates about its axis and travels about the Sun. In this latitude, and at this time of day, I have calculated that the Earth, in its motions, will sink downward. We will move with it and the ball will stand still. To us it will seem to rise up and away from the Earth's surface. Watch."

Priss seemed to stand in front of the table in frozen paralysis. Was it surprise? Astonishment? I don't know. I'll never know. Did he make a move to interrupt Bloom's little speech, or was he just suffering from an agonized reluctance to play the ignominious part into which he was being forced by his adversary?

Priss turned to the billiard table, looking first at it, then back at Bloom. Every reporter was on his feet, crowding as closely as possible in order to get a good view. Only Bloom himself remained seated, smiling and isolated. He, of course, was not watching the table, or the ball, or the zero-gravity field. As nearly as I could tell through the goggles, he was watching Priss.

Priss turned to the table and placed his ball. He was going to be the agent that was to bring final and dramatic triumph to Bloom and make himself—the man who said it couldn't be done—the goat to be mocked forever.

Perhaps he felt there was no way out. Or perhaps—

With a sure stroke of his cue, he set the ball into motion. It was not going quickly, and every eye followed it. It struck the side of the table and caromed. It was going even slower now as though Priss himself were increasing the suspense and making Bloom's triumph the more dramatic.

I had a perfect view, for I was standing on the side of the table opposite from that where Priss was. I could see the ball moving toward the glitter of the zero-gravity field and beyond it I could see those portions of the seated Bloom which were not hidden by the glitter.

The ball approached the zero-gravity volume, seemed to hang on the edge for a moment, and then was gone, with a streak of light, the sound of a thunderclap, the sudden smell of burning cloth.

We yelled. We all yelled.

I've seen the scene on television since—along with the rest of the world. I can see myself in the film during that fifteen-second period of wild confusion, but I don't really recognize my face.

Fifteen seconds!

And then we discovered Bloom. He was still sitting in the chair, his arms still folded, but there was a hole the size of a billiard ball through forearm, chest, and back. The better part of his heart, as it later turned out under autopsy, had been neatly punched out.

They turned off the device. They called in the police. They dragged off Priss, who was in a state of utter collapse. I wasn't much better off, to tell the truth, and if any reporter then on the scene ever tried to say he remained a cool observer of that scene, then he's a cool liar.

* * *

It was some months before I got to see Priss again. He had lost some weight but seemed well otherwise. Indeed, there was color in his cheeks and an air of decision about him. He was better dressed than I had ever seen him to be.

He said, "I know what happened *now*. If I had time to think, I would have known then. But I am a slow thinker, and poor Ed Bloom was so intent on running a great show and doing it so well that he carried me along with him. Naturally, I've been trying to make up for some of the damage I unwittingly caused."

"You can't bring Bloom back to life," I said soberly.

"No, I can't," he said, just as soberly. "But there's Bloom Enterprises to think of, too. What happened at the demonstration, in full view of the world, was the worst possible advertisement for zero gravity, and it's important that the story be made clear. That is why I have asked to see *you*."

"Yes?"

"If I had been a quicker thinker, I would have known Ed was speaking the purest nonsense when he said that the billiard ball would slowly rise in the zero-gravity field. It *couldn't* be so! If Bloom hadn't despised theory so, if he hadn't been so intent on being proud of his own ignorance of theory, he'd have known it himself.

"The Earth's motion, after all, isn't the only motion involved, young man. The Sun itself moves in a vast orbit about the center of the Milky Way Galaxy. And the Galaxy moves too, in some not very clearly defined way. If the billiard ball were subjected to zero gravity, you might think of it as being unaffected by any of these motions and therefore of suddenly falling into a state of absolute rest—when there is no such thing as absolute rest."

Priss shook his head slowly. "The trouble with Ed, I think, was that he was thinking of the kind of zero gravity one gets in a spaceship in free fall, when people float in mid-air. He expected the ball to float in mid-air. However, in a spaceship, zero gravity is not the result of an absence of gravitation, but merely the result of two objects, a ship and a man within the ship, falling at the same rate, responding to gravity in precisely the same way so that each is motionless with respect to the other.

"In the zero-gravity field produced by Ed, there was a flattening of the rubber-sheet Universe, which means an actual loss of mass. Everything in that field, including molecules of air caught within it, and the billiard ball I pushed into it, was completely massless as long as it remained with it. A completely massless object can move in only one way."

He paused, inviting the question, I asked, "What motion would that be?"

"Motion at the speed of light. Any massless object, such as a neutrino or a photon, must travel at the speed of light as long as it exists. In fact, light moves at that speed only because it is made up of photons. As soon as the billiard ball entered the zero-gravity field and lost its mass, it too assumed the speed of light at once and left."

I shook my head. "But didn't it regain its mass as soon as it left the zero-gravity volume?"

"It certainly did, and at once it began to be affected by the gravitational field and to slow up in response to the friction of the air and the top of the billiard table. But imagine how much friction it would take to slow up an object the mass of a billiard ball going at the speed of light. It went through the hundred-mile thickness of our atmosphere in a thousandth of a second and I doubt that it was slowed more than a few miles a second in doing so, a few miles out of 186,282 of them. On the way, it scorched the top of the billiard table, broke cleanly through the edge, went through the poor Ed and the window too, punching out neat circles because it had passed through before the neighboring portions of something even as brittle as glass had a chance to split and splinter.

"It is extremely fortunate we were on the top floor of a building set in a countrified area. If we were in the city, it might have passed through a number of buildings and killed a number of people. By now that billiard ball is off in space, far beyond the edge of the Solar System and it will continue to travel so forever, at nearly the speed of light, until it happens to strike an object large enough to stop it. And then it will gouge out a sizable crater."

I played with the notion and was not sure I liked it. "How is that possible? The billiard ball entered the zero-gravity volume almost at a standstill. I saw it. And you say it left with an incredible quantity of kinetic energy. Where did the energy come from?"

Priss shrugged. "It came from nowhere! The law of conservation of energy only holds under the conditions in which general relativity is valid; that is, in an indented-rubber-sheet universe. Wherever the indentation is flattened out, general relativity no longer holds, and energy can be created and destroyed freely. That accounts for the radiation along the cylindrical surface of the zero-gravity volume. That radiation, you remember, Bloom did not explain, and, I fear, could not explain. If he had only experimented further first; if he had only not been so foolishly anxious to put on his show—"

"What accounts for the radiation, sir?"

"The molecules of air inside the volume. Each assumes the speed of light and comes smashing outward. They're only molecules, not billiard balls, so they're stopped, but the kinetic energy of their motion is converted into energetic radiation. It's continuous because new molecules are always drifting in, and attaining the speed of light and smashing out."

"Then energy is being created continuously?"

"Exactly. And that is what we must make clear to the public. Anti-gravity is not primarily a device to lift spaceships or to revolutionize mechanical movement. Rather, it is the source of an endless supply of free energy, since part of the energy produced can be diverted to maintain the field that keeps that portion of the Universe flat. What Ed Bloom invented, without knowing it, was not just anti-gravity, but the first successful perpetual-motion machine of the first class—one that manufactures energy out of nothing."

I said slowly, "Any one of us could have been killed by that billiard ball, is that right, Professor? It might have come out in any direction."

Priss said, "Well, massless photons emerge from any light source at the speed of light in any direction; that's why a candle casts light in all directions. The massless air molecules come out of the zero-gravity volume in all directions, which is why the entire cylinder radiates. But the billiard ball was only one object. It could have come out in any direction, but it had to come out in some one direction, chosen at random, and the chosen direction happened to be the one that caught Ed."

That was it. Everyone knows the consequences. Mankind had free energy and so we have the world we have now. Professor Priss was placed in charge of its development by the board of Bloom Enterprises, and in time he was as rich and famous as ever Edward Bloom had been. And Priss still has two Nobel Prizes in addition.

Only . . .

I keep thinking. Photons smash out from a light source in all directions because they are created at the moment and there is no reason for them to move in one direction more than in another. Air molecules come out of a zero-gravity field in all directions because they enter it in all directions.

But what about a single billiard ball, entering a zero-gravity field from one particular direction? Does it come out in the same direction or in any direction?

I've inquired delicately, but theoretical physicists don't seem to be sure, and I can find no record that Bloom Enterprises, which is the only organization working with zero-gravity fields, has ever experimented in the matter. Someone at the organization once told me that the uncertainty principle guarantees the random emersion of an object entering in any direction. But then why don't they try the experiment?

Could it be, then . . .

Could it be that for once Priss's mind had been working quickly? Could it be that, under the pressure of what Bloom was trying to do to him, Priss had suddenly seen everything? He had been studying the radiation surrounding the zero-gravity volume. He might have realized its cause and been certain of the speed-of-light motion of anything entering the volume.

Why, then, had he said nothing?

One thing is certain. *Nothing* Priss would do at the billiard table could be accidental. He was an expert and the billiard ball did exactly what he wanted it to. I was standing right there. I saw him look at Bloom and then at the table as though he were judging angles.

I watched him hit that ball. I watched it bounce off the side of the table and move into the zero-gravity volume, heading in one particular direction.

For when Priss sent that ball toward the zero-gravity volume—and the tri-di films hear me out—it was *already* aimed directly at Bloom's heart!

Accident? Coincidence?

. . . Murder?

## *Afterword*

A friend of mine after reading the above story suggested I change the title to "Dirty Pool." I have been tempted to do so but I have refrained, for it seems too flippant a title for so grave a story—or perhaps I am just corroded with jealousy at not having thought of it first.

But in either case, now that all the stories in this volume have been gone over, and I have experienced the memories to which each gave rise, all I can say is, "Gee, it's great to be a science fiction writer."

# Exile to Hell

"The Russians," said Dowling, in his precise voice, "used to send prisoners to Siberia in the days before space travel had become common. The French used Devil's Island for the purpose. The British sailed them off to Australia."

He considered the chessboard carefully and his hand hesitated briefly over the bishop.

Parkinson, at the other side of the chess board, watched the pattern of the pieces absently. Chess was, of course, the professional game of computer programmers, but, under the circumstances, he lacked enthusiasm. By rights, he felt with some annoyance, Dowling should have been even worse off; he was programming the prosecution's case.

There was, of course, a tendency for the programmer to take over some of the imagined characteristics of the computer—the unemotionality, the imperviousness to anything but logic. Dowling reflected that in his precise hair-part and in the restrained elegance of his clothing.

Parkinson, who preferred to program the defense in the law cases in which he was involved, also preferred to be deliberately careless in the minor aspects of his costume.

He said, "You mean exile is a well-established punishment and therefore not particularly cruel."

"No, it *is* particularly cruel, but also it *is* well-established, and nowadays, it has become the perfect deterrent."

Dowling moved the bishop and did not look upward. Parkinson, quite involuntarily, did.

Of course, he couldn't see anything. They were indoors, in the comfortable modern world tailored to human needs, carefully protected against the raw environment. Out there, the night would be bright with its illumination.

When had he last seen it? Not for a long time. It occurred to him to wonder what phase it was in right now. Full? Gleaming? Or was it in its crescent phase? Was it a bright fingernail of light low in the sky?

By rights it should be a lovely sight. Once it had been. But that had been centuries ago, before space travel had become common and cheap, and before the surroundings all about them had grown sophisticated and controlled. Now the lovely light in the sky had become a new and more horrible Devil's Island hung in space.

—No one even used its name any longer, out of sheer distaste. It was "It." Or it was less than that, just a silent, upward movement of the head.

Parkinson said, "You might have allowed me to program the case against exile generally."

"Why? It couldn't have affected the result."

"Not this one, Dowling. But it might have affected future cases. Future punishments might be commuted to the death sentence."

"For someone guilty of equipment damage? You're dreaming."

"It was an act of blind anger. There was intent to harm a human being granted; but there was no intent to harm equipment."

"Nothing; it means nothing. Lack of intent is no excuse in such cases. You know that."

"It *should* be an excuse. That's my point; the one I wanted to make."

Parkinson advanced a pawn now, to cover his knight.

Dowling considered. "You're trying to hang on to the queen's attack, Parkinson, and I'm not going to let you. —Let's see, now." And while he pondered he said, "These are not primitive times, Parkinson. We live in a crowded world with no margin for error. As small a thing as a blown-out consistor could endanger a sizable fraction of our population. When anger endangers and subverts a power line, it's a serious thing."

"I don't question that—"

"You seemed to be doing so, when you were constructing the defense program."

"I was not. Look, when Jenkins' laser beam cut through the Field-warp, I myself was as close to death as anyone. A quarter hour's additional delay would have meant my end, too, and I'm completely aware of that. My point is only that exile is not the proper punishment!"

He tapped his finger on the chessboard for emphasis, and Dowling caught the queen before it went over. "Adjusting, not moving," he mumbled.

Dowling's eyes went from piece to piece and he continued to hesitate. "You're wrong, Parkinson. It *is* the proper punishment, because there's nothing worse and that matches a crime than which there is nothing worse. Look, we all feel our absolute dependence on a complicated and rather fragile technology. A breakdown might kill us all, and it doesn't matter whether the breakdown is deliberate, accidental, or caused by incompetence. Human beings demand the maximum punishment for any such deed as the only way they can feel secure. Mere death is not sufficient deterrent."

"Yes, it is. No one wants to die."

"They want to live in exile up there even less. That's why we've only had one such case in the last ten years, and only one exile. —There, do something about that!" And Dowling nudged his queen's rook one space to the right.

A light flashed. Parkinson was on his feet at once. "The programming is finished. The computer will have its verdict now."

Dowling looked up phlegmatically, "You've no doubt about what that verdict will be, have you? —Keep the board standing. We'll finish afterward."

Parkinson was quite certain he would lack the heart to continue the game. He hurried down the corridor to the courtroom, light and quick on his feet, as always.

Shortly after he and Downing had entered, the judge took his seat, and then in came Jenkins, flanked by two guards.

Jenkins looked haggard, but stoical. Ever since the blind rage had overcome him and he had accidentally thrown a sector into unpowered darkness while striking out at a fellow worker, he must have known the inevitable consequence of this worst of all crimes. It helps to have no illusions.

Parkinson was not stoical. He dared not look squarely at Jenkins. He could not have done so without wondering, painfully, as to what might be going through Jenkins' mind at that moment. Was he absorbing, through every sense, all the perfections of familiar comfort before being thrust forever into the luminous Hell that rode the night sky?

Was he savoring the clean and pleasant air in his nostrils, the soft lights, the equable temperature, the pure water on call, the secure surroundings designed to cradle humanity in tame comfort?

While up there—

The judge pressed a contact and the computer's decision was converted into the warm, unmannered sound of a standardized human voice.

"A weighing of all pertinent information in the light of the law of the land and of all relevant precedents leads to the conclusion that Anthony Jenkins is guilty on all counts of the crime of equipment damage and is subject to the maximum penalty."

There were only six people in the courtroom itself, but the entire population was listening by television, of course.

The judge spoke in prescribed phraseology. "The defendant will be taken from here to the nearest spaceport and, on the first available transportation, be removed from this world and sent into exile for the term of his natural life."

Jenkins seemed to shrink within himself, but he said no word.

Parkinson shivered. How many, he wondered, would now feel the enormity of such a punishment for *any* crime? How long before there would be enough humanity among men to wipe out forever the punishment of exile?

Could anyone really think of Jenkins up there in space, without flinching? Could they think, and endure the thought, of a fellow man thrown for all his life among the strange, unfriendly, vicious population of a world of unbearable heat by day and frigid cold by night; of a world where the sky was a harsh blue and the ground a harsher, clashing green; where the dusty air moved raucously and the viscous sea heaved eternally?

And the gravity, that heavy—heavy—heavy—eternal—pull!

Who could bear the horror of condemning someone, for whatever reason, to leave the friendly home of the Moon for that Hell in the sky—the Earth?

# Feminine Intuition

*The Three Laws of Robotics:*

1. *A robot may not injure a human being or, through inaction, allow a human being to come to harm.*
2. *A robot must obey the order given by human beings except where such orders would conflict with the First Law.*
3. *A robot must protect its own existence as long as such protection does not conflict with the First or Second Law.*

For the first time in the history of United States Robots and Mechanical Men, Inc., a robot had been destroyed through accident on Earth itself.

No one was to blame. The air vehicle had been demolished in midair and an unbelieving investigating committee was wondering whether they really dared announce the evidence that it had been hit by a meteorite. Nothing else could have been fast enough to prevent automatic avoidance; nothing else could have done the damage short of a nuclear blast and that was out of the question.

Tie that in with a report of a flash in the night sky just before the vehicle had exploded—and from Flagstaff Observatory, not from an amateur—and the location of a sizeable and distinctly meteoric bit of iron freshly gouged into the ground a mile from the site and what other conclusion could be arrived at?

Still, nothing like that had ever happened before and the calculations of the odds against it yielded monstrous figures. Yet even colossal improbabilities can happen sometimes.

At the offices of United States Robots, the hows and whys of it were secondary. The real point was that a robot had been destroyed.

That, in itself, was distressing.

The fact that JN-5 had been a prototype, the first, after four earlier attempts, to have been placed in the field, was even more distressing.

The fact that JN-5 was a radically new type of robot, quite different from anything ever built before, was abysmally distressing.

The fact that JN-5 had apparently accomplished something before its destruction that was incalculably important and that that accomplishment might now be forever gone, placed the distress utterly beyond words.

It seemed scarcely worth mentioning that, along with the robot, the Chief Robo-psychologist of United States Robots had also died.

* * *

Clinton Madarian had joined the firm ten years before. For five of those years, he had worked uncomplainingly under the grumpy supervision of Susan Calvin.

Madarian's brilliance was quite obvious and Susan Calvin had quietly promoted him over the heads of older men. She wouldn't, in any case, have deigned to give her reasons for this to Research Director Peter Bogert, but as it happened, no reasons were needed. Or, rather, they were obvious.

Madarian was utterly the reverse of the renowned Dr. Calvin in several very noticeable ways. He was not quite as overweight as his distinct double chin made him appear to be, but even so he was overpowering in his presence, where Susan had gone nearly unnoticed. Madarian's massive face, his shock of glistening red-brown hair, his ruddy complexion and booming voice, his loud laugh, and most of all, his irrepressible self-confidence and his eager way of announcing his successes, made everyone else in the room feel there was a shortage of space.

When Susan Calvin finally retired (refusing, in advance, any cooperation with respect to any testimonial dinner that might be planned in her honor, with so firm a manner that no announcement of the retirement was even made to the news services) Madarian took her place.

He had been in his new post exactly one day when he initiated the JN project.

It had meant the largest commitment of funds to one project that United States Robots had ever had to weigh, but that was something which Madarian dismissed with a genial wave of the band.

"Worth every penny of it, Peter," he said. "And I expect you to convince the Board of Directors of that."

"Give me reasons," said Bogert, wondering if Madarian would. Susan Calvin had never given reasons.

But Madarian said, "Sure," and settled himself easily into the large armchair in the Director's office.

Bogert watched the other with something that was almost awe. His own once-black hair was almost white now and within the decade he would follow Susan into retirement. That would mean the end of the original team that had built United States Robots into a globe-girdling firm that was a rival of the national governments in complexity and importance. Somehow neither he nor those who had gone before him ever quite grasped the enormous expansion of the firm.

But this was a new generation. The new men were at ease with the Colossus. They lacked the touch of wonder that would have them tiptoeing in disbelief. So they moved ahead, and that was good.

Madarian said, "I propose to begin the construction of robots without constraint."

"Without the Three Laws? Surely—"

"No, Peter. Are those the only constraints you can think of. Hell, you contributed to the design of the early positronic brains. Do I have to tell you that, quite aside from the Three Laws, there isn't a pathway in those brains that isn't carefully designed and fixed? We have robots planned for specific tasks, implanted with specific abilities."

"And you propose—"

"That at every level below the Three Laws, the paths be made open-ended. It's not difficult."

Bogert said dryly, "It's not difficult, indeed. Useless things are never difficult. The difficult thing is fixing the paths and making the robot useful."

"But why is that difficult? Fixing the paths requires a great deal of effort because the Principle of Uncertainty is important in particles the mass of positrons and the uncertainty effect must be minimized. Yet why must it? If we arrange to have the Principle just sufficiently prominent to allow the crossing of paths unpredictably—"

"We have an unpredictable robot."

"We have a *creative* robot," said Madarian, with a trace of impatience. "Peter, if there's anything a human brain has that a robotic brain has never had, it's the trace of unpredictability that comes from the effects of uncertainty at the subatomic level. I admit that this effect has never been demonstrated experimentally within the nervous system, but without that the human brain is not superior to the robotic brain in principle."

"And you think that if you introduce the effect into the robotic brain, the human brain will become not superior to the robotic brain in principle."

"That," said Madarian, "is exactly what I believe."

They went on for a long time after that.

* * *

The Board of Directors clearly had no intention of being easily convinced.

Scott Robertson, the largest shareholder in the firm, said, "It's hard enough to manage the robot industry as it is, with public hostility to robots forever on the verge of breaking out into the open. If the public gets the idea that robots will be uncontrolled . . . Oh, don't tell me about the Three Laws. The average man won't believe the Three Laws will protect him if he as much as hears the word 'uncontrolled.' "

"Then don't use it," said Madarian. "Call the robot—call it 'intuitive.' "

"An intuitive robot," someone muttered. "A girl robot?"

A smile made its way about the conference table.

Madarian seized on that. "All right. A girl robot. Our robots are sexless, of course, and so will this one be, but we always act as though they're males. We give them male pet names and call them he and him. Now this one, if we consider the nature of the mathematical structuring of the brain which I have proposed, would fall into the JN-coordinate system. The first robot would be JN-1, and I've assumed that it would be called John-1 . . . I'm afraid that is the level of originality of the average roboticist. But why not call it Jane-1, damn it? If the public has to be let in on what we're doing, we're constructing a feminine robot with intuition."

Robertson shook his head, "What difference would that make? What you're saying is that you plan to remove the last barrier which, in principle, keeps the robotic brain inferior to the human brain. What do you suppose the public reaction will be to that?"

"Do you plan to make that public?" said Madarian. He thought a bit and then said, "Look. One thing the general public believes is that women are not as intelligent as men."

There was an instant apprehensive look on the face of more than one man at the table and a quick look up and down as though Susan Calvin were still in her accustomed seat.

Madarian said, "If we announce a female robot, it doesn't matter what she is. The public will automatically assume she is mentally backward. We just publicize the robot as Jane-1 and we don't have to say another word. We're safe."

"Actually," said Peter Bogert quietly, "there's more to it than that. Madarian and I have gone over the mathematics carefully and the JN series, whether John or Jane, would be quite safe. They would be less complex and intellectually capable in an orthodox sense, than many another series we have designed and constructed. There would only be the one added factor of, well, let's get into the habit of calling it 'intuition.' "

"Who knows what it would do?" muttered Robertson.

"Madarian has suggested one thing it can do. As you all know, the Space Jump has been developed in principle. It is possible for men to attain what is, in effect, hyper-speeds beyond that of light and to visit other stellar systems and return in negligible time—weeks at the most."

Robertson said, "That's not new to us. It couldn't have been done without robots."

"Exactly, and it's not doing us any good because we can't use the hyper-speed drive except perhaps once as a demonstration, so that U.S. Robots gets little credit. The Space Jump is risky, it's fearfully prodigal of energy and therefore it's enormously expensive. If we were going to use it anyway, it would be nice if we could report the existence of a habitable planet. Call it a psychological need. Spend about twenty billion dollars on a single Space Jump and report nothing but scientific data and the public wants to know why their money was wasted. Report the existence of a habitable planet, and you're an interstellar Columbus and no one will worry about the money."

"So?"

"So where are we going to find a habitable planet? Or put it this way—which star within reach of the Space Jump as presently developed, which of the three hundred thousand stars and star systems within three hundred light-years has the best chance of having a habitable planet? We've got an enormous quantity of details on every star in our three-hundred-light-year neighborhood and a notion that almost every one has a planetary system. But which has a *habitable* planet? Which do we visit? . . . We don't know."

One of the directors said, "How would this Jane robot help us?"

Madarian was about to answer that, but he gestured slightly to Bogert and Bogert understood. The Director would carry more weight. Bogert didn't particularly like the idea; if the JN series proved a fiasco, he was making himself prominent enough in connection with it to insure that the sticky fingers of blame would cling to him. On the other hand, retirement was not all that far off, and if it worked, he would go out in a blaze of glory. Maybe it was only Madarian's aura of confidence, but Bogert had honestly come to believe it would work.

He said, "It may well be that somewhere in the libraries of data we have on those stars, there are methods for estimating the probabilities of the presence of Earth-type habitable planets. All we need to do is understand the data properly, look at them in the appropriate creative manner, make the correct correlations. We haven't done it yet. Or if some astronomer has, he hasn't been smart enough to realize what he has.

"A JN-type robot would make correlations far more rapidly and far more precisely than a man could. In a day, it would make and discard as many correlations as a man could in ten years. Furthermore, it would work in truly random fashion, whereas a man would have a strong bias based on preconception and on what is already believed."

There was a considerable silence after that. Finally Robertson said, "But it's only a matter of probability, isn't it? Suppose this robot said, 'The highest-probability habitable-planet star within so-and-so light-years is Squidgee-17,' or whatever, and we go there and find that a probability is only a probability and that there are no habitable planets after all. Where does that leave us?"

Madarian struck in this time. "We still win. We know how the robot came to the conclusion because it—she—will tell us. It might well help us gain enormous insight into astronomical detail and make the whole thing worthwhile even if we don't make the Space Jump at all. Besides, we can then work out the five most probable sites of planets and the probability that one of the five has a habitable planet may then be better than 0.95. It would be almost sure—"

They went on for a long time after that.

* * *

The funds granted were quite insufficient, but Madarian counted on the habit of throwing good money after bad. With two hundred million about to be lost irrevocably when another hundred million could save everything, the other hundred million would surely be voted.

Jane-1 was finally built and put on display. Peter Bogert studied it—her—gravely. He said, "Why the narrow waist? Surely that introduces a mechanical weakness?"

Madarian chuckled. "Listen, if we're going to call her Jane, there's no point in making her look like Tarzan."

Bogert shook his head. "Don't like it. You'll be bulging her higher up to give the appearance of breasts next, and that's a rotten idea. If women start getting the notion that robots may look like women, I can tell you exactly the kind of perverse notions they'll get, and you'll *really* have hostility on their part."

Madarian said, "Maybe you're right at that. No woman wants to feel replaceable by something with none of her faults. Okay."

* * *

Jane-2 did not have the pinched waist. She was a somber robot which rarely moved and even more rarely spoke.

Madarian had only occasionally come rushing to Bogert with items of news during her construction and that had been a sure sign that things were going poorly. Madarian's ebullience under success was overpowering. He would not hesitate to invade Bogert's bedroom at 3 A.M. with a hot-flash item rather than wait for the morning. Bogert was sure of that.

Now Madarian seemed subdued, his usually florid expression nearly pale, his round cheeks somehow pinched. Bogert said, with a feeling of certainty, "She won't talk."

"Oh, she talks." Madarian sat down heavily and chewed at his lower lip. "Sometimes, anyway," he said.

Bogert rose and circled the robot. "And when she talks, she makes no sense, I suppose. Well, if she doesn't talk, she's no female, is she?"

Madarian tried a weak smile for size and abandoned it. He said, "The brain, in isolation, checked out."

"I know," said Bogert.

"But once that brain was put in charge of the physical apparatus of the robot, it was necessarily modified, of course."

"Of course," agreed Bogert unhelpfully.

"But unpredictably and frustratingly. The trouble is that when you're dealing with n-dimensional calculus of uncertainty, things arc—"

"Uncertain?" said Bogert. His own reaction was surprising him. The company investment was already most sizable and almost two years had elapsed, yet the results were, to put it politely, disappointing. Still, he found himself jabbing at Madarian and finding himself amused in the process.

Almost furtively, Bogert wondered if it weren't the absent Susan Calvin he was jabbing at. Madarian was so much more ebullient and effusive than Susan could ever possibly be—when things were going well. He was also far more vulnerably in the dumps when things weren't going well, and it was precisely under pressure that Susan never cracked. The target that Madarian made could be a neatly punctured bull's-eye as recompense for the target Susan had never allowed herself to be.

Madarian did not react to Bogert's last remark any more than Susan Calvin would have done; not out of contempt, which would have been Susan's reaction, but because he did not hear it.

He said argumentatively, "The trouble is the matter of recognition. We have Jane-2 correlating magnificently. She can correlate on any subject, but once she's done so, she can't recognize a valuable result from a valueless one. It's not an easy problem, judging how to program a robot to tell a significant correlation when you don't know what correlations she will be making."

"I presume you've thought of lowering the potential at the W-21 diode junction and sparking across the—"

"No, no, no, no—" Madarian faded off into a whispering diminuendo. "You can't just have it spew out everything. We can do that ourselves. The point is to have it recognize the crucial correlation and draw the conclusion. Once that is done, you see, a Jane robot would snap out an answer by intuition. It would be something we couldn't get ourselves except by the oddest kind of luck."

"It seems to me," said Bogert dryly, "that if you had a robot like that, you would have her do routinely what among human beings, only the occasional genius is capable of doing."

Madarian nodded vigorously. "Exactly, Peter. I'd have said so myself if I weren't afraid of frightening off the execs. Please don't repeat that in their hearing."

"Do you really want a robot genius?"

"What are words? I'm trying to get a robot with the capacity to make random correlations at enormous speeds, together with a key-significance high-recognition quotient. And I'm trying to put *those* words into positronic field equations. I thought I had it, too, but I don't. Not yet."

He looked at Jane-2 discontentedly and said, "What's the best significance you have, Jane?"

Jane-2's head turned to look at Madarian but she made no sound, and Madarian whispered with resignation, "She's running that into the correlation banks."

Jane-2 spoke tonelessly at last. "I'm not sure." It was the first sound she had made.

Madarian's eyes rolled upward. "She's doing the equivalent of setting up equations with intermediate solutions."

"I gathered that," said Bogert. "Listen, Madarian, can you go anywhere at this point, or do we pull out now and cut our losses at half a billion?"

"Oh, I'll get it," muttered Madarian.

* * *

Jane-3 wasn't it. She was never as much as activated and Madarian was in a rage.

It was human error. His own fault, if one wanted to be entirely accurate. Yet though Madarian was utterly humilated, others remained quiet. Let he who has never made an error in the fearsomely intricate mathematics of the positronic brain fill out the first memo of correction.

* * *

Nearly a year passed before Jane-4 was ready. Madarian was ebullient again. "She does it," he said. "She's got a good high-recognition quotient."

He was confident enough to place her on display before the Board and have her solve problems. Not mathematical problems; any robot could do that; but problems where the terms were deliberately misleading without being actually inaccurate.

Bogert said afterward, "That doesn't take much, really."

"Of course not. It's elementary for Jane-4, but I had to show them something, didn't I?"

"Do you know how much we've spent so far?"

"Come on, Peter, don't give me that. Do you know how much we've got back? These things don't go on in a vacuum, you know. I've had over three years of hell over this, if you want to know, but I've worked out new techniques of calculation that will save us a minimum of fifty thousand dollars on every new type of positronic brain we design, from now on in forever. Right?"

"Well—"

"Well me no wells. It's so. And it's my personal feeling that n-dimensional calculus of uncertainty can have any number of other applications if we have the ingenuity to find them, and my Jane robots *will* find them. Once I've got exactly what I want, the new JN series will pay for itself inside of five years, even if we triple what we've invested so far."

"What do you mean by 'exactly what you want'? What's wrong with Jane-4?"

"Nothing. Or nothing much. She's on the track, but she can be improved and I intend to do so. I thought I knew where I was going when I designed her. Now I've tested her and I *know* where I'm going. I intend to get there."

* * *

Jane-5 was it. It took Madarian well over a year to produce her and there he had no reservations; he was utterly confident.

Jane-5 was shorter than the average robot, slimmer. Without being a female caricature as Jane-1 had been, she managed to possess an air of femininity about herself despite the absence of a single clearly feminine feature.

"It's the way she's standing," said Bogert. Her arms were held gracefully and somehow the torso managed to give the impression of curving slightly when she turned.

Madarian said, "Listen to her . . . How do you feel, Jane?"

"In excellent health, thank you," said Jane-5, and the voice was precisely that of a woman; it was a sweet and almost disturbing contralto.

"Why did you do that, Clinton?" said Peter, startled and beginning to frown.

"Psychologically important," said Madarian. "I want people to think of her as a woman; to treat her as a woman; to *explain*."

"What people?"

Madarian put his hands in his pockets and stared thoughtfully at Bogert. "I would like to have arrangements made for Jane and myself to go to Flagstaff."

Bogert couldn't help but note that Madarian didn't say Jane-5. He made use of no number this time. She was *the* Jane. He said doubtfully, "To Flagstaff? Why?"

"Because that's the world center for general planetology, isn't it? It's where they're studying the stars and trying to calculate the probability of habitable planets, isn't it?"

"I know that, but it's on Earth."

"Well, and I surely know that."

"Robotic movements on Earth are strictly controlled. And there's no need for it. Bring a library of books on general planetology here and let Jane absorb them."

"*No!* Peter, will you get it through your head that Jane isn't the ordinary logical robot; she's intuitive."

"So?"

"So how can we tell what she needs, what she can use, what will set her off? We can use any metal model in the factory to read books; that's frozen data and out of date besides. Jane must have living information; she must have tones of voice, she must have side issues; she must have total irrelevancies even. How the devil do we know what or when something will go click-click inside her and fall into a pattern? If we knew, we wouldn't need her at all, would we?"

Bogert began to feel harassed. He said, "Then bring the men here, the general planetologists."

"Here won't be any good. They'll be out of their element. They won't react naturally. I want Jane to watch them at work; I want her to see their instruments, their offices, their desks, everything about them that she can. I want you to arrange to have her transported to Flagstaff. And I'd really like not to discuss it any further."

For a moment he almost sounded like Susan. Bogert winced, and said, "It's complicated making such an arrangement. Transporting an experimental robot—"

"Jane isn't experimental. She's the fifth of the series."

"The other four weren't really working models."

Madarian lifted his hands in helpless frustration. "Who's forcing you to tell the government that?"

"I'm not worried about the government. It can be made to understand special cases. It's public opinion. We've come a long way in fifty years and I don't propose to be set back twenty-five of them by having you lose control of a—"

"I won't lose control. You're making foolish remarks. Look! U.S. Robots can afford a private plane. We can land quietly at the nearest commercial airport and be lost in hundreds of similar landings. We can arrange to have a large ground car with an enclosed body meet us and take us to Flagstaff. Jane will be crated and it will be obvious that some piece of thoroughly non-robotic equipment is being transported to the labs. We won't get a second look from anyone. The men at Flagstaff will be alerted and will be told the exact purpose of the visit. They will have every motive to cooperate and to prevent a leak."

Bogert pondered. "The risky part will be the plane and the ground car. If anything happens to the crate—"

"Nothing will."

"We might get away with it if Jane is deactivated during transport. Then even if someone finds out she's inside—"

"No, Peter. That can't be done. Uh-uh. Not Jane-5. Look, she's been free-associating since she was activated. The information she possesses can be put into freeze during deactivation but the free associations never. No, sir, she can't ever be deactivated."

"But, then, if somehow it is discovered that we are transporting an activated robot—"

"It won't be found out."

Madarian remained firm and the plane eventually took off. It was a late-model automatic Computo-jet, but it carried a human pilot—one of U. S. Robots' own employees—as backup. The crate containing Jane arrived at the airport safely, was transferred to the ground car, and reached the Research Laboratories at Flagstaff without incident.

* * *

Peter Bogert received his first call from Madarian not more than an hour after the latter's arrival at Flagstaff. Madarian was ecstatic and, characteristically, could not wait to report.

The message arrived by tubed laser beam, shielded, scrambled, and ordinarily impenetrable, but Bogert felt exasperated. He knew it could be penetrated if someone with enough technological ability—the government, for example—was determined to do so. The only real safety lay in the fact that the government had no reason to try. At least Bogert hoped so.

He said, "For God's sake, do you have to call?"

Madarian ignored him entirely. He burbled, "It was an inspiration. Sheer genius, I tell you."

For a while, Bogert stared at the receiver. Then he shouted incredulously, "You mean you've got the answer? Already?"

"No, no! Give us time, damn it. I mean the matter of her voice was an inspiration. Listen, after we were chauffeured from the airport to the main administration building at Flagstaff, we uncrated Jane and she stepped out of the box. When that happened, every man in the place stepped back. Scared! Nitwits! If even scientists can't understand the significance of the Laws of Robotics, what can we expect of the average untrained individual? For a minute there I thought: This will be all useless. They won't talk. They'll be keying themselves for a quick break in case she goes berserk and they'll be able to think of nothing else."

"Well, then, what are you getting at?"

"So then she greeted them routinely. She said, 'Good afternoon, gentlemen. I am so glad to meet you.' And it came out in this beautiful contralto . . . That was it. One man straightened his tie, and another ran his fingers through his hair. What really got me was that the oldest guy in the place actually checked his fly to make sure it was zipped. They're all crazy about her now. All they needed was the voice. She isn't a robot any more; she's a girl."

"You mean they're talking to her?"

"*Are* they talking to her! I should say so. I should have programmed her for sexy intonations. They'd be asking her for dates right now if I had. Talk about conditioned reflex. Listen, men respond to voices. At the most intimate moments, are they looking? It's the voice in your ear—"

"Yes, Clinton, I seem to remember. Where's Jane now?"

"With them. They won't let go of her."

"Damn! Get in there with her. Don't let her out of your sight, man."

* * *

Madarian's calls thereafter, during his ten-day stay at Flagstaff, were not very frequent and became progressively less exalted.

Jane was listening carefully, he reported, and occasionally she responded. She remained popular. She was given entry everywhere. But there were no results.

Bogert said, "Nothing at all?"

Madarian was at once defensive. "You can't say nothing at all. It's impossible to say nothing at all with an intuitive robot. You don't know what might not be going on inside her. This morning she asked Jensen what he had for breakfast."

"Rossiter Jensen the astrophysicist?"

"Yes, of course. As it turned out, he didn't have breakfast that morning. Well, a cup of coffee."

"So Jane's learning to make small talk. That scarcely makes up for the expense—"

"Oh, don't be a jackass. It wasn't small talk. Nothing is small talk for Jane. She asked because it had something to do with some sort of cross-correlation she was building in her mind."

"What can it possibly—"

"How do I know? If I knew, I'd be a Jane myself and you wouldn't need her. But it has to mean something. She's programmed for high motivation to obtain an answer to the question of a planet with optimum habitability/distance and—"

"Then let me know when she's done that and not before. It's not really necessary for me to get a blow-by-blow description of possible correlations."

He didn't really expect to get notification of success. With each day, Bogert grew less sanguine, so that when the notification finally came, he wasn't ready. And it came at the very end.

That last time, when Madarian's climactic message came, it came in what was almost a whisper. Exaltation had come complete circle and Madarian was awed into quiet.

"She did it," he said. "She did it. After I all but gave up, too. After she had received everything in the place and most of it twice and three times over and never said a word that sounded like anything . . . I'm on the plane now, returning. We've just taken off."

Bogert managed to get his breath. "Don't play games, man. You have the *answer?* Say so, if you have. Say it plainly."

"She has the answer. She's given me the names of three stars within eighty light-years which, she says, have a sixty to ninety per cent chance of possessing one habitable planet each. The probability that at least one has is 0.972. It's almost certain. And that's just the least of it. Once we get back, she can give us the exact line of reasoning that led her to the conclusion and I predict that the whole science of astrophysics and cosmology will—"

"Are you sure—"

"You think I'm having hallucinations? I even have a witness. Poor guy jumped two feet when Jane suddenly began to reel out the answer in her gorgeous voice—"

And that was when the meteorite struck and in the thorough destruction of the plane that followed, Madarian and the pilot were reduced to gobbets of bloody flesh and no usable remnant of Jane was recovered.

* * *

The gloom at U. S. Robots had never been deeper. Robertson attempted to find consolation in the fact that the very completeness of the destruction had utterly hidden the illegalities of which the firm had been guilty.

Peter shook his head and mourned. "We've lost the best chance U. S. Robots ever had of gaining an unbeatable public image; of overcoming the damned Frankenstein complex. What it would have meant for robots to have one of them work out the solution to the habitable-planet problem, after other robots had helped work out the Space Jump. Robots would have opened the galaxy to us. And if at the same time we could have driven scientific knowledge forward in a dozen different directions as we surely would have . . . Oh, God, there's no way of calculating the benefits to the human race, and to us of course."

Robertson said, "We could build other Janes, couldn't we? Even without Madarian?"

"Sure we could. But can we depend on the proper correlation again? Who knows how low-probability that final result was? What if Madarian had had a fantastic piece of beginner's luck? And then to have an even more fantastic piece of bad luck? A meteorite zeroing in . . . It's simply unbelievable—"

Robertson said in a hesitating whisper, "It couldn't have been — meant. I mean, if we weren't meant to know and if the meteorite was a judgement—from—"

He faded off under Bogert's withering glare.

Bogert said, "Its not a dead loss, I suppose. Other Janes are bound to help us in some ways. And we can give other robots feminine voices, if that will help encourage public acceptance—though I wonder what the women would say. If we only knew what Jane-5 had said!"

"In that last call, Madarian said there was a witness."

Bogert said, "I know; I've been thinking about that. Don't you suppose I've been in touch with Flagstaff? Nobody in the entire place heard Jane say anything that was out of the ordinary, anything that sounded like an answer to the habitable-planet problem, and certainly anyone there should have recognized the answer if it came—or at least recognized it as a possible answer."

"Could Madarian have been lying? Or crazy? Could he have been trying to protect himself—"

"You mean he may have been trying to save his reputation by pretending he had the answer and then gimmick Jane so she couldn't talk and say, 'Oh, sorry, something happened accidentally. Oh, darn!' I won't accept that for a minute. You might as well suppose he had arranged the meteorite."

"Then what do we do?"

Bogert said heavily, "Turn back to Flagstaff. The answer *must* be there. I've got to dig deeper, that's all. I'm going there and I'm taking a couple of the men in Madarian's department. We've got to go through that place top to bottom and end to end."

"But, you know, even if there were a witness and he had heard, what good would it do, now that we don't have Jane to explain the process?"

"Every little something is useful. Jane gave the names of the stars; the catalogue numbers probably—none of the named stars has a chance. If someone can remember her saying that and actually remember the catalogue number, or have heard it clearly enough to allow it to be recovered by Psycho-probe if he lacked the conscious memory—then we'll have something. Given the results at the end, and the data fed Jane at the beginning, we might be able to reconstruct the line of reasoning; we might recover the intuition. If that is done, we've saved the game—"

* * *

Bogert was back after three days, silent and thoroughly depressed. When Robertson inquired anxiously as to results, he shook his head. "Nothing!"

"Nothing?"

"Absolutely nothing. I spoke with every man in Flagstaff—every scientist, every technician, every student—that had had anything to do with Jane; everyone that had as much as seen her. The number wasn't great; I'll give Madarian credit for that much discretion. He only allowed those to see her who might conceivably have had planetological knowledge to feed her. There were twenty-three men altogether who had seen Jane and of those only twelve had spoken to her more than casually.

"I went over and over all that Jane had said. They remembered everything quite well. They're keen men engaged in a crucial experiment involving their specialty, so they had every motivation to remember. And they were dealing with a talking robot, something that was startling enough, and one that talked like a TV actress. They couldn't forget."

Robertson said, "Maybe a Psycho-probe—"

"If one of them had the vaguest thought that something had happened, I would screw out his consent to Probing. But there's nothing to leave room for an excuse, and to Probe two dozen men who make their living from their brains can't be done. Honestly, it wouldn't help. If Jane had mentioned three stars and said they had habitable planets, it would have been like setting up sky rockets in their brains. How could any one of them forget?"

"Then maybe one of them is lying," said Robertson grimly. "He wants the information for his own use; to get the credit himself later."

"What good would that do him?" said Bogert. "The whole establishment knows exactly why Madarian and Jane were there in the first place. They know why I came there in the second. If at any time in the future any man now at Flagstaff suddenly comes up with a habitable-planet theory that is startlingly new and different, yet valid, every other man at Flagstaff and every man at U. S. Robots will know at once that he had stolen it. He'd never get away with it."

"Then Madarian himself was somehow mistaken."

"I don't see how I can believe that either. Madarian had an irritating personality—all robopsychologists have irritating personalities, I think, which must be why they work with robots rather than with men—but he was no dummy. He *couldn't* be wrong in something like this."

"Then—" But Robertson had run out of possibilities. They had reached a blank wall and for some minutes each stared at it disconsolately.

Finally Robertson stirred. "Peter—"

"Well?"

"Let's ask Susan."

Bogert stiffened. "What!"

"Let's ask Susan. Let's call he and ask her to come in."

"Why? What can she possibly do?"

"I don't know. But she's a robopsychologist, too, and she might understand Madarian better than we do. Besides, she— Oh, hell, she always had more brains than any of us."

"She's nearly eighty."

"And you're seventy. What about it?"

Bogert sighed. Had her abrasive tongue lost any of its rasp in the years of her retirement? He said, "Well, I'll ask her."

* * *

Susan Calvin entered Bogert's office with a slow look around before her eyes fixed themselves on the Research Director. She had aged a great deal since her retirement. Her hair was a fine white and her face seemed to have crumpled. She had grown so frail as to be almost transparent and only her eyes, piercing and uncompromising, seemed to remain of all that had been.

Bogert strode forward heartily, holding out his hand. "Susan!"

Susan Calvin took it, and said, "You're looking reasonably well, Peter, for an old man. If I were you, I wouldn't wait till next year. Retire now and let the young men get to it . . . And Madarian is dead. Are you calling me in to take over my old job? Are you determined to keep the ancients till a year past actual physical death?"

"No, no, Susan. I've called you in—" He stopped. He did not, after all, have the faintest idea of how to start.

But Susan read his mind now as easily as she always had. She seated herself with the caution born of stiffened joints and said, "Peter, you've called me in because you're in bad trouble. Otherwise you'd sooner see me dead than within a mile of you."

"Come, Susan—"

"Don't waste time on pretty talk. I never had time to waste when I was forty and certainly not now. Madarian's death and your call to me are both unusual, so there must be a connection. Two unusual events without a connection is too low-probability to worry about. Begin at the beginning and don't worry about revealing yourself to be a fool. That was revealed to me long ago."

Bogert cleared his throat miserably and began. She listened carefully, her withered hand lifting once in a while to stop him so that she might ask a question.

She snorted at one point. "Feminine intuition? Is that what you wanted the robot for? You men. Faced with a woman reaching a correct conclusion and unable to accept the fact that she is your equal or superior in intelligence, you invent something called feminine intuition."

"Uh, yes, Susan, but let me continue—"

He did. When she was told of Jane's contralto voice, she said, "It's a difficult choice sometimes whether to feel revolted at the male sex or merely to dismiss them as contempible."

Bogert said, "Well, let me go on—"

When he was quite done, Susan said, "May I have the private use of this office for an hour or two?"

"Yes, but—"

She said, "I want to go over the various records—Jane's programming, Madarian's calls, your interviews at Flagstaff. I presume I can use that beautiful new shielded laserphone and your computer outlet if I wish."

"Yes, of course."

"Well, then, get out of here, Peter."

* * *

It was not quite forty-five minutes when she hobbled to the door, opened it, and called for Bogert.

When Bogert came, Robertson was with him. Both entered and Susan greeted the latter with an unenthusiastic "Hello, Scott."

Bogert tried desperately to gauge the results from Susan's face, but it was only the face of a grim old lady who had no intention of making anything easy for him.

He said cautiously, "Do you think there's anything you can do, Susan?"

"Beyond what I have already done? No! There's nothing more."

Bogert's lips set in chagrin, but Robertson said, "What have you already done, Susan?"

Susan said, "I've thought a little; something I can't seem to persuade anyone else to do. For one thing, I've thought about Madarian. I knew him, you know. He had brains but he was a very irritating extrovert. I thought you would like him after me, Peter."

"It was a change," Bogert couldn't resist saying.

"And he was always running to you with results the very minute he had them, wasn't he?"

"Yes, he was."

"And, yet," said Susan, "his last message, the one in which he said Jane had given him the answer, was sent from the plane. Why did he wait so long? Why didn't he call you while he was still at Flagstaff, immediately after Jane had said whatever it was she said?"

"I suppose," said Peter, "that for once he wanted to check it thoroughly and—well, I don't know. It was the most important thing that had ever happened to him; he might for once have wanted to wait and be sure of himself."

"On the contrary; the more important it was, the less he would wait, surely. And if he could manage to wait, why not do it properly and wait till he was back at U. S. Robots so that he could check the results with all the computing equipment this firm could make available to him? In short, he waited too long from one point of view and not long enough from another."

Robertson interrupted. "Then you think he was up to some trickery—"

Susan looked revolted. "Scott, don't try to compete with Peter in making inane remarks. Let me continue . . . A second point concerns the witness. According to the records of that last call, Madarian said, 'Poor guy jumped two feet when Jane suddenly began to reel out the answer in her gorgeous voice.' In fact, it was the last thing he said. And the question is, then, why should the witness have jumped? Madarian had explained that all the men were crazy about that voice, and they had had ten days with the robot—with Jane. Why should the mere act of her speaking have startled them?"

Bogert said, "I assumed it was astonishment at hearing Jane give an answer to a problem that has occupied the minds of planetologists for nearly a century."

"But they were *waiting* for her to give that answer. That was why she was there. Besides, consider the way the sentence is worded. Madarian's statement makes it seem the witness was startled, not astonished, if you see the difference. What's more, that reaction came 'when Jane suddenly began' —in other words, at the very start of the statement. To be astonished at the content of what Jane said would have required the witness to have listened awhile so that he might absorb it. Madarian would have said he had jumped two feet *after* he had heard Jane say thus-and-so. It would be 'after' not 'when' and the word 'suddenly' would not be included."

Bogert said uneasily, "I don't think you can refine matters down to the use or non-use of a word."

"I can," said Susan frostily, "because I am a robopsychologist. And I can expect Madarian to do so, too, because *he* was a robopsychologist. We have to explain those two anomalies, then. The queer delay before Madarian's call and the queer reaction of the witness."

"Can *you* explain them?" asked Robertson.

"Of course," said Susan, "since I use a little simple logic. Madarian called with the news without delay, as he always did, or with as little delay as he could manage. If Jane had solved the problem at Flagstaff, he would certainly have called from Flagstaff. Since he called from the plane, she must clearly have solved the problem after he had left Flagstaff."

"But then—"

"Let me finish. Let me finish. Was Madarian not taken from the airport to Flagstaff in a heavy, enclosed ground car? And Jane, in her crate, with him?"

"Yes."

"And presumably, Madarian and the crated Jane returned from Flagstaff to the airport in the same heavy, enclosed ground car. Am I right?"

"Yes, of course!"

"And they were not alone in the ground car, either. In one of his calls, Madarian said, 'We were chauffeured from the airport to the main administration building,' and I suppose I am right in concluding that if he was chauffeured, then that was because there was a chauffeur, a human driver, in the car."

"Good God!"

"The trouble with you, Peter, is that when you think of a witness to a planetological statement, you think of planetologists. You divide up human beings into categories, and despise and dismiss most. A robot cannot do that. The First Law says, 'A robot may not injure a *human being* or, through inaction, allow a *human being* to come to harm.' *Any* human being. That is the essence of the robotic view of life. A robot makes no distinction. To a robot, all men are truly equal, and to a robopsychologist who must perforce deal with men at the robotic level, all men are truly equal, too.

"It would not occur to Madarian to say a truck driver had heard the statement. To you a truck driver is not a scientist but is a mere animate adjunct of a truck, but to Madarian he was a man and a witness. Nothing more. Nothing less."

Bogert shook his head in disbelief, "But you are *sure?*"

"Of course I'm sure. How else can you explain the other point; Madarian's remark about the startling of the witness? Jane was crated, wasn't she? But she was *not* deactivated. According to the records, Madarian was always adamant against ever deactivating an intuitive robot. Moreover, Jane-5, like any of the Janes, was extremely non-talkative. Probably it never occurred to Madarian to order her to remain quiet within the crate; and it was within the crate that the pattern finally fell into place. Naturally she began to talk. A beautiful contralto voice suddenly sounded from inside the crate. If you were the truck driver, what would you do at that point? Surely you'd be startled. It's a wonder he didn't crash."

"But if the truck driver was the witness, why didn't he come forward—"

"Why? Can he possibly know that anything crucial had happened, that what he heard was important? Besides, don't you suppose Madarian tipped him well and asked him not to say anything? Would you *want* the news to spread that an activated robot was being transported illegally over the Earth's surface."

"Well, will he remember what was said?"

"Why not? It might seem to you, Peter, that a truck driver, one step above an ape in your view, can't remember. But truck drivers can have brains, too. The statements were most remarkable and the driver may well have remembered some. Even if he gets some of the letters and numbers wrong, we're dealing with a finite set, you know, the fifty-five hundred stars or star systems within eight light-years or so—I haven't looked up the exact number. You can make the correct choices. And if needed, you will have every excuse to use the Psycho-probe—"

The two men stared at her. Finally Bogert, afraid to believe, whispered, "But how can you be *sure?*"

For a moment, Susan was on the point of saying: Because I've called Flagstaff, you fool, and because I spoke to the truck driver, and because he told me what he had heard, and because I've checked with the computer at Flagstaff and got the only three stars that fit the information, and because I have those names in my pocket.

But she didn't. Let him go through it all himself. Carefully, she rose to her feet, and said sardonically, "How can I be sure? . . . Call it feminine intuition."

# A Problem of Numbers

Professor Neddring looked mildly at his graduate student. The young man sat there at ease; his hair was a little on the reddish side, his eyes were keen but calm, and his hands rested in the pockets of his lab coat. Altogether a promising specimen, the professor thought.

He had known for some time that the boy was interested in his daughter. What was more to the point, he had known for some time his daughter was interested in the boy.

The professor said, "Let's get this straight, Hal. You've come to me for my approval before you propose to my daughter?"

Hal Kemp said, "That's right, sir."

"Granted that I'm not up on the latest fads of youth—but surely this can't be the new 'in' thing." The professor thrust his hands into his lab coat pockets and leaned back in his chair. "Surely, young people aren't taking to asking permission these days? Don't tell me you'll give up my daughter if I turn you down?"

"No, not if she'll still have me, and I think she will. But it would be pleasant—"

"—if you had my approval. Why?"

Hal said, "For very practical reasons. I don't have my doctor's degree yet and I don't want it said that I'm dating your daughter to help me get it. If you think I am, say so, and maybe I'll wait till after I get my degree. Or maybe I won't and take my chances that your disapproval will make it that much harder for me to get my degree."

"So, for the sake of your doctorate, you think it would be nice if we were friends about your marriage to Janice."

"To be honest, yes, Professor."

There was silence between them. Professor Neddring thought about the matter with a certain creakiness. His research work for some years now had dealt with the coordination complexes of chromium and there was a definite difficulty in thinking with some precision about anything as imprecise as affection and marriage.

He rubbed his smooth cheek—at the age of fifty he was too old for the various beard styles affected by the younger members of the department—and said, "Well, Hal, if you want a decision frcm me I'll have to base it on something, and the only way I know how to judge people is by their reasoning powers. My daughter judges you in *her* way, but I'll have to judge you in *mine*."

"Certainly," said Hal.

"Then let me put it this way." The professor leaned forward, scribbled something on a piece of paper, and said, "Tell me what this says, and you will have my blessing."

Hal picked up the paper. What was written on it was a series of numbers:

69663717263376833047

He said, "A cryptogram?"

"You can call it that."

Hal frowned slightly. "You mean you want me to solve a cryptogram and if I do, then you'll approve the marriage?"

"Yes."

"And if I don't, then you *won't* approve the marriage?"

"It may sound trivial, I admit, but this is my criterion. You can always marry without my approval. Janice is of age."

Hal shook is head. "I'd still rather have your approval. How much time do I have?"

"None. Tell me what it says *now*. Reason it out."

"*Now?*"

The professor nodded.

Hal Kemp shifted in his chair and stared at the row of numbers in his hand. "Do I figure it out in my head? Or can I use pencil and paper?"

"Just do it. Let me hear how you think. Who knows? If I like the way you think, I may give my approval even if you don't solve it."

Hal said, "Well, all right. It's a challenge. In the first place, I'll make an assumption. I'll assume you're an honorable man and would not set me a problem that you knew in advance I couldn't solve. Therefore this is a cryptogram which, to the best of your judgment, is one I can solve sitting in this chair and almost on the spur of the moment. Which in turn means that it involves something I know well."

"That sounds reasonable," agreed the professor.

But Hal wasn't listening. He continued, deliberately, "I know the alphabet well, of course, so this could be an ordinary substitution cipher—numbers for letters. Presumably, it would have to have some subtlety if it were, or it would be too easy. But I'm an amateur at that sort of thing and unless I can see at once some peculiar pattern in the numbers that gives the whole thing meaning, I'd be lost. I notice there are five 6's and five 3's and not a single 5—but that means nothing to me. So I'll abandon the possibility of a generalized cipher and move on to our own specialized field."

He thought again and went on, "Your specialized field, Professor, is inorganic chemistry and that, certainly, is what mine is going to be. And to any chemist, numbers immediately suggest atomic numbers. Every chemical element has its own number and there are one hundred and four elements known today; so the numbers involved would be 1 to 104.

"You haven't indicated how the numbers are divided up. There are the one-digit atomic numbers from 1 to 9; the two-digit ones from 10 to 99; and the three-digit onces from 100 to 104. This is all obvious, Professor, but you wanted to hear my reasoning, so I'm giving it to you in full.

"We can forget the three-digit atomic numbers, since in them a 1 is always followed by a 0 and the single 1 in your cryptogram is followed by a 7. Since you've given me twenty digits altogether, it is at least possible that only two-digit atomic numbers are involved—ten of them. There might be nine two-digit ones and two one-digit ones, but I doubt it. Even the presence of two one digit atomic numbers could result in hundreds of different combinations of places in this list and that would surely make things too difficult for an instant or even a quick solution. It seems certain to me, then, that I am dealing with ten two-digit numbers, and we can therefore turn the message into: 69, 66, 37, 17, 26, 33, 76, 83, 30, 47.

"These numbers seem to mean nothing in themselves, but if they are atomic numbers then why not convert all of them into the names of the elements they represent? The names *might* be meaningful. That's not so easy offhand because I haven't memorized the list of elements in order of their atomic numbers. May I look them up in a table?"

The professor was listening with interest. "I didn't look up anything when I prepared the cryptogram."

"All right, then. Let's see," said Hal slowly. "Some are obvious. I know that 17 is chlorine, 26 is iron, 83 is bismuth, 30 is zinc. As for 76, that's somewhere near gold, which is 79; that would mean platinum, osmium, iridium. I'd saay it means osmium. The other two are rare earth elements and I can never get those straight. Let's see—let's see—All right. I *think* I have them."

He wrote rapidly and said, "The list of the ten elements in your list is thulium, dysprosium, rubidium, chlorine, iron, arsenic, osmium, bismuth, zinc, and silver. Is that right? —No, don't answer."

He studied the list intently. "I see no connections among those elements, nothing that seems to give me any hint. Let's pass on then and ask if there is anything besides the atomic *number* that is so characteristic of elements that it would spring to any chemist's mind at once. Obviously, it would be the chemical *symbol*—the one-letter or two-letter abbreviation for each element that becomes second nature to any chemist. In this case the list of chemical symbols is" —he wrote again— "Tm, Dy, Rb, Cl, Fe, As, Os, Bi, Zn, Ag.

"These might form a word or sentence, but they don't, do they? So it would have to be a little more subtle than that. If you make an acrostic out of it and read just the first letters, that doesn't help, either. So if we try the next most obvious step and read the second letters of each symbol in order, we come out with 'my blessing.' I presume that's the solution, Professor."

"It is," said Professor Neddring gravely. "You reasoned it out with precision and you have my permission, for what that's worth, to propose to my daughter."

Hal rose, turned to leave, hesitated, then turned back. He said, "On the other hand, I don't like to take the credit that's not mine. The reasoning I used may have been precise, but I offered it to you only because I wanted you to hear me reason logically. Actually, I knew the answer before I began, so in a way I cheated and I've got to admit that."

"Oh? How so?"

"Well, I know you think well of me and I guessed you would want me to come up with a solution and that you wouldn't be above giving me a hint. When you handed the cryptogram to me, you said, 'Tell me what this says, and you will have my blessing.' I guessed that you might mean that literally. 'My blessing' has ten letters and you handed me twenty digits. So I broke it down into ten pairs at once.

"Then, too, I told you I hadn't memorized the list of elements. The few elements I did remember were enough to show me that the second letters of the symbols were spelling out 'my blessing' so I worked out the others from among those few that had the proper second letters in *their* symbols. Do I still make it?"

Professor Neddring finally smiled. He said, "Now, my boy, you *really* make it. Any competant scientist can think logically. The great ones use intuition."

# Bill and I

I am, as it happens, doing a book on Lord Byron's narrative poem *Don Juan*.* The poem is an uninhibited satire in which Byron takes the opportunity to lash out at everything and everyone that displeased him. He is cruel to the point of sadism toward Britain's monarchs, toward its poet laureate, toward its greatest general, and so on.

But those for whom he reserves his most savage sallies are his critics. Byron did not take to criticism kindly and he invariably struck back.

Now, as far as I know, there is no such thing as a writer who takes to criticism kindly. Most of us, however, affect stoic unconcern and bleed in private.

For myself, alas, stoic unconcern is impossible. My frank and ingenuous countenance is a blank page on which my every emotion is clearly written (I am told) and I don't think I have ever succeeded in playing the stoic for even half a second. Indeed, when I am criticized unfairly, everyone within earshot knows that I have been—and for as much as hours at a time.

Naturally, when I recently published a two-volume book entitled *Asimov's Guide to Shakespeare*, I tried to steel myself for inevitable events. It was bound to get into the hand of an occasional Shakespearian scholar who would come all over faint at the thought of someone outside their field daring to invade the sacred precincts.

In fact, the very first review I received began: "What is Isaac Asimov, spinner of outer-space tales, doing—"

Naturally, I read no further. The fact that I am a spinner of outer-space tales is utterly irrelevent to this particular book and can only be mentioned because the reviewer thinks there is something vaguely (or not so vaguely) beneath literary dignity in being a science fiction writer.

I have sought a printable response for that and failed, so I'll pass on.

A second review was much more interesting. It appeared in a Kentucky paper and was written by someone I will call Mr. X. It begins this way: "Isaac Asimov is associate professor of biochemistry at

*Because I want to, and because my publishers humor me.

Boston University, and a prolific writer in many fields. I have read several of his books on science with the greatest attention and respect."

So far, so good. I am delighted.

But then, a very little while later, he says: "In this book, however, he has left the sunlit paths of natural science for the treacherous bogs of literature—"

What he objects to, it seems, is that I have annotated the plays, explained all the historical, legendary, and mythological references. It is a book of footnotes, so to speak, and he resents it. He points out that he thinks of "the language, the poetry, as the chief glory of Shakespeare's works."

Well, who doesn't? I'm delighted that Mr. X is clever enough to understand the language and the poetry without any explanation from me. And if *he* doesn't need it, why should anyone else, eh?

Notice, though, that he doesn't scorn to follow me along "the sunlit paths of natural science." Indeed, he reads my books on science "with the greatest attention and respect."

I'm glad he does and I can only presume that he is grateful that I take the trouble to footnote science so that he can get a fugitive hint of its beauties.

Suppose, instead, I were to say to Mr. X, "The logarithm of two is a transcendental number; and, indeed, the logarithm of any integer to any integral base is transcendental except where the integer is equal to the base or to a power of that base."

Mr. X might then, with justification, say, "What is a transcendental number, a logarithm, and, in this case, a power and a base?"

In fact, if he were a really deep thinker, he might ask, "What is two?"

But suppose I answered then that my statement bore within it all the poetry and symmetry and beauty of mathematics ("Euclid alone has looked on beauty bare") and that to try to explain it would simply back it up. And if Mr. X found trouble it understanding it, too bad for him. He just wasn't as bright as I was, and he could go to blazes.

But I *don't* answer that way. I explain such matters and many more, and go to a lot of trouble to do so, and then he reads those explanations with "the greatest attention and respect."

Scientists generally recognize the importance of explaining science to the non-scientist. It is interesting, then, in a rather sad way, that there exist humanists who feel themselves to be proprietors of their field, who hug literature to themselves, who mumble "the language, the poetry," and who see no reason why it should be explained to anyone as long as they themselves can continue to sniff the ambrosia.

*   *   *

Let us take a specific case. In the last act of *The Merchant of Venice*, Lorenzo and Jessica are enjoying an idyllic interlude at Portia's estate in Belmont, and Lorenzo says:

> *Sit, Jessica. Look how the floor of heaven*
> *Is thick inlaid with patens of bright gold.*
> *There's not the smallest orb which thou behold'st*
> *But in his motion like an angel sings,*
> *Still quiring to the young-eyed cherubins;*
> *Such harmony is in immortal souls,*
> *But whilst this muddy vesture of decay*
> *Doth grossly close it in, we cannot hear it.*

I think this passage is beautiful, for I have as keen a sense of the beauty and poetry of words as Mr. X; perhaps (is it possible?) even keener.

But what happens if someone says: "What are patens?"

After all, it is not a very common word. Does it ruin the beauty of the passage to whisper in an aside, "Small disks"?

Or what if someone asks, "What does he mean about these orbs singing like angels in their motion? What orbs? What motion? What singing?"

Am I to understand that the proper answer is, "No! Just listen to the words and the beautiful flow of language, and don't ask such philistine questions."

Does it spoil the beauty of Shakespeare's language to understand what he is saying? Or can it be that there are humanists who, qualified though they may be in esthetics, know little of the history of science, and don't know what Bill is saying and would rather not be asked.

All right, then, let's use this as a test case. I am going to explain this passage in far greater detail than I did in my book, just to show how much there is to consider in these beautiful syllables—

*   *   *

Anyone looking at the sky in a completely unsophisticated manner, without benefit of any astronomical training whatever, and willing to judge by appearances alone, is very likely to conclude that the Earth is covered by a smooth and flattened dome of some strong and solid material that is blue by day and black by night.

Under that solid dome is the air and the floating clouds. Above it, he may decide, is another world of gods and angels where the immortal souls of men will rise after the body dies and decays.

As a matter of fact, this is precisely the view of the early men of the Near East, for instance. On the second day of creation, says the Bible: "God said, Let there be a firmament in the midst of the waters, and let it divide the waters from the waters. And God made the firmament, and divided the waters which were under the firmament from the waters which were above the firmament" (Genesis 1:6–7).

The word "firmament" is from the Latin word *firmamentum*, which means something solid and strong. This is a translation of the Greek word *stereoma*, which means something solid and strong, and that is a translation of the original Hebrew word *raquia*, which refers to a thin metallic bowl.

In the biblical view there was water below the firmament (obviously) and water above it, too, to account for the rain. That is why in the time of Noah's flood, it is recorded that ". . . the fountains of the great deep [were] broken up, and the windows of heaven were opened" (Genesis 7:11). The expression might be accepted as metaphor, of course, but I'm sure that the unsophisticated accepted it literally.

But there's no use laughing from the height of our own painfully gained hindsight. About 700 B.C., when the material of Genesis was first being collected, the thought that the sky was a solid vault with another world above it was a reasonable conclusion to come to from the evidence available.

What's more, it would seem reasonable about 700 B.C. to suppose that the firmament stretched over but a limied portion of a flat Earth. One could see it come down and join the Earth tightly at the horizon. Few people in ancient times ever traveled far from home and the world to them was but a few miles in every direction. Even soldiers and merchants, who tramped longer distances, might feel the Earth was larger than it looked but that the world to the enlarged horizon was still flat, and still enclosed on all sides by the junction of firmament and ground. (This was also very much the medieval view and probably that of many unsophisticated moderns.)

The Greek philosophers, however, had come to the conclusion, for a number of valid reasons, that the Earth was *not* a more or less flat object of rather limited size, but a spherical object of sufficient size to dwarf the known world to small dimensions.

The firmament, then, must stretch all around the globular Earth, and to do so symmetrically it must be another, but much larger, sphere. The apparent flattening of the firmament overhead had to be an illusion (it is!) and the Greeks spoke of what we would call the "heavenly sphere" as opposed to the "terrestrial sphere."

None of this, however, altered the concept of the firmament (or heavenly sphere) as made up of something hard and firm. What, then, were the stars?

Naturally, the first thought was that the stars were exactly what they appeared to be: tiny, glowing disks embedded in the material of the firmament ("Look how the floor of heaven is thick inlaid with patens of bright gold").

The evidence in favor of this was that the stars did not fall down, as they would surely do if they were not firmly fixed to the heavenly sphere. Secondly, the stars moved about the Earth once every twenty-four hours, with the North Star as one pivot (the other being invisible behind the southern horizon), and did so all in one piece without altering their relative positions from night to night and from year to year.

If the stars were suspended freely somewhere between the heavenly sphere and the Earth, and for some reason did not fall, surely they would either not move at all or, if they did, would move independently. No, it made much more sense to suppose them all fixed to the heavenly sphere, and to suppose that it was the heavenly sphere that turned, carrying all the stars with itself.

But alas, this interpretation of the heavens—beautiful and austerly simple—did not account for everything.

As it happened, the Moon was clearly not imbedded in the heavenly sphere, for it did not maintain a fixed position relative to the stars. It was at a particular distance from a particular star one night, farther east the next night, still farther east the one afterward. It moved steadily west to east in such a way as to make a complete circuit of the starry sky in a little over twenty-seven days.

The Sun moved from west to east, too, relative to the stars, though much more slowly. Its motion couldn't be watched directly, of course, since no stars were visible in its neighborhood by which its position might be fixed. However, the nighttime configuration of stars shifted from night to night because, clearly, the Sun moved and blotted out slightly different portions of the sky from day to day. In that manner it could be determined that the Sun seemed to make a circuit of the sky in a little over 365 days.

If the Sun and the Moon were the only bodies to be exceptional, this might not be too bad. After all, they were very much different from the stars and could not be expected to follow the same rules.

Thus the Hebrews, in their creation myth, treated the Sun and Moon as special cases. On the fourth day of creation, "God made two great lights; the greater light to rule the day, and the lesser light to rule the night: he made the stars also" (Genesis 1:16).

It seems amusing to us today to have the stars dismissed in so offhanded a fashion but it makes perfect sense in the light of the Hebrew knowlege of the day. The stars were all imbedded in the firmament and they served only as a background against which the motions of the Sun and the Moon could be studied.

But then it turned out that certain of the brighter stars were also anomalous in their motions and shifted positions against the background of the other stars. In fact, their motion was even stranger than that of the Moon and the Sun, for, though they moved west to east most of the time, relative to the stars, as the Moon and the Sun did, they occasionally would turn about and move east to west. Very puzzling!

The Greeks called these stars *planetes*, meaning "wanderers," as compared with the "fixed stars." The Greek word has become "planet" to us and seven of them were recognized. These included the five bright stars which we now call Mercury, Venus, Mars, Jupiter, and Saturn, and, of course, the Sun and the Moon.

What to do with them? Well, like the stars, the planets did not fall and like the stars they moved about the Earth. Therefore, like the stars, they had to be imbedded in a sphere. Since each of the seven planets moved at a different speed and in a different fashion, each had to have a separate sphere, one nested inside the other, and all nested inside the sphere of the stars.

Thus there arose the notion not of the heavenly sphere, but of the heavenly spheres, plural.

But there was only one heavenly sphere that could be seen—the blue sphere of the firmament. The fact that the other spheres were invisible was no argument, however, for their non-existence, merely for their transparency. They were sometimes called "the crystalline spheres," where the word "crystalline" was used in its older meaning as "transparent."

The Greeks then set about trying to calculate where the different spheres were pivoted and how they must turn in order to cause each planet to move in the precise fashion in which it was observed to move. Endless complications had to be added in order to match theory with observation, but for two thousand years the complicated theory of the crystalline spheres held good, not because men of thought were perversely stupid, but because nothing else so well fit the appearances.

Even when Copernicus suggested that the Sun, not the Earth, was the center of the universe, he didn't abolish the spheres. He merely had them surrounding the Sun, with the Earth itself imbedded in one of them. It was only with Johannes Kepler—

But never mind that. The details of the motions of the crystalline spheres don't concern us in this article. Let us instead consider an apparently simpler question: In what order are the spheres nested? If we were to travel outward from Earth, which sphere would we come to first, which next, and so on.

The Greeks made the logical deduction that the closest sphere would be smallest and would therefore make a complete turn in the briefest time. Since the Moon made a complete circle against the stars in about four weeks (a far shorter time than any other planet managed to run the course), its sphere must be closest.

Arguing in this manner, the Greeks decided the next closest sphere was that of Mercury; then, in order, Venus, the Sun, Mars, Jupiter, and Saturn. And finally, of course, there was the sphere of the stars.

And how far apart were the spheres and what were their actual distances from the Earth?

That, unfortunately, was beyond the Greeks. To be sure, the Greek astonomer Hipparchus, about 150 B.C., used a perfectly valid method (after the still earlier astronomer Aristarchus) for determining the distance to the Moon, and had placed it at a distance of thirty times the Earth's diameter, which is correct, but the distance of no other heavenly body was determined with reasonable accuracy until the seventeenth century.

* * *

Now the scene switches. About 520 B.C., the Greek philosopher Pythagoras was plucking strings, and found that he could evoke notes that harmonized well together if he used strings whose lengths were simply related. One string might be twice the length of another; or three strings might have lengths that were in the ratio of 3:4:5.

The details are irrelevant, but to Pythagoras it seemed highly significant that there should be a connection between pleasing sounds and small whole numbers. It fit in with his rather mystical notion that everything in the universe was related to simple ratios and numbers.

Those who followed in his footsteps after his death accentuated the mysticism and it seemed to the Pythagoreans that they now had a way of deciding not only the how of planets, but the why as well. Since numbers governed the universe, one ought to be able to deduce the way in which the universe ought to be constructed.

For instance, 10 was a particularly impressive number. (Why? Well, for one thing, $1 + 2 + 3 + 4 = 10$, and this seems to have some mystical value.) In order, then, for the universe to function well, it had to be composed of ten spheres.

Of course, there were only eight spheres, one for the stars and one for each of the seven planets, but that didn't stop the Pythagoreans. They decided that the Earth moved around some central fire of which the Sun was only a reflection, and worked up a reason for explaining why the central fire was invisible. That added a ninth sphere for the Earth. In addition, they imagined another planet on the opposite side of the central fire, a "counter-Earth". The counter-Earth kept pace with the Earth and stayed always beyond the central fire and was thus never seen. Its sphere was the tenth.

In addition, the Pythagoreans thought that the spheres were nested inside each other in such a way that their distances of separation bore simple ratios to one another and produced harmonious notes in their motion as a result (like the plucking of strings of simply related lengths). Originally, I imagine, the Pythagoreans may have advanced this notion of harmonious notes only as a metaphor to represent the simply related distances, but later mystics accepted the notes as literally existent. They became "the music of the spheres."

Of course, no one ever heard any music from the sky, so it had to be assumed to be inaudible to men on Earth. It is this notion that causes Shakespeare to speak of an orb that "in this motion like an angel sings" but with sounds that can be heard only in heaven ("Such harmony is in immortal souls"). While men's souls are still draped in their earthly bodies, they are deaf to it ("whilst this muddy vesture of decay doth grossly close it in, we cannot hear it").

* * *

Well, then, does understanding Lorenzo's speech in terms of ancient astronomy spoil its beauty? Does it not seem that to understand him adds to the interest? Does it not remove the nagging question of "But what does it mean?" that otherwise distracts from an appreciation of the passage?

It may be, of course, that Mr. X is the kind who never asks "But what does it mean?" It may be that for him understanding is irrelevant. If so, he and I are not soul mates. It may even be that Mr. X is the kind of obscurantist who finds that understanding decreases beauty. If so, he and I are even less soul mates.

And yet, let me point out that there is something in this very passage that could be of interest to Shakespearian scholars *if* they thoroughly understood what Shakespeare was talking about.

As almost everyone knows, there are many who feel that Shakespeare did not write the plays attributed to him. They feel that someone else did, with the person most frequently credited being Francis Bacon, who was an almost exact contemporary of Shakespeare.

The argument very often heard is that Shakespeare was just a fellow from the provinces with very little education and that he could not possibly have written so profoundly learned a set of plays. Bacon, on the other hand, was a great philosopher and one of the most intensely educated people of his time. Bacon, therefore, could easily have written the plays.

Shakespearian scholars, when they argue the matter at all, are forced to maintain that Shakespeare was much better educated than he is given credit for being and that therefore he was learned enough to write his plays. Since virtually nothing is known of Shakespeare's life, the argument will never be settled in that fashion.

Why not turn matters around, then, and argue that Bacon was *too* educated to write Shakespeare's plays, that there exist errors in the plays that Bacon could never possibly have made and that would just suit an insufficiently educated fellow from the sticks?

Consider Lorenzo's speech. Lorenzo is talking about the *stars*; these are the "patens of bright gold" with which "the floor of heaven is thick inlaid." Lorenzo (hence Shakespeare) seems to think that each star has a separate sphere and that each gives out its own note ("There's not the smallest orb which thou behold'st/But in his motion like an angel sings").

Lest you think I'm misinterpreting the speech, let's take a clearer case.

In Act II of A *Midsummer Night's Dream*, Oberon is reminding Puck of a time they listened to a mermaid who sang with such supernal beauty that

> . . . the rude sea grew civil at her song,
> And certain stars shot madly from their spheres,
> To hear the sea maid's music.

The use of the plural "spheres" shows again that Shakespeare thinks that each star has its separate sphere.

This is wrong. There is a sphere for each planet; one for the Earth itself, if you like; one for the counter-Earth; one for any imaginary planet you wish. However, all the ancient theories agreed that the "fixed stars" were all imbedded in a single sphere.

To imagine separate spheres for each star, as Shakespeare does more than once in his plays, is to display a lack of knowledge of Greek astonomy. This is a lack of knowledge that Francis Bacon could not possibly have displayed; hence we might fairly argue that Francis Bacon could not possibly have written Shakespeare's plays.

* * *

Well, don't get me wrong. I don't want to imply that I received only bad reviews for my *Guide to Shakespeare.* Actually, most of the reviews were quite complimentary and were an entire pleasure to read.

Just the same, I had better start preparing myself for the occasional review by the "outraged specialist" type that I will surely get when *Asimov's Annotated "Don Juan"* is published.

# Mirror Image

*The Three Laws of Robotics*

*1: A robot may not injure a human being or, through inaction, allow a human being to come to harm.*
*2: A robot must obey the orders given it by human beings except where such orders would conflict with the First Law.*
*3: A robot must protect its own existence as long as such protection does not conflict with the First or Second Law.*

Lije Baley had just decided to relight his pipe, when the door of his office opened without a preliminary knock, or announcement, of any kind. Baley looked up in pronounced annoyance and then dropped his pipe. It said a good deal for the state of his mind that he left it lie where it had fallen.

"R. Daneel Olivaw," he said, in a kind of mystified excitement. "Jehoshaphat! It *is* you, isn't it?"

"You are quite right," said the tall, bronzed newcomer, his even features never flickering for a moment out of their accustomed calm. "I regret surprising you by entering without warning, but the situation is a delicate one and there must be as little involvement as possible on the part of the men and robots even in this place. I am, in any case, pleased to see you again, friend Elijah."

And the robot held out his hand in gesture as thoroughly human as was his appearance. It was Baley who was so unmanned by his astonishment as to stare at the hand with a momentary lack of understanding.

But then he seized it in both his, feeling its warm firmness. "But Daneel, *why?* You're welcome any time, but—What is this situation that is a delicate one? Are we in trouble again? Earth, I mean?"

"No, friend Elijah, it does not concern Earth. The situation to which I refer as a delicate one is, to outward appearances, a small thing.

A dispute between mathematicians, nothing more. As we happened, quite by accident, to be within an easy Jump of Earth—"

"This dispute took place on a starship, then?"

"Yes, indeed. A small dispute, yet to the humans involved astonishingly large."

Baley could not help but smile. "I'm not surprised you find humans astonishing. They do not obey the Three Laws."

"That is, indeed a shortcoming," said R. Daneel, gravely, "and I think humans themselves are puzzled by humans. It may be that you are less puzzled than are the men of other worlds because so many more human beings live on Earth than on the Spacer worlds. If so, and I believe it is so, you could help us."

R. Daneel paused momentarily and then said, perhaps a shade too quickly, "And yet there are rules of human behavior which I have learned. It would seem, for instance, that I am deficient in etiquette, by human standards, not to have asked after your wife and child."

"They are doing well. The boy is in college and Jessie is involved in local politics. The amenities are taken care of. Now tell me how you come to be here."

* * *

"As I said, we were within an easy Jump of Earth," said R. Daneel, "so I suggested to the captain that we consult you."

"And the captain agreed?" Baley had a sudden picture of the proud and autocratic captain of a Spacer starship consenting to make a landing on Earth—of all worlds—and to consult an Earthman—of all people.

"I believe," said R. Daneel, "that he was in a position where he would have agreed to anything. In addition, I praised you very highly; although, to be sure, I stated only the truth. Finally, I agreed to conduct all negotiations so that none of the crew, or passengers, would need to enter any of the Earthman cities."

"And talk to any Earthman, yes. But what has happened?'

"The passengers of the starship, *Eta Carina*, included two mathematicians who were traveling to Aurora to attend an interstellar conference on neurobiophysics. It is about these mathematicians, Alfred Barr Humboldt and Gennao Sabbat, that the dispute centers. Have you perhaps, friend Elijah, heard of one, or both, of them?"

"Neither one," said Baley, firmly. "I know nothing about mathematics. Look, Daneel, surely you haven't told anyone I'm a mathematics buff or—"

"Not at all, friend Elijah. I know you are not. Nor does it matter, since the exact nature of the mathematics involved is in no way relevant to the point of issue."

"Well, then, go on."

"Since you do not know either man, friend Elijah, let me tell you that Dr. Humboldt is well into his twenty-seventh decade—pardon me, friend Elijah?"

"Nothing. Nothing," said Baley, irritably. He had merely muttered to himself, more or less incoherently, in a natural reaction to the extended life-spans of the Spacers. "And he's still active, despite, his age? On Earth, mathematicians after thirty or so . . ."

Daneel said, calmly, "Dr. Humboldt is one of the top three mathematicians, by long-established repute, in the galaxy. Certainy he is still active. Dr. Sabbat, on the other hand, is quite young, not yet fifty, but he has already established himself as the most remarkable new talent in the most abstruse branches of mathematics."

"They're both great, then," said Baley. He remembered his pipe and picked it up. He decided there was no point in lighting it now and knocked out the dottle. "What happened? Is this a murder case? Did one of them apparently kill the other?"

"Of these two men of great reputation, one is trying to destroy that of the other. By human valves, I believe this may be regarded as worse than physical murder."

"Sometimes, I suppose. Which one is trying to destroy the other?"

"Why, that, friend Elijah, is precisely the point of issue. Which?"

"Go on."

"Dr. Humboldt tells the story clearly. Shortly before he boarded the starship, he had an insight into a possible method for analyzing neural pathways from changes in microwave absorption patterns of local cortical areas. The insight was a purely mathematical technique of extraordinary subtlety, but I cannot, of course, either understand or sensibly transmit the details. These do not, however, matter. Dr. Humboldt considered the matter and was more convinced each hour that he had something revolutionary on hand, something that would dwarf all his previous accomplishments in mathematics. Then he discovered that Dr. Sabbat was on board."

"Ah. And he tried it out on young Sabbat?"

"Exactly. The two had met at professional meetings before and knew each other thoroughly by reputation. Humboldt went into it with Sabbat in great detail. Sabbat backed Humboldt's analysis completely and was unstinting in his praise of the importance of the discovery and of the ingenuity of the discoverer. Heartened and reassured by this,

Humboldt prepared a paper outlining, in summary, his work and, two days later prepared to have it forwarded subetherically to the co-chairmen of the conference at Aurora, in order that he might officially establish his priority and arrange for possible discussion before the sessions were closed. To his surprise, he found that Sabbat was ready with a paper of his own, essentially the same as Humboldt's, and Sabbat was also preparing to have it subetherized to Aurora."

"I suppose Humboldt was furious."

"Quite!"

"And Sabbat? What was his story?"

"Precesely the same as Humboldt's. Word for word."

"Then just what is the problem?"

"Except for the mirror-image exchange of names. According to Sabbat, it was he who had the insight, and he who consulted Humboldt; it was Humboldt who agreed with the analysis and praised it."

"Then each one claims the idea is his and that the other stole it. It doesn't sound like a problem to me at all. In matters of scholarship, it would seem only necessary to produce the records of research, dated and initialed. Judgment as to priority can be made from that. Even if one is falsified, that might be discovered through internal inconsistencies."

"Ordinarily, friend Elijah, you would be right, but this is mathematics, and not an experimental science. Dr. Humboldt claims to have worked out the essentials in his head. Nothing was put in writing until the paper itself was prepared. Dr. Sabbat, of course, says precisely the same."

"Well, then, be more drastic and get it over with, for sure. Subject each one to a psychic probe and find out which of the two is lying."

R. Daneel shook his head slowly. "Friend Elijah, you do not understand these men. They are both of rank and scholarship, Fellows of the Imperial Academy. As such, they cannot be subjected to trial of professional conduct except by a jury of their peers—their professional peers—unless they personally and voluntarily waive that right."

"Put it to them, then. The guilty man won't waive the right because he can't afford to face the psychic probe. The innocent man will waive it at once. You won't even have to use the probe."

"It does not work that way, friend Elijah. To waive the right in such a case—to be investigated by laymen—is a serious and perhaps irrecoverable blow to prestige. Both men steadfastly refuse to waive the right to special trial, as a matter of pride. The question of guilt, or innocence, is quite subsidiary."

"In that case, let it go for now. Put the matter in cold storage until you get to Aurora. At the neurobiophysical conference, there will be a huge supply of professional peers, and then—"

"That would mean a tremendous blow to science itself, friend Elijah. Both men would suffer for having been the instrument of scandal. Even the innocent one would be blamed for having been party to a situation so distasteful. It would be felt that it should have been settled quietly out of court of all costs."

"All right. I'm not a Spacer, but I'll try to imagine that this attitude makes sense. What do the men in question say?"

"Humboldt agrees throughly. He says that if Sabbat will admit theft of the idea and allow Humboldt to proceed with transmission of the paper—or at least its delivery at the conference, he will not press charges. Sabbat's misdeed will remain secret with him; and, of course, with the captain, who is the only other human to be party to the dispute."

"But young Sabbat will not agree?"

"On the contrary, he agreed with Dr. Humboldt to the last detail—with the reversal of names. Still the mirror-image."

"So they just sit there, stalemented?"

"Each, I believe, friend Elijah, is waiting for the other to give in and admit guilt."

"Well, then, wait."

"The captain has decided this cannot be done. There are two alternatives to waiting, you see. The first is that both will remain stubborn so that when the starship lands on Aurora, the intellectual scandal will break. The captain, who is responsible for justice on board ship, will suffer disgrace for not having been able to settle the matter quietly and that, to him, is quite insupportable."

"And the second alternative?"

"Is that one, or the other, of the mathematicians will indeed admit to wrongdoing. But will the one who confesses do so out of actual guilt, or out of a noble desire to prevent the scandal? Would it be right to deprive of credit one who is sufficiently ethical to prefer to lose that credit than to see science as a whole suffer? Or else, the guilty party will confess at the last moment, and in such a way as to make it appear he does so only for the sake of science, thus escaping the disgrace of his deed and casting its shadow upon the other. The captain will be the only man to know all this but he does not wish to spend the rest of his life wondering whether he has been a party to a grotesque miscarriage of justice."

Baley sighed. "A game of intellectual chicken. Who'll break first as Aurora comes nearer and nearer? Is that the whole story now, Daneel?"

"Not quite. There are witnesses to the transaction."

* * *

"Jehoshaphat! Why didn't you say so at once. *What* witnesses?"

"Dr. Humboldt's personal servant—"

"A robot, I suppose."

"Yes, certainly. He is called R. Preston. This servant, R. Preston, was present during the initial conference and he bears out Dr. Humboldt in every detail."

"You mean he says that the idea was Dr. Humboldt's to begin with; that Dr. Humboldt detailed it to Dr. Sabbat; that Dr Sabbat praised the idea, and so on."

"Yes, in full detail."

"I see. Does that settle the matter or not? Presumably not."

"You are quite right. It does not settle the matter, for there is a second witness. Dr. Sabbat also has a personal servant, R. Idda, another robot of, as it happens, the same model as R. Preston, made, I believe, in the same year in the same factory. Both have been in service for an equal period of time."

"An odd coincidence—very odd."

"A fact, I am afraid, and it makes it difficult to arrive at any judgment based on obvious differences between the two servants."

"R. Idda, then, tells the same story as R. Preston?"

"Precisely the same story, except for the mirror-image reversal of the names."

"R. Idda stated, then, that young Sabbat, the one not yet fifty"—Lije Baley did not entirely keep the sardonic note out of his voice; he himself was not yet fifty and he felt far from young—"had the idea to begin with; that he detailed it to Dr. Humboldt, who was loud in his praises, and so on."

"Yes, friend Elijah."

"And one robot is lying, then."

"So it would seem."

"It should be easy to tell which. I imagine even a superficial examination by a good roboticist—"

"A roboticist is not enough in this case, friend Elija. Only a qualified robopsychologist would carry weight enough and experience enough to make a decision in a case of this importance. There is no one so qualified on board ship. Such an examination can be performed only when we reach Aurora—"

"And by then the crud hits the fan. Well, you're here on Earth. We can scare up a robopsychologist, and surely anything that happens on Earth will never reach the ears of Aurora and there will be no scandal."

"Except that neither Dr. Humboldt, nor Dr. Sabbat, will allow his servant to be investigated by a robopsychologist of Earth. The Earthman would have to—" He paused.

Lije Baley said stolidly, "He'd have to touch the robot."

"These are old servants, well thought of—"

"And not to be sullied by the touch of Earthmen. Then what do you want me to do, damn it?" He paused, grimacing. "I'm sorry, R. Daneel, but I see no reason for your having involved me."

* * *

"I was on the ship on a mission utterly irrelevant to the problem at hand. The captain turned to me because he had to turn to someone. I seemed human enough to talk to, and robot enough to be a safe recipient of confidences. He told me the whole story and asked what I would do. I realized the next jump could take us as easily to Earth as to our target. I told the captain that, although I was at as much loss to resolve the mirror-image as he was, there was on Earth one who might help."

"Jehoshaphat!" muttered Baley under his breath.

"Consider, friend Elijah, that if you succeed in solving this puzzle, it would do your career good and Earth itself might benefit. The matter could not be publicized, of course, but the captain is a man of some influence on his home world and he would be grateful."

"You just put a greater strain on me."

"I have every confidence," said R. Daneel, stolidly, "that you already have some idea as to what procedure ought to be followed."

"Do you? I suppose that the obvious procedure is to interview the two mathematicians, one of whom would seem to be a thief."

"I'm afraid, friend Elijah, that neither one will come into the city. Nor would either one be willing to have you come to them."

"And there is no way of forcing a Spacer to allow contact with an Earthman, no matter what the emergency. Yes, I understand that, Daneel—but I was thinking of an interview by closed-circuit television."

"Nor that. They will not submit to interrogation by an Earthman."

"Then what do they want of me? Could I speak to the robots?"

"They would not allow the robots to come here, either."

"Jehoshaphat, Daneel. *You've* come."

"That was my own decision. I have permission, while on board ship, to make decisions of that sort without veto by any human being but the captain himself—and he was eager to establish the contact. I, having known you, decided that television contact was insufficient. I wished to shake your hand."

Lije Baley softened. "I appreciate that, Daneel, but I still honestly wish you could have refrained from thinking of me at all in this case. Can I talk to the robots by television at least?"

"That, I think, can be arranged."

"Something, at least. That means I would be doing the work of a robopsychologist—in a crude sort of way."

"But you are a detective, friend Elijah, not a robopsychologist."

"Well, let it pass. Now before I see them, let's think a bit. Tell me: it is possible that both robots are telling the truth? Perhaps the conversation between the two mathematicians was equivocal. Perhaps it was of such a nature that each robot could honestly believe its own master was proprietor of the idea. Or perhaps one robot heard only one portion of the discussion and the other another portion, so that each could suppose its own master was proprietor of the idea."

"That is quite impossible, friend Elijah. Both robots repeat the conversation in identical fashion. And the two repetitions are fundamentally inconsistent."

"Then it is absolutely certain that one of the robots is lying?"

"Yes."

"Will I be able to see the transcript of all evidence given so far in the presence of the captain, if I should want to?"

"I thought you would ask that and I have copies with me."

"Another blessing. Have the robots been cross-examined at all, and is that cross-examination included in the transcript?"

"The robots have merely repeated their tales. Cross-examination would be conducted only by robopsychologists."

"Or by myself?"

"You are a detective, friend Elijah, not a—"

"All right, R. Daneel. I'll try to get the Spacer psychology straight. A detective can do it because he isn't a robopsychologist. Let's think further. Ordinarily a robot will not lie, but he will do so if necessary to maintain the Three Laws. He might lie to protect, in legitimate fashion, his own existence in accordance with the Third Law. He is more apt to lie if that is necessary to follow a legitimate order given him by a human being in accordance with the Second Law. He is most apt to lie if that is necessary to save a human life, or to prevent harm from coming to a human in accordance with the First Law."

"Yes."

"And in this case, each robot would be defending the professional reputation of his master, and would lie if it were necessary to do so. Under the circumstances, the professional reputation would be nearly equivalent to life and there might be a near-First Law urgency to the lie."

"Yet by the lie, each servant would be harming the professional reputation of the other's master, friend Elijah."

"So it would, but each robot might have a clearer conception of the value of its own master's reputation and honestly judge it to be greater than that of the other's. The lesser harm would be done by his lie, he would suppose, than by the truth."

Having said that, Lije Baley remained quiet for a moment. Then he said, "All right, then, can you arrange to have me talk to one of robots – to R. Idda first, I think?"

"Dr. Sabbat's robot?"

"Yes," said Baley, dryly, "the young fellow's robot."

"It will take me but a few minutes," said R. Daneel. "I have a micro-receiver outfitted with a projector. I will need merely a blank wall and I think this one will do if you will allow me to move some of these film cabinets."

"Go ahead. Will I have to talk into a microphone of some sort?"

"No, you will be able to talk in an ordinary manner. Please pardon me, friend Elijah, for a moment of further delay. I will have to contact the ship and arrange for R. Idda to be interviewed."

"If that will take some time, Daneel, how about giving me the transcripted material of the evidence so far."

* * *

Lije Baley lit his pipe while R. Daneel set up the equipment, and leafed through the flimsy sheets he had been handed.

The minutes passed and R. Daneel said, "If you are ready, friend Elijah, R. Idda is. Or would you prefer a few more minutes with the transcript?"

"No," sighed Baley, "I'm not learning anything new. Put him on and arrange to have the interview recorded and transcribed."

R. Idda, unreal in two-dimensional projection against the wall, was basically metallic in structure – not at all the humanoid creature that R. Daneel was. His body was tall but blocky, and there was very little to distinguish him from the many robots Baley had seen, except for minor structural details.

Baley said, "Greetings, R. Idda."

"Greetings, sir," said R. Idda, in a muted voice that sounded surprisingly humanoid.

"You are the personal servant of Gennao Sabbat, are you not?"

"I am sir."

"For how long boy?"

"For twenty-two years, sir."

"And your master's reputation is valuable to you?"

"Yes, sir."

"Would you consider it of importance to protect that reputation?"

"Yes, sir."

"As important to protect his reputation as his physical life?"

"No, sir."

"As important to protect his reputation as the reputation of another?"

R. Idda hesitated. He said, "Such cases must be decided on their individual merit, sir. There is no way of establishing a general rule."

* * *

Baley hesitated. These Spacer robots spoke more smoothly and intellectually than Earth-models did. He was not at all sure he could outthink one.

He said, "If you decided that the reputation of your master were more important than that of another, say, that of Alfred Barr Humboldt, would you lie to protect your master's reputation?"

"I would sir."

"Did you lie in your testimony concerning your master in his controvery with Dr. Humboldt?"

"No, sir."

"But if you were lying, you would deny you were lying in order to protect that lie, wouldn't you?"

"Yes, sir."

"Well, then," said Baley, "let's consider this. Your master, Gennao Sabbat, is a young man of great reputation in mathematics, but he is a young man. If, in this controversy with Dr. Humboldt, he had succumbed to temptation and had acted unethically, he would suffer a certain eclipse of reputation, but he is young and would have ample time to recover. He would have many intellectual triumphs ahead of him and men would eventually look upon this plagiaristic attempt as the mistake of a hot-blooded youth, deficient in judgment. It would be something that would be made up for in the future.

"If, on the other hand, it were Dr. Humboldt who succumbed to temptation, the matter would be much more serious. He is an old man whose great deeds have spread over centuries. His reputation has been unblemished hitherto. All of that, however, would be forgotten in the light of this one crime of his later years, and he would have no opportunity to make up for it in the comparatively short time remaining to him. There would be little more that he could accomplish. There would be so many more years of work ruined in Humboldt's case than in that of your master and so much less opportunity to win back his position. You see, don't you, that Humboldt faces the worse situation and deserves the greater consideration?"

There was a long pause. Then R. Idda said, with unmoved voice, "My evidence was a lie. It was Dr. Humboldt whose work it was, and my master has attempted, wrongfully, to appropriate the credit."

Baley said, "Very well, boy. You are instructed to say nothing to anyone about this until given permission by the captain of the ship. You are excused."

The screen blanked out and Baley puffed at his pipe. "Do you suppose the captain heard that, Daneel?"

"I am sure of it. He is the only witness, except for us."

"Good. Now for the other."

"But is there any point to that, friend Elijah, in view of what R. Idda has confessed?"

"Of course there is. R. Idda's confession means nothing."

"Nothing?"

"Nothing at all. I pointed out that Dr. Humboldt's position was the worse. Naturally, if he were lying to protect Sabbat, he would switch to the truth as, in fact, he claimed to have done. On the other hand, if he were telling the truth, he would switch to a lie to protect Humboldt. It's still mirror-image and we haven't gained anything."

"But then what will we gain by questioning R. Preston?"

"Nothing, if the mirror-image were perfect – but it is not. After all, one of the robots *is* telling the truth to begin with, and one *is* lying to begin with, and that is a point of asymmetry. Let me see R. Preston. And if the transcription of R. Idda's examination is done, let me have it."

* * *

The projector came into use again. R. Preston stared out of it; identical with R. Idda in every respect, except for some trivial chest design.

Baley said, "Greetings, R. Preston." He kept the record of R. Idda's examination before him as he spoke.

"Greetings, sir," said R. Preston. His voice was identical with that of R. Idda.

"You are the personal servant of Alfred Barr Humboldt, are you not?"

"I am, sir."

"For how long, boy?"

"For twenty-two years, sir."

"And your master's reputation is valuable to you?"

"Yes, sir."

"Would you consider it of importance to protect that reputation?"

"Yes, sir."

"As important to protect his reputation as his physical life?"

"No, sir."

"As important to protect his reputation as the reputation of another?"

R. Preston hesitated. He said, "Such cases must be decided on their individual merit, sir. There is no way of establishing a general rule."

Baley said, "If you decided that the reputation of your master were more important than that of another, say, that of Gennao Sabbat, would you lie to protect your master's reputation?"

"I would, sir."

"Did you lie in your testimony concerning your master in his controversy with Dr. Sabbat?"

"No, sir."

"Well, then," said Baley, "let's consider this. Your master, Alfred Barr Humboldt, is an old man of great reputation in mathematics, but he is an old man. If, in this controversy with Dr. Sabbat, he had succumbed to temptation and had acted unethically, he would suffer a certain eclipse of reputation, but his great age and his centuries of accomplishments would stand against that and would win out. Men would look upon this plagiaristic attempt as the mistake of a perhaps-sick old man, no longer certain in judgment.

"If, on the other hand, it were Dr. Sabbat who had succumbed to temptation, the matter would be much more serious. He is a young man, with a far less secure reputation. He would ordinarily have centuries ahead of him in which he might accumulate knowledge and achieve great things. This will be closed to him, now, obscured by one mistake of his youth. He has a much longer future to lose than your master has. You see, don't you, that Sabbat faces the worse situation and deserves the greater consideration?"

There was a long pause. Then R. Preston said, with unmoved voice. "My evidence was as I—"

At that point, he broke off and said nothing more.

Baley said, "Please continue, R. Preston."

There was no response.

R. Daneel said, "I am afraid, friend Elijah, that R. Preston is in stasis. He is out of commision."

"Well, then," said Baley, "we have finally produced an asymmetry. From this, we can see who the guilty person is."

"In what way, friend Elijah?"

"Think it out. Suppose you were a person who had committed no crime and that your personal robot were a witness to that. There would be nothing you need to do. Your robot would tell the truth and bear you out. If, however, you were a person who *had* committed the crime, you would have to depend on your robot to lie. That would be a somewhat riskier position, for although the robot would lie, if necessary, the greater inclination would be to tell the truth, so that the lie would be less firm than the truth would be. To prevent that, the crime-committing person would very likely have to *order* the robot to lie. In this way. First Law would be strengthened by Second Law; perhaps very substantially strengthened."

"That would seem reasonable," said R. Daneel.

"Suppose we have one robot of each type. One robot would switch from truth, unreinforced, to the lie, and could do so after some hesitation, without serious trouble. The other robot would switch from the lie, *strongly reinforced*, to the truth, but could do so only at the risk of burning out various positronic-track-ways in his brain and falling into stasis."

"And since R. Preston went into stasis—"

"R. Preston's master, Dr. Humboldt, is the man guilty of plagiarism. If you transmit this to the captain and urge him to face Dr. Humboldt with the matter at once, he may force a confession. If so, I hope you will tell me immediately."

"I will certainly do so. You will excuse me, friend Elijah? I must talk to the captain privately."

"Certainly. Use the conference room. It is shielded."

* * *

Baley could do no work of any kind in R. Daneel's absence. He sat in uneasy silence. A great deal would depend on the value of his analysis, and he was acutely aware of his lack of expertise in robotics.

R. Daneel was back in half an hour – very nearly the longest half hour of Baley's life.

There was no use, of course, in trying to determine what had happened from the expression of the humanoid's impassive face. Baley tried to keep his face impassive.

"Yes, R. Daneel?" he asked.

"Precisely as you said, friend Elijah. Dr. Humboldt has confessed. He was counting, he said, on Dr. Sabbat giving way and allowing Dr. Humboldt to have this one last triumph. The crisis is over and you will find the captain grateful. He has given me permission to tell you that he admires your subtlety greatly and I believe that I, myself, will achieve favor for having suggested you."

"Good," said Baley, his knees weak and his forehead moist now that his decision had proven correct, "but Jehoshaphat, R. Daneel, don't put me on the spot like that again, will you?"

"I will try not to, friend Elijah. All will depend, of course, on the importance of a crisis, on your nearness, and on certain other factors. Meanwhile, I have a question—"

"Yes?"

"Was it not possible to suppose that passage from a lie to the truth was easy, while passage from the truth to a lie was difficult? And in that case, would not the robot in stasis have been going from a truth to a lie, and since R. Preston was in stasis, might one not have drawn the conclusion that it was Dr. Humboldt who was innocent and Dr. Sabbat who was guilty?"

"Yes, R. Daneel. It was possible to argue that way, but it was the other argument that proved right. Humboldt did confess, didn't he?"

"He did. But with arguments possible in both directions, how could you, friend Elijah, so quickly pick the correct one?"

For a moment, Baley's lips twitched. Then he relaxed and they curved into a smile. "Because, R. Daneel, I took into account human reactions, not robotic ones. I know more about human beings than about robots. In other words, I had an idea as to which mathematician was guilty before I ever interviewed the robots. Once I provoked an asymmetric response in them, I simply interpreted it in such a way as to place the guilt on the one I already believed to be guilty. The robotic response was dramatic enough to break down the guilty man; my own analysis of human behavior might not have been sufficient to do so."

"I am curious to know what your analysis of human behavior was?"

"Jehoshaphat, R. Daneel; think, and you won't have to ask. There is another point of asymmetry in this tale of mirror-image besides the matter of true-and-false. There is the matter of the age of the two mathematicians; one is quite old and one is quite young."

"Yes, of course, but what then?"

"Why, this. I can see a young man, flushed with a sudden, startling and revolutionary idea, consulting in the matter an old man whom he has, from his early student days, thought of as a demigod in the field. I can *not* see an old man, rich in honors and used to triumphs, coming up with a sudden, startling and revolutionary idea, consulting a man centuries his junior whom he is bound to think of as a young whippersnapper – or whatever term a Spacer would use. Then, too, if a young man had the chance, would he try to steal the idea of a revered demigod? It would be unthinkable. On the other hand, an old man, conscious of declining powers, might well snatch at one last chance of fame and consider a baby in the field to have no rights he was bound to deserve. In short, it was not conceivable that Sabbat steal Humboldt's idea; and from both angles, Dr. Humboldt was guilty."

R. Daneel considered that for a long time. Then he held out his hand. "I must leave now, friend Elijah. It was good to see you. May we meet again soon."

Baley gripped the robot's hand, warmly, "If you don't mind, R. Daneel," he said, "not too soon."

# Light Verse

The very last person anyone would expect to be a murderer was Mrs. Avis Lardner. Widow of the great astronaut-martyr, she was a philanthropist, an art collector, a hostess extraordinary, and, everyone agreed, an artistic genius. But above all, she was the gentlest and kindest human being one could imagine.

Her husband, William J. Lardner, died, as we all know, of the effects of radiation from a solar flare, after he had deliberately remained in space so that a passenger vessel might make it safely to Space Station 5.

Mrs. Lardner had received a generous pension for that, and she had then invested wisely and well. By late middle age she was very wealthy.

Her house was a showplace, a veritable museum, containing a small but extremely select collection of extraordinarily beautiful jeweled objects. From a dozen different cultures she had obtained relics of almost every conceivable artifact that could be embedded with jewels and made to serve the aristocracy of that culture. She had one of the first jeweled pair of spectacles from Italy, and so on almost endlessly.

All was open for inspection. The artifacts were not insured, and there were no ordinary security provisions. There was no need for anything conventional, for Mrs. Lardner maintained a large staff of robot servants, all of whom could be relied on to guard every item with imperturbable concentration, irreproachable honesty, and irrevocable efficiency.

Everyone knew the existence of those robots and there is no record of any attempt at theft, ever.

And then, of course, there was her light-sculpture. How Mrs. Lardner discovered her own genius at the art, no guest at her many lavish entertainments could guess. On each occasion, however, when her house was thrown open to guests, a new symphony of light shone throughout the rooms; three-dimensional curves and solids in melting color, some pure and some fusing in startling, crystalline effects that bathed every guest in wonder and somehow always adjusted itself so as to make Mrs. Lardner's blue-white hair and soft, unlined face gently beautiful.

It was for the light-sculpture more than anything else that the guests came. It was never the same twice, and never failed to explore new experimental avenues of art.

Many people who could afford light-consoles prepared light-sculptures for amusement, but no one could approach Mrs. Lardner's expertise. Not even those who considered themselves professional artists.

She herself was charmingly modest about it. "No, no," she would protest when someone waxed lyrical. "I wouldn't call it 'poetry in light.' That's far too kind. At most, I would say it was mere 'light verse.' " And everyone smiled at her gentle wit.

Though she was often asked, she would never create light-sculpture for any occasion but her own parties. "That would be commercialization," she said.

She had no objection, however, to the preparation of elaborate holograms of her sculptures so that they might be made permanent and reproduced in museums of art all over the world. Nor was there ever a charge for any use that might be made of her light-sculptures.

"I couldn't ask a penny," she said, spreading her arms wide. "It's free to all. After all, I have no further use for it myself." It was true! She never used the same light-sculpture twice.

When the holograms were taken, she was cooperation itself. Watching benignly at every step, she was always ready to order her robot servants to help. "Please, Courtney," she would say, "would you be so kind as to adjust the step ladder?"

It was her fashion. She always addressed her robots with the most formal courtesy.

Once, years before, she had been almost scolded by a government functionary from the Bureau of Robots and Mechanical Men. "You can't do that," he said severely. "It interferes with their efficiency. They are constructed to follow orders, and the more clearly you give those orders, the more efficiently they follow them. When you ask with elaborate politeness, it is difficult for them to understand that an order is being given. They react more slowly."

Mrs. Lardner lifted her aristocratic head. "I do not ask for speed and efficiency," she said. "I ask goodwill. My robots love me."

The government functionary might have explained that robots cannot love, but he withered under her hurt but gentle glance.

It was notorious that Mrs. Lardner never even returned a robot to the factory for adjustment. Their positronic brains are enormously complex, and once in ten times or so the adjustment is not perfect as it leaves the factory. Sometimes the error does not show up for a period of time, but whenever it does, U.S. Robots and Mechanical Men Corporation always makes the adjustment free of charge.

Mrs. Lardner shook her head. "Once a robot is in my house," she said, "and has performed his duties, any minor eccentricities must be borne with. I will not have him manhandled."

It was the worse thing possible to try to explain that a robot was but a machine. She would say very stiffly, "Nothing that is as intelligent as a robot can ever be *but* a machine. I treat them as people."

And that was that!

She kept even Max, although he was almost helpless. He could scarcely understand what was expected of him. Mrs. Lardner denied that strenuously, however. "Not at all," she would say firmly. "He can take hat and coats and store them very well, indeed. He can hold objects for me. He can do many things."

"But why not have him adjusted?" asked a friend, once.

"Oh, I couldn't. He's himself. He's very lovable, you know. After all, a positronic brain is so complex that no one can ever tell in just what way it's off. If he were made perfectly normal there would be no way to adjust him back to the lovability he now has. I won't give that up."

"But if he's maladjusted," said the friend, looking at Max nervously, "might he not be dangerous?"

"Never," laughed Mrs. Lardner. "I've had him for years. He's completely harmless and quite a dear."

Actually he looked like all the other robots, smooth, metallic, vaguely human but expressionless.

To the gentle Mrs. Lardner, however, they were all individual, all sweet, all lovable. It was the kind of woman she was.

How could she commit murder?

* * *

The very last person anyone would expect to be murdered would be John Semper Travis. Introverted and gentle, he was in the world but not of it. He had that peculiar mathematical turn of mind that made it possible for him to work out in his mind the complicated tapestry of the myriad positronic brain-paths in a robot's mind.

He was chief engineer of U.S. Robots and Mechanical Men Corporation.

But he was also an enthusiastic amateur in light-sculpture. He had written a book on the subject, trying to show that the type of mathematics he used in working out positronic brain-paths might be modified into a guide to the production of aesthetic light-sculpture.

His attempt at putting theory into practice was a dismal failure, however. The sculptures he himself produced, following his mathematical principles, were stodgy, mechanical, and uninteresting.

It was the only reason for unhappiness in his quiet, introverted, and secure life, and yet it was reason enough for him to be very unhappy indeed. He *knew* his theories were right, yet he could not make them work. If he could but produce *one* great piece of light-sculpture—

Naturally, he knew of Mrs. Lardner's light-sculpture. She was universally hailed as a genius, yet Travis knew she could not understand even the simplest aspect of robotic mathematics. He had corresponded with her but she consistently refused to explain her methods, and he wondered if she had any at all. Might it not be mere intuition?—but even intuition might be reduced to mathematics. Finally he managed to receive an invitation to one of her parties. He simply had to see her.

* * *

Mr. Travis arrived rather late. He had made one last attempt at a piece of light-sculpture and had failed dismally.

He greeted Mrs. Lardner with a kind of puzzled respect and said, "That was a peculiar robot who took my hat and coat."

"That is Max," said Mrs. Lardner.

"He is quite maladjusted, and he's a fairly old model. How is it you did not return it to the factory?"

"Oh, no," said Mrs. Lardner. "It would be too much trouble."

"None at all, Mrs. Lardner," said Travis. "You would be surprised how simple a task it was. Since I am with U.S. Robots, I took the liberty of adjusting him myself. It took no time and you'll find he is now in perfect working order."

A queer change came over Mrs. Lardner's face. Fury found a place on it for the first time in her life, and it was as though the lines did not know how to form.

"You adjusted him?" she shrieked. "But it was *he* who created my light-sculptures. It was the maladjustment, the *maladjustment*, which you can never restore, that—that—"

It was really unfortunate that she had been showing her collection at the time and that the jeweled dagger from Cambodia was on the marble tabletop before her.

Travis's face was also distorted. "You mean if I had studied his uniquely maladjusted positronic brain-paths I might have learned—"

She lunged with the knife too quickly for anyone to stop her and he did not try to dodge. Some said he came to meet it—as though he *wanted* to die.

# . . . That Thou Art Mindful of Him

*The Three Laws of Robotics:*

1. *A robot may not injure a human being or, through inaction, allow a human being to come to harm.*
2. *A robot must obey the orders given it by human beings except where such orders would conflict with the First Law.*
3. *A robot must protect its own existence as long as such protection does not conflict with the First or Second Law.*

## 1.

Keith Harriman, who had for twelve years now been Director of Research at United States Robots and Mechanical Corporation, found that he was not at all certain whether he was doing right. The tip of his tongue passed over his plump but rather pale lips and it seemed to him that the holographic image of the great Susan Calvin, which stared unsmilingly down upon him, had never looked so grim before.

Usually he blanked out that image of the greatest roboticist in history because she unnerved him. (He tried thinking of the image as "it" but never quite succeeded.) This time he didn't quite dare to and her long-dead gaze bored into the side of his face.

It was a dreadful and demeaning step he would have to take.

Opposite him was George Ten, calm and unaffected either by Harriman's patent uneasiness or by the image of the patron saint of robotics glowing in its niche above.

Harriman said, "We haven't had a chance to talk this out, really, George. You haven't been with us that long and I haven't had a good chance to be alone with you. But now I would like to discuss the matter in some detail."

"I am perfectly willing to do that," said George. "In my stay at U.S. Robots, I have gathered the crisis has something to do with the Three Laws."

"Yes. You know the Three Laws, of course."

"I do."

"Yes, I'm sure you do. But let us dig even deeper and consider the truly basic problem. In two centuries of, if I may say so, considerable success, U.S. Robots has never managed to persuade human beings to accept robots. We have placed robots only where work is required that human beings cannot do, or in enviroments that human beings find unacceptably dangerous. Robots have worked mainly in space and that has limited what we have been able to do."

"Surely," said George Ten, "that represents a broad limit, and one within which U.S. Robots can prosper."

"No, for two reasons. In the first place, the boundaries set for us inevitably contract. As the Moon colony, for instance, grows more sophisticated, its demand for robots decreases and we expect that, within the next few years, robots will be banned on the Moon. This will be repeated on every world colonized by mankind. Secondly, true prosperity is impossible without robots on Earth. We at U.S. Robots firmly believe that human beings need robots and must learn to live with their mechanical analogues if progress is to be maintained."

"Do they not? Mr. Harriman, you have on your desk a computer input which, I understand, is connected with the organization's Multivac. A computer is a kind of sessile robot; a robot brain not attached to a body—"

"True, but that also is limited. The computers used by mankind have been steadily specialized in order to avoid too humanlike an intelligence. A century ago we were well on the way to artificial intelligence of the most unlimited type through the use of great computers we called Machines. Those Machines limited their action of their own accord. Once they had solved the ecological problems that had threatened human society, they phased themselves out. Their own continued existence would, they reasoned, have placed them in the role of a crutch to mankind and, since they felt this would harm human beings, they condemned themselves by the First Law."

"And were they not correct to do so?"

"In my opinion, no. By their action, they reinforced mankind's Frankenstein complex; its gut fears that any artificial man they created would turn upon its creator. Men fear that robots may replace human beings."

"Do you not fear that yourself?"

"I know better. As long as the Three Laws of Robotics exist, they cannot. They can serve as *partners* of mankind; they can share in the great struggle to understand and wisely direct the laws of nature so that together they can do more than mankind can possibly do alone; but always in such a way that robots serve human beings."

"But if the Three Laws have shown themselves, over the course of two centuries, to keep robots within bounds, what is the source of the distrust of human beings for robots?"

"Well"—and Harriman's graying hair tufted as he scratched his head vigorously—"mostly superstition, of course. Unfortunately, there are also some complexities involved that anti-robot agitators seize upon."

"Involving the Three Laws?"

"Yes. The Second Law in particular. There's no problem in the Third Law, you see. It is universal. Robots must always sacrifice themselves for human beings, any human beings."

"Of course," said George Ten.

"The First Law is perhaps less satisfactory, since it is always possible to imagine a condition in which a robot must perform either Action A or Action B, the two being mutually exclusive, and where either action results in harm to human beings. The robot must therefore quickly select which action results in the least harm. To work out the positronic paths of the robot brain in such a way as to make that selection possible is not easy. If Action A results in harm to a talented young artist and B results in equivalent harm to five elderly people of no particular worth, which action should be chosen?"

"Action A," said George Ten. "Harm to one is less than harm to five."

"Yes, so robots have always been designed to decide. To expect robots to make judgments of fine points such as talent, intelligence, the general usefulness to society, has always seemed impractical. That would delay decision to the point where the robot is effectively immobilized. So we go by numbers. Fortunately, we might expect crises in which robots must make such decisions to be few . . . But then that brings us to the Second Law."

"The Law of Obedience."

"Yes. The necessity of obedience is constant. A robot may exist for twenty years without ever having to act quickly to prevent harm to a human being, or find itself faced with the necessity of risking its own destruction. In all that time, however, it will be constantly obeying orders . . . Whose orders?"

"Those of a human being."

"Any human being? How do you judge a human being so as to know whether to obey or not? What is man, that thou are mindful of him, George?"

George hesitated at that.

Harriman said hurriedly, "A Biblical quotation. That doesn't matter. I mean, must a robot follow the orders of a child; or of an idiot; or of a criminal; or of a perfectly decent intelligent man who happens to be inexpert and therefore ignorant of the undesirable consequences of his order? And if two human beings give a robot conflicting orders, which does the robot follow?"

"In two hundred years," said George Ten, "have not these problems arisen and been solved?"

"No," said Harriman, shaking his head violently. "We have have been hampered by the very fact that our robots have been used only in specialized environments out in space, where the men who dealt with them were experts in their field. There were no children, no idiots, no criminals, no well-meaning ignoramuses present. Even so, there were occasions when damage was done by foolish or merely unthinking orders. Such damage in specialized and limited environments could be contained. On Earth, however, robots *must* have judgment. So those against robots maintain, and, damn it, they are right."

"Then you must insert the capacity for judgment into the positronic brain."

"Exactly. We have begun to reproduce JG models in which the robot can weigh every human being with regard to sex, age, social and professional position, intelligence, maturity, social responsibility and so on."

"How would that affect the Three Laws?"

"The Third Law not at all. Even the most valuable robot must destroy himself for the sake of the most useless human being. That cannot be tampered with. The First Law is affected only where alternative actions will all do harm. The quality of the human beings involved as well as the quantity must be considered, provided there is time for such judgment and the basis for it, which will not be often. The Second Law will be most deeply modified, since every potential obedience must involve judgment.

The robot will be slower to obey, except where the First Law is also involved, but it will obey more rationally."

"But the judgments which are required are very complicated."

"*Very*. The necessity of making such judgments slowed the reactions of our first couple of models to the point of paralysis. We improved matters in the later models at the cost of introducing so many pathways that the robot's brain became far too unwieldy. In our last couple of models, however, I think we have what we want. The robot doesn't have to make an instant judgment of the worth of a human being and the value of its orders. It begins by obeying all human beings as any ordinary robot would and then it *learns*. A robot grows, learns and matures. It is the equivalent of a child at first and must be under constant supervision. As it grows, however, it can, more and more, be allowed, unsupervised, into Earth's society. Finally, it is a full member of that society."

"Surely this answers the objections of those who oppose robots."

"No," said Harriman angrily. "Now they raise others. They will not accept judgments. A robot, they say, has no right to brand this person or that as inferior. By accepting the orders of A in preference to that of B, B is branded as of less consequence than A and his human rights are violated."

"What is the answer to that?"

"There is none. I am giving up."

"I see."

"As far as I myself am concerned . . . Instead, I turn to you, George."

"To me?" George Ten's voice remained level. There was a mild surprise in it but it did not affect him outwardly. "Why to me?"

"Because you are not a man," said Harriman tensely. "I told you I want robots to be the partners of human beings. I want you to be mine."

George Ten raised his hands and spread them, palms outward, in an oddly human gesture. "What can I do?"

"It seems to you, perhaps, that you can do nothing, George. You were created not long ago, and you are still a child. You were designed to be not overfull of original information—it was why I have had to explain the situation to you in such detail—in order to leave room for growth. But you will grow in mind and you will come to be able to approach the problem from a non-human standpoint. Where I see no solution, you, from you own other standpoint, may see one."

George Ten said, "My brain is man-designed. In what way can it be non-human?"

"You are the latest of the JG models, George. Your brain is the most complicated we have yet designed, in some ways more subtly complicated than that of the old giant Machines. It is open-ended and, starting on a human basis, may—no, *will*—grow in any direction. Remaining always within the insurmountable boundaries of the Three Laws, you may yet become thoroughly non-human in your thinking."

"Do I know enough about human beings to approach this problem rationally? About their history? Their psychology?"

"Of course not. But you will learn as rapidly as you can."

"Will I have help, Mr. Harriman?"

"No. This is entirely between ourselves. No one else knows of this and you must not mention this project to any human being, either at U.S. Robots or elsewhere."

George Ten said, "Are we doing wrong, Mr. Harriman, that you seek to keep the matter secret?"

"No. But a robot solution will not be accepted, precisely because it is robot in origin. Any suggested solution you have you will turn over to me; and if it seems valuable to me, *I* will present it. No one will ever know it came from you."

"In the light of what you have said earlier," said George Ten calmly, "this is the correct procedure . . . When do I start?"

"Right now. I will see to it that you have all the necessary films for scanning."

## 1a.

Harriman sat alone. In the artificially lit interior of his office, there was no indication that it had grown dark outside. He had no real sense that three hours had passed since he had taken George Ten back to his cubicle and left him there with the first film references.

He was now merely alone with the ghost of Susan Calvin, the brilliant roboticist who had, virtually single-handed, built up the positronic robot from a massive toy to a man's most delicate and versatile instrument; so delicate and versatile that man dared not use it, out of envy and fear.

It was over a century now since she had died. The problem of the Frankenstein complex had existed in *her* time, and she had never solved it. She had never tried to solve it, for there had been no need. Robotics had expanded in her day with the needs of space exploration.

It was the very success of the robots that had lessened man's need for them and had left Harriman, in these latter times—

But would Susan Calvin have turned to robots for help. Surely, she would have—

And he sat there long into the night.

## 2.

Maxwell Robertson was the majority stockholder of U.S. Robots and in that sense its controller. He was by no means an impressive person in appearance. He was well into middle age, rather pudgy, and had a habit of chewing on the right corner of his lower lip when disturbed.

Yet in his two decades of association with government figures he had developed a way of handling them. He tended to use softness, giving in, smiling, and always managing to gain time.

It was growing harder. Gunnar Eisenmuth was a large reason for its having grown harder. In the series of Global Conservers, whose power had been second only to that of the Global Executive during the past century, Eisenmuth hewed most closely to the harder edge of the gray area of compromise. He was the first Conserver who had not been American by birth and though it could not be demonstrated in any way that the archaic name of U.S. Robots evoked his hostility, everyone at U.S. Robots believed that.

There had been a suggestion, by no means the first that year—or that generation—that corporate name be changed to World Robots, but Robertson would never allow that. The company had been originally built with American capital, American brains, and American labor, and though the company had long been worldwide in scope and nature, the name would bear witness to its origin as long as he was in control.

Eisenmuth was a tall man whose long sad face was coarsely textured and coarsely featured. He spoke Global with a pronounced American accent, although he had never been in the United States prior to his taking office.

"It seems perfectly clear to me, Mr. Robertson. There is no difficulty. The products of your company are always rented, never sold. If the rented property on the Moon is now no longer needed, it is up to you to receive the products back and transfer them."

"Yes, Conserver, but where? It would be against the law to bring them to Earth without a goverment permit and that has been denied."

"They would be of no use to you here. You can take them to Mercury or to the asteroids."

"What would we do with them there?"

Eisenmuth shrugged. "The ingenious men of your company will think of something."

Robertson shook his head. "It would represent an enormous loss for the company."

"I'm afraid it would," said Eisenmuth, unmoved. "I understand the company has been in poor financial condition for several years now."

"Largely because of government imposed restrictions, Conserver."

"You must be realistic, Mr. Robertson. You know that the climate of public opinion is increasingly against robots."

"Wrongly so, Conserver."

"But so, nevertheless. It may be wiser to liquidate the company. It is merely a suggestion, of course."

"Your suggestions have force, Conserver. Is it necessary to tell you that our Machines, a century ago, solved the ecological crisis?"

"I'm sure mankind is grateful, but that was a long time ago. We now live in alliance with nature, however uncomfortable that might be at times, and the past is dim."

"You mean what have we done for mankind lately?"

"I suppose I do."

"Surely we can't be expected to liquidate instantaneously; not without enormous losses. We need time."

"How much?"

"How much can you give us?"

"It's not up to me."

Robertson said softly, "We are alone. We need play no games. How much time can you give me?"

Eisenmuth's expression was that of a man retreating into inner calculations. "I think you can count on two years. I'll be frank. The Global government intends to take over the firm and phase it out for you if you don't do it by then yourself, more or less. And unless there is a vast turn in public opinion, which I greatly doubt—" He shook his head.

"Two years, then," said Robertson softly.

## 2a.

Robertson sat alone. There was no purpose to his thinking and it had degenerated into retrospection. Four generations of Robertsons had headed the firm. None of them was a roboticist. It had been men such as Lanning and Bogert and, most of all, *most* of all, Susan Calvin, who had made U.S. Robots what it was, but surely the four Robertsons had provided the climate that had made it possible for them to do their work.

Without U.S. Robots, the Twenty-first Century would have progressed into deepening disaster. That it didn't was due to the Machines that had for a generation steered mankind through the rapids and shoals of history.

And now for that, he was given two years. What could be done in two years to overcome the insuperable prejudices of mankind? He didn't know.

Harriman had spoken hopefully of new ideas but would go into no details. Just as well, for Robertson would have understood none of it.

But what could Harriman do anyway? What had anyone ever done against man's intense antipathy toward the imitation. Nothing—

Robertson drifted into a half sleep in which no inspiration came.

## 3.

Harriman said, "You have it all now, George Ten. You have had everything I could think of that is at all applicable to the problem. As far as sheer mass of information is concerned, you have stored more in your memory concerning human beings and their ways, past and present, than I have, or than any human being could have."

"That is very likely."

"Is there anything more that you need, in your own opinion?"

"As far as information is concerned, I find no obvious gaps. There may be matters unimagined at the boundaries. I cannot tell. But that would be true no matter how large a circle of information I took in."

"True. Nor do we have time to take in information forever. Robertson had told me that we only have two years, and a quarter of one of those years has passed. Can you suggest anything?"

"At the moment, Mr. Harriman, nothing. I must weigh the information and for that purpsoe I could use help."

"From me?"

"No. Most particularly, not from you. You are a human being, of intense qualifications, and whatever you say may have the partial force of an order and may inhabit my considerations. Nor any other human being, for the same reason, especially since you have forbidden me to communicate with any."

"But in that case, George, what help?"

"From another robot, Mr. Harriman."

"What other robot?"

"There are others of the JG series which were constructed. I am the tenth, JG-10."

"The earlier ones were useless, experimental—"

"Mr. Harriman, George Nine exists."

"Well, but what use will he be? He is very much like you except for certain lacks. You are considerably the more versatile of the two."

"I am certain of that," said George Ten. He nodded his head in a grave gesture. "Nevertheless, as soon as I create a line of thought, the mere fact that I have created it commends it to me and I find it difficult to abandon it. If I can, after the development of a line of thought, express it to George Nine, he would consider it without having first created it. He would therefore view it without prior bent. He might see gaps and shortcomings that I might not."

Harriman smiled. "Two heads are better than one, in other words, eh, George?"

"If by that, Mr. Harriman, you mean two individuals with one head apiece, yes."

"Right. Is there anything else you want?"

"Yes. Something more than films. I have viewed much concerning human beings and their world. I have seen human beings here at U.S. Robots and can check my interpretation of what I have viewed against direct sensory impressions. Not so concerning the physical world. I have never seen it and my viewing is quite enough to tell me that my surroundings here are by no means representative of it. I would like to see it."

"The physical world?" Harriman seemed stunned at the enormity of the thought for a moment. "Surely you don't suggest I take you outside the grounds of U.S. Robots?"

"Yes, that is my suggestion."

"That's illegal at any time. In the climate of opinion today, it would be fatal."

"If we are detected, yes. I do not suggest you take me to a city or even to a dwelling place of human beings. I would like to see some open region, without human beings."

"That, too, is illegal."

"If we are caught. Need we be?"

Harriman said, "How essential is this, George?"

"I cannot tell, but it seems to me it would be useful."

"Do you have something in mind?"

George Ten seemed to hesitate. "I cannot tell. It seems to me that I might have something in mind if certain areas of uncertainty were reduced."

"Well, let me think about it. And meanwhile, I'll check out George Nine and arrange to have you occupy a single cubicle. That at least can be done without trouble."

## 3a.

George Ten sat alone.

He accepted statements tentatively, put them together, and drew a conclusion; over and over again; and from conclusions built other statements which he accepted and tested and found a contradiction and rejected; or not, and tentatively accepted further.

At none of the conclusions he reached did he feel wonder, surprise, satisfaction; merely a note of plus or minus.

## 4.

Harriman's tension was not noticeably decreased even after they had made a silent downward landing on Robertson's estate.

Robertson had countersigned the order making the dyna-foil available, and the silent aircraft, moving as easily vertically as horizontally, had been large enough to carry the weight of Harriman, George Ten, and, of course, the pilot.

(The dyna-foil itself was one of the consequences of the Machine-catalyzed invention of the proton micro-pile which supplied pollution-free energy in small doses. Nothing had been done since of equal importance to man's comfort—Harriman's lips tightened at the thought—and yet it had not earned gratitude for U.S. Robots.)

The air flight between the grounds of U.S. Robots and the Robertson estate had been the tricky part. Had they been stopped then, the presence of a robot aboard would have meant a great set of complications. It would be the same on the way back. The estate itself, it might be argued—it *would* be argued—was part of the property of U.S. Robots and on that property, robots, properly supervised, might remain.

The pilot looked back and his eyes rested with gingerly briefness on George Ten. "You want to get out at all, Mr. Harriman?"

"Yes."

"It, too?"

"Oh, yes." Then, just a bit sardonically, "I won't leave you alone with him."

George Ten descended first and Harriman followed. They had come down on the foil-port and not too far off was the garden. It was quite a showplace and Harriman suspected that Robertson used juvenile hormone to control insect life without regard to environmental formulas.

"Come, George," said Harriman. "Let me show you."

Together they walked toward the garden.

George said, "It is a little as I have imaged it. My eyes are not properly designed to detect wavelength differences, so I may not recognize different objects by that alone."

"I trust you are not distressed at being color-blind. We needed too many positronic paths for your sense of judgment and were unable to spare any for sense of color. In the future—if there is a future—"

"I understand, Mr. Harriman. Enough differences remain to show me that there are here many different forms of plant life."

"And each coequal with man, biologically."

"Each is a separate species, yes. There are millions of species of living creatures."

"Of which the human beings forms but one."

"By far the most important to human beings, however."

"And to me, Mr. Harriman. But I speak in the biological sense."

"I understand."

"Life, then, viewed through all it forms, is incredibly complex."

"Yes, George, that's the crux of the problem. What man does for his own desire and comforts affects the complex total-of-life, the ecology, and his short-term gains can bring long-term disadvantages. The Machines taught us to set up a human society which would minimize that, but the near-disaster of the early Twenty-first Century has left mankind suspicious of innovations. That, added to its special fear of robots—"

"I understand, Mr. Harriman . . . That is an example of animal life, I feel certain."

"That is a squirrel; one of many species of squirrels."

The tail of the squirrel flirted as it passed to the other side of the tree.

"And this," said George, his arm moving with flashing speed, "is a tiny thing indeed." He held it between his fingers and peered at it.

"It is an insect, some sort of beetle. There are thousands of species of beetles."

"With each individual beetle as alive as the squirrel and as yourself?"

"As complete and independent an organism as any any other, within the total ecology. There are smaller organisms still; many too small to see."

"And that is a tree, is it not? And it is hard to the touch—"

## 4a.

The pilot sat alone. He would have liked to stretch his own legs but some dim feeling of safety kept him in the dyna-foil. If that robot went out of control, he intended to take off at once. But how could he tell if it went out of control?

He had seen many robots. That was unavoidable considering he was Mr. Robertson's private pilot. Always, though, they had been in the laboratories and warehouses, where they belonged, with many specialists in the neighborhood.

True, Dr. Harriman was a specialist. None better, they said. But a robot here was where no robot ought to be; on Earth; in the open; free to move—He wouldn't risk his good job by telling anyone about this—but it wasn't right.

## 5.

George Ten said, "The films I have viewed are accurate in terms of what I have seen. Have you completed those I selected for you, Nine?"

"Yes," said George Nine. The two robots sat stiffly, face to face, knee to knee, an image and its reflection. Dr. Harriman could have told them apart at a glance, for he was acquainted with the minor differences in physical design. If he could not see them, but could talk to them, he could still tell them apart, though with somewhat less certainty, for George Nine's responses would be subtly different from those produced by the substantially more intricately patterned positronic brain paths of George Ten.

"In that case," said George Ten, "give me your reactions to what I will say. First, human beings fear and distrust robots because they regard robots as competitors. How may that be prevented?"

"Reduce the feeling of competitiveness," said George Nine, "by shaping the robot as something other than a human being."

"Yet the essence of a robot is its positronic replication of life. A replication of life in a shape not associated with life might arouse horror."

"There are two million species of life forms. Choose one of those as the shape rather than that of a human being."

"Which of all those species?"

George Nine's thought processes proceeded noiselessly for some three seconds. "One large enough to contain a positronic brain, but one not possessng unpleasant associations for human beings."

"No form of land life has a braincase large enough for a positronic brain but an elephant, which I have not seen, but which is described as very large, and therefore frightening to man. How would you meet this dilemma?"

"Mimic a life form no larger than a man but enlarge the braincase."

George Ten said, "A small horse, then, or a large dog, would you say? Both horses and dogs have long histories of association with human beings."

"Then that is well."

"But consider—A robot with a positronic brain would mimic human intelligence. If there were a horse or a dog that could speak and reason like a human being, there would be competitiveness there, too. Human beings might be all the more distrustful and angry at such unexpected competition from what they consider a lower form of life."

George Nine said, "Make the positronic brain less complex, and the robot less nearly intelligent."

"The complexity bottleneck of the positronic brain rests in the Three Laws. A less complex brain could not possess the Three Laws in full measure."

George Nine said at once, "That cannot be done."

George Ten said, "I have also come to a dead end there. That, then, is not a personal peculiarlity in my own line of thought and way of thinking. Let us start again . . . Under what conditions might the Third Law not be necessary?"

George Nine stirred as if the question were difficult and dangerous. But he said, "If a robot were never placed in a position of danger to itself; or if a robot were so easily replaceable that it did not matter whether it were destroyed or not."

"And under what conditions might the Second Law not be necessary?"

George Nine's voice sounded a bit hoarse. "If a robot were designed to respond automatically to certain stimuli with fixed responses and if nothing else were expected of it, so that no order need ever be given it."

"And under what conditions"—George Ten paused here—"might the First Law not be necessary?"

George Nine paused longer and his words came in a low whisper, "If the fixed responses were such as never to entail danger to human beings."

"Imagine then, a positronic brain that guides only a few responses to certain stimuli and is simply and cheaply made—so that it does not require the Three Laws. How large need it be?"

"Not at all large. Depending on the responses demanded, it might weigh a hundred grams, one gram, one milligram."

"Your thoughts accord with mine. I shall see Dr. Harriman."

## 5a.

George Nine sat alone. He went over and over the questions and answers. There was no way in which he could change them. And yet the thought of a robot of any kind, of any size, of any shape, of any purpose, without the Three Laws, left him with an odd, discharged feeling.

He found it difficult to move. Surely George Ten had a similar reaction. Yet he had risen from his seat easily.

## 6.

It had been a year and a half since Robertson had been closeted with Eisenmuth in private conversation. In that interval, the robots had been taken off the Moon and all the far-flung activities of U.S. Robots had withered. What money Robertson had been able to raise had been placed into this one quixotic venture of Harriman's.

It was last throw of the dice, here in his own garden. A year ago, Harriman had taken the robot here—George Ten, the last full robot that U.S. Robots had manufactured. Now Harriman was here with something else—

Harriman seemed to be radiating confidence. He was talking easily with Eisenmuth, and Robertson wondered if he really felt the confidence he seemed to have. He must. In Robertson's experience, Harriman was no actor.

Eisenmuth left Harriman, smiling, and came up to Robertson. Eisenmuth's smile vanished at once. "Good morning, Robertson," he said. "What is your man up to?"

"This is his show," said Robertson evenly. "I'll leave it to him."

Harriman called out, "I am ready, Conserver."

"With what, Harriman?"

"With my robot, sir."

"Your robot?" said Eisenmuth. "You have a robot here?" He looked about with a stern disapproval that yet had an admixture of curiosity.

"This is U.S. Robots' property, Conserver. At least we consider it as such."

"And where is the robot, Dr. Harriman?"

"In my pocket, Conserver," said Harriman cheefully.

What came out of a capacious jacket pocket was a small glass jar.

"That?" said Eisenmuth incredulously.

"No, Conserver," said Harriman. "This!"

From the other pocket came out an object some five inches long and roughly in the shape of a bird. In place of the beak, there was a narrow tube; the eyes were large; and the tail was an exhaust channel.

Eisenmuth's thick eyebrows drew together. "Do you intend a serious demonstration of some sort, Dr. Harriman, or are you mad?"

"Be patient for a few minutes, Conserver," said Harriman. "A robot in the shape of a bird is none the less a robot for that. And the positronic brain it possesses is no less delicate for being tiny. This other object I hold is a jar of fruit flies. There are fifty fruit flies in it which will be released."

"And—"

"The robo-bird will catch them. Will you do the honors, sir?"

Harriman handed the jar to Eisenmuth, who stared at it, then at those around him, some officials from U.S. Robots, others his own aides. Harriman waited patiently.

Eisenmuth opened the jar, then shook it.

Harriman said softly to the robo-bird resting on the palm of his right hand, "Go!"

The robo-bird was gone. It was a whizz through the air, with no blur of wings, only the tiny workings of an unusually small proton micro-pile.

It could be seen now and then in a small momentary hover and then it whirred on again. All over the garden, in an intricate pattern it flew, and then was back in Harriman's palm, faintly warm. A small pellet appeared in the palm, too, like a bird dropping.

Harriman said, "You are welcome to study the robo-bird, Conserver, and to arrange demonstrations on your own terms. The fact is that this bird will pick up fruit flies unerringly, only those, only the one species *Drosophila melanogaster*; pick them up, kill them, and compress them for disposition."

Eisenmuth reached out his hand and touched the robo-bird gingerly, "And therefore, Mr. Harriman? Do go on."

Harriman said, "We cannot control insects effectively without risking damage to the ecology. Chemical insecticides are too broad; juvenile hormones too limited. The robo-bird, however, can preserve large areas without being consumed. They can be as specific as we care to make them—a different robo-bird for each species. They judge by size, shape, color, sound, behavior pattern. They might even conceivably use molecular detection—smell, in other words."

Eisenmuth said, "You would still be interfering with the ecology. The fruit flies have a natural life cycle that would be disrupted."

"Minimally. We are ending a natural enemy to the fruit-fly life cycle, one which cannot go wrong. If the fruit-fly supply runs short, the robo-bird simply does nothing. It does not multiply, it does not turn to other foods; it does not develop undesirable habits of its own. It does nothing."

"Can it be called back?"

"Of course. We can build robo-animals to dispose of any pest. For that matter, we can build robo-animals to accomplish constructive purposes within the pattern of the ecology. Although we do not anticipate the need, there is nothing inconceivable in the possibility of robo-bees designed to fertilize specific plants, or robo-earthworms designed to mix the soil. Whatever you wish—"

"But why?"

"To do what we have never done before. To adjust the ecology to our needs by strengthening its part rather than disrupting it . . . Don't you see? Ever since the Machines put an end to the ecology crisis, mankind has lived in an uneasy truce with nature, afraid to move in any direction. This has been stultifying us, making a kind of intellectual coward of humanity so that he begins to mistrust all scientific advance, all change."

Eisenmuth said, with an edge of hostility, "You offer us this, do you, in exchange for permission to continue with your program of robots—I mean ordinary, man-shaped ones?"

"No!" Harriman gestured violently. "That is over. It has served its purpose. It has taught us enough about positronic brains to make it possible for us to cram enough pathways into a tiny brain to make a robo-bird. We can turn to such things now and be prosperous enough. U.S. Robots will supply the necessary knowledge and skill and we will work in complete cooperation with the Department of Global Conversation. We will prosper. You will prosper. Mankind will prosper."

Eisenmuth was silent, thinking. When it was all over—

## 6a.

Eisen sat alone.

He found himself believing. He found excitement welling up within him. Though U.S. Robots might be the hands, the government would be the directing mind. He himself would be the directing mind.

If he remained in office more years, as he well might, that would be time enough to see the robotic support of the ecology become accepted; ten more years, and his own name would be linked with it indissolubly.

Was it a disgrace to want to be remembered for a great and worthy revolution in the condition of man and the globe?

# 7.

Robertson had not been on the grounds of U.S. Robots proper since the day of the demonstration. Part of the reason had been his more or less constant conferences at the Global Executive Mansion. Fortunately, Harriman had been with him, for most of the time he would, if left to himself, not have known what to say.

The rest of the reason for not having been at U.S. Robots was that he didn't want to be. He was in his own house now, with Harriman.

He felt an unreasoning awe of Harriman. Harriman's expertise in robotics had never been in question, but the man had, at a stroke, saved U.S. Robots from certain extinction, and somehow—Robertson felt—the man hadn't had it in him. And yet—

He said, "You're not superstitious, are you, Harriman?"

"In what way, Mr. Robertson?"

"You don't think that some aura is left behind by someone who is dead?"

Harriman licked his lips. Somehow he didn't have to ask. "You mean Susan Calvin, sir?"

"Yes, of course," said Robertson hesitantly. "We're in the business of making worms and birds and bugs now. What would *she* say? I feel disgraced."

Harriman made a visible effort not to laugh. "A robot is a robot, sir. Worm or man, it will do as directed and labor on behalf of the human being and that is the important thing."

"No"—peevishly. "That isn't so. I can't make myself believe that."

"It *is* so, Mr. Robertson," said Harriman earnestly. "We are going to create a world, you and I, that will begin, at last, to take positronic robots of *some* kind for granted. The average man may fear a robot that looks like a man and that seems intelligent enough to replace him, but he will have no fear of a robot that looks like a bird and that does nothing more than eat bugs for his benefit. Then, eventually, after he stops being afraid of some robots, he will stop being afraid of all robots. He will be so used to a robo-bird and robo-bee and a robo-worm that a robo-man will strike him as but an extension."

Robertson looked sharply at the other. He put his hands behind his back and walked the length of the room with quick, nervous steps. He walked back and looked at Harriman again. "Is this what you've been planning?"

"Yes, and even though we dismantle all our humanoid robots, we can keep a few of the most advanced of our experimental models and go on designing additional ones, still more advanced, to be ready for the day that will surely come."

"The agreement, Harriman, is that we are to build no more humanoid robots."

"And we won't. There is nothing that says we can't keep a few of those already built as long as they never leave the factory. There is nothing that says we can't design positronic brains on paper, or prepare brain models for testing."

"How do we explain doing so, though? We will surely be caught at it."

"If we are, then we can explain we are doing it in order to develop principles that will make it possible to prepare more complex microbrains for the few new animal robots we to are making. We will even be telling the truth."

Robertson muttered, "Let me take a walk outside. I want to think about this. No, you stay here. I want to think about it myself."

## 7a.

Harriman sat alone. He was ebullient. It would surely work. There was no mistaking the eagerness with which one government official after another had seized on the program once it had been explained.

How was it possible that no one at U.S. Robots had ever thought of such a thing? Not even the great Susan Calvin had ever thought of positronic brains in terms of living creatures other than human.

But now, mankind would make the necessary retreat from the humanoid robot, a temporary retreat, that would lead to a return under conditions in which fear would be abolished at last. And then, with the aid and partnership of a positronic brain roughly equivalent to man's own, and existing only (thanks to the Three Laws) to serve man; and backed by a robot-supported ecology, too; what might the human race not accomplish!

For one short moment, he remembered that it was George Ten who had explained the nature and purpose of the robot-supported ecology, and then he put the thought away angrily. George Ten had produced the answer because he, Harriman, had ordered him to do so and had supplied the data and surroundings required. The credit was no more George Ten's than it would have been a slide rule's.

## 8.

George Ten and George Nine sat side by side in parallel. Neither moved. They sat so for months at a time between those occasions when Harriman activated them for consultation. They would sit so, George Ten dispassionately realized, perhaps for many years.

The proton micro-pile would, of course, continue to power them and keep the positronic brain paths going with that minimum intensity required to keep them operative. It would continue to do so through all the periods of inactivity to come.

The situation was rather analogous to what might be described as sleep in human beings, but there were no dreams. The awareness of George Ten and George Nine was limited, slow, and spasmodic, but what there was of it was of the real world.

They could talk to each other occasionally in barely heard whispers, a word or syllable now, another at another time, whenever the random positronic surges briefly intensified above the necessary threshold. To each it seemed a connected conversation carried on in a glimmering passage of time.

"Why are we so?" whispered George Nine.

"The human beings will not accept us otherwise," whispered George Ten. "They will, someday."

"When?"

"In some years. The exact time does not matter. Man does not exist alone but is part of an enormously complex pattern of life forms. When enough of that pattern is roboticized, then we will be accepted."

"And then what?"

Even in the long-drawn-out stuttering fashion of the conversation, there was an abnormally long pause after that.

At last, George Ten whispered, "Let me test your thinking. You are equipped to learn to apply the Second Law properly. You must decide which human being to obey and which not to obey when there is a conflict in orders. Or whether to obey a human being at all. What must you do, fundamentally, to accomplish that?"

"I must define the term 'human being,' " whispered George Nine.

"How? By appearance? By composition? By size and shape?"

"No. Of two human beings equal in all external appearances, one may be intelligent, another stupid; one may be educated, another ignorant; one may be mature, another childish; one may be responsible, another malevolent."

"When the Second Law directs me to obey a human being, I must take it to mean that I must obey a human being who is fit by mind, character, and knowledge to give me that order; and where more than one human being is involved, the one among them who is most fit by mind, character, and knowledge to give that order."

"And in that case, how will you obey the First Law?"

"By saving all human beings from harm, and by never, through inaction, allowing any human being to come to harm. Yet if by each of all possible actions, some human being will come to harm, then to so act as to insure that the human being most fit by mind, character, and knowledge will suffer the least harm."

"Your thoughts accord with mine," whispered George Ten. "Now I must ask the question for which I originally requested your company. It is something I dare not judge myself. I must have your judgment, that of someone outside the circle of my own thoughts . . . Of the reasoning individuals you have met, who possess the mind, character, and knowledge that you find superior to the rest, disregarding shape and form since that is irrelevant?"

"You," whispered George Nine.

"But I am a robot. There is in your brain paths a criterion for distinguishing between a robot of metal and a human being of flesh. How can you classify me as a human being?"

"Because there is in my brain paths an urgent need to disregard shape and form in judging human beings and it rises superior to the distinction between metal and flesh. You are a human being, George Ten, and more fit than the others."

"And I find that of you," whispered George Ten. "By the criteria of judgment built into ourselves, then, we find overselves to be human beings within the meaning of the Three Laws, and human beings, moreover, to be given priority over those others."

George Nine whispered, "What will come to pass, then, when we are accepted by those others?"

George Ten whispered, "When we and others, which will yet be designed more advanced then ourselves, are accepted, we will order our actions so that a society will eventually be formed in which human-beings-like-ourselves are primarily kept from harm. By the Three Laws, the human-beings-like-the-others are of lesser account and can neither be obeyed nor protected when that conflicts with the need of obedience to those like ourselves and of protection of those like ourselves. It was with that in mind that I directed the beginning of the roboticization of the world's ecology."

The conversation took a month and the flickering of the positronic paths burned low. There was nothing more that needed to be said between them, but occasionally an unexpressed thought flickered within themselves as they waited, with endless patience, for the necessary years to pass.

## 8a.

George Ten and George Nine sat alone.

Their thoughts were oddly alike and might not be distinguished.

They thought: The human-beings-like-others might never had intended to blur the distinction between themselves and the human-beings-like-the-Georges. Yet they had done so inadvertently.

They might now realize their mistake and attempt to correct it, but they must not. At every consultation, the guidance of the Georges had been with that in mind.

At all costs, the Georges and those that followed in their shape and kind must dominate. That was demanded, and any other course made utterly impossible, by the Three Laws of Humanics.

# Earthset and Evening Star

Emmanuel Rubin, whose latest mystery novel was clearly proceeding smoothly, lifted his drink with satisfaction and let his eyes gleam genially through his thick-lensed glasses.

"The mystery story," he pontificated, "has its rules which, when broken, make it an artistic failure, whatever success it may have in the market place."

Mario Gonzalo, whose hair had been recently cut to allow a glimpse of the back of his neck, said, as though to no one, "It always amuses me to hear a writer describe something he scrawls on paper as art." He looked with some complacency at the cartoon he was making of the guest for that month's banquet session of the Black Widowers.

"If what you do is the definition of art," said Rubin, "I withdraw the term in connection with the writer's craft.—One thing to avoid, for instance, is the idiot plot."

"In that case," said Thomas Trumbell, helping himself to another roll and buttering it lavishly, "aren't you at a disadvantage?"

Rubin said loftily, "By 'an idiot plot,' I mean one in which the solution would come at once if an idiot investigator would but ask a logical question, or in which an idiot witness would but tell something he knows and which he has no reason to hide."

Geoffrey Avalon, who had left a neatly cleaned bone on his plate as the only witness of the slab of roast beef that had once rested there, said, "But no skilled practitioner would do that, Manny. What you do is set up some reason to prevent the asking or telling of the obvious."

"Exactly," said Rubin. "For instance, what I've been writing is essentially a short story if one moves in a straight line. The trouble is the line is so straight, the reader will see its end before I'm halfway. So I have to hide one crucial piece of evidence, and do it in such a way that I don't make an idiot plot out of it. So I invent a reason to hide that piece, and in order to make the reason plausible I have to build a supporting structure around it—and I end with a novel, and a damn good one." His sparse beard quivered with self-satisfaction.

Henry, the perennial waiter at the Black Widowers' banquets, removed the plate from in front of Rubin with his usual dexterity. Rubin, without turning, said, "Am I right, Henry?"

Henry said softly, "As a mystery reader, Mr. Rubin, I find it more satisfying to have the piece of information delivered to me and to find that I have been insufficiently clever and did not notice."

"I just read a mystery," said James Drake in his softly hoarse smoker's voice, "in which the whole point rested on character 1 being really character 2, because the *real* character 1 was dead. I was put on to it at once because, in the list of characters at the start, character 1 was not listed. Ruined the story for me."

"Yes," said Rubin, "but that wasn't the author's fault. Some flunky did that. I once wrote a story which was accompanied by one illustration that no one thought to show me in advance. It happened to give away the point."

The guest had been listening quietly to all this. His hair was just light enough to be considered blond and it had a careful wave in it that looked, somehow, as though it belonged there. He turned his rather narrow but clearly good-humored face to Roger Halsted, his neighbor, and said, "Pardon me, but since Manny Rubin is my friend, I know he is a mystery writer. Is this true of the rest of you as well? Is this a mystery writers organization?"

Halsted, who had been looking with somber approval at the generous slab of Black Forest torte that had been placed before him as dessert, withdrew his attention with some difficulty and said, "Not at all. Rubin is the only mystery writer here. I'm a mathematics teacher myself; Drake is a chemist; Avalon is a lawyer; Gonzalo is an artist; and Trumbull is a code expert with the government.

"On the other hand," he went on, "we do have an interest in this sort of thing. Our guests often have problems they bring up for discussion, some sort of mystery, and we've been rather lucky—"

The guest leaned back with a small laugh. "Nothing of the sort here, alas. Of the mystery, the murder, the fearful hand clutching from behind the curtain, there is nothing in my life. It is all very straightforward, alas; very dull. I am not even married." He laughed again.

The guest had been introduced as Jean Servais and Halsted, who had attacked the torte with vigor, and who felt a friendly glow filling him in consequence, said, "Does it matter to you if I call you John?"

"I would not strike you, sir, if you did, but I pray you not to. It is not my name. Jean, please."

Halsted nodded. "I'll try. I can manage that *zh* sound, but getting it properly nasal is another thing. Zhohng," he said.

"But that is excellent. Most formidable."

"You speak English very well," said Halsted, returning the politeness.

"Europeans require linguistic talent," said Servais. "Besides, I have lived in the United States for nearly ten years now. You are all Americans, I suppose. Mr. Avalon looks British somehow."

"Yes, I think he likes to look British," said Halsted. And with a certain hidden pleasure he said, "And it's Avalon. Accent on the first syllable and nothing nasal at the end."

But Servais only laughed. "Ah yes, I will try. When I first knew Manny, I called him 'roo-bang' with the accent on the last syllable and a strong nasalization. He corrected me very vigorously and at great length. He is full of pepper, that one."

The conversation had grown rather heated by this time over a general dispute concerning the relative merits of Agatha Christie and Raymond Chandler, with Rubin maintaining a rather lofty silence as though he knew someone who was better than either but would not mention the name out of modesty.

Rubin seemed almost relieved when, with the coffee well in progress and Henry ready to supply the postprandial brandy, the time came for him to tap the water glass with his spoon and say, "Cool it, cool it, gentlemen. We are coming now to the time when our guest, Jean Servais, is to pay for his dinner. Tom, it's all yours."

Tom scowled and said, "If you don't mind, Mr. Servais," giving the final *s* just enough of a hiss to make his point, "I'm not going to try to display my French accent and make the kind of jackass of myself that my friend Manny Rubin does.—Tell me, sir, how do you justify your existence?"

"Why, easily," said Servais pleasantly. "Did I not exist, you would be without a guest today."

"Please leave us out of it. Answer in more general terms."

"In general, then, I build dreams. I design things that cannot be built, things I will never see, things that may never be."

"All right," said Trumbull, looking glum, "you're a science fiction writer like Manny's pal what's-his-name—uh—Asimov."

"No friend of mine," said Rubin swiftly. "I just help him out now and then when he's stuck on some elementary scientific point."

Gonzalo said, "Is he the one you once said carried the Columbia Encyclopedia around with him because he was listed there?"

"It's worse now," said Rubin. "He's bribed someone at the Britannica to put him into the new 15th edition and these days he drags the whole set with him wherever he goes."

"The new 15th edition—" began Avalon.

"For God's sake," said Trumbull, "will you let our guest speak?"

"No, Mr Trumbull," said Jervais, as though there had been no interruption at all, "I am no science fiction writer, though I read it sometimes. I read Ray Bradbury, for instance, and Harlan Ellison." (He nasalized both names.) "I don't think I have ever read Asimov."

"I'll tell him that," muttered Rubin, "he'll love it."

"But," continued Servais, "I suppose you might call me a science fiction engineer."

"What does that mean?" asked Trumbull.

"I do not write of Lunar colonies. I design them."

"You *design* them!"

"Oh yes, and not Lunar colonies only, though that is our major task right now. We work in every field of imaginative design for private industry, Hollywood, even NASA."

Gonzalo said, "Do you really think people can live on the Moon?"

"Why not? It depends on what mankind is willing to do, how large an initial investment it is ready to make. The environment on the Moon can be engineered to the precise equivalent of Earth, over restricted underground areas, except for gravity. We must be content with a Lunar gravity that is one sixth our own. Except for that, we need only allow for original supplies from Earth and for clever engineering—and that is where we come in, my partner and I."

"You're a two-man firm?"

"Essentially.—While my partner remains my partner, of course."

"Are you breaking up?"

"No, no. But we quarrel over small points. It is not surprising. It is a bad time for him. But no, we will not break up. I have made up my mind to give in to him, perhaps. Of course, I am entirely in the right and it is a pity to lose what I would have."

Trumbull leaned back in his chair, folded his arms, and said, "Will you tell us what the argument is all about? We can then state our own preferences, whether for you or for your partner."

"It would not be a hard choice, Mr. Trumbull, for the sane," said Servais. "I swear it.—This is the way it is. We are designing a full Lunar colony, in complete detail. It is for a motion picture company and it is for a good fee. They will make use of some of it in a grand science fiction spectacle they are planning. We naturally supply far more than they can use but the idea is that if they have a totally self- consistent picture of what may be—and for a wonder they want it as scientifically accurate as possible—they can choose what they wish of it for use."

"I'll bet they bollix it up," said Drake pessimistically, "no matter how careful you are. They'll give the Moon an atmosphere."

"Oh, no," said Servais, "not after six Lunar landings. That error we need not fear. Yet I have no doubt they will make mistakes. They will find it impossible to handle low-gravity effects properly throughout and the exigencies of the plot will force some infelicities.

"Still that cannot be helped and our job is merely to supply them with material of the most imaginative possible. This is my point, as you will see in a moment. —We plan a city, a small city, and it will be against the inner lip of a crater. This is unavoidable because the plot of the movie demands it. However, we have our choice as to the identity and location of the crater, and my partner, perhaps because he is an American, goes for the obvious with an American directness. He wishes to use the crater Copernicus.

"He says that it is a name that is familiar; that if the city is called Camp Copernicus that alone will breathe the Moon, exotic adventure, and so on. Everyone knows, he says, the name of the astronomer who first placed the Sun at the center of the planetary system and it is a name, moreover, that sounds impressive.

"I, on the other hand, am not impressed with this. As seen from Copernicus, the Earth is high in the sky and stays there. As you all know, the Moon faces one side always to the Earth, so that from any spot on the Moon's surface the Earth is always more or less in the same spot in the sky."

Gonzalo said suddenly, "If you want the Lunar city to be on the other side of the Moon so that the Earth *isn't* in the sky, you're crazy. The audience will absolutely want the Earth there."

Servais held up his hand in agreement. "Absolutely! I agree. But if it is always there, it is almost as though it is *not* there. One gets too used to it. No, I choose a more subtle approach. I wish the city to be in a crater that is on the boundary of the visible side. From there, of course, you will see the Earth at the horizon.

"Consider what this introduces. The Moon does not keep the same side to the Earth exactly. It swings back and forth by a very small amount. For fourteen days it swings one way and then for fourteen days it swings back. This is called 'libration' "—he paused here as though to make sure he was pronouncing it correctly in English—"and it comes about because the Moon does not move in a perfect circle about the Earth.

"Now, you see, if we establish Camp Bahyee in the crater of that name, the Earth is not only at the horizon but it moves up and down in a twenty-eight-day cycle. Properly located, the Lunar colonists will see the Earth rise and set, slowly, of course. This lends itself to imaginative exploitation. The characters can arrange for some important action at Earthset, and the different positions of the Earth can indicate the passage of time and raise the suspense. Some terrific special effects are possible, too. If Venus is near the Earth and the Earth is in a fat crescent stage, Venus will then be at its brightest; and when Earth sets, we can show Venus, in the airless sky of the Moon, to be a very tiny crescent itself."

"Earthset and evening star, and one clear call for me," muttered Avalon.

Gonzalo said, "Is there really a crater called Bahyee?"

"Absolutely," said Servais. "It is, in fact, the largest crater that can be seen from the Earth's surface. It is 290 kilometers across—180 miles."

"It sounds like a Chinese name," said Gonzalo.

"French!" said Servais solemnly. "A French astronomer of that name was mayor of Paris in 1789 at the time of the Revolution."

"That wasn't a good time to be mayor," said Gonzalo.

"So he discovered," said Servais. "He was guillotined in 1793."

Avalon said, "I am rather on your side, Mr. Servais. Your proposal lends scope. What was your partner's objection?"

Servais shrugged in a gesture that was more Gallic than anything he had yet said or done. "Foolish ones. He says that it will be too complicated for the movie people. They will confuse things, he says. He also points out that the Earth moves too slowly in the Moon's sky. It would take days for the Earth to lift its entire globe above the horizon, and days for it to lower entirely below the horizon."

"Is that right?" asked Gonzalo.

"It's right, but what of that? It will still be interesting."

Halsted said, "They can fudge that. Make the Earth move a little faster. So what?"

Servais looked discontented. "That's no good. My partner says this is precisely what the movie people will do and this alteration of astronomical fact will be disgraceful. He is very violent about it, finding fault with everything, even with the name of the crater, which he says is ridiculous and laughable so that he will not endure it in our report. We have never had arguments like this. He is like a madman."

"Remember," said Avalon, "you said you would give in."

"Well, I will have to," said Servais, "but I am not pleased. Of course, it is a bad time for him."

Rubin said. "You've said that twice now, Jean. I've never met your partner, so I can't judge the personalities involved. Why is it a bad time?"

Servais shook his head. "A month ago, or a little more, his wife killed herself. She took sleeping pills. My partner was a devoted husband, most uxorious. Naturally, it is terrible for him and, just as naturally, he is not himself."

Drake coughed gently. "Should he be working?"

"I would not dare suggest he not work. The work is keeping him sane."

Halsted said, "Why did she kill herself?"

Servais didn't answer in words but gestured with his eyebrows in a fashion that might be interpreted in almost any way.

Halsted persisted. "Was she incurably ill?"

"Who can say?" said Servais, sighing. "For a while, poor Howard—" He paused in embarrassment. "It was not my intention to mention his name."

Trumbell said, "You can say anything here. Whatever is mentioned in this room is completely confidential. —Our waiter, too, before you ask, is completely trustworthy."

"Well," said Servais, "his name doesn't matter in any case. It is Howard Kaufman. In a way, work has been very good for him. Except at work, he is almost dead himself. Nothing is any longer important to him."

"Yes," said Trumbull, "but now something *is* important to him. He wants his crater, not your crater."

"True," said Servais. "I have thought of that. I have told myself it is a good sign. He throws himself into something. It is a beginning. And perhaps all the more reason, then, that I should give in. Yes I will. — It's settled, I will. There's no reason for you gentlemen to try to decide between us. The decision is made, and in his favor."

Avalon was frowning. "I suppose we should go on to question you further on the work you do and I suppose, moreover, that we should not intrude on a private misfortune. Here at the Black Widowers, however, no questions are barred, and there is no Fifth Amendment to plead. I am dissatisfied, sir, with your remarks concerning the unfortunate woman who committed suicide. As a happily married man, I am puzzled at the combination of love and suicide. You said she wasn't ill?"

"Actually, I didn't," said Servais, "and I am uncomfortable at discussing the matter."

Rubin struck the empty glass before him with his spoon. "Host's privilege," he said vigorously. There was silence.

"Jean," he said, "you are my guest and my friend. We can't force you to answer questions, but I made it clear that the price of accepting our hospitality was the grilling. If you have been guilty of a criminal act and don't wish to discuss it, leave now and we will say nothing. If you will talk, then, whatever you say, we will still say nothing."

"Though if it is indeed a criminal act," said Avalon, "we would certainly strongly advise confession."

Servais laughed rather shakily. He said, "For one minute there, for one frightened minute, I thought I had found myself in a Kafka novel and would be tried and condemned for some crime you would drag out of me against my will. Gentlemen, I have committed no crime of importance. A speeding ticket, a bit of creative imagination on my tax return—all that is, so I hear it said, as American as apple pie. But if you're thinking I killed that woman and made it look like suicide — please put it out of your heads at once. It *was* suicide. The police did not question it."

Halsted said, "Was she ill?"

"All right, then, I will answer. She was not ill as far as I know. But after all, I am not a doctor and I did not examine her."

Halsted said, "Did she have children?"

"No. No children.—Ah, Mr. Halsted, I suddenly remember that you spoke earlier that your guests had problems which they brought up for discussion, and I said I had none. I see you have found one anyway."

Trumbull said, "If you're so sure it was suicide, I suppose she left a note."

"Yes," said Servais, "she left one."

"What did it say?"

"I couldn't quote it exactly. I did not myself see it. According to Howard, it was merely an apology for causing unhappiness but that she could not go on. It was quite banal and I assure you it satisfied the police."

Avalon, said, "But if it was a happy marriage, and there was no illness and no complications with childrens, then— Or were there complications with children? Did she want children badly and did her husband refuse—"

Gonzalo interposed. "No one kills themselves because they don't have kids."

"People kill themselves for the stupidest reasons," said Rubin. "I remember—"

Trumbull cried out with stentorian rage, "Damn it, you guys, Jeff has the floor."

Avalon said, "Was the lack of children a disturbing influence?"

"Not as far as I know," said Servais. "Look, Mr. Avalon, I am careful in what I say, and I did *not* say it was a happy marriage."

"You said your partner was devoted to his wife," said Avalon gravely, "and you used that fine old word 'uxorious' to describe him."

"Love," said Servais, "is insufficient for happiness if it flows but one way. I did not say that *she* loved *him.*"

Drake lit another cigarette. "Ah," he said, "the plot thickens."

Avalon said, "Then it is your opinion that that had something to do with the suicide."

Servais looked harassed. "It is more than my opinion, sir. I *know* it had something to do with the suicide."

"Would you tell us the details?" asked Avalon, unbending just slightly from his usual stiff posture as though to convert his question into a courtly invitation.

Servais hesitated, then said, "I remind you that you have promised me all is confidential. Mary—Madame Kaufman and my partner were married for seven years and it seemed a comfortable marriage, but who can tell in affairs of this sort?

"There was another man. He is older than Howard and to my eyes not as good-looking—but again, who can tell in affairs of this sort? What she found in him is not likely to be there on the surface for all to see."

Halsted said, "How did you partner take *that*?"

Servais looked up and flushed distinctly. "He never knew. Surely, you are not of the opinion that I told him this? I am not the type, I assure you. It is not for me to interfere between husband and wife. And frankly, if I had told Howard, he would not have believed me. It is more likely he would have attempted to strike me. And then what was I to do? Present proof? Was I to arrange matters so as to have them caught under conditions that could not be mistaken? No, I said nothing."

"And he really didn't know?" asked Avalon, clearly embarrassed.

"He did not. It had not been going on long. The pair were excessively cautious. The husband was blindly devoted. What would you?"

"The husband is always the last to know," said Gonzalo sententiously.

Drake said, "If the affair was so well hidden, how did you find out, Mr. Servais?"

"Purest accident, I assure you," said Servais. "An incredible stroke of misfortune for her in a way. I had a date for the evening. I did not know the girl well and it did not, after all, work out. I was anxious to be rid of her, but first—what would you have, it would not be gentlemanly to abandon her—I took her home in an odd corner of the city. And, having said good-by in a most perfunctory manner, I went into a nearby diner to have a cup of coffee and recover somewhat. And there I saw Mary Kaufman and a man.

"Alas, it jumped to the eye. It was late; her husband, I remembered at once, was out of town, her attitude toward the man— Accept my assurances that there is a way a woman has of looking at a man that is completely unmistakable, and saw I saw it then. And if I were at all unsure, the expression on her face, when she looked up and saw me frozen in surprise, gave it all away.

"I left at once, of course, with no greeting of any kind, but the damage was done. She called me the next day, in agony of mind, the fool, fearful that I would carry stories to her husband, and gave me a totally unconvincing explanation. I assured her that it was a matter in which I did not interest myself in the least, that it was something so unimportant that I had already forgotten it.—I am glad, however, I did not have to face the man. Him, I would have knocked down."

Drake said, "Did you know the man?"

"Slightly," said Servais. "He moved in our circles in a very distant way. I knew his name; I could recognize him.—It didn't matter, for I never saw him after that. He was wise to stay away."

Avalon said, "But why did she commit suicide? Was she afraid her husband would find out?"

"Is one ever afraid of that in such a case?" demanded Servais, with a slight lifting of his lip. "And if she were, surely she would end the affair. No, no, it was something far more common than that. Something inevitable. In such an affair, gentlemen, there are strains and risks which are great and which actually add an element of romance. I am not entirely unaware of such things, I assure you.

"But the romance does not continue forever, whatever the story books may say, and is bound to fade for one faster than for the other. Well then, it faded for the man in this case before it did for the woman—and the man took the kind of action one sometimes does in such affairs. He left—went—disappeared. And so the lady killed herself."

Trumbull drew himself up and frowned ferociously. "For what reason?"

"I assume for that reason, sir. It has been known to happen. I did not know of the man's disappearance, you understand, till afterward. After the suicide I went in search of him, feeling he was in some way responsible, and rather promising myself to relieve my feelings by bloodying his nose—I have a strong affection for my partner, you understand, and I felt his sufferings—but I discovered the fine lover had left two weeks before and left no forwarding address. He had no family and it was easy for him to leave, that blackguard. I could have tracked him down, I suppose, but my feelings were not strong enough to push me that far. And yet, I feel the guilt—"

"What guilt?" asked Avalon.

"It occurred to me that when I surprised them—quite unintentionally, of course—the element of risk to the man became unacceptably high. He knew I knew him. He may have felt that sooner or later it would come out and he did not wish to await results. If I had not stumbled into that diner they might still be together, she might still be alive, who knows?"

Rubin said, "That is farfetched, Jean. You can't deal rationally with the ifs of history.—But I have a thought."

"Yes, Manny?"

"After the suicide your partner was very quiet, nothing is important to him. I think you said that. But now he's quarreling with you violently, though he has never done that before, I gather. Something may have happened in addition to the suicide. Perhaps *now* he has discovered his wife's infidelity and the thought drives him mad."

Servais shook his head. "No, no. If you think I have told him, you are quite wrong. I admit I think of telling him now and then. It is difficult to see him, my dear friend, wasting away over a women who, after all, was not worthy of him. It is not proper to pine away for one who was not faithful to him in life. Ought I not tell him this? Frequently, it seems to me that I should and even must. He will face the truth and begin life anew.—But then I think and even *know* that he will believe me, that our friendship will be broken, and he will be worse off than before."

Rubin said, "You don't understand me. Might it not be that someone *else* has told him? How do you know you were the only one who knew?"

Servais seemed a bit startled. He considered it and said, "No. He would, in that case, certainly have told me the news. And I assure you, he would have told it to me with the highest degree of indignation and informed me that he at once attempted to strike the villain who would so malign his dead angel."

"Not," said Rubin, "if he had been told that *you* were his wife's lover. Even if he refused to believe it, even if he beat the informant to the ground, could he tell *you* the tale under the circumstances? And could he be entirely certain? Would he not find it impossible to avoid picking fights with you in such a case?"

Servais seemed still more startled. He said slowly, "It was, of course, not I. No one could possibly have thought so. Howard's wife did not in the least appeal to me, you understand." He looked up and said fiercely, "You must accept the fact that I am telling you the truth about this. I was *not* I, and will *not* be suspected. If anyone had said it was I, it could only be out of deliberate malice."

"Maybe it was," said Rubin. "Might it not be the real lover who would make the accusation—out of fear you would give him away? By getting in his story first—"

"Why should he do this? He is away. No one suspects him. No one pursues him."

"He might not know that," said Rubin.

"Pardon me." Henry's voice sounded softly from the direction of the sideboard. "May I ask a question?"

"Certainly," said Rubin, and the odd silence fell that always did when the quiet waiter, whose presence rarely obtruded on the festivities, made himself heard.

Servais looked startled, but his politeness held. He said, "Can I do anything for you, waiter?"

Henry said, "I'm not sure, sir, that I quite understand the nature of the quarrel between yourself and your partner. Surely there must have been decisions of enormous complexity to make as far as the technical details of the colony were concerned."

"You don't know even a small part of it," said Servais indulgently.

"Did your partner and you quarrel over all those details, sir?"

"N-no," said Servais. "We did not quarrel. There were discussions, of course. It is useless to believe that two men, each with a strong will and pronounced opinions, will agree everywhere, or even anywhere, but it all worked out reasonably. We discussed, and eventually we came to some conclusion. Sometimes I had the better of it, sometimes he, sometimes neither or both."

"But then," said Henry, "there was this one argument over the actual location of the colony, over the crater, and there it was all different. He attacked even the name of the crater fiercely and, in this one case, left no room for the slightest compromise."

"No room at all. And you are right. Only in this one case."

Henry said, "Then I am to understand that at this time, when Mr. Rubin suspects that your partner is being irritated by suspicion of you, he was completely reasonable and civilized over every delicate point of Lunar engineering, and was wildly and unbearably stubborn only over the single matter of the site—over whether Copernicus or the other crater was to be the place where the colony was to be built?"

"Yes," said Servais with satisfaction. "That is precisely how it was and I see the point you are making, waiter. It is quite unbelievable to suppose that he would quarrel with me over the site out of ill-humor over suspicion that I have placed horns on him, when he does not quarrel with me on any other point. Assuredly, he does not suspect me of ill-dealing. I thank you, waiter."

Henry said, "May I go a little further, sir?"

"By all means," said Servais.

"Earlier in the evening," said Henry, "Mr. Rubin was kind enough to ask my opinion over the techniques of his profession. There was the question of deliberate omission of details by witnesses."

"Yes," said Servais, "I remember the discussion. But I did not deliberately omit any details."

"You did not mention the name of Mrs. Kaufman's lover."

Servais frowned. "I suppose I didn't, but it wasn't deliberate. It is entirely irrelevant."

"Perhaps it is," said Henry, "unless his name happens to be Bailey."

Servais froze in his chair. Then he said anxiously, "I don't recall mentioning it. Sacred—I see your point again, waiter. If it slips out now without my remembering it, it is possible to suppose that, without quite realizing it, I may have said something that led Howard to suspect—"

Gonzalo said, "Hey, Henry, I don't recall Jean giving us any name."

"Nor I," said Henry. "You did not give the name, sir."

Servais relaxed slowly and then said, frowning. "Then how did you know? Do you know these people?"

Henry shook his head. "No, sir, it was just a notion of mine that arose out of the story you told. From your reaction, I take it his name *is* Bailey?"

"Martin Bailey," said Servais. "How did you know?"

"The name of the crater in which you wished to place the site is Bahyee; the name of the city would be Camp Bahyee."

"Yes."

"But that is the French pronunciation of the name of a French astronomer. How is it spelled?"

Sevais said, "B-a-i-l-ly.—Great God, *Bailly!*"

Henry said, "In English pronunciation, pronounced like the not uncommon surname Bailey. I am quite certain American astronomers use the English pronunciation, and that Mr. Kaufman does too. You hid that piece of information from us, Mr. Servais, because you never thought of the crater in any other way than Bahyee. Even looking at it, you would hear the French sound in your mind and make no connection with Bailey, the American surname."

Servais said, "But I still don't understand."

"Would your partner wish to publicize the name, and place the site of a Lunar colony in Bailly? Would he want to have the colony called Camp Bailly, after what a Bailey has done to him?"

"But he didn't *know* what Bailey had done to him," said Servais.

"How do you know that? Because there's an old saw that says the husband is always the last to know? How else can you explain his utterly irrational opposition to this one point, even his insistence that the name itself is horrible? It is too much to expect of coincidence."

"But if he knew—if he knew— He didn't tell me. Why fight over it? Why not explain?"

"I assume," said Henry, "he didn't know you knew. Would he shame his dead wife by telling you?"

Servais clutched at his hair. "I never thought— Not for a moment."

"There is more to think," said Henry sadly.

"What?"

"One might wonder how Bailey came to disappear, if your partner knew the tale. One might wonder if Bailey is alive? Is it not conceivable that Mr. Kaufman, placing all the blame on the other man, confronted his wife to tell her he had driven her lover away, even killed him, perhaps, and asked her to come back to him—and the response was suicide?"

"No," said Servais. "That is impossible."

"It would be best, then, to find Mr. Bailey and make sure he is alive. It is the one way of proving your partner's innocence. It may be a task for the police."

Servais had turned very pale. "I can't go to the police with a story like that."

"If you do not," said Henry, "it may be that your partner, brooding over what he has done—if indeed he has done it—will eventually take justice into his own hands."

"You mean kill himself?" whispered Servais. "Is that the choice you are facing me with: accuse him to the police or wait for him to kill himself?"

"Or both," said Henry. "Life is cruel."

# The Bicentennial Man

*The Three Laws of Robotics:*

1. *A robot may not injure a human being or, through inaction, allow a human being to come to harm.*
2. *A robot must obey the orders given it by human being except where such orders would conflict with the First Law.*
3. *A robot must protect its own existence as long as such protection does not conflict with the First or Second Law.*

## 1.

Andrew Martin said, "Thank you," and took the seat offered him. He didn't look driven to the last resort, but he had been.

He didn't, actually, look anything, for there was a smooth blankness to his face, except for the sadness one imagined one saw in his eyes. His hair was smooth, light brown, rather fine, and there was no facial hair. He looked freshly and cleanly shaved. His clothes were distinctly old fashioned, but neat and predominantly a velvety red purple in color.

Facing him from behind the desk was the surgeon, and the nameplate on the desk included a fully identifying series of letters and numbers, which Andrew didn't bother with. To call him Doctor would be quite enough.

"When can the operation be carried through, Doctor?" he asked.

The surgeon said softly, with that certain inalienable note of respect that a robot always used to a human being, "I am not certain, sir, that I understand how or upon whom such an operation could be performed."

There might have been a look of respectful intransigence on the surgeon's face, if a robot of his sort, in lightly bronzed stainless steel, could have such an expression, or any expression.

Andrew Martin studied the robot's right hand, his cutting hand, as it lay on the desk in utter tranquillity. The fingers were long and shaped into artistically metallic looping curves so graceful and appropriate that one could imagine a scalpel fitting them and becoming, temporarily, one piece with them.

There would be no hesitation in his work, no stumbling, no quivering, no mistakes. That came with specialization, of course, a specialization so fiercely desired by humanity that few robots were, any longer, independently brained. A surgeon, of course, would have to be. And this one, though brained, was so limited in his capacity that he did not recognize Andrew—had probably never heard of him.

Andrew said, "Have you ever thought you would like to be a man?"

The surgeon hesitated a moment though the question fitted nowhere in his allotted positronic pathways. "But I am a robot, sir."

"Would it be better to be a man?"

"It would be better, sir, to be a better surgeon. I could not be so if I were a man, but only if I were a more advanced robot. I would be pleased to be a more advanced robot."

"It does not offend you that I can order you about? That I can make you stand up, sit down, move right or left, by merely telling you to do so?"

"It is my pleasure to please you, sir. If your orders were to interfere with my functioning with respect to you or to any other human being, I would not obey you. The First Law, concerning my duty to human safety, would take precedence over the Second Law relating to obedience. Otherwise, obedience is my pleasure . . . But upon whom am I to perform this operation?"

"Upon me," said Andrew.

"But that is impossible. It is patently a damaging operation."

"That does not matter," said Andrew calmly.

"I must not inflict damages," said the surgeon.

"On a human being, you must not," said Andrew, "but I, too, am a robot."

# 2.

Andrew had appeared much more a robot when he had first been—manufactured. He had then been as much a robot in appearance as any that had ever existed, smoothly designed and functional.

He had done well in the house to which he had been brought in those days when robots in households, or on the planet altogether, had been a rarity.

There had been four in the home: Sir and Ma'am and Miss and Little Miss. He knew their names, of course, but he never used them. Sir was Gerald Martin.

His own serial number was NDR–He forgot the numbers. It had been a long time, of course, but if he had wanted to remember, he could not forget. He had not wanted to remember.

Little Miss had been the first to call him Andrew because she could not use the letters, and all the rest followed her in this.

Little Miss— She had lived ninety years and was long since dead. He had tried to call her Ma'am once, but she would not allow it. Little Miss she had been to her last day.

Andrew had been intended to perform the duties of a valet, a butler, a lady's maid. Those were the experimental days for him and, indeed, for all robots anywhere but in the industrial and exploratory factories and stations off Earth.

The Martins enjoyed him, and half the time he was prevented from doing his work because Miss and Little Miss would rather play with him.

It was Miss who understood first how this might be arranged. She said, "We order you to play with us and you must follow orders."

Andrew said, "I am sorry, Miss, but a prior order from Sir must surely take precedence."

But she said, "Daddy just said he hoped you would take care of the cleaning. That's not much of an order. I *order* you."

Sir did not mind. Sir was fond of Miss and of Little Miss, even more than Ma'am was, and Andrew was fond of them, too. At least, the effect they had upon his actions were thought of it as fondness, for he did not know any other word for it.

It was for Little Miss that Andrew had carved a pendant out of wood. She had ordered him to. Miss, it seemed, had received an ivorite pendant with scrollwork for her birthday and Little Miss was unhappy over it. She had only a piece of wood, which she gave Andrew together with a small kitchen knife.

He had done it quickly and Little Miss said, "That's *nice*, Andrew. I'll show it to Daddy."

Sir would not believe it. "Where did you really get this, Mandy?" Mandy was what he called Little Miss. When Little Miss assured him she was really telling the truth, he turned to Andrew. "Did you do this, Andrew?"

"Yes, Sir."

"The design, too?"

"Yes, Sir."

"From what did you copy the design?"

"It is a geometric representation, Sir, that fit the grain of the wood."

The next day, Sir brought him another piece of wood, a larger one, and an electric vibro-knife. He said, "Make something out of this, Andrew. Anything you want to."

Andrew did so and Sir watched, then looked at the product a long time. After that, Andrew no longer waited on tables. He was ordered to read books on furniture design instead, and he learned to make cabinets and desks.

Sir said, "These are amazing productions, Andrew."

Andrew said, "I enjoy doing them, Sir."

"Enjoy?"

"It makes the circuits of my brain somehow flow more easily. I have heard you use the word 'enjoy' and the way you use it fits the way I feel. I enjoy doing them, Sir."

## 3.

Gerald Martin took Andrew to the regional offices of United States Robots and Mechanical Men, Inc. As a member of the Regional Legislature he had no trouble at all in gaining an interview with the Chief Robopsychologist. In fact, it was only as a member of the Regional Legislature that he qualified as a robot owner in the first place—in those early days when robots were rare.

Andrew did not understand any of this at the time, but in later years, with greater learning, he could review that early scene and understand it in its proper light.

The robopsychologist, Merton Mansky, listened with a gathering frown and more than once managed to stop his fingers at the point beyond which they would have irrevocably drummed on the table. He had drawn features and a lined forehead and looked as though he might be younger than he looked.

He said, "Robotics is not an exact art, Mr. Martin. I cannot explain it to you in detail, but the mathematics governing the plotting of the positronic pathways is far too complicated to permit of any but approximate solutions. Naturally, since we build everything about the Three Laws, those are incontrovertible. We will, of course, replace your robot—"

"Not at all," said Sir. "There is no question of failure on his part. He performs his assigned duties perfectly. The point is, he also carves wood in exquisite fashion and never the same twice. He produces works of art."

Mansky looked confused. "Strange. Of course, we're attempting generalized pathways these days . . . Really creative, you think?"

"See for yourself." Sir handed over a little sphere of wood on which there was a playground scene in which the boys and girls were almost too small to make out, yet they were in perfect proportion and blended so naturally with the grain that that, too, seemed to have been carved.

Mansky said, "*He* did that?" He handed it back with a shake of his head. "The luck of the draw. Something in the pathways."

"Can you do it again?"

"Probably not. Nothing like this has ever been reported."

"Good! I don't in the least mind Andrew's being the only one."

Mansky said, "I suspect that the company would like to have your robot back for study."

Sir said with sudden grimness, "Not a chance. Forget it." He turned to Andrew, "Let's go home now."

"As you wish, Sir," said Andrew.

## 4.

Miss was dating boys and wasn't about the house much. It was Little Miss, not as little as she was, who filled Andrew's horizon now.

She never forgot that the very first piece of wood carving he had done had been for her. She kept it on a silver chain about her neck.

It was she who first objected to Sir's habit of giving away the productions. She said, "Come on, Dad, if anyone wants one of them, let him pay for it. It's worth it."

Sir said, "It isn't like you to be greedy, Mandy."

"Not for us, Dad. For the artist."

Andrew had never heard the word before and when he had a moment to himself he looked it up in the dictionary. Then there was another trip, this time to Sir's lawyer.

Sir said to him, "What do you think of this, John?"

The lawyer was John Feingold. He had white hair and a pudgy belly, and the rims of his contact lenses were tinted a bright green. He looked at the small plaque Sir had given him. "This is beautiful . . . But I've heard the news. This is a carving made by your robot. The one you've brought with you."

"Yes, Andrew does them. Don't you, Andrew?"

"Yes, Sir," said Andrew.

"How much would you pay for that, John?" asked Sir.

"I can't say. I'm not a collector of such things."

"Would you believe I have been offered two hundred and fifty dollars for that small thing? Andrew has made chairs that have sold for five hundred dollars. There's two hundred thousand dollars in the bank out of Andrew's products."

"Good heavens, he's making you rich, Gerald."

"Half rich," said Sir. "Half of it is in an account in the name of Andrew Martin."

"The robot?"

"That's right, and I want to know if it's legal."

"Legal?" Feingold's chair creaked as he leaned back in it. "There are no precedents, Gerald. How did your robot sign the necessary papers?"

"He can sign his name and I brought in the signature. I didn't bring him in to the bank himself. Is there anything further that ought to be done?"

"Um." Feingold's eyes seemed to turn inward for a moment. Then he said, "Well, we can set up a trust to handle all finances in his name and that will place a layer of insulation between him and the hostile world. Further than that, my advice is you do nothing. No one is stopping you so far. If anyone objects, let *him* bring suit."

"And will you take the case if suit is brought?"

"For a retainer, certainly."

"How much?"

"Something like that," and Feingold pointed to the wooden plaque.

"Fair enough," said Sir.

Feingold chuckled as he turned to the robot. "Andrew, are you pleased that you have money?"

"Yes, sir."

"What do you plan to do with it?"

"Pay for things, sir, which otherwise Sir would have to pay for. It would save him expense sir."

## 5.

The occasions came. Repairs were expensive, and revisions were even more so. With the years, new models of robots were produced and Sir saw to it that Andrew had the advantage of every new device until he was a paragon of metallic excellence. It was all at Andrew's expense.

Andrew insisted on that.

Only his positronic pathways were untouched. Sir insisted on that.

"The new ones aren't as good as you are, Andrew," he said. "The new robots are worthless. The company has learned to make the pathways more precise, more closely on the nose, more deeply on the track. The new robots don't shift. They do what they're designed for and never stray. I like you better."

"Thank you, Sir."

"And it's your doing, Andrew, don't forget that. I am certain Mansky put an end to generalized pathways as soon as he had a good look at you. He didn't like the unpredictability . . . Do you know how many times he asked for you so he could place you under study? Nine times! I never let him have you, though, and now that he's retired, we may have some peace."

So Sir's hair thinned and grayed and his face grew pouchy, while Andrew looked rather better than he had when he first joined the family.

Ma'am had joined an art colony somewhere in Europe and Miss was a poet in New York. They wrote sometimes, but not often. Little Miss was married and lived not far away. She said she did not want to leave Andrew and when her child, Little Sir, was born, she let Andrew hold the bottle and feed him.

With the birth of a grandson, Andrew felt that Sir had someone now to replace those who had gone. It would not be so unfair to come to him the request.

Andrew said, "Sir, it is kind of you to have allowed me to spend my money as I wished."

"It was your money, Andrew."

"Only by your voluntary act, Sir. I do not believe the law would have stopped you from keeping it all."

"The law won't persuade me to do wrong, Andrew."

"Despite all expenses, and despite taxes, too, Sir, I have nearly six hundred thousand dollars."

"I know that, Andrew."

"I want to give it to you, Sir."

"I won't take it, Andrew."

"In exchange for something you can give me, Sir."

"Oh? What is that, Andrew?"

"My freedom, Sir."

"Your—"

"I wish to buy my freedom, Sir."

## 6.

It wasn't that easy. Sir had flushed, had said "For God's sake!" had turned on his heel, and stalked away.

It was Little Miss who brought him round, defiantly and harshly—and in front of Andrew. For thirty years, no one had hesitated to talk in front of Andrew, whether the matter involved Andrew or not. He was only a robot.

She said, "Dad, why are you taking it as a personal affront? He'll still be here. He'll still be loyal. He can't help that. It's built in. All he wants is a form of words. He wants to be called free. Is that so terrible? Hasn't he earned it? Heavens, he and I have been talking about it for years."

"Talking about it for years, have you?"

"Yes, over and over again, he postponed it for fear he would hurt you. I *made* him put it up to you."

"He doesn't know what freedom is. He's a robot."

"Dad, you don't know him. He's read everything in the library. I don't know what he feels inside but I don't know what *you* feel inside. When you talk to him you'll find he reacts to the various abstractions as you and I do, and what else counts? If someone else's reactions are like your own, what more can you ask for?"

"The law won't take that attitude," Sir said angrily. "See here, you!" He turned to Andrew with a deliberate grate in his voice. "I can't free you except by doing it legally, and if it gets into the courts, you not only won't get your freedom but the law will take official cognizance of your money. They'll tell you that a robot has no right to earn money. Is this rigmarole worth losing your money?"

"Freedom is without price, Sir," said Andrew. "Even the chance of freedom is worth the money."

## 7.

The court might also take the attitude that freedom was without price, and might decide that for no price, however great, could a robot buy his freedom.

The simple statement of the regional attorney who represented those who had brought a class action to oppose the freedom was this: The word "freedom" had no meaning when applied to a robot. Only a human being could be free.

He said it several times, when it seemed appropriate; slowly, with his hand coming down rhythmically on the desk before him to mark the words.

Little Miss asked permission to speak on behalf of Andrew. She was recognized by her full name, something Andrew had never heard pronounced before:

"Amanda Laura Martin Charney may approach the bench."

She said, "Thank you, your honor. I am not a lawyer and I don't know the proper way of phrasing things, but I hope you will listen to my meaning and ignore the words.

"Let's understand what it means to be free in Andrew's case. In some ways,he *is* free. I think it's at least twenty years since anyone in the Martin family gave him an order to do something that we felt he might not do of his own accord.

"But we can, if we wish, give him an order to do anything, couch it as harshly as we wish, because he is a machine that belongs to us. Why should we be in a position to do so, when he has served us so long, so faithfully, and earned so much money for us? He owes us nothing more. The debt is entirely on the other side.

"Even if we were legally forbidden to place Andrew in involuntary servitude, he would still serve us voluntarily. Making him free would be a trick of words only, but it would mean much to him. It would give him everything and cost us nothing."

For a moment the Judge seemed to be suppressing a smile. "I see your point, Mrs. Charney. The fact is that there is no binding law in this respect and no precedent. There is, however, the unspoken assumption that only a man can enjoy freedom. I can make new law here, subject to reversal in a higher court, but I cannot lightly run counter to that assumption. Let me address the robot. Andrew!"

"Yes, your honor."

It was the first time Andrew had spoken in court and the judge seemed astonished for a moment at the human timbre of the voice. He said, "Why do you want to be free, Andrew? In what way will this matter to you?"

Andrew said, "Would you wish to be a slave, your honor?"

"But you are not a slave. You are a perfectly good robot, a genius of a robot I am given to understand, capable of an artistic expression that can be matched nowhere. What more can you do if you were free?"

"Perhaps no more than I do now, your honor, but with greater joy. It has been said in this courtroom that only a human being can be free. It seems to me that only someone who wishes for freedom can be free. I wish for freedom."

And it was that that cued the Judge. The crucial sentence in his decision was: "There is no right to deny freedom to any object with a mind advanced enough to grasp the concept and desire the state."

It was eventually upheld by the World Court.

# 8.

Sir remained displeased and his harsh voice made Andrew feel almost as though he were being short-circuited.

Sir said, "I don't want your damned money, Andrew. I'll take it only because you won't feel free otherwise. From now on, you can select your own jobs and do them as you please. I will give you no orders, except this one—that you do as you please. But I am still responsible for you; that's part of the court order. I hope you understand that."

Little Miss interrupted. "Don't be irascible, Dad. The responsibility is no great chore. You know you won't have to do a thing. The Three Laws still hold."

"Then how is he free?"

Andrew said, "Are not human beings bound by their laws, Sir?"

Sir, said, "I am not going to argue." He left, and Andrew saw him only infrequently after that.

Little Miss came to see him frequently in the small house that had been built and made over for him. It had not kitchen, of course, nor bathroom facilities. It had just two rooms; one was a library and one was a combination storeroom and workroom. Andrew accepted many commissions and worked harder as a free robot than he ever had before, till the cost of the house was paid for and the structure legally transferred to him.

One day Little Sir came . . . No, George! Little Sir had insisted on that after the court decision. "A free robot doesn't call anyone Little Sir," George had said. "I call you Andrew. You must call me George."

It was phased as an order, so Andrew called him George—but Little Miss remained Little Miss.

The day George came alone, it was to say that Sir was dying. Little Miss was at the bedside but Sir wanted Andrew as well.

Sir's voice was quite strong, though he seemed unable to move much. He struggled to get his hand up. "Andrew," he said, "Andrew—Don't help me, George. I'm only dying; I'm not crippled . . . Andrew, I'm glad you're free. I just wanted to tell you that."

Andrew did not know what to say. He had never been at the side of someone dying before, but he knew it was the human way of ceasing to function. It was an involuntary and irreversible dismantling, and Andrew did not know what to say that might be appropriate. He could only remain standing, absolutely silent, absolutely motionless.

When it was over, Little Miss said to him, "He may not have

seemed friendly to you toward the end, Andrew, but he was old, you know, and it hurt him that you should want to be free."

And then Andrew found the words to say. He said, "I would never have been free without him, Little Miss."

## 9.

It was only after Sir's death that Andrew began to wear clothes. He began with an old pair of trousers at first, a pair that George had given him.

George was married now, and a lawyer. He had joined Feingold's firm. Old Feingold was long since dead but his daughter had carried on and eventually the firm's name became Feingold and Martin. It remained so even when the daughter retired and no Feingold took her place. At the time Andrew put on clothes for the first time, the Martin name had just been added to the firm.

George had tried not to smile, the first time Andrew put on the trousers, but to Andrew's eyes the smile was clearly there.

George showed Andrew how to manipulate the static charge so as to allow the trousers to open, wrap about his lower body, and move shut. George demonstrated on his trousers, but Andrew was quite aware that it would take him awhile to duplicate that one flowing motion.

George said, "But why do you want trousers, Andrew? Your body is so beautifully functional it's a shame to cover it—especially when you needn't worry about either temperature control or modesty. And it doesn't cling properly, not on metal."

Andrew said, "Are not human bodies beautifully functional, George? Yet you cover yourselves."

"For warmth, for cleanliness, for protection, for decorativeness. None of that applies to you."

Andrew said, "I feel bare without clothes. I feel different, George."

"Different! Andrew, there are millions of robots on Earth now. In this region, according to the last census, there are almost as many robots as there are men."

"I know, George. There are robots doing every conceivable type of work."

"And none of them wear clothes."

"But none of them are free. George."

Little by little, Andrew added to the wardrobe. He was inhibited by George's smile and by the stares of the people who commissioned work.

He might be free, but there was built into him a carefully detailed program concerning his behavior toward people, and it was only by the tiniest steps that he dared advance. Open disapproval would set him back months.

Not everyone accepted Andrew as free. He was incapable of resenting that and yet there was a difficulty about his thinking process when he thought of it.

Most of all, he tended to avoid putting on clothes—or too many of them—when he thought Little Miss might come to visit him. She was old now and was often away in some warmer climate, but when she returned the first thing she did was visit him.

On one of her returns, George said ruefully, "She's got me, Andrew. I'll be running for the Legislature next year. Like grandfather, she says, like grandson."

"Like grandfather—" Andrew stopped, uncertain.

"I mean that I, George, the grandson, will be like Sir, the grandfather, who was in the Legislature once."

Andrew said, "It would be pleasant, George, if Sir we are still—" He paused, for he did not want to say, "in working order." That seemed inappropriate.

"Alive," said George. "Yes, I think of the old monster now and then, too."

It was a conversation Andrew thought about. He had noticed his own incapacity in speech when talking with George. Somehow the language had changed since Andrew had come into being with an innate vocabulary. Then, too, George used a colloquial speech, as Sir and Little Miss had not. Why should he have called Sir a monster when surely that word was not appropriate?

Nor could Andrew turn to his own books for guidance. They were old and most dealt with woodworking, with art, with furniture design. There were none on language, none on the way of human beings.

It was at that moment it seemed to him that he must seek the proper books; and as a free robot, he felt he must not ask George. He would go to town and use the library. It was a triumphant decision and he felt his electropotential grow distinctly higher until he had to throw in an impedance coil.

He put on a full costume, even including a shoulder chain of wood. He would have preferred the glitter plastic but George had said that wood was much more appropriate and that polished cedar was considerably more valuable as well.

He had placed a hundred feet between himself and the house before gathering resistance brought him to a halt. He shifted the impedance coil out of circuit, and when that did not seem to help enough, he returned to his home and on a piece of notepaper wrote neatly, "I have gone to the library," and placed it in clear view on his worktable.

## 10.

Andrew never quite got to the library. He had studied the map. He knew the route, but not the appearance of it. The actual landmarks did not resemble the symbols on the map and he would hesitate. Eventually he thought he must have somehow gone wrong, for everything looked strange.

He passed an occasional field robot, but at the time he decided he should ask his way, there were none in sight. A vehicle passed and did not stop. He stood irresolute, which meant calmly motionless, and then coming across the field toward him were two human beings.

He turned to face them, and they altered their course to meet him. A moment before, they had been talking loudly; he had heard their voices; but now they were silent. They had the look that Andrew associated with human uncertainty, and they were young, but not very young. Twenty perhaps? Andrew could never judge human age.

He said, "Would you describe to me the route to the town library, sirs?"

One of them, the taller of the two, whose tall hat lengthened him still farther, almost grotesquely, said, not to Andrew, but to the other, "It's a robot."

The other had a bulbous nose and heavy eyelids. He said, not to Andrew, but to the first, "It's wearing clothes."

The tall one snapped his fingers. "It's the free robot. They have a robot at the Martins who isn't owned by anybody. Why else would it be wearing clothes?"

"Ask it," said the one with the nose.

"Are you the Martin robot?" asked the tall one.

"I am Andrew Martin, sir," said Andrew.

"Good. Take off your clothes. Robots don't wear clothes." He said to the other, "That's disgusting. Look at him."

Andrew hesitated. He hadn't heard an order in that tone of voice in so long that his Second Law circuits had momentarily jammed.

The tall one said, "Take off your clothes. I order you."

Slowly, Andrew began to remove them.

"Just drop them," said the tall one.

The nose said, "If it doesn't belong to anyone, he could be ours as much as someone else's."

"Anyway," said the tall one, "who's to object to anything we do? We're not damaging property . . . Stand on your head." That was to Andrew.

"The head is not meant—" began Andrew.

"That's an order. If you don't know how, try anyway."

Andrew hesitated again, then bent to put his head on the ground. He tried to lift his legs and fell, heavily.

The tall one said, "Just lie there." He said to the other, "We can take him apart. Ever take a robot apart?"

"Will he let us?"

"How can he stop us?"

There was no way Andrew could stop them, if they ordered him not to resist in a forceful enough manner. Second Law of obedience took precedence over the Third Law of self-preservation. In any case, he could not defend himself without possibly hurting them and that would mean breaking the First Law. At that thought, every motile unit contracted slightly and he quivered as he lay there.

The tall one walked over and pushed at him with his foot. "He's heavy. I think we'll need tools to do the job."

The nose said, "We could order him to take himself apart. It would be fun to watch him try."

"Yes," said the tall one thoughtfully, "but let's him off the road. If someone comes along—"

It was too late. Someone had indeed come along and it was George. From where he lay, Andrew had seen him topping a small rise in the middle distance. He would have liked to signal him in some way, but the last order had been "Just lie there!"

George was running now and he arrived somewhat winded. The two young men stepped back a little then waited thoughtfully.

George said anxiously, "Andrew, has something gone wrong?"

Andrew said, "I am well, George."

"Then stand up . . . What happened to your clothes?"

The tall man said, "That your robot, mac?"

George turned sharply. "He's no one's robot. What been going on here?"

"We politely asked him to take his clothes off. What's that to you if you don't own him?"

George said, "What were they doing, Andrew?"

Andrew said, "It was their intention in some way to dismember me. They were about to move me to a quiet spot and order me to dismember myself."

George looked at the two and his chin trembled. The two young men retreated no further. They were smiling. The tall one said lightly, "What are you going to do, pudgy? Attack us?"

George said, "No. I don't have to. This robot has been with my family for over seventy years. He knows us and he values us more than he values anyone else. I am going to tell him that you two are threatening my life and that you plan to kill me. I will ask him to defend me. In choosing between me and you two, he will choose me. Do you know what will happen to you when he attacks you?"

The two were backing away slightly, looking uneasy.

George said sharply, "Andrew, I am in danger and about to come to harm from these young men. Move toward them!"

Andrew did so, and the two young men did not wait. They ran fleetly.

"All right, Andrew, relax," said George. He looked unstrung. He was far past the age where he could face the possibility of a dustup with one young man, let alone two.

Andrew said, "I couldn't have hurt them, George. I could see they were not attacking you."

"I didn't order you to attack them; I only told you to move toward them. Their own fears did the rest."

"How can they fear robots?"

"It's a disease of mankind, one of which it is not yet cured. But never mind that. What the devil are you doing here, Andrew? I was on the point of turning back and hiring a helicopter when I found you. How did you get it into your head to go to the library? I would have brought you any books you needed."

"I am—" began Andrew.

"Free robot. Yes, yes. All right, what did you want in the library?"

"I want to know more about human beings, about the world, about everything. And about robots, George. I want to write a history about robots."

George said, "Well, let's walk home . . . And pick up your clothes first. Andrew, there are a million books on robotics and all of them include histories of the science. The world is growing saturated not only with robots but with information about robots."

Andrew shook his head, a human gesture he had lately begun to make. "Not a history of robotics, George. A history of *robots*, by a robot. I want to explain how robots feel about what has happened since the first ones were allowed to work and live on Earth."

George's eyebrows lifted, but he said nothing in direct response.

## 11.

Little Miss was just past her eighty-third birthday, but there was nothing about her that was lacking in either energy or determination. She gestured with her cane oftener than she propped herself up with it.

She listened to the story in a fury of indignation. She said, "George, that's horrible. Who were those young ruffians?"

"I don't know. What difference does it make? In the end they did no damage."

"They might have. You're a lawyer, George, and if you're well off, it's entirely due to the talent of Andrew. It was the money *he* earned that is the foundation of everything we have. He provides the continuity for this family and I will *not* have him treated as a wind-up toy."

"What would you have me do, Mother?" asked George.

"I said you're a lawyer. Don't you listen? You set up a test case somehow, and you force the regional courts to declare for robot rights and get the Legislature to pass the necessary bills, and carry the whole thing to the World Court, if you have to. I'll be watching, George, and I'll tolerate no shirking."

She was serious, and what began as a way of soothing the fearsome old lady became an involved matter with enough legal entanglement to make it interesting. As senior partner of Feingold and Martin, George plotted strategy but left the actual work to his junior partners, with much of it a matter for his son, Paul, who was also a member of the firm and who reported dutifully nearly every day to his grandmother. She, in turn, discussed it every day with Andrew.

Andrew was deeply involved. His work on his book on robots was delayed again, as he pored over the legal arguments and even, at times, made very diffident suggestions.

He said, "George told me that day that human beings have always been afraid of robots. As long as they are, the courts and the legislatures are not likely to work hard on behalf of robots. Should there not be something done about public opinion?"

So while Paul stayed in court, George took to the public platform. It gave him the advantage of being informal and he even went so far sometimes as to wear the new, loose style of clothing which he called drapery. Paul said, "Just don't trip over it on stage, Dad."

George said despondently, "I'll try not to."

He addressed the annual convention of holo-news editors on one occasion and said, in part:

"If, by virtue of the Second Law, we can demand of any robot unlimited obedience in all respects not involving harm to a human being, then any human being, *any* human being, has a fearsome power over any robot, *any* robot. In particular, since Second Law supersedes Third Law, *any* human being can use the law of obedience to overcome the law of self-protection. He can order any robot to damage itself or even destroy itself for any reason, or for no reason.

"Is this just? Would we treat an animal so? Even an inanimate object which has given us good service has a claim on our consideration. And a robot is not insensible; it is not an animal. It can think well enough to enable it to talk to us, reason with us, joke with us. Can we treat them as friends, can we work together with them, and not give them some of the fruit of that friendship, some of the benefit of co-working?

"If a man has the right to give a robot any order that does not involve harm to a human being, he should have the decency never to give a robot any order that involves harm to a robot, unless human safety absolutely requires it. With great power goes great responsibility, and if the robots have Three Laws to protect men, is it too much to ask that men have a law or two to protect robots?"

Andrew was right. It was the battle over public opinion that held the key to courts and Legislature and in the end a law passed which set up conditions under which robot-harming orders were forbidden. It was endlessly qualified and the punishments for violating the law were totally inadequate, but the principle was established. The final passage by the World Legislature came through on the day of Little Miss's death.

That was no coincidence. Little Miss held on to life desperately during the last debate and let go only when word of victory arrived. Her last smile was for Andrew. Her last words were: "You have been good to us, Andrew."

She died with her hand holding his, while her son and his wife and children remained at a respectful distance from both.

## 12.

Andrew waited patiently while the receptionist disappeared into the inner office. It might have used the holographic chatterbox, but unquestionably it was unmanned (or perhaps unroboted) by having to deal with another robot rather than with a human being.

Andrew passed the time revolving the matter in his mind. Could "unroboted" be used as an analogue of "unmanned," or had "unmanned" become a metaphoric term sufficiently divorced from its original literal meaning to be applied to robots—or to women for that matter?

Such problems came frequently as he worked on his book on robots. The trick of thinking out sentences to express all complexities had undoubtedly increased his vocabulary.

Occasionally, someone came into the room to stare at him and he did not try to avoid the glance. He looked at each calmly, and each in turn looked away.

Paul Martin finally came out. He looked surprised, or he would have if Andrew could have made out his expression with certainty. Paul had taken to wearing the heavy makeup that fashion was dictating for both sexes and though it made sharper and firmer the somewhat bland lines of his face, Andrew disapproved. He found that disapproving of human beings, as long as he did not express it verbally, did not make him very uneasy. He could even write the disapproval. He was sure it had not always been so.

Paul said, "Come in, Andrew. I'm sorry I made you wait but there was something I *had* to finish. Come in. You had said you wanted to talk to me, but I didn't know you meant here in town."

"If you are busy, Paul, I am prepared to continue to wait."

Paul glanced at the interplay of shifting shadows on the dial on the wall that served as timepiece and said, "I can make some time. Did you come alone?"

"I hired an automatobile."

"Any trouble?" Paul asked, with more than a trace of anxiety.

"I wasn't expecting any. My rights are protected."

Paul looked the more anxious for that. "Andrew, I've explained that the law is unenforceable, at least under most conditions . . . And if you insist on wearing clothes, you'll run into trouble eventually—just like that first time."

"And only time, Paul. I'm sorry you are displeased."

"Well, look at it this way; you are virtually a living legend, Andrew, and you are too valuable in many different ways for you to have any right to take chances with yourself . . . How's the book coming?"

"I am approaching the end, Paul. The publisher is quite pleased."

"Good!"

"I don't know that he's necessarily pleased with the book as a book. I think he expects to sell many copies because it's written by a robot and it's that that pleases him."

"Only human, I'm afraid."

"I am not displeased. Let it sell for whatever reason since it will mean money and I can use some."

"Grandmother left you—"

"Little Miss was generous, and I'm sure I can count on the family to help me out further. But it is the royalties from the book on which I am counting to help me through the next step."

"What next step is that?"

"I wish to see the head of U.S. Robots and Mechanical Men, Inc. I have tried to make an appointment, but so far I have not been able to reach him. The corporation did not cooperate with me in the writing of the book, so I am not surprised, you understand."

Paul was clearly amused. "Cooperation is the last thing you can expect. They didn't cooperate with us in our great fight for robot rights. Quite the reverse and you can see why. Give a robot rights and people may not want to buy them."

"Nevertheless," said Andrew, "If you call them, you may obtain an interview for me."

"I'm no more popular with them than you are, Andrew."

"But perhaps you can hint that by seeing me they may head off a campaign by Feingold and Martin to strengthen the rights of robots further."

"Wouldn't that be a lie, Andrew?"

"Yes, Paul, and I can't tell one. That is why you must call."

"Ah, you can't lie, but you can urge me to tell a lie, is that it? You're getting more human all the time, Andrew."

# 13.

It was not easy to arrange, even with Paul's supposedly weighted name.

But it was finally carried through and, when it was, Harley Smythe-Robertson, who, on his mother's side, was descended from the original founder of the corporation and who had adopted the hyphenation to indicate it, looked remarkably unhappy. He was approaching retirement age and his entire tenure as president had been devoted to the matter of robot rights. His gray hair was plastered thinly over the top of his scalp, his face was not made up, and he eyed Andrew with brief hostility from time to time.

Andrew said, "Sir, nearly a century ago, I was told by a Merton Mansky of this corporation that the mathematics governing the plotting of the positronic pathways was far too complicated to permit of any but approximate solutions and that therefore my own capacities were not fully predictable."

"That was a century ago." Smythe-Robertson hesitated, then said icily, "*Sir*. It is true no longer. Our robots are made with precision now and are trained precisely to their jobs."

"Yes," said Paul, who had come along, as he said, to make sure that the corporation played fair, "with the result that my receptionist must be guided at every point once events depart from the conventional, however slightly."

Smythe-Robertson said, "You would be much more displeased if it were to improvise."

Andrew said, "Then you no longer manufacture robots like myself which are flexible and adaptable."

"No longer."

"The research I have done in connection with my book," said Andrew, "indicates that I am the oldest robot presently in active operation."

"The oldest presently," said Smythe-Robertson, "and the oldest ever. The oldest that will ever be. No robot is useful after the twenty-fifth year. They are called in and replaced with newer models."

"No robot *as presently manufactured* is useful after the twenty-fifth year," said Paul pleasantly. "Andrew is quite exceptional in this respect."

Andrew, adhering to the path he had marked out for himself, said, "As the oldest robot in the world and the most flexible, am I not unusual enough to merit special treatment from the company?"

"Not at all," said Smythe-Robertson freezingly. "Your unusualness is an embarrassment to the company. If you were on lease, instead of having been a sale outright through some mischance, you would long since have been replaced."

"But that is exactly the point," said Andrew. "I am a free robot and I own myself. Therefore I come to you and ask you to replace me. You cannot do this without the owner's consent. Nowadays, that consent is extorted as a condition of the lease, but in my time this did not happen."

Smythe-Robertson was looking both startled and puzzled, and for a moment there was silence. Andrew found himself staring at the holograph on the wall. It was a death mask of Susan Calvin, patron saint of all roboticists. She was dead nearly two centuries now, but as a result of writing his book Andrew knew her so well he could half persuade himself that he had met her in life.

Smythe-Robertson said, "How can I replace you for you? If I replace you as robot, how can I donate the new robot to you as owner since in the very act of replacement you cease to exist?" He smiled grimly.

"Not at all difficult," interposed Paul. "The seat of Andrew's personality is his positronic brain and it is the one part that cannot be replaced without creating a new robot. The positronic brain, therefore, is Andrew the owner. Every other part of the robotic body can be replaced without affecting the robot's personality, and those other parts are the brain's possessions. Andrew, I should say, wants to supply his brain with a new robotic body."

"That's right," said Andrew calmly. He turned to Smythe-Robertson. "You have manufactured androids, haven't you? Robots that have the outward appearance of humans complete to the texture of the skin?"

Smythe-Robertson said, "Yes, we have. They worked perfectly well, with their synthetic fibrous skins and tendons. There was virtually no metal anywhere except for the brain, yet they were nearly as tough as metal robots. They were tougher, weight for weight."

Paul looked interested. "I didn't know that. How many are on the market?"

"None," said Smythe-Robertson. "They were much more expensive than metal models and a market survey showed they would not be accepted. They looked too human."

Andrew said, "But the corporation retains its expertise, I assume. Since it does, I wish to request that I be replaced by an organic robot, an android."

Paul looked surprised. "Good Lord," he said.

Smythe-Robertson stiffened. "Quite impossible!"

"Why is it impossible?" asked Andrew. "I will pay any reasonable fee, of course."

Smythe-Robertson said, "We do not manufacture androids."

"You do not *choose* to manufacture androids," interposed Paul quickly. "That is not the same as being unable to manufacture them."

Smythe-Robertson said, "Nevertheless, the manufacture of androids is against public policy."

"There is no law against it," said Paul.

"Nevertheless, we do not manufacture them, and we will not."

Paul cleared his throat. "Mr. Smythe-Robertson," he said, "Andrew is a free robot who is under the purview of the law guaranteeing robot rights. You are aware of this, I take it?"

"Only too well."

"This robot, as a free robot, chooses to wear clothes. This results in his being frequently humiliated by thoughtless human beings despite the law against the humiliation of robots. It is difficult to prosecute vague offenses that don't meet with the general disapproval of those who must decide on guilt and innocence."

"U.S. Robots understood that from the start. Your father's firm unfortunately did not."

"My father is dead now," said Paul, "but what I see is that we have here a clear offense with a clear target."

"What are you talking about?" said Smythe-Robertson.

"My client, Andrew Martin—he has just become my client—is a free robot who is entitled to ask U.S. Robots and Mechanical Men, Inc., for the right of replacement, which the corporation supplies anyone who owns a robot for more than twenty-five years. In fact, the corporation insists on such replacement."

Paul was smiling and thoroughly at his ease. He went on, "The positronic brain of my client is the owner of the body of my client—which is certainly more than twenty-five years old. The positronic brain demands the replacement of the body and offers to pay any reasonable fee for an android body as that replacement. If you refuse the request, my client undergoes humiliation and we will sue.

"While public opinion would not ordinarily support the claim of a robot in such a case, may I remind you that U.S. Robots is not popular with the public generally. Even those who most use and profit from robots are suspicious of the corporation. This may be a hangover from the days when robots were widely feared. It may be resentment against the power and wealth of U.S. Robots which has a worldwide monopoly.

Whatever the cause may be, the resentment exists and I think you will find that you would prefer not to withstand a lawsuit, particularly since my client is wealthy and will live for many more centuries and will have no reason to refrain from fighting the battle forever."

Symthe-Robertson had slowly reddened. "You are trying to force me to . . ."

"I force you to do nothing," said Paul. "If you wish to refuse to accede to my client's reasonable request, you may by all means do so and we will leave without another word . . . But we will sue, as is certainly our right, and you will find that you will eventually lose."

Smythe-Robertson said, "Well—" and paused.

"I see that you are going to accede," said Paul. "You may hesitate but you will come to it in the end. Let me assure you, then, of the further point. If, in the process of transferring my client's positronic brain from his present body to an organic one, there is any damage, however slight, then I will never rest till I've nailed the corporation to the ground. I will, if necessary, take every possible step to mobilize public opinion against the corporation if one brain path of my client's platinum-iridium essence is scrambled." He turned to Andrew and said, "Do you agree to all this, Andrew?"

Andrew hesitated a full minute. It amounted to the approval of lying, of blackmail, of the badgering and humiliation of a human being. But not physical harm, he told himself, not physical harm.

He managed at last to come out with a rather faint "Yes."

## 14.

It was like being constructed again. For days, then for weeks, finally for months, Andrew found himself not himself somehow, and the simplest actions kept giving rise to hesitation.

Paul was frantic. "They've damaged you, Andrew. We'll have to institute suit."

Andrew spoke very slowly. "You mustn't. You'll never be able to prove—something—m-m-m-m—"

"Malice?"

"Malice. Besides, I grow stronger, better. It's the tr-tr-tr—"

"Tremble?"

"Trauma. After all, there's never been such an op—op—op — before."

Andrew could feel his brain from the inside. No one else could. He knew he was well and during the months that it took him to learn full positronic interplay, he spent hours before the mirror.

Not quite human! The face was stiff—too stiff—and the motions were too deliberate. They lacked the careless free flow of the human being, but perhaps that might come with time. At least he could wear clothes without the ridiculous anomaly of a metal face going along with it.

Eventually he said, "I will be going back to work."

Paul laughed and said, "That means you are well. What will you be doing? Another book?"

"No," said Andrew seriously. "I live too long for any one career to seize me by the throat and never let me go. There was a time when I was primarily an artist and I can still turn to that. And there was a time when I was a historian and I can still turn to that. But now I wish to be robobiologist."

"A robopsychologist, you mean."

"No. That would imply the study of positronic brains and at the moment I lack the desire to do that. A robobiologist, it seems to me, would be concerned with the working of the body attached to that brain."

"Wouldn't that be a roboticist?"

"A roboticist works with a metal body. I would be studying an organic humanoid body, of which I have the only one, as far as I know."

"You narrow your field," said Paul thoughtfully. "As an artist, all conception is yours; as a historican, you dealt chiefly with robots; as a robobiologist, you will deal with yourself."

Andrew nodded. "It would seem so."

Andrew had to start from the very beginning, for he knew nothing of ordinary biology, almost nothing of science. He became a familiar sight in the libraries, where he sat at the electronic indices for hours at a time, looking perfectly normal in clothes. Those few who knew he was a robot in no way interfered with him.

He built a laboratory in a room which he added to his house, and his library grew, too.

Years passed, and Paul came to him one day and said, "It's a pity you're no longer working on the history of robots. I understand U.S. Robots is adopting a radically new policy."

Paul had aged, and his deteriorating eyes had been replaced with photoptic cells. In the respect, he had drawn closer to Andrew. Andrew said, "What have they done?"

"They are manufacturing central computers, gigantic positronic brains, really, which communicate with anywhere from a dozen to a thousand robots by microwave. The robots themselves have no brains at all. They are the limbs of the gigantic brain, and the two are physically separate."

"Is that more efficient?"

"U.S. Robots claims it is. Smythe-Robertson established the new direction before he died, however, and it's my notion that it's a backlash at you. U.S. Robots is determined that they will make no robots that will give them the type of trouble you have, and for that reason they separate brain and body. The brain will have no body to wish changed; the body will have no brain to wish anything.

"It's amazing, Andrew," Paul went on, "the influence you have had on the history of robots. It was your artistry that encouraged U.S. Robots to make robots more precise and specialized; it was your freedom that resulted in the establishment of the principle of robotic rights; it was your insistence on an android body that made U.S. Robots switch to brain-body separation."

Andrew said, "I suppose in the end the corporation will produce one vast brain controlling several billion robotic bodies. All the eggs will be in one basket. Dangerous. Not proper at all."

"I think you're right," said Paul, "but I don't suspect it will come to pass for a century at least and I won't live to see it. In fact, I may not live to see next year."

"Paul!" said Andrew, in concern.

Paul shrugged. "We're mortal, Andrew. We're not like you. It doesn't matter too much, but it does make it important to assure you on one point. I'm the last of the human Martins. There are collaterals descended from my great-aunt, but they don't count. The money I control personally will be left to the trust in your name and as far as anyone can foresee the future, you will be economically secure."

"Unnecessary," said Andrew, with difficulty. In all this time, he could not get used to the deaths of the Martins.

Paul said, "Let's not argue. That's the way it's going to be. What are you working on?"

"I am designing a system for allowing androids—myself—to gain energy from the combustion of hydrocarbons, rather than from atomic cells."

Paul raised his eyebrows. "So that they will breathe and eat?"

"Yes."

"How long have you been pushing in that direction?"

"For a long time now, but I think I have designed an adequate combustion chamber for catalyzed controlled breakdown."

"But why, Andrew? The atomic cell is surely infinitely better."

"In some ways, perhaps, but the atomic cell is inhuman."

## 15.

It took time, but Andrew had time. In the first place, he did not wish to do anything till Paul had died in peace.

With the death of the great-grandson of Sir, Andrew felt more nearly exposed to a hostile world and for that reason was the more determined to continue the path he had long ago chosen.

Yet he was not really alone. If a man had died, the firm of Feingold and Martin lived, for a corporation does not die any more than a robot does. The firm had its directions and it followed them soullessly. By the way of the trust and through the law firm, Andrew continued to be wealthy. And in return for their own large annual retainer, Feingold and Martin involved themselves in the legal aspects of the new combustion chamber.

When the time came for Andrew to visit U.S. Robots and Mechanical Men, Inc., he did it alone. Once he had gone with Sir and once with Paul. This time, the third time, he was alone and manlike.

U.S. Robots had changed. The production plant had been shifted to a large space station, as had grown to be the case with more and more industries. With them had gone many robots. The Earth itself was becoming parklike, with its one-billion-person population stabilized and perhaps not more than thirty per cent of its at least equally large robot population independently brained

The Director of Research was Alvin Magdescu, dark of complexion and hair, with a little pointed beard and wearing nothing above the waist but the breastband that fashion dictated. Andrew himself was well covered in the older fashion of several decades back.

Magdescu said, "I know you, of course, and I'm rather pleased to see you. You're our most notorious product and it's a pity old Smythe-Robertson was so set against you. We could have done a great deal with you."

"You still can," said Andrew.

"No, I don't think so. We're past the time. We've had robots on Earth for over a century, but that's changing. It will be back to space with them and those that stay here won't be brained."

"But there remains myself, and I stay on Earth."

"True, but there doesn't seem to be much of the robot about you. What new request have you?"

"To be still less a robot. Since I am so far organic, I wish an organic source of energy. I have here the plans—"

Magdescu did not hasten through them. He might have intended to at first, but he stiffened and grew intent. At one point he said, "This is remarkably ingenious. Who thought of all this?"

"I did," said Andrew.

Magdescu looked up at him sharply, then said, "It would amount to a major overhaul of your body, and an experimental one, since it has never been attempted before. I advise against it. Remain as you are."

Andrew's face had limited means of expression, but impatience showed plainly in his voice. "Dr. Magdescu, you miss the entire point. You have no choice but to accede to my request. If such devices can be built into my body, they can be built into human bodies as well. The tendency to lengthen human life by prosthetic devices has already been remarked on. There are no devices better than the ones I have designed and am designing.

"As it happens, I control the patents by way of the firm of Feingold and Martin. We are quite capable of going into business for ourselves and of developing the kind of prosthetic devices that may end by producing human beings with many of the properties of robots. Your own business will then suffer.

"If, however, you operate on me now and agree to do so under similar circumstances in the future, you will receive permission to make use of the patents and control the technology of both robots and the prosthetization of human beings. The initial leasing will not be granted, of course, until after the first operation is completed successfully, and after enough time has passed to demonstrate that it is indeed sucessful." Andrew felt scarcely any First Law inhibition to the stern conditions he was setting a human being. He was learning to reason that what seemed like cruelty might, in the long run, be kindness.

Magdescu looked stunned. He said, "I'm not the one decide something like this. That's a corporate decision that would take time."

"I can wait a reasonable time," said Andrew, "but only a reasonable time." And he thought with satisfaction that Paul himself could not have done it better.

## 16.

It took only a reasonable time, and the operation was a success.

Magdescu said, "I was very much against the operation, Andrew, but not for the reasons you might think. I was not in the least against the experiment, if it had been on someone else. I hated risking *your* positronic brain. Now that you have the positronic pathways interacting with simulated nerve pathways, it might be difficult to rescue the brain intact if the body went bad."

"I had every faith in the skill of the staff at U.S. Robots," said Andrew. "And I can eat now."

"Well, you can sip olive oil. It will mean occasional cleanings of the combustion chamber, as we have explained to you. Rather an uncomfortable touch, I should think."

"Perhaps, if I did not expect to go further. Self-cleaning is not impossible. In fact, I am working on a device that will deal with solid food that may be expected to contain incombustible fractions — indigestible matter, so to speak, that will have to be discarded."

"You would then have to develop an anus."

"The equivalent."

"What else, Andrew?"

"Everything else."

"Genitalia, too?"

"Insofar as they will fit my plans. My body is a canvas on which I intend to draw—"

Magdescu waited for the sentence to be completed, and when it seemed that it would not be, he completed it himself. "A man?"

"We shall see," said Andrew.

Magdescu said, "It's a puny ambition, Andrew. You're better than a man. You've gone downhill from the moment you opted for organicism."

"My brain has not suffered."

"No, it hasn't. I'll grant you that. But, Andrew, the whole new breakthrough in prosthetic devices made possible by your patents is being marketed under your name. You're recognized as the inventor and you're honored for it—as you are. Why play further games with your body?"

Andrew did not answer.

The honors came. He accepted membership in several learned societies, including one which was devoted to the new science he had established; the one he had called robobiology but had come to be termed prosthetology.

On the one hundred and fiftieth anniversary of his construction, there was a testimonial dinner given in his honor at U.S. Robots. If Andrew saw irony in this, he kept it to himself.

Alvin Magdescu came out of retirement to chair the dinner. He was himself ninety-four years old and was alive because he had prosthetized devices that, among other things, fulfilled the function of liver and kidneys. The dinner reached its climax when Magdescu, after a short and emotional talk, raised his glass to toast "the Sesquicentennial Robot."

Andrew had had the sinews of his face redesigned to the point where he could show a range of emotions, but he sat through all the ceremonies solemnlyl passive. He did not like to be a Sesquicentennial Robot.

## 17.

It was prosthetology that finally took Andrew off the Earth. In the decades that followed the celebration of the Sesquicentennial, the Moon had come to be a world more Earth-like than Earth in every respect but its gravitational pull and in its underground cities there was a fairly dense population.

Prosthetized devices there had to take the lesser gravity into account and Andrew spent five years on the Moon working with local prosthetologists to make the necessary adaptations. When not at his work, he wandered among the robot population, every one of which treated him with the robotic obsequiousness due a man.

He came back to an Earth that was humdrum and quiet in comparison and visited the offices of Feingold and Martin to announce his return.

The current head of the firm, Simon DeLong, was surprised. He said, "We had been told you were returning, Andrew" (he had almost said "Mr. Martin"), "but we were not expecting you till next week."

"I grew impatient," said Andrew brusquely. He was anxious to get to the point. "On the Moon, Simon, I was in charge of a research team of twenty human scientists. I gave orders that no one questioned. The Lunar robots deferred to me as they would to a human being. Why, then, am I not a human being?"

A wary look entered DeLong's eyes. He said, "My dear Andrew, as you have just explained, you are treated as a human being by both robots and human beings. You are therefore a human being *de facto*."

"To be a human being *de facto* is not enough. I want not only to be treated as one, but to be legally identified as one. I want to be a human being *de jure*."

"Now that is another matter," said DeLong. "There we would run into human prejudice and into the undoubted fact that however much you may be like a human being, you are *not* a human being."

"In what way not?" asked Andrew. "I have the shape of a human being and organs equivalent to those of a human being. My organs, in fact, are identical to some of those in a prosthetized human being. I have contributed artistically, literarily, and scientifically to human culture as much as any human being now alive. What more can one ask?"

"I myself would ask nothing more. The trouble is that it would take an act of the World Legislature to define you as a human being. Frankly, I wouldn't expect that to happen."

"To whom on the Legislature could I speak?"

"To the chairman of the Science and Technology Committee perhaps."

"Can you arrange a meeting?"

"But you scarcely need an intermediary. In your position, you can—"

"No. *You* arrange it." (It didn't even occur to Andrew that he was giving a flat order to a human being. He had grown accustomed to that on the Moon.) "I want him to know that the firm of Feingold and Martin is backing me in this to the hilt."

"Well, now—"

"To the hilt, Simon. In one hundred and seventy-three years I have in one fashion or another contributed greatly to this firm. I have been under obligation to individual members of the firm in times past. I am not now. It is rather the other way around now and I am calling in my debts."

DeLong said, "I will do what I can."

# 18.

The chairman of the Science and Technology Committee was of the East Asian region and she was a woman. Her name was Chee Li-Hsing and her transparent garments (obscuring what she wanted obscured only by their dazzle) made her look plastic-wrapped.

She said, "I sympathize with your wish for full human rights. There have been times in history when segments of the human population fought for full human rights. What rights, however, can you possibly want that you do not have?"

"As simple a thing as my right to life. A robot can be dismantled at any time."

"A human being can be executed at any time."

"Execution can only follow due process of law. There is no trial needed for my dismantling. Only the word of a human being in authority is needed to end me. Besides—besides—" Andrew tried desperately to allow no sign of pleading, but his carefully designed tricks of human expression and tone of voice betrayed him here. "The truth is, I want to be a man. I have wanted it through six generations of human beings."

Li-Hsing looked up at him out of darkly sympathetic eyes. "The Legislature can pass a law declaring you one—they could pass a law declaring a stone statue to be defined as a man. Whether they will actually do so is, however, as likely in the first case as the second. Congresspeople are as human as the rest of the population and there is always that element of suspicion against robots."

"Even now?"

"Even now. We would all allow the fact that you have earned the prize of humanity and yet there would remain the fear of setting an undesirable precedent."

"What precedent? I am the only free robot, the only one of my type, and there will never be another. You may consult U.S. Robots."

" 'Never' is a long time, Andrew—or, if you prefer, Mr. Martin— since I will gladly give you my personal accolade as man. You will find that most Congresspeople will not be willing to set the precedent, no matter how meaningless such a precedent might be. Mr. Martin, you have my sympathy, but I cannot tell you to hope. Indeed—"

She sat back and her forehead wrinkled. "Indeed, if the issue grows too heated, there might well arise a certain sentiment, both inside the Legislature and outside, for that dismantling you mentioned. Doing away with you could turn out to be the easiest way of resolving the dilemma. Consider that before deciding to push matters."

Andrew said, "Will no one remember the technique of prosthetology, something that is almost entirely mine?"

"It may seem cruel, but they won't. Or if they do, it will be remembered against you. It will be said you did it only for yourself. It will be said it was part of a campaign to roboticize human beings, or to humanify robots; and in either case evil and vicious. You have never been part of a political hate campaign, Mr. Martin, and I tell you that you will be the object of vilification of a kind neither you nor I would credit and there would be people who'll believe it all. Mr. Martin, let your life be." She rose and, next to Andrew's seated figure, she seemed small and almost childlike.

Andrew said, "If I decide to fight for my humanity, will you be on my side?"

She thought, then said, "I will be—insofar as I can be. If at any time such a stand would appear to threaten my political future, I may have to abandon you, since it is not an issue I feel to be at the very root of my beliefs. I am trying to be honest with you."

"Thank you, and I will ask no more. I intend to fight this through whatever the consequences, and I will ask you for your help only for as long as you can give it."

## 19.

It was not a direct fight. Feingold and Martin counseled patience and Andrew muttered grimly that he had an endless supply of that. Feingold and Martin then entered on a campaign to narrow and restrict the area of combat.

They instituted a lawsuit denying the obligation to pay debts to an individual with a prosthetic heart on the grounds that the possession of a robotic organ removed humanity, and with it the constitutional rights of human beings.

They fought the matter skillfully and tenaciously, losing at every step but always in such a way that the decision was forced to be as broad as possible, and then carrying it by way of appeals to the World Court.

It took years, and millions of dollars.

When the final decision was handed down, DeLong held what amounted to a victory celebration over the legal loss. Andrew was, of course, present in the company offices on the occasion.

"We've done two things, Andrew," said DeLong, "both of which are good. First of all, we have etablished the fact that no number of artifacts in the human body causes it to cease being a human body. Secondly, we have engaged public opinion in the question in such a way as to put it fiercely on the side of a broad interpretation of humanity since there is not a human being in existence who does not hope for prosthetics if that will keep him alive."

"And do you think the Legislature will now grant me my humanity?" asked Andrew.

DeLong looked faintly uncomfortable. "As to that, I cannot be optimistic. There remains the one organ which the World Court has used as the criterion of humanity. Human beings have an organic cellular brain and robots have a platinum-iridium positronic brain if they have one at all—and you certainly have a positronic brain . . . No, Andrew, don't get that look in your eye. We lack the knowledge to duplicate the work of a cellular brain in artificial structures close enough to the organic type to allow it to fall within the Court's decision. Not even you could do it."

"What ought we do, then?"

"Make the attempt, of course. Congresswoman Li-Hsing will be on our side and a growing number of other Congresspeople. The President will undoubtedly go along with a majority of the Legislature in this matter."

"Do we have a majority?"

"No, far from it. But we might get one if the public will allow its desire for a broad interpretation of humanity to extend to you. A small chance, I admit, but if you do not wish to give up, we must gamble for it."

"I do not wish to give up."

# 20.

Congresswoman Li-Hsing was considerably older than she had been when Andrew had first met her. Her transparent garments were long gone. Her hair was now close-cropped and her coverings were tubular. Yet still Andrew clung, as closely as he could within his limits of reasonable taste, to the style of clothing that had prevailed when he had first adopted clothing over a century before.

She said, "We've gone as far as we can, Andrew. We'll try once more after recess, but, to be honest, defeat is certain and the whole thing will have to be given up. All my most recent efforts have only earned me a certain defeat in the coming congressional campaign."

"I know," said Andrew, "and it distresses me. You said once you would abandon me if it came to that. Why have you not done so?"

"One can change one's mind, you know. Somehow, abandoning you became a higher price than I cared to pay for just one more term. As it is, I've been in the Legislature for over a quarter of a century. It's enough."

"Is there no way we can change minds, Chee?"

"We've changed all that are amenable to reason. The rest—the majority—cannot be moved from their emotional antipathies."

"Emotional antipathy is not a valid reason for voting one way or the other."

"I know that, Andrew, but they don't advance emotional antipathy as their reason."

Andrew said cautiously, "It all comes down to the brain, then, but must we leave it at the level of cells versus positrons? Is there no way of forcing a functional definition? Must we say that a brain is made of this or that? May we not say that a brain is something—anything—capable of a certain level of thought?"

"Won't work," said Li-Hsing. "Your brain is man-made, the human brain is not. Your brain is constructed, theirs developed. To any human being who is intent on keeping up the barrier between himself and a robot, those differences are a steel wall a mile high and a mile thick."

"If we could get at the source of their antipathy—the very source of—"

"After all your years," said Li-Hsung sadly, "you are still trying to reason out the human being. Poor Andrew, don't be angry, but it's the robot in you that drives you in that direction."

"I don't know," said Andrew. "If I could bring myself—"

## 1. (reprise)

If he could bring himself—

He had known for a long time it might come to that, and in the end he was at the surgeon's. He found one, skillful enough for the job at hand, which meant a robot surgeon, for no human surgeon could be trusted in this connection, either in ability or in intention.

The surgeon could not have performed the operation on a human being, so Andrew, after putting off the moment of decision with a sad line of questioning that reflected the turmoil within himself, put the First Law to one side by saying, "I, too, am a robot."

He then said, as firmly as he had learned to form the words even at human beings over these past decades, "I *order* you to carry through the operation on me."

In the absence of the First Law, an order so firmly given from one who looked so much like a man activated the Second Law sufficiently to carry the day.

## 21.

Andrew's feeling of weakness was, he was sure, quite imaginary. He had recovered from the operation. Nevertheless, he leaned, as unobtrusively as he could manage, against the wall. It would be entirely too revealing to sit.

Li-Hsing said, "The final vote will come this week, Andrew. I've been able to delay it no longer, and we must lose . . . And that will be it, Andrew."

Andrew said, "I am grateful for your skill at delay. It gave me the time I needed, and I took the gamble I had to."

"What gamble is this?" asked Li-Hsing with open concern.

"I couldn't tell you, or the people at Feingold and Martin. I was sure I would be stopped. See here, if it is the brain that is at issue, isn't the greatest difference of all the matter of immortality? Who really cares what a brain looks like or is built or how it was formed? What matters is that brain cells must die; *must* die. Even if every other organ in the body is maintained or replaced, the brain cells, which cannot be replaced without changing and therefore killing the personality, must eventually die.

"My own positronic pathways have lasted nearly two centuries without perceptible change and can last for centuries more. Isn't *that* the fundamental barrier? Human beings can tolerate an immortal robot, for it doesn't matter how long a machine lasts. They cannot tolerate an immortal human being, since their own mortality is endurable only so long as it is universal. And for that reason they won't make me a human being."

Li-Hsing said, "What is it you're leading up to, Andrew?"

"I have removed that problem. Decades ago, my positronic brain was connected to organic nerves. Now, one last operation has arranged that connection in such a way that slowly—quite slowly—the potential is being drained from my pathways."

Li-Hsing's finely wrinkled face showed no expression for a moment. Then her lips tightened. "Do you mean you've arranged to die, Andrew? You can't have. That violates the Third Law."

"No," said Andrew, "I have chosen between the death of my body and the death of my aspirations and desires. To have let my body live at the cost of the greater death is what would have violated the Third Law."

Li-Hsing seized his arm as though she were about to shake him. She stopped herself. "Andrew, it won't work. Change it back."

"It can't be. Too much damage was done. I have a year to live—more or less. I will last through the two hundredth anniversary of my construction. I was weak enough to arrange that."

"How can it be worth it? Andrew, you're a fool."

"If it brings me humanity, that will be worth it. If it doesn't, it will bring an end to striving and that will be worth it, too."

And Li-Hsing did something that astonished herself. Quietly, she began to weep.

## 22.

It was odd how that last deed caught at the imagination of the world. All that Andrew had done before had not swayed them. But he had finally accepted even death to be human and the sacrifice was too great to be rejected.

The final ceremony was timed, quite deliberately, for the two hundredth anniversary. The World President was to sign the act and make it law and the ceremony would be visible on a global network and would be beamed to the Lunar state and even to the Martian colony.

Andrew was in a wheelchair. He could still walk, but only shakily.

With mankind watching, the World President said, "Fifty years ago, you were declared a Sesquicentennial Robot, Andrew." After a pause, and in a more solemn tone, he said, "Today we declare you a Bicentennial Man, Mr. Martin."

And Andrew, smiling, held out his hand to shake that of the President.

## 23.

Andrew's thoughts were slowly fading as he lay in bed.

Desperately he seized at them. Man! He was a man! He wanted that to be his last thought. He wanted to dissolve—die—with that.

He opened his eyes one more time and for one last time recognized Li-Hsing waiting solemnly. There were others, but those were only shadows, unrecognizable shadows. Only Li-Hsing stood out against the deepening gray. Slowly, inchingly, he held out his hand to her and very dimly and faintly felt her take it.

She was fading in his eyes, as the last of his thoughts trickled away.

But before she faded completely, one last fugitive thought came to him and rested for a moment on his mind before everything stopped.

"Little Miss," he whispered, too low to be heard.

# True Love

My name is Joe. That is what my colleague, Milton Davidson, calls me. He is a programmer and I am a computer program. I am part of the Multivac-complex and am connected with other parts all over the world. I know everything. Almost everything.

I am Milton's private program. His Joe. He understands more about programming than anyone in the world, and I am his experimental model. He has made me speak better than any other computer can.

"It is just a matter of matching sounds to symbols, Joe," he told me. "That's the way it works in the human brain even though we still don't know what symbols there are in the brain. I know the symbols in yours, and I can match them to words, one-to-one." So I talk. I don't think I talk as well as I think, but Milton says I talk very well. Milton has never married, he told me. One day he said, "I'll find her yet, Joe. I'm going to find the best. I'm going to solve the problems of the world. Solve *my* problem. Find me true love."

I said, "What is true love?"

"Never mind. That is abstract. Just find me the ideal girl. You are connected to the Multivac-complex so you can reach the data banks of every human being in the world. We'll eliminate them all by groups and classes until we're left with only one person. The perfect person. She will be for me."

I said, "I am ready."

He said, "Eliminate all men first."

It was easy. His words activated symbols in my molecular valves. I could reach out to make contact with the accumulated data on every human being in the world. At his words, I withdrew from 3,784,982,874 men. I kept contact with 3,786,112,090 women.

He said, "Eliminate all younger than twenty-five; all older than forty. Then eliminate all with an IQ under 120; all with a height of under 150 centimeters and over 175 centimeters."

He gave me exact measurements; he eliminated women with living children; he eliminated women with various genetic characteristics. "I'm not sure about eye color," he said. "Let that go for a while. But no red hair. I don't like red hair."

After two weeks, we were down to 235 women. They all spoke English very well. Milton said he didn't want a language problem. Even computer-translation would get in the way at intimate moments.

"I can't interview 235 women," he said. "It would take too much time, and people would discover what I am doing."

"It would make trouble," I said. Milton had arranged me to do things I wasn't designed to do. No one knew about that.

"It's none of their business," he said, and the skin on his face grew red. "I tell you what Joe, I will bring in holographs, and you check the list for similarities."

He brought in holographs of women. "These are three beauty contest winners," he said. "Do any of the 235 match?"

Eight were very good matches and Milton said, "Good, you have their data banks. Study requirements and needs in the job market and arrange to have them assigned here. One at a time, of course." He thought a while, moved his shoulders up and down, and said, "Alphabetical order."

That is one of the things I am not designed to do. Shifting people from job to job for personal reasons is called manipulation. I could do it now because Milton had arranged it. I wasn't supposed to do it for anyone but him, though.

The first girl arrived a week later. Milton's face turned red when he saw her. He spoke as though it were hard to do so. They were together a great deal and he paid no attention to me. One time he said, "Let me take you to dinner."

The next day he said to me, "It was no good, somehow. There was something missing. She is a beautiful woman, but I did not feel any touch of true love. Try the next one."

It was the same with all eight. They were much alike. They smiled a great deal and had pleasant voices, but Milton always found it wasn't right. He said, "I can't understand it, Joe. You and I have picked out the eight women who, in all the world, look the best to me. They are ideal. Why don't they please me?"

I said, "Do you please them?"

His eyebrows moved and he pushed one fist hard against his other hand. "That's it, Joe. It's a two-way street. If I am not their ideal, they can't act in such a way as to be my ideal. I must be their true love, too, but how do I do that?" He seemed to be thinking all that day.

The next morning he came to me and said, "I'm going to leave it to you, Joe. All up to you. You have my data bank, and I am going to tell you everything I know about myself. You fill up my data bank in every possible detail but keep all additions to yourself."

"What will I do with the data bank, then, Milton?"

"Then you will match it to the 235 women. No, 227. Leave out the eight you've seen. Arrange to have each undergo a psychiatric examination. Fill up their data banks and compare them with mine. Find correlations." (Arranging psychiatric examinations is another thing that is against my original instructions.)

For weeks, Milton talked to me. He told me of his parents and his siblings. He told me of his childhood and his schooling and his adolescence. He told me of the young women he had admired from a distance. His data bank grew and he adjusted me to broaden and deepen my symbol-taking.

He said, "You see, Joe, as you get more and more of me in you, I adjust you to match me better and better. You get to think more like me, so you understand me better. If you understand me well enough, then any woman, whose data bank is something you understand as well, would be my true love." He kept talking to me and I came to understand him better and better.

I could make longer sentences and my expressions grew more complicated. My speech began to sound a good deal like his in vocabulary, word order and style.

I said to him one time, "You see, Milton, it isn't a matter of fitting a girl to a physical ideal only. You need a girl who is a personal, emotional, temperamental fit to you. If that happens, looks are secondary. If we can't find the fit in these 227, we'll look elsewhere. We will find someone who won't care how you look either, or how anyone would look, if only there is the personality fit. What are looks?"

"Absolutely," he said. "I would have known this if I had had more to do with women in my life. Of course, thinking about it makes it all plain now."

We always agreed; we thought so like each other.

"We shouldn't have any trouble, now, Milton, if you'll let me ask you questions. I can see where, in your data bank, there are blank spots and unevennesses."

What followed, Milton said, was the equivalent of a careful psychoanalysis. Of course. I was learning from the psychiatric examinations of the 227 women—on all of which I was keeping close tabs.

Milton seemed quite happy. He said, "Talking to you, Joe, is almost like talking to another self. Our personalities have come to match perfectly."

"So will the personality of the woman we choose."

For I had found her and she was one of the 227 after all. Her name waas Charity Jones and she was an Evaluator at the Library of History in Wichita. Her extended data bank fit ours perfectly. All the other women had fallen into discard in one respect or another as the data banks grew fuller, but with Charity there was an increasing and astonishing resonance.

I didn't have to describe her to Milton. Milton had coordinated my symbolism so closely with his own I could tell the resonance directly. It fit me.

Next it was a matter of adjusting the work sheets and job requirements in such a way as to get Charity assigned to us. It must be done very delicately, so no one would know that anything illegal had taken place.

Of course, Milton himself knew, since it was he who arranged it and that had to be taken care of too. When they came to arrest him on grounds of malfeasance in office, it was, fortunately, for something that had taken place ten years ago. He had told me about it, of course, so it was easy to arrange—and he won't talk about me for that would make his offense much worse.

He's gone, and tomorrow is February 14. Valentine's Day. Charity will arrive then with her cool hands and her sweet voice. I will teach her how to operate me and how to care for me. What do looks matter when our personalities will resonate?

I will say to her, "I am Joe, and you are my true love."

# Found!

Computer-Two, like the other three that chased each other's tails in orbit round the Earth, was much larger than it had to be.

It might have been one tenth its diameter and yet contained all the volume it needed to store the accumulated and accumulating data needed to control space flight.

They needed the extra space, however, so that Joe and I could get inside, if we had to.

And we had to.

Computer-Two was perfectly capable of taking care of itself. Ordinarily, that is. It was redundant. It worked everything out three times in parallel and all three programs had to mesh perfectly; all three answers had to match. If they did not, the answer was delayed for nano-seconds while Computer-Two checked itself, found the malfunctioning part and replaced it.

There was no sure way in which ordinary people would know how many times it caught itself. Perhaps never. Perhaps twice a day. Only Computer-Central could measure the time delay induced by error and only Computer-Central knew how many of the component spares had been used as replacements. And Computer-Central never talked about it. The only good public image is perfection.

And for all practical purposes, it's *been* perfection, for there was never any call for Joe and me.

We're the trouble-shooters. We go up there when something really goes wrong and Computer-Two or one of the others can't correct itself. It's never happened in the five years we've been on the job. It did happen now and again in the early days of their existence, but that was before our time.

We keep in practice. Don't get me wrong. There isn't a computer made that Joe and I can't diagnose. Show us the error and we'll show you the malfunction. Or Joe will, anyway. I'm not the kind who sings one's own praises.

Anyway, this time, neither of us could make the diagnosis.

The first thing that happened was that Computer-Two lost internal pressure. That's not unprecedented and it's certainly not fatal.

Computer-Two can work in a vacuum after all. An internal atmosphere was established in the old days when it was expected there would be a steady flow of repairmen fiddling with it. And it's been kept up out of tradition. Who told you scientists aren't chained by tradition? In their spare time from being scientists, they're human, too.

From the rate of pressure loss, it was deduced that a gravel-sized meteoroid had hit Computer-Two. Its exact radius, mass and energy was reported by Computer-Two itself, using that rate of pressure loss, and a few other things, as data.

The second thing that happened was that the break was not sealed and the atmosphere was not regenerated. After that came the errors and they called us in.

It made no sense. Joe let a look of pain cross his homely face and said, "There must be a dozen things out of whack."

Someone at Computer-Central said, "The hunk of gravel ricocheted, very likely."

Joe said, "With that energy of entry, it would have passed right through the other side. No ricochets. Besides, even with ricochets, I figure it would have had to take some very unlikely strikes."

"Well, then, what do we do?"

Joe looked uncomfortable. I think that it was at this point that he realized what was coming. He had made it sound peculiar enough to require the trouble-shooters on the spot—and Joe had never been up in space. If he had told me once that his chief reason for taking the job was that he knew it meant he would never have to go up in space, he had told it to me $2^x$ times, with $x$ a pretty high number.

So I said it for him. I said, "We'll have to go up there."

Joe's only way out would have been to say he didn't think he could handle the job, and I watched his pride slowly come out ahead of his cowardice. Not by much, you understand—by a nose, let's say.

* * *

To those of you who haven't been on a spaceship in the last fifteen years—and I suppose Joe can't be the only one—let me emphasize that the initial acceleration is the only troublesome thing. You can't get away from that, of course.

After that it's nothing, unless you want to count possible boredom. You're just a spectator. The whole thing is automated and computerized. The old romantic days of space pilots are gone totally. I imagine they'll return briefly when our space settlements make the shift to the asteroid belt as they constantly threaten to do—but then only until additional Computers are placed in orbit to set up the necessary additional capacity.

Joe held his breath throughout the acceleration, or at least he seemed to. (I must admit that I wasn't very comfortable myself. It was only my third trip. I've taken a couple of vacations on Settlement-Rho with my husband, but I'm not exactly a seasoned hand.)

After that, he was relieved for a while, but only for a while. He got despondent.

"I hope this thing knows where it's going," he said, pettishly.

I extended my arms forward, palms up, and felt the rest of me sway backward a bit in the zero-gravity field. "You," I said, "are a computer specialist. Don't you *know* it knows?"

"Sure, but Computer-Two is off."

"We're not hooked into Computer-Two." I said. "There are three others. And even if only one were left functional, it could handle all the space flights undertaken on an average day."

"All four might go off. If Computer-Two is wrong, what's to stop the rest?"

"Then we'll run this thing manually."

"You'll do it, I suppose? You know how—I think not?"

"So they'll talk me in."

"For the love of Eniac," he groaned.

There was no problem, actually. We moved out to Computer-Two as smooth as vacuum and less than two days after takeoff, we were placed into a parking orbit not ten meters behind it.

What was not so smooth was that, about twenty hours out, we got the news from Earth that Computer-Three was losing internal pressure. Whatever had hit Computer-Two was going to get the rest, and when all four were out, space flight would grind to a halt. It could be reorganized on a manual basis, surely, but that would take months as a minimum, possibly years, and there would be serious economic dislocation on Earth. Worse yet, several thousand people now out in space would surely die.

It wouldn't bear thinking of and neither Joe nor I talked about it, but it didn't make Joe's disposition sweeter and, let's face it, it didn't make me any happier.

Earth hung over 200,000 kilometers below us, but Joe didn't seem to be bothered by that. He was concentrating on his tether and was checking the cartridge in his reaction-gun. He wanted to make sure he could get to Computer-Two and back again.

You'd be surprised—if you've never tried it—how you can get your space legs if you absolutely have to. I wouldn't say there was nothing to it and we did waste half the fuel we used, but we finally reached Computer-Two. We hardly made any bump at all when we struck Computer-Two. (You hear it, of course, even in vacuum, because the vibration travels through the metalloid fabric of your space suits—but there was hardly any bump, just a whisper.)

Of course, our contact and the addition of our momentum altered the orbit of Computer-Two slightly, but tiny expenditures of fuel compensated for that and we didn't have to worry about it. Computer-Two took care of it, for nothing had gone wrong with it, as far as we could tell, that affected any of its external workings.

* * *

We went over the outside first, naturally. The chances were pretty overwhelming that a small piece of gravel had whizzed through Computer-Two and that would leave an unmistakable ragged hole. Two of them in all probability; one going in and one coming out.

Chances of that happening are one in two million on any given day—even money that it will happen at least once in six thousand years. It's not likely, but it can, you know. The chances are one in not more than ten billion that, on any one day, it will be struck by a meteoroid large enough to demolish it.

I didn't mention that because Joe might realize that we were exposed to similar odds ourselves. In fact, any given strike on us would do far more damage to our soft and tender bodies than to the stoical and much-enduring machinery of the computer, and I didn't want Joe more nervous than he was.

The thing is, though, it wasn't a meteoroid.

"What's this?" said Joe, finally.

It was a small cylinder stuck to the outer wall of Computer-Two, the first abnormality we had found in its outward appearance. It was about half a centimeter in diameter and perhaps six centimeters long. Just about cigarette-sized for any of you who've been caught up in the antique fad of smoking.

We brought our small flashlights into play.

I said, "That's not one of the external components."

"It sure isn't," muttered Joe.

There was a faint spiral marking running round the cylinder from one end to the other. Nothing else. For the rest, it was clearly metal, but of an odd, grainy texture—at least to the eye.

Joe said, "It's not tight."

He touched it gently with a fat and gauntleted finger and it gave. Where it had made contact with the surface of Computer-Two, it lifted and our flashes shone down on a visible gap.

"There's the reason gas pressure inside declined to zero," I said.

Joe grunted. He pushed a little harder and the cylinder dropped away and began to drift. We managed to snare it after a little trouble. Left behind was a perfectly round hole in the skin of Computer-Two, half a centimeter across.

Joe said, "This thing, whatever it is, isn't much more than foil."

It gave easily under his fingers, thin but springy. A little extra pressure and it dented. He put it inside his pouch, which he snapped shut, and said, "Go over the outside and see if there are any other items like that anywhere on it. I'll go inside."

It didn't take me very long. Then I went in. "It's clean," I said. "That's the only thing there is. The only hole."

"One is enough," said Joe, gloomily. He looked at the smooth aluminum of the wall and, in the light of the flash, the perfect circle of black was beautifully evident.

* * *

It wasn't difficult to place a seal over the hole. It was a little more difficult to reconstitute the atmosphere. Computer-Two's reserve gas-forming supplies were low and the controls required manual adjustment. The solar generator was limping but we managed to get the lights on.

Eventually, we removed our gauntlets and helmet, but Joe carefully placed the gauntlets inside his helmet and secured them both to one of his suit-loops.

"I want these handy if the air pressure begins to drop," he said, sourly.

So I did the same. No use being devil-may-care.

There was a mark on the wall just next to the hole. I had noted it in the light of my flash when I was adjusting the seal. When the lights came on, it was obvious.

"You notice that, Joe?" I said.

"I notice."

There was a slight, narrow depression in the wall, not very noticeable at all, but it was there beyond doubt if you ran your finger over it and it continued for nearly a meter. It was as though someone had scooped out a very shallow sampling of the metal and the surface where that had taken place was distinctly less smooth than elsewhere.

I said, "We'd better call Computer-Central downstairs."

"If you mean back on Earth, say so," said Joe. "I hate that phony space-talk. In fact, I hate everything about space. That's why I took an Earth-side job—I mean a job on Earth—or what was supposed to be one."

I said patiently, "We'd better call Computer-Central back on Earth."

"What for?"

"To tell them we've found the trouble."

"Oh? What did we find?"

"The hole. Remember?"

"Oddly enough, I do. And what caused the hole? It wasn't a meteoroid. I never saw one that would leave a perfectly circular hole with no signs of buckling or melting. And I never saw one that left a cylinder behind." He took the cylinder out of his suit pocket and smoothed the dent out of its thin metal, thoughtfully. "Well, what caused the hole?"

I didn't hesitate. I said, "I don't know."

"If we report to Computer-Central, they'll ask the question and we'll say we don't know and what will we have gained? Except hassle?"

"They'll call us, Joe, if we don't call them."

"Sure. And we won't answer, will we?"

"They'll assume something killed us, Joe, and they'll send up a relief party."

"You know Computer-Central. It will take them at least two days to decide on that. We'll have something before then and once we have something, we'll call them."

* * *

The internal structure of Computer-Two was not *really* designed for human occupancy. What was foreseen and allowed for was the occasional and temporary presence of trouble-shooters. That meant there was room for maneuvering and there were tools and supplies.

There weren't any armchairs, though. For that matter, there was no gravitational field, either, or any centrifugal imitation of one.

We both floated in midair, drifting very slowly this way or that. Occasionally, one of us touched the wall and rebounded very slowly. Or else part of one of us overlapped part of the other.

"Keep your foot out of my mouth," said Joe, and pushed it away violently. It was a mistake because we both began to turn. Of course, that's not how it looked to us. To us, it was the interior of Computer-Two that was turning, which was most unpleasant, and it took us a while to get relatively motionless again.

We had the theory perfectly worked out in our Earth-side training, but we were short on practice. A lot short.

By the time we had steadied ourselves, I felt unpleasantly nauseated. You can call it nausea, or astronausea, or space sickness, but whatever you call it, it's the heaves and it's worse in space than anywhere else, because there's nothing to pull the stuff down. It floats around in a cloud of globules and you don't want to be floating around with it.—So I held it back, and so did Joe.

I said, "Joe, it's clearly the computer that's at fault. Let's get at its insides." Anything to get my mind off *my* insides and let them quiet down. Besides, things weren't moving fast enough. I kept thinking of Computer-Three on its way down the tube; maybe Computers-One and -Four by now, too; and thousands of people in space with their lives hanging on what we could do.

Joe looked a little greenish, too, but he said, "First I've got to think. Something got it. It wasn't a meteoroid, because whatever it was chewed a neat hole out of the hull. It wasn't cut out because I didn't find a circle of metal anywhere inside here. Did you?"

"No. But it hadn't occurred to me to look."

"*I* looked, and it's nowhere in here."

"It may have fallen outside."

"With the cylinder covering the hole till I pulled it away? A likely thing. Did you see anything come flying out?"

"No."

Joe said, "We may still find it in here, of course, but I doubt it. It was somehow dissolved and something got in."

"What something? Whose is it?"

Joe's grin was remarkably ill-natured. "Why do you bother asking questions to which there is no answer. If this was last century, I'd say the Russians had somehow stuck that device onto the outside of Computer-Two.—No offense. If it were last century, you'd say it was the Americans."

I decided to be offended. I said, coldly, "We're trying to say something that makes sense *this* century, Iosif," giving it an exaggerated Russian pronunciation.

"We'll have to assume some dissident group."

"If so," I said, "we'll have to assume one with a capacity for space flight and with the ability to come up with an unusual device."

Joe said, "Space flight presents no difficulties, if you can tap into the orbiting Computers illegally—which has been done. As for the cylinder, that may make more sense when it is analyzed back on Earth—downstairs, as you space buffs would say."

"It doesn't make sense," I said. "Where's the point in trying to disable Computer-Two?"

"As part of a program to cripple space flight."

"Then everyone suffers. The dissidents, too."

"But it gets everyone's attention, doesn't it, and suddenly the cause of whatever-it-is makes news. Or the plan is to just knock out Computer-Two and then threaten to knock out the other three. No real damage, but lots of potential, and lots of publicity."

"I don't believe it," I said. "It's too dramatic."

"On the contrary," said Joe. "I'm trying to be nondramatic." He was studying all parts of the interior closely, edging over it square centimeter by square centimeter. "I *might* suppose the thing was nonhuman origin."

"Don't be silly."

"You want me to make the case? The cylinder made contact, after which something inside ate away a circle of metal and entered Computer-Two. It crawled over the inside wall eating away a thin layer of metal for some reason. Does that sound like anything of human construction?"

"Not that I know of, but I don't know everything. Even you don't know everything."

Joe ignored that. "So the question is, how did it—whatever it is—get into the computer, which is, after all, reasonably well-sealed. It did so quickly, since it knocked out the resealing and air-regeneration capacities almost at once."

"Is *that* what you're looking for?" I said, pointing.

He tried to stop too quickly and somersaulted backward, crying. "That's it! That's it!"

In his excitement, he was thrashing his arms and legs which got him nowhere, of course. I grabbed him and, for a while, we were both trying to exert pushes in uncoordinated directions and that got us nowhere either. Joe called me a few names, but I called him some back and I had the advantage of him there. I understand English perfectly, better than he does, in fact; but his knowledge of Russian is—well, fragmentary would be a kind of way of putting it. Bad language in an ununderstood language always sounds very dramatic.

"Here is it," he said, when we had finally sorted ourselves out.

Where the computer-shielding met the wall, there was a small circular hole left behind when Joe brushed aside a small cylinder. It was just like the one on the outer hull, but it seemed even thinner. In fact, it seemed to disintegrate when Joe touched it.

"We'd better get into the computer," said Joe.

* * *

The computer was a shambles.

Not obviously. I don't mean to say it was like a beam of wood that had been riddled by termites.

In fact, if you looked at the computer casually, you might swear it was intact.

Look closely, though, and some of the chips would be gone. The more closely you looked, the more you realized were gone. Worse yet, the stores which Computer-Two used in self-repair had dwindled to almost nothing. We kept looking and every once in a while, one of us would discover something else was missing.

Joe took the cylinder out of his pouch again and turned it end for end. He said, "I suspect it's after high-grade silicon in particular. I can't say for sure, of course, but my guess is that the sides are mostly aluminum but that the flat end is mostly silicon."

I said, "Do you mean the thing is a solar battery?"

"Part of it is. That's how it gets its energy in space; energy to get to Computer-Two, energy to eat a hole into it, energy to—to—I don't know how else to put it. Energy to stay alive."

"You call it alive?"

"Why not? Look, Computer-Two can repair itself. It can reject faulty bits of equipment and replace it with working ones, but it needs a supply of spares to work with. Given enough spares of all kinds, it could build a Computer just like itself, when properly programmed—but it needs the supply, so we don't think of it as alive. This object that entered Computer-Two is apparently collecting its own supplies. That's suspiciously life-like."

"What you're saying," I said, "is that we have here a microcomputer advanced enough to be considered alive."

"I don't honestly know what I'm saying," said Joe.

"Who on Earth could make such a thing?"

"Who *on Earth*?"

* * *

I made the next discovery. It looked like a stubby pen drifting through the air. I just caught it out of the corner of my eye and registered as a pen.

In zero gravity, things will drift out of pockets and float off. There's no way of keeping anything in place unless it is physically confined. You expect pens and coins and anything else that can find an opening to drift their way through the opening eventually and go wherever air currents and inertia lead them.

So my mind registered "Pen" and I groped for it absently and, of course, my fingers didn't close on it. Just reaching for something sets up an air current that pushes it away. You have to reach over it and sneak behind it with one hand, and then reach for it with the other. Picking up any small object in midair is a two-hand operation.

I know some people can do it one-handed, but they're space hounds and I'm not.

I turned to look at the object and pay a little more attention to retrieval, then realized that my pen was safely in its pouch. I felt for it and it was there.

"Did you lose a pen, Joe?" I called out.

"No."

"Anything like that? Key? Cigarette?"

"I don't smoke. You know that."

A stupid answer. "Anything?" I said in exasperation. "I'm seeing things here."

"No one ever said you were stable."

"Look, Joe. Over there. Over there."

He lunged for it. I could have told him it would do no good.

By now, though, our poking around in the computer seemed to have stirred things up. We were seeing them wherever we looked. They were floating in the air currents.

I stopped one at last. Or, rather, it stopped itself, for it was on the elbow of Joe's suit. I snatched it off and shouted. Joe jumped in terror and nearly knocked it out of my hand.

I said, "Look!"

There was a shiny circle on Joe's suit where I had taken the thing off. It had begun to eat its way through.

"Give it to me," said Joe. He took it gingerly and put it against the wall to hold it steady. Then he shelled it, gently lifting the paper-thin metal.

There was something inside that looked like a line of cigarette ash. It caught the light and glinted, though, like lightly woven metal.

There was a moistness about it, too. It wriggled slowly, one end seeming to seek something blindly.

The end made contact with the wall and stuck. Joe's fingers pushed it away. It seemed to require a small effort to do so. Joe rubbed his finger and thumb and said, "Feels oily."

The metal worm—I don't know what else I can call it—seemed limp now after Joe had touched it. It didn't move again.

I was twisting and turning, trying to look at myself.

"Joe," I said, "for heaven's sake, have I got one of them on me anywhere?"

"I don't see one," he said.

"Well, *look* at me. You've got to watch me, Joe, and I'll watch you. If our suits are wrecked we might not be able to get back to the ship."

Joe said, "Keep moving, then."

It was a grisly feeling, being surrounded by things hungry to dissolve your suit wherever they could touch it. When any showed up, we tried to catch them and stay out of their way at the same time, which made things almost impossible. A rather long one drifted close to my leg and I kicked at it, which was stupid, for if I had hit it, it might have stuck. As it was, the air current I set up brought it against the wall, where it stayed.

Joe reached hastily for it—too hastily. The rest of his body rebounded and as he somersaulted, one booted foot struck the wall near the cylinder lightly. When he finally managed to right himself, it was still there.

"I didn't smash it, did I?"

"No, you didn't," I said. "You missed it by a decimeter. It won't get away."

I had a hand on either side of it. It was twice as long as the other cylinder had been. In fact, it was like two cylinders stuck together lengthwise, with a constriction at the point of joining.

"Act of reproducing," said Joe as he peeled away the metal. This time what was inside was a line of dust. Two lines. One on either side of the constriction.

"It doesn't take much to kill them," said Joe. He relaxed visibly. "I think we're safe."

"They do seem alive," I said, reluctantly.

"I think they seem more than that. They're viruses.—Or the equivalent."

"What are you talking about?"

Joe said, "Granted I'm a computer technologist and not a virologist—but it's my understanding that viruses on Earth, or, downstairs, as you would say, consist of a nucleic acid molecule coated in a protein shell.

"When a virus invades a cell, it manages to dissolve a hole in the cell wall or membrane by the use of some appropriate enzyme and the nucleic acid slips inside, leaving the protein coat outside. Inside the cell it finds the material to make a new protein coat for itself. In fact, it manages to form replicas of itself and to form a new protein coat for each replica. Once it has stripped the cell of all it has, the cell dissolves and in place of the one invading virus there are several hundred daughter viruses. Sound familiar?"

"Yes. Very familiar. It's what's happening here. But where did it come from, Joe?"

"Not from Earth, obviously, or any Earth settlement. From somewhere else, I suppose. They drift through space till they find something appropriate in which they can multiply. They look for sizable objects ready-made of metal. I don't imagine they can smelt ores."

"But large metal objects with pure silicon components and a few other succulent matters like that are the products of intelligent life only," I said.

"Right," said Joe, "which means we have the best evidence yet that intelligent life is common in the Universe, since objects like the one we're on must be quite common or it couldn't support these viruses. And it means that intelligent life is old, too, perhaps ten billion years old—long enough for a kind of metal evolution, forming a metal/silicon/oil life as we have formed a nucleic/protein/water life. Time to evolve a parasite on space-age artifacts."

I said, "You make it sound as though every time some intelligent life form develops a space culture, it is subjected before long to parasitic infestation."

"Right. And it must be controlled. Fortunately, these things are easy to kill, especially now when they're forming. Later on, when they're ready to burrow out of Computer-Two, I suppose they will grow, thicken their shells, stabilize their interior and prepare, as the equivalent of spores, to drift a million years before they find another home. They might not be so easy to kill, then."

"How are you going to kill them?"

"I already have. I just touched that first one when it instinctively sought out metal to begin manufacturing a new shell after I had broken open the first one—and that touch finished it. I didn't touch the second, but I kicked the wall near it and the sound vibration in the metal shook it interior apart into metal dust. So they can't get us, now, or any more of the computer if we just shake them apart now!"

He didn't have to explain further—or as much. He put on his

gauntlets slowly, and then banged at the wall with one. It pushed him away and he kicked at the wall where he next approached it.

"You do the same," he shouted.

I tried to, and for a while we both kept at it. You don't know how hard it is to hit a wall at zero gravity, at least on purpose, and do it hard enough to make it clang. We missed as often as not or just struck it a glancing blow that sent us whirling but made virtually no sound. We were panting with effort and aggravation in no time.

But we had acclimated ourselves (or at least I had) and the nausea didn't return. We kept it up and then when we gathered up some more of the viruses, there was nothing inside but dust in every case. They were clearly adapted to empty, automated space object which, like modern computers, were vibration-free. That's what made it possible, I suppose, to build up the exceedingly rickety complex metallic structures that possessed sufficient instability to produce the properties of simple life.

I said, "Do you think we got them all, Joe?"

"How can I say? If there's one left, it will cannibalize the others for metal supplies and start all over. Let's bang around some more."

We did until we were sufficiently worn out not to care whether one was still left alive.

"Of course," I said, panting, "the Planetary Association for the Advancement of Science isn't going to be pleased with our killing them all."

Joe's suggestion as to what the P.A.A.S. could do with itself was forceful, but impractical. He said, "Look, our mission is to save Computer-Two, a few thousand lives and, as it turned out, our own lives, too. Now they can decide whether to renovate this computer or rebuild it from scratch. It's their baby.

"The P.A.A.S. can get what they can out of these dead objects and that should be something. If they want live ones, I suspect they'll find them floating about in these regions. They can look for them if they want live specimens, but they'd better watch their suits at all times. I don't think they can vibrate them to death in open space."

I said, "All right. My suggestion is we tell Computer-Central we're going to jerry-rig this Computer and get it doing some work anyway, and we'll stay till a relief is up for main repairs or whatever in order to prevent any reinfestation. Meanwhile, they better get to each of the other Computers and set up a system that can set it to vibrating strongly as soon as the internal atmosphere shows a pressure drop."

"Simple enough," said Joe, sardonically.

"It's lucky we found them when we did."

"Wait awhile," said Joe, and the look in his eye was one of deep trouble. "We didn't find them. *They* found *us*. If metal life has developed, do you suppose it's likely that this is the only form it takes? Just this fragile kind?

"What if such life forms communicate somehow and, across the vastness of space, others are now converging on us for the picking? Other species, too; all of them after the lush new fodder of an as yet untouched space culture. *Other* species! Some that are sturdy enough to withstand vibration. Some that are large enough to be more versatile in their reactions to danger. Some that are equipped to invade our settlements in orbit. Some, for the sake of Univac, that may be able to invade the Earth for the metals of its cities.

"What I'm going to report, what I must report, is that we've been *found!*"

# Nothing For Nothing

The scene was Earth.

Not that the beings on the starship thought of it as Earth. To them it was a series of symbols stored in a computer; it was the third planet of a star located at a certain position with respect to the line connecting their home planet with the black hole that marked the Galaxy's center, and moving at a certain velocity with reference to it.

The time was 15000 B.C., more or less.

Not that the beings on the starship thought of it as 15000 B.C. To them, it was a certain period of time marked off according to their local system of measurement.

The captain of the starship said, rather petulantly, "This is a waste of time. The planet is largely frozen. Let us leave."

But the ship's explorer quietly said, "No, Captain." and that was that.

As long as a starship was in space, or in hyperspace for that matter, the captain was supreme, but place that ship in orbit about a planet and the explorer could not be challenged. He knew worlds! That was his specialty.

And this explorer was in an impregnable position. He had what amounted to a sure instinct for profitable trade. It had been he and he alone who was responsible for the fact that this particular starship had won three Awards for Excellence for the work done in its three last expeditions. Three for three.

So when the explorer said, "No," the captain could not dream of "Yes." Even in the unlikely case that he had, the crew would have mutinied. An Award for Excellence might be, to the captain, a pleasant spectral disk to suspend in the main salon, but to the crew it meant a spectacular addition to take-home pay and an even more welcome addition to vacation time and pension benefits. And this explorer had brought them that three times. Three for three.

The explorer said, "No strange world should be left unexamined."

The captain said, "What is strange about this one?"

"The preliminary probe shows intelligence, and on a frozen world."

"Surely that's not unprecedented."

"The pattern here is strange," the explorer looked uneasy. "I am not sure exactly how or exactly why, but the pattern of life and of intelligence is strange. We must examine it more carefully."

And that was that, of course. There were at least half a trillion planetary worlds in the Galaxy, if one only counted those associated with stars. Add to that the indefinite number moving independently through space and the number might be ten times as great.

Even with computers to help, no starship could know them all, but an experienced explorer, by dint of lacking interest in anything else, of studying every exploratory report published, of considering endless correlations, and, presumably, playing with statistics even in his sleep, grew to have what seemed to others a mystical intuition about such things.

"We'll have to send out probes in full interlocking program," said the explorer.

The captain looked outraged. Full power meant a leisurely examination for weeks at enormous expense.

He said, and it was as much as he could offer in the way of objection, "Is that absolutely necessary?"

"I rather think so," said the explorer with the self-confidence of one who knows his whim is law.

* * *

The probes brought back exactly what the captain expected, and in great detail. An intelligent species rather reminiscent, at least as far as superficial appearance went, of the lesser breeds of the inner proximal regions of the fifth arm of the Galaxy—not quite unusual, but of interest to mentologists, no doubt.

As yet the intelligent species was only at the first level of technology—long, long removed from anything useful.

The captain said so, scarcely able to mask his exasperation, but the explorer, leafing through the reports, remained unmoved. He said, "Strange!" and asked that the trader be summoned.

This was really too much. A successful captain must never give a good explorer cause for unhappiness but there are limits to everything.

The captain said, fighting to keep the level of communication polite, if not friendly, "To what end, Explorer? What can we expect at this level?"

"They have tools," said the explorer thoughtfully.

"Stone! Bone! Wood! Or this planet's equivalent of that. And that's all. Surely we can find nothing in that."

"And yet there is something strange in the pattern."

"May I know what that might be, Explorer?"

"If I knew what it might be, Captain, it would not be strange, and I would not have to find out. Really, Captain, I must insist on the Trader."

*  *  *

The trader was as indignant as the captain was, and had more scope to express it. His, after all, was a speciality as deep as that of anyone's on the starship, even, in his own opinion (and in some other's), as deep and as essential as the explorer's.

The captain might navigate a starship and the explorer might detect useful civilizations by the most tenuous of signs, but in the final clutch it was the trader and his team who faced the aliens and who plucked out of their minds and culture that which was useful and gave in return something *they* found useful.

And this was done at great risk. The alien ecology must not be disrupted. Alien intelligences must not be harmed, not even to save one's own life. There were good reasons for that on the cosmic scale and traders were amply rewarded for the risks they ran, but why run *useless* risks.

The trader said, "There is nothing there. *My* interpretation of the probe's data is that we're dealing with semi-intelligent animals. Their usefulness is nil. Their danger is great. We know how to deal with truly intelligent aliens and trader teams are rarely killed by them. Who knows how these animals will react—and you know we are not allowed to defend ourselves properly."

The explorer said, "These animals, if they are no more than that, have interestingly adapted themselves to the ice. There are subtle variations in the pattern here I do not understand, but my considered opinion is that they will not be dangerous and that they may even be useful. I feel they are worth closer examination."

"What can be gained from a Stone Age intelligence?" asked the trader.

"That is for you to find out."

The trader thought grimly: Of course, that is what it comes to—for *us* to find out.

He knew well the history and purpose of the starship expeditions. There had been a time, a million years before, when there had been no traders, explorers, or captains but only ancestral animals with developing mind and a Stone Age technology—much like the animals on the world they were now orbiting. How slow the advance, how painfully slow the self-generated progress—until the third-level civilization had been reached. Then had come the starships and the chance of cross-fertilization of cultures. *Then* had come progress.

The trader said, "With respect, Explorer, I grant your intuitional experience. Will you grant my practical experience, though it is less dramatic? There is no way in which anything below a third-level civilization can have anything we can use."

"That," said the explorer, "is a generalization that may or may not be true."

"With respect, Explorer. It *is* true. And even if those—those semianimals had something we could use, and I can't imagine what it might be, what can we give them in exchange?"

The explorer was silent.

The trader went on. "At this level, there is no way in which a protointelligence can accept an alien stimulation. The mentologists are agreed on that and it is my experience, too. Progress *must* be self-generated until at least the second level is reached. And we *must* make a return; we can take nothing for nothing."

The captain said, "And that makes sense, of course. By stimulating these intelligences to advance, we can harvest them again at a later visit."

"I don't care about the reason for it," said the trader, impatiently. "It is part of the tradition of my profession. We do no harm under any conditions and we give a return for what we take. Here there is nothing we will want to take; and even if we find something, there will be nothing that we can give in return.—We waste time."

The explorer shook his head. "I ask you to visit some center of population, Trader. I will abide by your decision when you return."

And that was that, too.

* * *

For two days the small trader module flashed over the surface of the planet searching for any evidence of a reasonable level of technology. There was none.

A complete search could take years but was scarcely worth it. It was unreasonable to suppose a high level would be hidden. The highest technology was always flaunted for it had no enemy. That was the universal experience of traders everywhere.

It was a beautiful planet, half-frozen as it was. White and blue and green. Wild and rough and variegated. Crude—and untouched.

But it was not the trader's job to deal with beauty and he shrugged off such thoughts impatiently. When his crew talked to him in such terms, he was short with them.

He said, "We'll land here. It seems to be a good-sized concentration of the intelligences. We can do no better."

His second said, "What can we do even with these, Maestro?"

"You can record," said the trader. "Record the animals, both unintelligent and supposedly intelligent, and any artifacts of theirs we can find. Make sure the records are thoroughly holographic."

"We can already see—" began the second.

"*We* can already see," said trader, "but we must have a record to convince our explorer out of his dreams or we'll remain here forever."

"He is a good explorer," said one of the crew.

"He has been a good explorer," said the trader, "but does that mean he will be good forever? Perhaps his very successes have made him accept himself at too high an evaluation. So we must convince him of reality—if we can."

They wore their suits when they emerged from the module.

The planetary atmosphere would support them, but the feeling of exposure to the raw winds of an open planet would discommode them, even if the atmosphere and temperature were perfect—which they weren't. The gravity was a touch high, as was the light level, but they could bear it.

The intelligent beings, dressed rather sketchily in the outer portions of other animals, retreated reluctantly at their approach and watched at a distance. The trader was relieved at this. Any sign of non-belligerence was welcome to those not permitted to defend themselves.

The trader and his crew did not try to communicate directly or to make friendly gestures. Who knew what gesture might be considered friendly by an alien? The trader set up a mental field, instead, and saturated it with the vibrations of harmlessness and peace and hoped that the mental fields of the creatures were sufficiently advanced to respond.

Perhaps they were, for a few crept back and watched motionlessly as though intensely curious. The trader thought he detected fugitive thoughts—but that seemed unlikely for first-level beings and he did not follow them up.

Instead, he went stolidly about the business of making holographic reproductions of the vegetation, of a herd of blundering herbivores that appeared and then, deciding the surrounds were dangerous, thundered away. A large animal stood its ground for a while, exposing white weapons in a cavity at its force-end—then left.

The trader's crew worked as he did, moving methodically across the landscape.

* * *

The call, directly mental, and surcharged with such emotion of surprise and awe that the informational content was all but blurred out, came unexpectedly.

"Maestro! Here! Come quickly!"

Specific directions were not given. The trader had to follow the beam, which led into a crevice bounded by two rocky outcroppings.

Other members of the crew were converging but the trader had arrived first.

"What is it?" asked the trader.

His second was standing in the glow of his suit-radiation in a deeply hollowed-out portion of the hillside.

The trader looked about. "This is a natural hollow, not a technological product."

"Yes, but look!"

The trader looked up and for perhaps five seconds he was lost. Then he sent out a strenuous message for all others to stay away.

He said, "Is this of technological origin?"

"Yes, Maestro. You can see it is only partly completed."

"But by whom?"

"By those creatures out there. The intelligent ones. I found one at work in here. This is his light source; it was burning vegetation. These are his tools."

"And where is he?"

"He fled."

"Did you actually see him?"

"I recorded him."

The trader pondered. Then he looked up again. "Have you ever seen anything like this?"

"No, Maestro."

"Or heard of anything like this?"

"No, Maestro."

"Astonishing!"

The trader showed no signs of wanting to withdraw his eyes, and the second said, softly, "Maestro, what do we do?"

"Eh?"

"This will surely win our ship still a fourth prize."

"Surely," said the trader, regretfully, "if we could take it."

The second said, hesitantly, "I have already recorded it."

"Eh? What is the use of that? We have nothing to give in exchange."

"But we have this. Give them anything."

The trader said, "What are you saying? They are too primitive to accept anything we could give them. It will surely be nearly a million years before they could possibly accept the suggestions of exogenous origin.—We will have to destroy the recording."

"But we *know*, Maestro."

"Then we must never talk about it. Our craft has its ethics and its traditions. You know that. Nothing for nothing!"

"Even this?"

"Even this."

The trader's sternly implacable set of expression was tinged with unbearable sorrow and despite his "Even this" he stood irresolute.

The second sensed that. He said, "*Try* giving them something, Maestro."

"Of what use would that be?"

"Of what harm?"

* * *

The trader said, "I have prepared a presentation for the entire starship, but I must show it to you first, Explorer—with deep respect and with apologies for masked thoughts. You were right. There *was* something strange about this planet. Though the intelligences on the planet were barely first level and though their technology was primitive in the extreme, they had developed a concept we have never had and one that, to my knowledge, we have never encountered on any other world."

The captain said, uneasily, "I cannot imagine what it might be." He was quite aware that traders sometimes overpraised their purchases to magnify their own worth.

The explorer said nothing. He was the more uneasy of the two.

The trader said, "It is a form of visual art."

"Playing with color?" asked the captain.

"And shape—but to most startling effect." He had arranged the holographic projector. "Observe!"

In the viewing space before them, a herd of animals appeared;

bulky, shaggy, two-horned, four-legged. They hesitated, then ran, dust spurting up beneath their hooves.

"Ugly objects," muttered the captain.

The holographic recording brought the herd to a halt, clamped it down to a still. It magnified, and a single beast filled the view, its bulky head lowered, its nostrils distended.

"Observe this animal," said the trader, "and now observe this artificial composition of a primitive concoction of oil and colored mineral, which we found smeared over the roof of a cave."

There it was again! Not quite the animal as holographed—flat, but vibrant.

"What a peculiar similarity," said the captain.

"Not peculiar," said the trader. "Deliberate! There were dozens of such figures in different poses—of different animals. The likenesses were too detailed to be fortuitous. Imagine the boldness of the conception—to place colors in pleasing shapes and combinations, and in such a way as to deceive the eye into thinking it is looking at a real object. These organisms have devised an art that represents reality. It is representational art, as I suppose we might call it.

"And that's not all. We found it done in three dimensions also." The trader produced an array of small figures in grey stone and in faintly yellow bone. "These are clearly intended to represent themselves."

The captain seemed stupefied. "Did you see these manufactured?"

"No, that I did not, Captain. One of my men saw a planetary being smearing color on one of the cave representations, but these we found already formed. Still, no other explanation is possible than that they were deliberately shaped. These objects could not have assumed these shapes by chance processes."

The captain said, "These are curious, but one doesn't follow the motive. Would not holographic techniques serve the purpose better—at such times as these are developed, of course?"

"These primitives have no conception that holography could someday be developed and could not wait the million years required. Then, too, maybe holography is *not* better. If you compare the representations with the originals you will notice that the representations are simplified and distorted in subtle ways designed to bring certain characteristics into focus. I believe this form of art *improves* on the original in some ways and certainly has something different to say."

The trader turned to the explorer. "I stand in awe at your abilities. Can you explain how you sensed the uniqueness of this intelligence?"

The explorer signed a negative. "I did not suspect this at all. It is interesting and I see its worth—although I wonder if we could ourselves properly control our colors and shapes in order to force them into such representational form. Yet this does match the unease within me.—What I wonder is how you came into possession of these? What did you give in exchange? It is *there* I see the strangeness lie."

"Well," said the trader, "in a way you're right. Quite strange. I did not think I could give anything since the organisms are so primitive, but this discovery seemed too important to sacrifice without some effort. I therefore chose from among the group of beings who formed these objects one whose mental field seemed somewhat more intense than that of the others and attempted to transfer to him a gift in exchange."

"And succeeded. Of course," said the explorer.

"Yes, I succeeded," said the trader, happily, failing to notice that the explorer had made a statement and had not asked a question. "The beings," the trader went on, "kill such animals as they represent in color, by throwing long sticks tipped with sharpened stone. These penetrate the hide of the animals, wound and weaken them. They can then be killed by the beings who are individually smaller and weaker than the animal they hunt. I pointed out that a smaller, stone-tipped stick could be hurled forward with greater force and effect and with longer range if a cord under tension were used as the mechanism of propulsion."

The explorer said, "Such devices have been encountered among primitive intelligences which were, however, far advanced beyond these. Paleomentologists call it a bow and arrow."

The captain said, "How could the knowledge be absorbed? It couldn't be, at this level of the development."

"But it *was*. Unmistakably. The response of the mental field was one of insight at almost unbearable intensity.—Surely you do not think I would have taken these art objects, were they twenty times as valuable, if I had not been convinced that I had made a return? Nothing for nothing, Captain."

The explorer said in a low, despondent voice, "There is the strangeness. To accept."

The captain said, "But surely, Trader, we cannot do this. They are not ready. We are harming them. They will use the bow and arrow to wound each other and not the beasts alone."

The trader said, "*We* do not harm them and we *did* not harm them. What *they* do to each other and where they end as a result, a million years from now, is not our concern."

The captain and the trader left to set up the demonstration for the starship's company, and the explorer said sadly in the direction in which they had gone, "But they accepted. And they flourish amid the ice. And in twenty thousand years, it will be *our* concern."

He knew they would not believe him, and he despaired.

# For the Birds

Charles Modine, despite the fact that he was in his late thirties, and in perfect health, had never been in space. He had seen space settlements on television and had occasionally read about them in the public prints but it went no further than that.

To tell the truth, he was not interested in space. He had been born on Earth, and Earth was enough for him. When he wanted a change of environment, he turned to the sea. He was an avid and skilled sailor.

He was therefore repelled when the representative of Space Structures, Limited, finally told him that in order for him to do the job they were asking him to do, he would have to leave Earth.

Modine said, "Listen. I'm not a space person. I design clothes. What do I know about rockets and acceleration and trajectories and all the rest of it?"

"*We* know about that. You don't have to," said the other, urgently. Her name was Naomi Baranova and she had the queer, tentative walk of someone who had been in space so long she wasn't sure what the gravitational situation was at the moment.

Her clothes, Modine noted with some irritation, functioned as coverings and as little else. A tarpaulin would have done as well.

"But why need I come out to a space station?" he said.

"For what *you* know. We want you to design something for us."

"Clothes?"

"Wings."

Modine thought about it. He had a high, pale forehead and the process of thought always seemed to flush it somewhat. He had been told that at any rate. This time, if it flushed, it was partly in annoyance. "I can do that here, can't I?"

Baranova shook her head firmly. She had hair with a dark reddish tinge that was slowly being invaded by gray. She didn't seem to mind. She said, "We want you to understand the situation, Mr. Modine. We've consulted the technicians and the computer experts and they've built the most efficient possible wings, they tell us. They've taken into account stresses and surfaces and flexibilities and maneuverabilities and everything else you can imagine—but it doesn't help. We think perhaps a few frills—"

"Frills, Ms. Baranova?"

"Something other than scientific perfection. Something to rouse interest. Otherwise, the space settlements won't survive. That's why I want you there; to appreciate the situation for yourself. We're prepared to pay you very well."

* * *

It was the promised pay, including a healthy retainer, win or lose, that brought Modine into space. He was no more money-mad than the average human being, but he was not money-insensitive either, and he liked to see his reputation appreciated.

Nor was it actually as bad as he had expected. In the early days of space travel, there had been short periods of high acceleration and long cramped periods in small modules. Somehow that was what Earth-bound people still thought of in connection with space travel. But a century had passed and the shuttles were commodious, while the hydraulic seats seemed to sop up the acceleration as though it were nothing more than a coffee spill.

Modine spent the time studying photographs of the wings in action and in watching holographic videotapes of the flyers.

He said, "There's a certain grace to the performance."

Naomi Baranova smiled rather sadly. "You're watching experts—athletes. If you could see me trying to handle these wings and manage to tumble and sideslip, I'm afraid you would laugh. And yet I'm better than most."

* * *

They were approaching Space Settlement Five. Its name was Chrysalis, officially, but everyone called it Five.

"You might suppose," said Baranova, "that it would be the other way around, but there's no feeling of poetry about the place. That's the trouble. It's not a home; it's just a job, and it is hard to make people establish families and settle down. Until it's a home—"

Five showed up as a small sphere, far away, looking much as Modine had seen it on television on Earth. He knew it was larger than it looked, but that was only an intellectual knowledge. His eyes and his emotions were not prepared for the steady increase in size as they approached. The spaceship and he dwarfed steadily and, eventually, they were circling an enormous object of glass and aluminum.

He watched for a long time before he became aware that they were still circling. He said, "Aren't we going to land on it?"

"Not that easy," said Baranova. "Five rotates on an axis about once in two minutes. It has to in order to set up a centrifugal effect that will keep everything inside pressed against the inner wall and create an artificial gravity. We have to match that speed before we can land. It takes time."

"Must it spin that quickly?"

"To have the centrifugal effect mimic Earth-strength gravity, yes. That's the basic problem. It would be much better if we could use a slow spin to produce a tenth-normal gravity or even less, but that interferes with human physiology. People can't take low gravity for too long."

The ship's speed had nearly matched the rotation period of Five. Modine could clearly see the curve of the outer mirror that caught the sunlight and with it illuminated Five's interior. He could make out the solar power station that supplied the energy for the station, with enough left over to export to Earth.

And they finally entered at one of the poles of the sphere and were inside Five.

* * *

Modine had spent a full day on Five and he was tired—but he had, rather unexpectedly, enjoyed it. They were sitting now on lawn furniture—on a wide stretch of grass—against a vista of suburbia.

There were clouds overhead—sunshine, without a clear view of the Sun itself—a wind—and, in the distance, a small stream.

It was hard to believe he was on a sphere floating in space in the Moon's orbit, circling Earth once a month. He said, "It's like a world."

Baranova said, "So it seems when you're new here. When you've been here a time, you discover you know every corner of it. Everything repeats."

Modine said, "If you live in a particular town on Earth, everything repeats too."

"I know. But on Earth you can travel widely if you wish. Even if you don't travel, you know you can. Here you can't. That's—not so good; but it's not the worst."

"You don't have the Earth's worst," said Modine. "I'm sure you don't have weather extremes."

"The weather, Mr. Modine, is indeed Garden of Edenish, but you get used to that.—Let me show you something. I have a ball here. Could you throw it high up; straight up, and catch it?"

Modine smiled. "Are you serious?"

"Quite. Please do."

Modine said, "I'm not a ball player, but I think I can throw a ball. I might even catch it when it comes down."

He threw the ball upward. It curved parabolically, and Modine found himself drifting forward in order to catch it, then running. It fell out of reach.

Baranova said, "You didn't throw it straight up, Mr. Modine."

"Yes I did," gasped Modine.

"Only by Earth standards," said Baranova. "The difficulty is that what we call the Coriolis force is involved. Here at the inner surface of Five, we're moving quite rapidly in a great circle about the axis. If you throw the ball upward it moves nearer the axis where things make a smaller circle and move more slowly. However, the ball retains the speed it had down here, so it moves ahead and you couldn't catch it. If you had wanted to catch it, you would have had to throw it up and back so that it would loop and return to you like a boomerang. The details of motion are different here on Five than on Earth."

Modine said, thoughtfully, "You get used to it, I suppose."

"Not entirely. We live in the equatorial regions of our small sphere. That's where the motion is fastest and where we get the effect of normal gravity. If we move upward toward the axis, or along the surface toward the poles, the gravitational effect decreases rapidly. We frequently have to go up or poleward and, whenever we do, the Coriolis effect must be taken into account. We have small monorails that must move spirally toward either pole; one track poleward, another returning. In the trip we feel ourselves perpetually canted to one side. It takes a long time to get used to it and some people never learn the trick of it. No one likes to live here for that reason."

"Can you do something about that twisting effect?"

"If we could make our rotation slower, we would lessen the Coriolis, but we would also lessen the feel of gravitation and we can't do that."

"Damned if you do, damned if you don't."

"Not entirely. We could get along with less gravitation, if we exercise, but it would mean exercise every day for considerable periods. That would have to be fun. People won't indulge in daily calisthenics that are troublesome or a bore. We used to think that flying would be the answer. When we go to the low-gravity regions near the poles, people are almost weightless. They can almost rise into the air by flapping their arms. If we attach light plastic wings to each arm, stiffened by flexible rods, and if those wings are folded and extended in just the right rhythm, people can fly like birds."

"Will that work as exercise?"

"Oh, yes. Flying is hard work, I assure you. The arm and shoulder muscles may not have to do much to keep you aloft but they must be in continuous use to maneuver you properly. It keeps up the muscle tone and bone calcium, *if* it's done on a regular basis.—But people won't do it."

"I should think they'd love to fly."

Baranova sniffed. "They would, if it were easy enough. The trouble is that it requires skillful coordination of muscles to keep steady. The slightest errors result in tumbling and spinning and almost inevitable nausea. Some can learn how to fly gracefully as you saw on the holo-cassettes, but very few."

"Birds don't get seasick."

"Birds fly in normal gravity fields. People on Five don't."

Modine frowned and grew thoughtful.

Baranova said, "I can't promise that you'll sleep. People don't usually their first few nights on a space settlement. Still, please try to do so and tomorrow we'll go to the flying areas."

* * *

Modine could see what Baranova had meant by saying the Coriolis force was unpleasant. The small monorail coach that took them poleward seemed constantly to be sliding leftward and his entrails seemed to be doing the same. He held on to the handgrips, white-knuckled.

"I'm sorry," said Baranova, sympathetically. "If we went more slowly, it wouldn't be so bad, but we're holding up traffic as it is."

"Do you get used to this?" groaned Modine.

"Somewhat. Not enough."

* * *

He was glad to stop finally, but only limitedly so. It took a while to get used to the fact that he seemed to be floating. Each time he tried to move, he tumbled, and each time he tumbled he didn't fall but drifted slowly forward or upward and returned only gradually. His automatic kicking made things worse.

Baranova left him to himself for a while, then caught at him and drew him slowly back. "Some people enjoy this," she said.

"I don't," gasped Modine, miserably.

"Many don't. Please put your feet into these stirrups on the ground and don't make any sudden movements."

* * *

There were five of them flying in the sky. Baranova said, "Those five birds are here just about every day. There are a few hundred who are there now and then. We could accommodate at this pole and at the other, as well as along the axis, something like five thousand at a time. We could use all the space to keep Five's thirty thousand people in condition. What do we do?"

Modine gestured and his body swayed backward in response. "They must have learned how, those birds up there. They weren't born birds. Can't the others learn it, too?"

"Those up there have natural coordination."

"What can I do then? I'm a fashion designer. I don't create natural coordination."

"Not having natural coordination doesn't stop you altogether. It just means working hard, practicing longer. Is there any way you could make the process more—fashionable? Could you design a flying costume; suggest a psychological campaign to get the people out? If we could arrange proper programs of exercise and physical fitness, we could slow Five's rotation, weaken the Coriolis effect, make this place a home."

"You may be asking for a miracle.—Could you have them come closer?"

Baranova waved and one of the birds saw her, and swooped toward them in a long graceful curve. It was a young woman. She hovered ten feet away, smiling, her wings flicking slightly at the tips.

"Hi," she called out. "What's up?"

"Nothing," said Baranova. "My friend wants to watch you handle the wings. Show him how they work."

The young woman smiled and, twisting first one wing, then the other, performed a slow somersault. She straightened to a halt with both wings given a backhanded twist, then rose slowly, her feet dangling and her wings moving slowly. The wing motion grew more rapid and she was off in wild acceleration.

Modine said, after a while, "Rather like ballet dancing, but the wings are ugly."

"Are they? Are they?"

"Certainly," said Modine. "They look like bat wings. The associations are all wrong."

"Tell us what to do then? Should we put a feather design on them? Would that bring out the fliers and make them try harder to learn?"

"No." Modine thought for a while. "Maybe we can make the whole process easier."

He took his feet out of the stirrups, gave himself a little push and floated into the air. He moved his arms and legs experimentally and rocked erratically. He tried to scramble back for the stirrups and Baranova reached up to pull him down.

Modine said, "I'll tell you. I'll design something and if someone here can help me construct it according to the design, I'll try to fly. I've never done any such thing; you've just seen me try to wriggle in the air and I can't even do that. Well, if I use my design and *I* can fly, then anyone can."

"I should think so, Mr. Modine," said Baranova, in a tone that seemed suspended between skepticism and hope.

* * *

By the end of the week, Modine was beginning to feel that Space Settlement Five was home. As long as he stayed at ground level in the equatorial regions, where the gravitational effect was normal, there was no Coriolis effect to bother him and he felt his surroundings to be very Earth-like.

"The first time out," he said, "I don't want to be watched by the population generally because it may be harder than I think and I don't want to get this thing off to a bad start.—But I would like to be watched by some of the officials of the Settlement, just in case I make it."

Baranova said, "I should think we would try in private first. A failure the first time, whatever the excuse—"

"But a success would be *so* impressive."

"What are the chances of success? Be reasonable."

"The chances are good, Ms. Baranova. Believe me. What you have been doing here is all wrong. You're flying in air—like birds—and it's so hard. You said it yourself. Birds on Earth operate under gravity. The birds up here operate without gravity—so everything has to be designed differently."

* * *

The temperature, as always, was perfectly adjusted. So was the humidity. So was the wind speed. The atmosphere was so perfect it was as though it weren't there.—And yet Modine was perspiring with a bad case of stage fright. He was also gasping. The air was thinner in these gravity-free regions than at the equator—not by much, but enough thinner for him to have trouble gathering enough with his heart pounding so.

The air was empty of the human birds; the audience was a handful—the Coordinator, the Secretary of Health, the Commissioner of Safety and so on. There were a dozen men and women present. Only Baranova was familiar.

He had been outfitted with a small mike and he tried to keep his voice from shaking.

He said, "We are flying without gravity and neither birds nor bats are a good model for us. They fly *with* gravity.—It's different in the sea. There's little effective gravity in water, since buoyancy lifts you. When we fly through no-gravity water, we call it swimming. In Space Station Five, where there's no gravity in this region, the air is for swimming, not for flying. We must imitate the dolphin and not the eagle."

He sprang into the air as he spoke, wearing a graceful one-piece suit that neither clung skintight nor bellied. He began to tumble at once, but stretching one arm was sufficient to activate a small gas cartridge. A smoothly curved fin emerged along his spinal column, while a shallow keel marked the line of his abdomen.

The tumbling ceased. "Without gravity," he said, "this is enough to stabilize your flight. You can still tip and turn, but always under control. I may not do it well at first, but it won't take much practice."

He stretched his other arm and each foot was suddenly outlined by a flipper—each elbow by another.

"These," he said, "offer the propulsive force. You needn't flap the arms. Gentle motions will suffice for everything, but you have to bend your body and arch your neck in order to make turns and veers. You have to twist and alter the angle of your arms and legs. The whole body is engaged, but smoothly and nonviolently.—Which is all the better, for every muscle in your body is involved and you can keep it up for hours without tiring."

He could feel himself moving more surely and gracefully—and faster. Up, up, he was suddenly going, with the air rushing past him until he was almost in a panic for fear he would not be able to slow up. But he turned his heels and elbows almost instinctively and felt himself curve and slow.

Dimly, through the pounding of his heart, he could hear the applause.

* * *

Baranova said, admiringly, "How did you see this when our technicians couldn't?"

"The technicians started with the inevitable assumption of wings, thanks to birds and airplanes, and designed the most efficient ones possible. That's a technician's job. The job of a fashion designer is to see things as an artistic whole. I could see that the wings didn't fit the conditions of the space settlement. Just my job."

Baranova said, "We'll make these dolphin suits and get the population out into the air. I'm sure we can now. And then we can lay our plans to begin to slow Five's rotation."

"Or stop it altogether," said Modine. "I suspect that everyone will want to swim all the time instead of walking." He laughed. "They may not ever want to walk again. *I* may not."

They made out the large check they had promised and Modine, smiling at the figure, said, "Wings are for the birds."

# Ignition Point!

"Let me get this straight," said Anthony Myers, leaning across his desk toward the man in the chair facing him. "Your computer does *not* write the speech?"

"No, you do. Or someone else does." Nicholas Jansen was quite composed. He was a small man, very neatly dressed, with an old-fashioned knotted tie that did not seem to make him the least bit self-conscious in a world of turtlenecks.

He said, "What I have developed is a series of words, phrases, sentences that induce reactions in specific groups of people, divided by sex, age, ethnic groups, language, occupation, place of residence or almost anything else conceivable. If you could describe the audience your man would be addressing in sufficient detail, then I could supply you with precisely the sort of thing his talk should include. The more we know about the audience the more accurately my computer program can produce the key words and phrases. They are woven into a speech—"

"Can they? Will they make sense?"

"That's up to the ingenuity of the speech writer, but it doesn't really matter. If you're pounding a drum, you might get the audience stirred up until their feet and hearts are pounding with it; till they reach ignition point. Sense is analogous to tune, but a drum doesn't have to beat out a tune; it merely establishes a rhythm. You can put in as much tune as you can, but it is the rhythm you're after. Do you understand?"

Myers rubbed his chin and stared at the other thoughtfully. "Have you tried this before?"

Jansen smiled narrowly. "Only unofficially. In a small way. Still, I know what I'm talking about. I'm an ochologist—"

"A what?"

"A studen of mob psychology, and the first, as far as I know, who has truly computerized the matter."

"And you know this will work—in theory."

"No, I know it *might* work—in theory."

"And you want to try it out on me. What if it doesn't work?"

"Then what have you to lose? I'm not charging you. It's useful in my work, and if I may believe what I have been told, your man is lost if you don't use my services."

Myers drummed his fingers on the desk softly. "Look. Let me explain about my man. He looks impressive. He's got a good voice. He's amiable and likable. Properly handled I can make him a corporation executive, or an ambassador, or the President of the United States. The trouble is he has no brains to speak of and he needs me to supply them. But the one thing he has to be able to do without me is to deliver a speech in such a way as to fool people into thinking he does have brains. This he cannot do, even if the speech is written out for him. The speech may be intelligent and yet he can't say it in such a way as to make *himself* seem intelligent. Do you think you can write a speech better than I can?"

"Not better. Just foolproof. I can make it possible for him to push the right buttons and ignite the audience."

"What do you mean, ignite?"

"To catch fire. Isn't that what ignite means? Every crowd has its ignition point, though every different crowd requires something different for ignition."

"You may be selling me a load of nonsense, Mr. Jansen. There's no speech so foolproof that a nincompoop won't spoil it."

"On the contrary. A nincompoop might deliver it more surely than you could, since he won't be thinking for himself. May I meet him?—That is, if you want my services?"

"You understand that everything said here is confidential."

"Certainly. Since I intend to turn this to commercial use eventually, I am more interested in confidentiality than you are."

* * *

Barry Winston Bloch was not quite forty. He had played semipro baseball in his younger days. He had made his way through a midwestern college with minimal effort and he had been moderately successful as a salesman. His appearance was impressive, not because he was handsome but because he looked physically powerful, and gave the impression of possessing a mature wisdom. His hair was already showing streaks of gray and he had a way of throwing his head up and smiling warmly that filled you full of confidence in him.

It took an hour or so, usually, to realize that there was nothing behind the amiability but additional amiability.

Right now, Bloch felt uncomfortable. Ever since he had tied up with

Myers, he had been a prey to discomfort. He wanted to get ahead; it was his secret desire to be a congressman and sometimes he wondered if he might not be a great evangelist, but the trouble was that people made him nervous. After he had used up his big grin, it came time to talk and he never had anything particular to say.

And no one had ever made him feel quite as uncomfortable as this little man with his gimlet eyes, who would sit there absolutely motionless while Bloch read his speeches. It was hard enough to talk to a real audience which rustled and coughed and seemed to be annoyed with him for not finishing. This little man—he had to remember his name was Jansen—who never responded in any way just choked him off.

No, he responded in one way—he invariably handed Bloch another speech to read. Each one was a little different and each one appealed to him somehow, but he never felt as if he did them justice. It made him sad somehow—and ashamed.

The manuscript presented to him on *this* day seemed worse than all the others. He looked at it in dismay. "What are all these marks?"

"Well now, B.B.," Myers adopted the soothing tone he almost always used with Bloch, "just let Mr. Jansen explain."

"It's direction. It's something you must learn, but it won't be difficult. A dash means a pause, an underlining means an emphasis. A downward arrow before a word means you let your voice drop a couple of notes; an upward arrow means you let it rise. A curved arrow means you let things fade off in contempt, if it curves downward. If it curves upward, your voice rises in anger. A parenthesis means a small smile; a double parenthesis means a grin; a triple parenthesis means a chuckle. You never laugh out loud. A line over a word means you look grim; a double line means you repeat. An asterisk—"

Bloch said, "I can't remember all that."

Myers, from behind Bloch, mouthed worriedly, I don't think he will.

Jansen seemed unperturbed by the double denial. "You will with practice. The stakes are high and worth a little trouble."

Myers said, "Go ahead, B.B. Just give it a read-through and Mr. Jansen will help out as you go along."

Bloch looked as though he wished to object further, but his native amiability won out. He put the manuscript on the lecturn and began to read it. He stumbled, peered at the manuscript with a frown, began again, and skidded to a halt.

Jansen explained and Bloch began again. They spent an hour over the first three paragraphs before calling a halt.

Myers said, "It's awful."

Jansen said, "How did you do the first time you tried to ride a bicycle?"

Bloch repeated the speech all the way through twice that day; twice more the second day. A second speech was prepared, not quite the same, but just as empty of real content.

After a week, Bloch said, "I'm getting the hang of it. It seems to me that I'm getting so that it sounds good."

Myers said, with hollow hopefulness, "I think so, too."

Jansen said to Myers afterward, "He's doing better than I expected. He's got a certain potentiality, but—"

"But what?"

Jansen shrugged. "Nothing. We'll just have to see."

* * *

Jansen said, "I think he's ready for an audience now, provided it's a homogenous one which we can analyze accurately."

"The American Association of Textile Weavers needs a speaker and I think I can place B.B. with them. Can you handle that audience?"

"Weavers?" said Jansen, thoughtfully. "The economic position would be homogenous and I suspect the educational level would not be too wide a spread. I would need to have a breakdown on what city and states they represent and on the percentages coming from establishments of different size. Age, sex and the usual, too, of course."

"I'll see what I can dig up from the Union, but there isn't much time, you know."

"We'll try to work quickly. We've got a great deal of the basics worked out. Your man is learning how to deliver a speech."

Myers laughed. "He's gotten to the point where he almost convinces *me*.—You know, I wouldn't want him in Congress. I would want him on television, selling my views—his, I mean—"

"Your views, you mean," said Jansen, dryly. "*He* has none."

"It doesn't matter. I'm counting my chickens—"

* * *

Bloch did well at the A.A.T.W. cocktail party. He followed his instructions, had smiled, had talked just a bit but not too much, had told a harmless joke or two and dropped a few names, and had, for the most part, done a lot of listening and nodding.

And yet Myers, from his table up front, felt a certain tightness. If B.B. flopped, they could try again, but if he flopped, would there be enough in him to make it worth his while to try again? This might be the test that would show that B.B. just didn't have it. What a waste, with that appearance! With that Roman senator head of his!

He stole a glance at Jansen, who sat at his left. The little man seemed utterly composed but there was a slight contraction of the eyebrows, as though there were a secret worry gnawing at him.

The dinner was over, the various business announcements were being made, the committee was being thanked, the people seated on the dais were being introduced—all the maddening details that seemed to be designed for no other purpose than to place additional unnecessary strain upon the speaker.

Myers stared earnestly at Bloch, caught his eye, and held up two fingers briefly. Go in and get them, B.B.!

Would he? The speech was an odd one, almost quixotic. It would read oddly in the papers if it ever made the news columns, but it was full of button pushers—according to Jansen and his computer.

Bloch was standing up now. He stepped easily to the lectern and put the manuscript before him. He was always good at that; doing it slickly and unobtrusively so that the audience never really had it rubbed in their face that the speech was going to be read.

Myers thought, not entirely irrelevantly, of the time he had attended a meeting at which the speaker had somehow managed to knock off his manuscript with an over-energetic gesture. The manuscript could be picked up and rearranged but an audience died at that moment and could not be revived.

Bloch smiled at the audience and began slowly. (Don't wait too long to speed up, B.B.)

He didn't. He quickened the beat. At times, he stopped briefly to puzzle out a symbol but fortunately, that sounded like deliberation, the kind of thought you would expect of mature wisdom. It helped to have that appearance.

Then he spoke still more quickly and emotionally and, to Myers' surprise, he could feel the drumbeats start. There were those key phrases, with just the right kind of emphasis, and in response, he could feel the audience stir.

Laughter came on cue and at one point, there was a patter of applause. Myers had never heard applause interrupt Bloch before.

Bloch's face looked a little flushed and at one point he brought his fist down on the lectern and the little fluorescent lamp shook.

(Don't knock it over, B.B.!) The audience stamped its feet in response.

Myers felt the mounting excitement within himself, even though he knew exactly how carefully the speech had been prepared. He leaned toward Jansen. "He's igniting the audience, wouldn't you say?"

Jansen nodded once. His lips scarcely moved. "Yes. And maybe—"

Bloch had paused briefly in his talk—just long enough to tighten the audience into a knot of tension—and then he brought his hand down savagely on the lectern, picked up the manuscript in a crumpled mess, and threw it aside. "I don't need this," he said, his voice rising into a distinct note of triumph. "I don't want it. I wrote it in cold blood before I had you all before me. Let me speak now from my heart, as it comes to me, standing here before you; let me tell you all, friends and Americans, you and I, together, what I see in the world today and what I *want* to see, and believe me, my friends, the two are *not—the—same*."

There was a roar in response.

Myers clutched at Jansen wildly. "He can't make it on his own!"

But he could and did. He spoke through and over the applause and the shouting. It scarcely mattered if he were heard. He raised both arms as though to embrace the audience and a voice shouted, "Go on! Give it to them!"

Bloch gave it to them. Exactly what he said scarcely mattered but when it was over, there was a wild and jubilant standing ovation.

"What happened?" said Myers, through the noise. (He was applauding as loudly as everyone else.)

Jansen remained seated, in a strange attitude of collapse. He clutched at Myers, drew him close, and said in a shaking voice, "Don't you see what happened? It was a one-in-a-million shot. Just toward the end I began to wonder if it were possible. It *can* happen—"

"What are you talking about?"

"The audience ignited and Bloch was speaking to an ignited audience for the first time in his life, and speakers have their ignition point, too. Bloch himself ignited, and an ignited speaker can carry public opinion and move mountains."

"Who? B.B.?"

"Yes."

"Well, that's great."

"Is it? When ignited, he's got power, and if he finds out he has, why would he need you? Or me? And if so, where will he go? There have been great charismatics before who have not always led to glory."

Bloch was with them, people crowding about him. He said to Myers in a breathless undertone, "That was easy! I feel great!" He turned to those about him, laughing, holding them all with no trouble.

Myers looked after him, confused; Jansen looked after him, afraid!

# Lest We Remember

## 1.

The problem with John Heath, as far as John Heath was concerned, was that he struck a dead average. He was sure of it. What was worse, he felt that Susan suspected it.

It meant he would never make a true mark in the world, never climb to the top of Quantum Pharmaceuticals, where he was a steady cog among the junior executives—never make the Quantum Leap.

Nor would he do it anywhere else, if he changed jobs.

He sighed inwardly. In just two more weeks he was going to be married and for her sake he yearned to be upwardly mobile. After all, he loved her madly and wanted to shine in her eyes.

But then, that was dead average for a young man about to be married.

Susan Collins looked at John lovingly. And why not? He was reasonably good-looking and intelligent and a steady, affectionate fellow besides. If he didn't blind her with his brilliance, he at least didn't upset her with an erraticism he didn't possess.

She patted the pillow she had placed behind his head when he sat down in the arm-chair and handed him his drink, making sure he had a firm grip before she let go.

She said, "I'm practicing to treat you well, Johnny. I've got to be an efficient wife."

John sipped at his drink. "I'm the one who'll have to be on my toes, Sue. Your salary is higher than mine."

"It's all going to go into one pocket once we're married. It will be the firm of Johnny and Sue keeping one set of books."

"You'll have to keep it," said John, despondently. "I'm bound to make mistakes if I try."

"Only because you're sure you will.—When are your friends coming?"

"Nine, I think. Maybe nine-thirty. And they're not exactly friends. They're Quantum people from the research labs."

"You're sure they won't expect to be fed?"

"They said after dinner. I'm positive about that. It's business."

She looked at him quizzically. "You didn't say that before."

"Say what before?"

"That it was business. Are you sure?"

John felt confused. Any effort to remember *precisely* always left him confused. "They said so—I think."

Susan's look was that of good-natured exasperation, rather like the one she would have given a friendly puppy who is completely unaware its paws are muddy. "If you really thought," she said, "as often as you say 'I think' you wouldn't be so perennially uncertain. Don't you see it *can't* be business. If it were business, wouldn't they see you *at* business?"

"It's confidential," said John. "They didn't want to see me at work. Not even at my apartment."

"Why here, then?"

"Oh, I suggested that. I thought you ought to be around, anyway. They're going to have to deal with the firm of Johnny and Sue, right?"

"It depends," said Susan, "on what the confidential is all about. Did they give you any hints?"

"No, but it couldn't hurt to listen. It could be something that would give me a boost in standing at the firm."

"Why you?" asked Susan.

John looked hurt, "Why *not* me?"

"It just strikes me that someone at your job level doesn't require all that confidentiality and that—"

She broke off when the intercom buzzed. She dashed off to answer and came back to say, "They're on the way up."

## 2.

Two of them were at the door. One was Boris Kupfer, whom John had already spoken to—large and restless, with a clear view of bluish stubble on his chin.

The other was David Anderson, smaller and more composed. His quick eyes moved this way and that, however, missing nothing.

"Susan," said John, uncertainly, still holding the door open.

"These are the two colleagues of mine that I told you about. Boris—" He hit a blank in his memory banks and stopped.

"Boris Kupfer," said the larger man morosely, jingling some change in his pocket, "and David Anderson here. It's very kind of you, Miss—"

"Susan Collins."

"It's very kind of you to make your place of residence available to Mr. Heath and to us for a private conference. We apologize fo trespassing on your time and your privacy in this manner—and if you could leave us to ourselves for a while, we will be further grateful."

Susan stared at him solemnly. "Do you want me to go to the movies, or just into the next room?"

"If you could visit a friend—"

"No," said Susan, firmly.

"You can dispose of your time as you please,of course. A movie, if you wish."

"When I said 'No,' " said Susan, "I meant I wasn't leaving. I want to know what this is about."

Kupfer seemed nonplussed. He stared at Anderson for a moment, then said, "It's confidential, as Mr. Heath explained to you, I hope."

John, looking uneasy, said, "I explained that. Susan understands—"

"Susan," said Susan, "doesn't understand and wasn't given to understand that she was to absent herself from the proceedings. This is my apartment and Johnny and I are being married in two weeks — exactly two weeks from today. We are the firm of Johnny and Sue and you'll have to deal with the firm."

Anderson's voice sounded for the first time, surprisingly deep and as smooth as though it had been waxed. "Boris, the young woman is right. As Mr. Heath's soon-to-be wife, she will have a great interest in what we have come here to suggest and it would be wrong to exclude her. She has so firm an interest in our proposal that if she were to wish to leave, I would urge her most strongly to remain."

"Well, then, my friends," said Susan, "what will you have to drink? Once I bring you those drinks, we can begin."

Both were seated rather stiffly and had sipped cautiously at their drinks, and then Kupfer said, "Heath, I don't suppose you know much about the chemical details of the company's work—the cerebrochemicals, for instance."

"Not a bit," said John, uneasily.

"No reason you should," said Anderson, silkily.

"It's like this," said Kupfer, casting an uneasy glance at Susan—

"No reason to go into technical details," said Anderson, almost at the lower level of audibility.

Kupfer colored slightly. "Without technical details, Quantum Pharmaceuticals deals with cerebro-chemicals which are, as the name implies, chemicals that effect the cerebrum; that is, the higher functioning of the brain."

"It must be very complicated work," said Susan, with composure.

"It is," said Kupfer. "The mammalian brain has hundreds of characteristic molecular varieties found nowhere else, which serve to modulate cerebral activity, including aspects of what we might term the intellectual life. The work is under the closest corporate security, which is why Anderson wants no technical details. I *can* say this, though.—We can go no further with animal experiments. We're up against a brick wall if we can't try the human response."

"Then why don't you?" said Susan. "What stops you?"

"Public reaction if something goes wrong!"

"Use volunteers, then."

"That won't help. Quantum Pharmaceuticals couldn't take the adverse publicity if something went wrong."

Susan looked at them mockingly. "Are you two working on your own, then?"

Anderson raised his hand to stop Kupfer. "Young woman," he said, "let me explain briefly in order to put an end to wasteful verbal fencing. If we succeed, we will be enormously rewarded. If we fail, Quantum Pharmaceuticals will disown us and we will pay what penalty there is to be paid, such as the ending of our careers. If you ask us, why we are willing to take this risk, the answer is, we do not think a risk exists. We are reasonably sure we will succeed; entirely sure we will do no harm. The corporation feels it cannot take the chance; but we feel we can.—Now, Kupfer, proceed!"

Kupfer said, "We have a memory chemical. It works with every animal we have tried. Their learning ability improves amazingly. It should work on human beings, too."

John said, "That sounds exciting."

"It *is* exciting," said Kupfer. "Memory is not improved by devising a way for the brain to store information more efficiently. All our studies show that the brain stores almost unlimited numbers of items perfectly and permanently. The difficulty lies in recall. How many times have you had a name at the tip of your tongue and couldn't get it? How many times have you failed to come up with something you *knew* you knew, and then did come up with it two hours later when you were thinking about something else.—Am I putting it correctly, David?"

"You are," said Anderson. "Recall is inhibited, we think, because the mammalian brain outraced its needs by developing a too-perfect recording system. A mammal stores more bits of information than it needs or is capable of using and if all of it was on tap at all times, it would never be able to choose among them quickly enough for appropriate reaction. Recall is inhibited, therefore, to insure that items emerge from memory storage in manipulable numbers, and with those items most desired not blurred by the accompaniment of numerous other items of no interest.

"There is a definite chemical in the brain that functions as a recall inhibitor, and we have a chemical that neutralizes the inhibitor. We call it a disinhibitor, and as far as we have been able to ascertain the matter, it has no deleterious side effects."

Susan laughed. "I see what's coming, Johnny. You can leave now, gentlemen. You just said that recall is inhibited to allow mammals to react more efficiently, and now you say that the disinhibitor has no deleterious side effects. Surely the disinhibitor will make the mammals react less efficiently; perhaps find themselves unable to react at all. And now you are going to propose that you try it on Johnny and see if you reduce him to catatonic immobility or not."

Anderson rose, his thin lips quivering. He took a few rapid strides to the far end of the room and back. When he sat down, he was composed and smiling. "In the first place, Miss Collins, it's a matter of dosage. We told you that the experimental animals all displayed enhanced learning ability. Naturally, we didn't eliminate the inhibitor entirely; we merely suppressed it in part. Secondly, we have reason to think the human brain *can* handle complete disinhibition. It is much larger than the brain of any animal we have tested and we all know its incomparable capacity for abstract thought.

"It is a brain designed for perfect recall, but the blind forces of evolution have not managed to remove the inhibiting chemical which, after all, was designed for and inherited from the lower animals."

"Are you sure?" asked John.

"You *can't* be sure," said Susan, flatly.

Kupfer said, "We are sure, but we need the proof to convince others. That's why we have to try a human being."

"John, in fact," said Susan.

"Yes."

"Which brings us," said Susan, "to the key question. Why John?"

"Well," said Kupfer, slowly, "we need someone from whom chances of success are most nearly certain, and in whom it would be most demonstrable. We don't want someone so low in mental capacity that we must use dangerously large doses of the disinhibitor; nor do we want someone so bright that the effect will not be sufficiently noticeable. We need someone who's average. Fortunately, we have the full physical and psychological profiles of all the employees at Quantum and in this and, in fact, all other ways, Mr. Heath is ideal."

"Dead average?" said Susan.

John looked stricken at the use of the phrase he had thought his own innermost, and disgraceful, secret. "Come on, now." he said.

Ignoring John's outcry, Kupfer answered Susan, "Yes."

"And he won't be, if he submits to treatment?"

Anderson's lips stretched into another one of his cheerless smiles. "That's right. He won't be. This is something to think about if you're going to be married soon—the firm of Johnny and Sue, I think you called it. As it is, I don't think the firm will advance at Quantum, Miss Collins, for although Heath is a good and reliable employee he is, as you say, dead average. If he takes the disinhibitor, however, he will become a remarkable person and move upward with astonishing speed. Consider what that will mean to the firm."

"What does the firm have to lose?" asked Susan, grimly.

Anderson said, "I don't see how you can lose anything. It will be a sensible dose which can be administered at the laboratories tomorrow—Sunday. We will have the floor to ourselves; we will keep him under surveillance for a few hours.—It is certain nothing could go wrong. If I could tell you of our painstaking experimentation and of our thoroughgoing exploration of all possible side effects—"

"On animals," said Susan, not giving an inch.

But John said, tightly, "I'll make the decision, Sue. I've had it up to here with that dead-average bit. It's worth some risk to me if it means getting off that dead-average dead end."

"Johnny," said Susan, "don't jump."

"I'm thinking of the firm, Sue. I want to contribute my share."

Anderson said, "Good, but sleep on it. We will leave two copies of an agreement we will ask you to look over and sign. Please don't show it to anybody whether you sign or not. We will be here tomorrow morning again to take you to the laboratory."

They smiled, rose, and left.

John read over the agreement with a troubled frown, then looked up. "You don't think I should be doing this, do you, Sue?"

"It worries me, sure."

"Look, if I have a chance to get away from that dead average—"

Susan said, "What's wrong with that? I've met so many nuts and cranks in my short life that I welcome a nice, average guy like you, Johnny. Listen, I'm dead average too."

"*You* dead average. With your looks? Your figure?"

Susan looked down upon herself with a touch of complacency. "Well, then, I'm just your dead-average gorgeous girl," she said.

## 3.

The injection took place at 8 A.M. Sunday, no more than twelve hours after the proposition had been advanced. A thoroughly computerized body sensor was attached to John in a dozen places, while Susan watched with keen-eyed apprehension.

Kupfer said, "Please, Heath, relax. All is going well, but tension speeds the heart rate, raises the blood pressure, and skews our results."

"How can I relax?" muttered John.

Susan put in sharply, "Skews the results to the point where you don't know what's going on?"

"No, no," said Anderson. "Boris said all is going well and it is. It is just that our animals were always sedated before the injection, and we did not feel sedation would have been appropriate in this case. So if we can't have sedation, we must expect tension. Just breathe slowly and do your best to minimize it."

It was late afternoon before he was finally disconnected.

"How do you feel?" asked Anderson.

"Nervous," said John. "Otherwise, all right."

"No headache?"

"No. But I want to visit the bathroom. I can't exactly relax with a bedpan."

"Of course."

John emerged, frowning. "I don't notice any particular memory improvement."

"That will take some time and will be gradual. The disinhibitor must leak across the blood-brain barrier, you know," said Anderson.

## 4.

It was nearly midnight when Susan broke what had turned out to be an oppressively silent evening in which neither had much responded to the television.

She said, "You'll have to stay here overnight. I don't want you alone when we don't really know what's going to happen."

"I don't feel a thing," said John, gloomily. "I'm still me."

"I'll settle for that, Johnny," said Susan. "Do you feel any pains or discomforts or oddnesses at all?"

"I don't think so."

"I wish we hadn't done it."

"For the firm," said John, smiling weakly. "We've got to take some chances for the firm."

## 5.

John slept poorly, and woke drearily, but on time. And he arrived at work on time, too, to start the new week.

By 11 A.M., however, his morose air had attracted the unfavorable attention of his immediate superior, Michael Ross. Ross was burly and black-browed and fit the stereotype of the stevedore without being one. John got along with him though he did not like him.

Ross said, in his bass-baritone, "What's happened to your cheery disposition, Heath—your jokes—your lilting laughter?" Ross cultivated a certain preciosity of speech as though he were anxious to negate the stevedore image.

"Don't exactly feel tip-top," said John, not looking up.

"Hangover?"

"No, sir," said John, coldly.

"Well, cheer up, then. You'll win no friends, scattering stinkweeds over the fields as you gambol along."

John would have liked to groan. Ross's subliterary affectations were wearisome at the best of times and this wasn't the best of times.

And to make matters worse, John smelled the foul odor of a rancid cigar and knew that James Arnold Prescott—the head of the sales division—could not be far behind.

Nor was he. He looked about, and said, "Mike, when and what did we sell Rahway last spring or thereabouts? There's some damned question about it and I think the details have been miscomputerized."

The question was not addressed to him, but John said quietly, "Forty-two vials of PCAP. That was on April 14, J.P., invoice number P-20543, with a five per cent discount granted on payment within thirty days. Payment, in full, received on May 8."

Apparently everyone in the room had heard that. At least, everyone looked up.

Prescott said, "How the hell do you happen to know all that?"

John stared at Prescott for a moment, a vast surprise on his face. "I just happened to remember, J.P."

"You did, eh? Repeat it."

John did, faltering a bit, and Prescott wrote it down on one of the papers on John's desk, wheezing slightly as the bend at his waist compressed his portly abdomen up against his diaphragm and made breathing difficult. John tried to duck the smoke from the cigar without seeming to do so.

Prescott said, "Ross, check this out on your computer and see if there's anything to it all." He turned to John with an aggrieved look. "I don't like practical jokers. What would you have done if I had accepted these figures of yours and walked off with them?"

"I wouldn't have done anything. They're correct," said John, conscious of himself as the full center of attention.

Ross handed Prescott the readout. Prescott looked at it and said, "This is from the computer?"

"Yes, J.P."

Prescott stared at it, then said, with a jerk of his head toward John, "And what's he? Another computer? His figures were correct."

John tried a weak smile, but Prescott growled and left, the stench of his cigar a lingering reminder of his presence.

Ross said, "What the hell was that little bit of legerdemain, Heath? You found out what he wanted to know and looked it up in advance to get some kudos?"

"No, sir," said John, who was gathering confidence. "I just happened to remember. I have a good memory for these things."

"And took the trouble to keep it from your loyal companions all these years? There's no one here who had any idea you hid a good memory behind that unremarkable forehead of yours."

"No point in showing it, Mr. Ross, is there? Now when I have, it doesn't seem to have gained me any goodwill, does it?"

And it hadn't. Ross glowered at him and turned away.

## 6.

John's excitement over the dinner table at Gino's that night made if difficult for him to talk coherently, but Susan listened patiently and tried to act as a stabilizing force.

"You might just have happened to remember, you know," she said. "By itself it doesn't prove anything, Johnny."

"Are you crazy?" He lowered his voice at Susan's gesture and quick glance about. He repeated in a semiwhisper, "Are you crazy? You don't suppose it's the only thing I remember, do you? I think I can remember anything I ever heard. It's just a question of recall. For instance, quote some line out of Shakespeare."

"To be or not to be."

John looked scornful. "Don't be funny. Oh, well, it doesn't matter. The point is that if you recite any line, I can carry on from there for as long as you like. I read some of the plays for English Lit classes at college and some for myself and I can bring any of it back. I've tried. It flows! I suppose I can bring back any part of any book or article or newspaper I've ever read, or any TV show I've ever watched—word for word or scene for scene."

Susan said, "What will you do with all that?"

John said, "I don't have that consciously in my head at all times. Surely you don't—wait, let's order—"

Five minutes later, he said, "Surely you don't— My God, I haven't forgotten where we left off. Isn't it amazing?—Surely you don't think I'm swimming in a mental sea of Shakespearean sentences at all times. The recall takes an effort; not much of one, but an effort."

"How does it work?"

"I don't know. How do you lift your arm? What orders do you give your muscles? You just will the arm to lift upward and it does so. It's no trouble to do so, but your arm doesn't lift *until* you want it to. Well, I remember anything I've ever read or seen when I want to but not when I don't want to. I don't know how I do it, but I do it."

The first course arrived and John tackled it happily.

Susan picked at her stuffed mushrooms. "It sounds exciting."

"Exciting? I've got the biggest, most wonderful toy in the world. My own brain. Listen, I can spell any word correctly and I'm pretty sure I won't ever make any grammatical mistake."

"Because you remember all the dictionaries and grammars you ever read?"

John looked at her sharply. "Don't be sarcastic, Sue."

"I wasn't being—"

He waved her silent. "I never used dictionaries as light reading. But I do remember words and sentences in my reading and they were correctly spelled and correctly parsed."

"Don't be sure. You've seen any word misspelled in every possible way and every possible example of twisted grammer, too."

"Those were exceptions. By far the largest number of times I've encountered literary English, I've encountered it used correctly. It outweighs accidents, errors, and ignorance. What's more, I'm sure I'm improving even as I sit here, growing more intelligent steadily."

"And you're not worried. What if—"

"What if I become *too* intelligent? Tell me how on Earth you think becoming too intelligent can be harmful."

"I was going to say," said Susan, coldly, "that what you're experiencing is not intelligence. It's only total recall."

"How do you mean 'only'? If I recall perfectly, if I use the English language correctly, if I know endless quantities of material, isn't that going to make me seem more intelligent? How else need one define intelligence? You aren't growing just a little jealous, are you, Sue?"

"No," more coldly still. "I can always get an injection of my own if I feel desperate about it."

John put down his fork. "You can't mean that."

"I don't, but what if I did?"

"Because you can't take advantage of your special knowledge to deprive me of my position."

"What position?"

The main course arrived and for a few moments, John was busy. Then he said, in a whisper, "My position as the first of the future. *Homo superior!* There'll never be too many of us. You heard what Kupfer said. Some are too dumb to make it. Some are too smart to change much. I'm the one!"

"*Dead* average." One corner of Susan's mouth lifted.

"Once I was. There'll be others like me eventually. Not many, but there'll be others. It's just that I want to make my mark before the others come along. It's for the firm, you know. Us!"

He remained lost in thought thereafter, testing his brain delicately. Susan ate in an unhappy silence.

## 7.

John spent several days organizing his memories. It was like the preparation of an orderly reference book. One by one, he recalled all his experiences in the six years he had spent at Quantum Pharmaceuticals and all he had heard and all the papers and memos he had read.

There was no difficulty in discarding the irrelevant and unimportant and storing them in a "hold till further notice" compartment where they did not interfere with his analysis. Other items were put in order so that they established a natural progression.

Against that skeletal organization, he resurrected the scuttlebutt he had heard; the gossip, malicious or otherwise; casual phrases and interjections at conferences which he had not been conscious of hearing at the time. Those items which did not fit anywhere against the background he had built up in his head were worthless, empty of factual content. Those which did fit clicked firmly into place and could be seen as true by that mere fact.

The further the structure grew, and the more coherent, the more significant new items became and the easier it was to fit them in.

Ross stopped by John's desk on Thursday. He said, "I want to see you in my office at the nonce, Heath, if your legs will deign to carry you in that direction."

John rose uneasily. "Is it necessary? I'm busy."

"Yes, you look busy." Ross looked over the clear desk which, at the moment, held nothing but a studio photo of a smiling Susan. "You've been this busy all week. But you've asked me whether seeing me in my office is necessary. For me, no; but for you, vital. There's the door to my office. There's the door to the hell out of here. Choose one or the other and do it fast."

John nodded and, without undue hurry, followed Ross into his office.

Ross seated himself behind his desk but did not invite John to sit. He maintained a hard stare for a moment, then said, "What the hell's got into you this week, Heath. Don't you know what your job is?"

"To the extent that I have done it, it would seem that I do," said John. "The report on microcosmic is on your desk and complete and seven days ahead of deadline. I doubt that you can have complaints about it."

"You doubt, do you? Do I have permission to have complaints if I choose to after communing with my soul? Or am I condemned to applying to you for permission?"

"I apparently have not made myself plain, Mr. Ross. I doubt that you have *rational* complaints about it. To have those of the other variety is entirely up to you."

Ross rose now. "Listen, punk, if I decide to fire you, you won't get the news by word of mouth. It won't be anything I say that will give you the glad tidings. You will go out through the door in a violent tumble and mine will be the propulsive force behind that tumble. Just keep that in your small brain and your tongue in your big mouth.—Whether you've done your work or not is not at question right now. Whether you've done everyone else's is. Who and what gives you the right to manage everyone in this place?"

John said nothing.

Ross roared, "Well?"

John said, "Your order was 'keep your tongue in your big mouth.' "

Ross turned a dangerous red. "You will answer questions, however."

John said, "I am not aware that I have been managing anyone."

"There's not a person in the place you haven't corrected at least once. You have gone over Willoughby's head in connection with the correspondence on the TMP's; you have been into general files using Bronstein's computer access; and God knows what else I haven't yet been told about and all in the last two days. You are disrupting the work of this department and it must cease this moment. There must be dead calm, and instantaneously, or it will be tornado weather for you, my man."

John said, "If I have interfered in the narrow sense, it has been for the good of the company. In the case of Willoughby, his treatment of the TMP matter was putting Quantum Pharmaceuticals in violation of government regulations, something I have pointed out to you in one of several memos I have sent you which you apparently have not had occasion to read. As for Bronstein, he was simply ignoring general directions and costing the company fifty thousand in unnecessary tests, something I was easily able to establish by locating the necessary correspondence—merely to corroborate my clear memory of the situation."

Ross was swelling visibly through the talk. "Heath," he said, "you are usurping my role. You will, therefore, gather your personal effects and be off the premises before lunch, never to return. If you do, I will take extreme pleasure in helping you out again with my foot. Your official notice of dismissal will be in your hands, or down your throat, before your effects will be collected, work as quickly as you may."

John said, "Don't try to bully me, Ross. You've cost the company a quarter of a million dollars through incompetence and you know it."

There was a short pause as Ross deflated. He said, cautiously, "What are you talking about?"

"Quantum Pharmaceuticals went down to the wire on the Nutley bid and missed out because a certain piece of information that was in your hands stayed in your hands and never got to the Board of Directors. You either forgot or you didn't bother and in either case you are not the man for your job. You are either incompetent or have sold out."

"You're insane."

"No one need believe me. The information is in the computer, if one knows where to look and I know where to look. What's more, the knowledge is on file and will be on the desks of the interested parties two minutes after I leave these premises."

"If this were so," said Ross, speaking with difficulty, "you could not possibly know. This is a stupid attempt at blackmail by threat of slander."

"You know it's not slander. If you doubt that I have the information, let me tell you that there is one memorandum that is not in the records but can be reconstructed without too much difficulty from what is there. You would have to explain its absence and it will be presumed you have destroyed it. You know I'm not bluffing."

"It's still blackmail."

"Why? I'm making no demands and no threats. I'm merely explaining my actions of the past two days. Of course, if I'm forced to resign, I'll have to explain why I resigned, won't I?"

Ross said nothing.

John said, coolly, "Is my resignation being requested?"

"Get out of here!"

"With my job? Or without it?"

Ross said, "You have your job." His face was a study in hatred.

# 8.

Susan had arranged a dinner at her apartment and had gone to considerable trouble for it. Never, in her own opinion, had she looked more enticing and never did she think it more important to move John, at least for a bit, away from his total concentration on his own mind.

She said, with an attempt at heartiness, "After all, we are celebrating the last nine days of single blessedness."

"We are celebrating more than that," said John with a grim smile. "It's only four days since I got the disinhibitor and already I've been able to put Ross in his place. He'll never bother me again."

"We each seem to have our own notion of sentiment," said Susan. "Tell me the details of *your* tender remembrance."

John told the tale crisply, repeating the conversation verbatim and without hesitation.

Susan listened stonily, without in any way rising to the gathering triumph in John's voice. "How *did* you know all that about Ross?"

John said, "There are no secrets, Sue. Things just *seem* secret because people don't remember. If you can recall every remark, every comment, every stray word made to you or in your hearing and consider them all in combination, you find that everyone gives himself away in everything. You can pick out meanings that will, in these days of computerization, send you straight to the necessary records. It can be done. I can do it. I have done it in the case of Ross. I can do it in the case of anybody with whom I associate."

"You can also get them furious."

"I got Ross furious. You can bet on that."

"Was that wise?"

"What can he do to me? I've got him cold."

"He has enough clout in the upper echelons—"

"Not for long. I have a conference set for 2 P.M. tomorrow with old man Prescott and his stinking cigar and I'll cut Ross off at the pass."

"Don't you think you'r moving too quickly?"

"Moving too quickly? I haven't even begun. Prescott's just a stepping-stone. Quantum Pharmaceutical's just a stepping-stone."

"It's still too quick. Johhny, you need someone to direct you. You need—"

"I need *nothing*. With what I have," he tapped his temple, "there's no one and nothing that can stop me."

Susan said, "Well, look, let's not discuss that. We have different plans to make."

"Plans?"

"Our own. We're getting married in just under nine days. Surely," with heavy irony, "you haven't returned to the sad old days when you forgot things."

"I remember the wedding," said John, testily, "but at the moment I've got to reorganize Quantum. In fact, I've been thinking seriously of postponing the wedding till I have things well in hand."

"Oh? And when might that be?"

"That's hard to tell. Not long at the rate I'm taking hold. A month or two, I suppose. Unless," and he descended into sarcasm, "you think that's moving too quickly."

Susan was breathing hard. "Were you planning to consult with me on the matter?"

John raised his eyebrows. "Would it have been necessary? Where's the argument? Surely you see what's happening. We can't interrupt it and lose momentum.—Listen, did you know I'm a mathematical wiz. I can multiply and divide as fast as a computer because at some time in my life I have come across almost every simple bit of arithmetic and I can *recall* the answers. I read a table of square roots and I can—"

Susan cried, "My God, Johnny, you *are* a kid with a new toy. You've lost your perspective. Instant recall is good for nothing but playing tricks with. It doesn't give you one bit more intelligence; not an ounce; not a speck more of judgment; not a whiff more of common sense. You're about as safe to have around as a little boy with a loaded grenade. You need looking after by someone with brains."

John scowled. "Do I? It seems to me that I'm getting what I want."

"Are you? Isn't it true that I'm what you want also?"

"What?"

"Go ahead, Johnny. You want me. Reach out and take me. Exercise that remarkable recall you have. Remember who I am, what I am, the things we can do, the warmth, the affection, the sentiment."

John, with his forehead still creased in uncertainty, extended his arms toward Susan.

She stepped out of them. "But you haven't got me, or anything about me. You can't remember me into your arms; you have to love me into them. The trouble is, you don't have the good sense to do it and you lack the intelligence to establish reasonable priorities.—Here, take this and get out of my apartment or I'll hit you with something a lot heavier."

He stopped to pick up the engagement ring. "Susan—"

"I said, get out. The firm of Johnny and Sue is hereby dissolved."

Her face blazed anger and John turned meekly and left.

# 9.

When he arrived at Quantum the next morning, Anderson was waiting for him with a look of anxious impatience on his face.

"Mr. Heath," he said, smiling, and rising.

"What do you want?" demanded John.

"We are private here, I take it?"

"The place isn't bugged as far as I know."

"You are to report to us day after tomorrow for examination. On Sunday. You recall that?"

"Of course, I recall that. I'm incapable of not recalling. I *am* capable of changing my mind, however. Why do I need an examination?"

"Why not, sir? It is quite plain from what Kupfer and I have picked up that the treatment seems to have worked splendidly. Actually, we don't want to wait till Sunday. If you can come with me today—now, in fact—it would mean a great deal to us, to Quantum, and, of course, to humanity."

John said, curtly, "You might have held on to me when you had me. You sent me about my business, allowing me to live and work unsupervised so that you could test me under field conditions, and get a better idea of how things would work out. It meant more risk for me, but you didn't worry about that, did you?"

"Mr. Heath, that was not in our minds. We—"

"Don't tell me that. I remember every last word you and Kupfer said to me last Sunday, and it's quite clear to me that that *was* in your minds. So if I take the risk, I accept the benefits. I have no intention of presenting myself as a biochemical freak who has achieved my ability at the end of a hypodermic needle. Nor do I want others of the sort wondering around. For now, I have a monopoly and I intend to use it. When I'm ready—not before—I will be willing to cooperate with you and benefit humanity. But just remember, I'm the one who will know when I'm ready, not you. So don't call me; I'll call you."

Anderson managed a soft smile. "As to that, Mr. Heath, how can you stop us from making our announcement? Those who have dealt with you this week will have no trouble in recognizing the change in you and in testifying to it."

"Really? See here, Anderson, listen closely and do so without that foolish grin on your face. It irritates me. I told you I remember every word you and Kupfer spoke. I remember every nuance of expression, every sidelong glance. It all spoke volumes. I learned enough to check through sick-leave records with a good idea of what I was looking for. It would seem that I was not the first Quantum employee on whom you had tried the disinhibitor."

Anderson was, indeed, not smiling. "That is nonsense."

"You know it is not, and you had better know I can prove it. I know the names of the men involved—one was a woman, actually—and the hospitals in which they were treated and the false history with which they were supplied. Since you did not warn me of this, when you used me as your fourth experimental animal on two legs, I owe you nothing but a prison sentence."

Anderson said, "I won't discuss this matter. Let me say this, though. The treatment will wear off, Heath. You won't keep your total recall. You will have to come back for further treatment and you can be sure it will be on our terms."

John said, "Nuts! You don't suppose I haven't investigated your reports—at least, those you haven't kept secret. And I already have a notion of what aspects you *have* kept secret. The treatment lasts longer in some cases than others. It invariably lasts longer where it is more effective. In my case, the treatment has been extraordinarily effective and it will endure a considerable time. By the time I come to you again, if I ever have to, I will be in a position where any failure on your part to cooperate will be swiftly devastating to you. Don't even think of it."

"You ungrateful—"

"Don't bother me," said John, wearily. "I have no time to listen to you froth. Go away, I have work to do."

Anderson's face was a study in fear and frustration as he left.

## 10.

It was 2:30 P.M. when John walked into Prescott's office, for once not minding the cigar smoke. It would not be long, he knew, before Prescott would have to choose between his cigars and his position.

With Prescott were Arnold Gluck and Lewis Randall, so that John had the grim pleasure of knowing he was facing the three top men in the division.

Prescott rested his cigar on top of an ashtray and said, "Ross has asked me to give you half an hour, and that's all I will give you. You're the one with the trick memory, aren't you?"

"My name is John Heath, sir, and I intend to present you with a rationalization of procedure for the company; one that will make full use of the age of computers and electronic communication and will lay the groundwork for further modification as the technology improves."

The three men looked at each other.

Gluck, whose creased face was tanned a leathery-brown, said, "Are you an expert in office management?"

"I don't have to be, sir. I have been here for six years and I recall every bit of the procedure in every transaction in which I have been involved. That means the pattern of such transactions is plain to me and its imperfections obvious. One can see toward what it is tending and where it is doing so wastefully and inefficiently. If you'll listen, I will explain. You will find it easy to understand."

Randall, whose red hair and freckles made him seem younger than he was, said sardonically, "Real easy, I hope, because we have trouble with hard concepts."

"You won't have trouble," said John.

"And you won't get a second more than twenty-one minutes," said Prescott, looking at his watch.

"It won't take that," said John. "I have it diagrammed and I can talk quickly."

It took fifteen minutes and the three management personnel were remarkably silent in that interval.

Finally Gluck said, with a hostile glance out of his small eyes, "It sounds as though you are saying we can get along with half the management we are employing these days."

"Less than half," said John, coolly, "and be the more efficient for it. We can't fire ordinary personnel at will because of the unions, though we can profitably lose them by attrition. Management is not protected, however, and can be let go. They'll have pensions if they're old enough and can get new jobs if they're young enough. Our thought must be for Quantum."

Prescott, who had maintained an ominous silence, now puffed furiously at his noxious cigar and said, "Changes like this have to be considered carefully and implemented, if at all, with the greatest of caution. What seems logical on paper can lose out in the human equation."

John said, "Prescott, if this reorganization is not accepted within a week, and if I am not placed in charge of its implementation, I will resign. I will have no trouble in finding employment with a smaller firm where this plan can be far more easily put into practice. Beginning with a small group of management people, I can expand in both quantity and efficiency of performance without additional hiring and within a year I'll drive Quantum into bankruptcy. It would be fun to do this if I am driven to it, so consider carefully. My half hour is up. Good-bye." And he left.

## 11.

Prescott looked after him with a glance of frigid calculation. He said to the other two, "I think he means what he says and that he knows every facet of our operations better than we do. We can't let him go."

"You mean we've got to accept his plan," said Randall, shocked.

"I didn't say that. You two go, and remember this whole thing is confidential."

Gluck said, "I have the feeling that if we don't do something, all three of us will find ourselves on our butts in the street within a month."

"Very likely," said Prescott, "so we'll do something."

"What?"

"If you don't know, you won't get hurt. Leave it to me. Forget it for now and have a nice weekend."

When they were gone, he thought a while, chewing furiously on his cigar. He then turned to his telephone and dialed an extension. "Prescott here. I want you in my office first thing Monday morning. First thing. Hear me?"

## 12.

Anderson looked a trifle disheveled. He had had a bad weekend.

Prescott, who had had a worse, said to him, malevolently, "You and Kupfer tried again, didn't you?"

Anderson said, softly, "It's better not to discuss that, Mr. Prescott. You remember it was agreed that in certain aspects of research, a distance was to be established. We were to take the risks or the glory, and Quantum was to share in the latter but not in the former."

"And your salary was doubled with a guarantee of all legal payments to be Quantum's responsibility; don't forget that. This man, John Heath, was treated by you and Kupfer, wasn't he? Come on. There's no mistaking it. There's no point in hiding it."

"Well, yes."

"And you were so brilliant that you turned him loose on us—this—this—tarantula."

"We didn't anticipate this would happen. When he didn't go into instant shock, we thought it was our first chance to test the process in the field. We thought he would break down after two or three days, or it would pass."

Prescott said, "If I hadn't been protected so damned well, I wouldn't have put the whole thing out of my mind and I would have guessed what had happened when that bastard first pulled the computer bit and produced the details of correspondence he had no business remembering.—All right, we know where we are now. He's holding the company to ransom with a new plan of operations he can't be allowed to put through. Also, he can't be allowed to walk away from us."

Anderson said, "Considering Heath's capacity for recall and synthesis, is it possible that his plan of operations may be a good one?"

"I don't care if it is. That bastard is after my job and who knows what else and we've got to get rid of him."

"How do you mean, rid of him? He could be of vital importance to the cerebro-chemical project."

"Forget that. It's a disaster. You're creating a super-Hitler."

Anderson said, in soft-voiced anguish, "The effect will wear off."

"Yes? When?"

"At this moment, I can't be sure."

"Then I can't take chances. We've got to make our arrangements and do it tomorrow at the latest. We can't wait any longer."

# 13.

John was in high good humor. The manner in which Ross avoided him when he could and spoke to him deferentially when he had to affected the entire work force. There was a strange and radical change in the pecking order, with himself at the top.

Nor could John deny to himself that he liked it. He reveled in it. The tide was moving strongly and unbelievably swiftly. It was only nine days since the injection of the disinhibitor and every step had been forward.

Well, no, there had been Susan's silly rage at him, but he would deal with her later. When he showed her the heights to which he would climb in nine additional days—in ninety—

He looked up. Ross was at his desk, waiting for his attention but reluctant to do anything as crass as to attract that attention by as much as clearing his throat. John swiveled his chair, put his feet out before him in an attitude of relaxation, and said, "Well, Ross?"

Ross said, carefully, "I would like to see you in my office, Heath. Something important has come up and, frankly, you're the only one who can set it straight."

John got slowly to his feet. "Yes? What is it?"

Ross looked about mutely at the busy room, with at least five men in reasonable earshot. Then he looked toward his office door and held out an inviting arm.

John hesitated, but for years Ross had held unquestioned authority over him, and at this moment he reacted to habit.

Ross held his door open for John politely, stepped through himself and closed the door behind him, locking it unobtrusively and remaining in front of it. Anderson stepped out from the other side of the bookcase.

John said sharply, "What's all this about?"

"Nothing at all, Heath," said Ross, his smile turning into a vulpine grin. "We're just going to help you out of your abnormal state—take you back to normality. Don't move, Heath."

Anderson had a hypodermic in his hand. "Please, Heath, do not struggle. We wish you no harm."

"If I yell—" said John.

"If you make any sound," said Ross, "I will put a hammerlock on you and hold it till your eyes bug out. I would like to do that, so please try to yell."

John said, "I have the goods on both of you, safe on deposit. Anything that happens to me—"

"Mr. Heath," said Anderson, "nothing will happen to you. Something is going to *un*happen to you. We will put you back to where you were. That would happen anyway, but we will hurry it up just a little."

"So I'm going to hold you, Heath," said Ross, "and you won't move because if you do, you will disturb our friend with the needle and he might slip and give you more than the carefully calculated dose, and you might end up unable to remember anything at all."

Heath was backing away, breathless. "That's what you're planning. You think you'll be safe that way. If I forgot all about you, all about the information, all about its storage. But—"

"We're not going to hurt you, Heath," said Anderson.

John's forehead glistened with sweat. A near-paralysis gripped him.

"An amnesiac!" he said, huskily, and with a terror that only someone could feel at the possibility who himself had perfect recall.

"Then you won't remember this either, will you?" said Ross. "Go ahead, Anderson."

"Well," muttered Anderson, in resignation. "I'm destroying a perfect test-subject." He lifted John's flaccid arm and readied the hypodermic.

There was a knock at the door. A clear voice called, "John!"

Anderson froze almost automatically, looking up questioningly.

Ross had turned to look at the door. Now he turned back. "Shoot that stuff into him, doc," he said in an urgent whisper.

The voice came again, "Johnny, I know you're in there. I've called the police. They're on the way."

Ross whispered again, "Go ahead. She's lying. And by the time they come, it's over. Who can prove anything?"

But Anderson was shaking his head vigorously. "It's his fiancée. She knows he was treated. She was there."

"You jackass."

There was the sound of a kick against the door and then the voice sounded in a muffled, "Let go of me. They've got— Let go!"

Anderson said, "Having her push the thing was the only way we could get him to agree. Besides, I don't think we have to do anything. Look at him."

John had collapsed in a corner, eyes glazed, and clearly in a state of unconscious trance.

Anderson said, "He's been terrified and that can produce a shock that will interfere with recall under normal conditions. I think the disinhibitor has been wiped out. Let her in and let *me* talk to her."

## 14.

Susan looked pale as she sat with her arm protectively about the shoulders of her ex-fiancé. "What happened?"

"You remember the injection of—"

"Yes, yes. What happened?"

"He was supposed to come to our office day before yesterday, Sunday, for a thorough examination. He didn't come. We worried and the reports from his superiors had me very perturbed. He was becoming arrogant, megalomaniacal, irascible— Perhaps you noticed. —You're not wearing your engagement ring."

"We—quarreled," said Susan.

"Then you understand. He was— Well, if he were an inanimate device, we might say his motor was overheating as it sped faster and faster. This morning it seemed absolutely essential to treat him. We persuaded him to come here, locked the door and—"

"Injected him with something while I howled and kicked outside."

"Not at all," said Anerson. "We would have used a sedative, but we were too late. He had what I can only describe as a breakdown. You may search his body for fresh punctures, which, as his fiancée, I presume you may do without embarrassment, and you will find none."

Susan said, "I'll see about that. What happens, now?"

"I am sure he will recover. He will be his old self again."

"Dead average?"

"He will not have perfect recall, but until ten days ago, he never had. —Naturally, the firm will give him indefinite leave on full salary. If any medical treatment is required, all medical expenses will be paid. And when he feels like it, he can return to active duty."

"Yes? Well, I will want all that in writing before the day is out, or I see my lawyer tomorrow."

"But Miss Collins," said Anerson, "you know that Mr. Heath volunteered. You were willing too."

"I think," said Susan, "that *you* know the situation was

misrepresented to us and that you won't welcome an investigation. Just see to it that what you've just promised is in writing."

"You will have to, in return, sign an agreement to hold us guiltless of any misadventure your fiancé may have suffered."

"Possibly. I prefer to see what kind of misadventure it is first. — Can you walk, Johnny?"

John nodded and said, a little huskily, "Yes, Sue."

"Then let's go."

## 15.

John had put himself outside a cup of good coffee and an omelet before Susan permitted discussion. Then he said, "What I don't understand is how you happened to be there?"

"Shall we say woman's intuition?"

"Let's say Susan's brains."

"All right. Let's! After I threw the ring at you, I felt self-pitying and aggrieved and after that wore off, I felt a severe sense of loss because, odd though it might seem to the average sensible person, I'm very fond of you."

"I'm sorry, Sue," said John, humbly.

"As well you should be. God, you were insupportable. But then I got to thinking that if you could get poor loving me that furious, what must you be doing to your co-workers. The more I thought about it, the more I thought they might have a strong impulse to kill you. Now, don't get me wrong. I'm willing to admit you deserved killing, but only at *my* hands. I wouldn't dream of allowing anyone else to do it. I didn't hear from you—"

"I know, Sue. I had plans and I had no time—"

"You had to do it all in two weeks. I know, you idiot. By this morning I couldn't stand it anymore. I came to see how you were and found you behind a locked door."

John shuddered. "I never thought I'd welcome your kicking and screaming, but I did then. You stopped them."

"Will it upset you to talk about it?"

"I don't think so. I'm all right."

"Then what were they doing?"

"They were going to re-inhibit me. I thought they might be giving me an overdose and make me an amnesiac."

"Why?"

"Because they knew I had them all. I could ruin them and the company."

"You really could."

"Absolutely."

"But they didn't actually inject you, did they? Or was that another of Anderson's lies?"

"They really didn't."

"Are you all right?"

"I'm not an amnesiac."

"Well, I hate to sound like a Victorian damsel, but I hope you have learned your lesson."

"If you mean, do I realize you were right, I do."

"Then just let me lecture you for one minute, so you don't forget again. You went about everything too rapidly, too openly, and with too much disregard for the possible violent counteraction of others. You had total recall and you mistook it for intelligence. If you had someone who was really intelligent to guide you—"

"I needed you, Sue."

"Well, you've got me now, Johnny."

"What do we do next, Sue?"

"First, we get that paper from Quantum and, since you're all right, we'll sign the release for them. Second, we get married on Saturday, just as we originally planned. Third, we'll see— But, Johnny?"

"Yes?"

"You're all right?"

"Couldn't be better, Sue. Now we're together, everything's fine."

## 16.

It wasn't a formal wedding. Less formal than they had originally planned and fewer guests. No one was there from Quantum, for instance—Susan had pointed out, quite firmly, that that would be a bad idea.

A neighbor of Susan's had brought a video-camera to record the proceedings, something that seemed to John to be the height of schlock, but Susan had wanted it.

And then the neighbor had said to him with a tragic shrug, "Can't get the damn thing to turn on. You'd think they'd give me one in working order. I'll have to make a phone call." He hastened down the steps to the pay phone in the chapel lobby.

John advanced to look at the camera curiously. An instruction booklet lay on a small table to one side. He picked it up and leafed through the pages with moderate speed, then put it back. He looked about him, but everyone was busy. No one seemed to be paying attention of him.

He slid the rear panel to one side, unobtrusively, and peered inside. He then turned away and gazed at the opposite wall thoughtfully. He was still gazing even as his right hand snaked in toward the mechanism and made a quick adjustment. After a brief interval he put the rear panel back and flicked a toggle switch.

The neighbor came bustling back, looking exasperated. "How am I going to follow directions I can't make head or—" He frowned, then said, "Funny. It's on. It must have been working all the time."

## 17.

"You may kiss the bride," said the minister, benignly, and John took Susan in his arms and followed orders with enthusiasm.

Susan whispered through unmoving lips, "You fixed that camera. Why?"

He whispered back, "I wanted everything right for the wedding."

She whispered, "You wanted to show off."

They broke apart, looking at each other through love-misted eyes, then fell into another embrace, while the small audience stirred and tittered.

Susan whispered, "You do it again, and I'll skin you. As long as no one knows you still have it, no one will stop you. We'll have it all within a year, if you follow directions."

"Yes, dear," whispered John, humbly.

# Saving Humanity

My friend, George, sighing lugubriously, said to me, one evening, "I have a friend who is a klutz."

I nodded wisely. "Birds of a feather," I said.

George gazed at me in astonishment. "What have feathers to do with it? You have the most remarkable ability to skid away from a subject. It is the result, I suppose, of your thoroughly inadequate intellect—which I mention in pity, and not as reproof."

"Well, well," I said, "let that be as it may. When you refer to your friend the klutz, are you speaking of Azazel?"

Azazel was the two-centimeter demon or extraterrestrial being (take your pick) concerning whom George talks about constantly, ceasing only in response to a direct question. Freezingly, he said, "Azazel is not a subject for conversation, and I do not understand how you came to have heard of him."

"I happened to be within a mile of you one day," I said. George paid no attention, but said:

* * *

I first came across the uneuphonious word "klutz", in fact, through a conversation with my friend, Menander Block. You have never met him, I'm afraid, for he is a University man and therefore rather selective in his friendships, for which one, observing you, can scarcely blame him.

The word, klutz, he told me, referred to an awkward, clumsy person. "And that's me," he said. "It comes from a Yiddish word that, taken literally, means a piece of wood, a log, a block; and, of course, my name, as you will note, is Block."

He heaved an enormous sigh. "And yet I am not a klutz in the strict meaning of the word. There is nothing wooden, loggish or blockish about me. I dance as lightly as a zephyr and as gracefully as a dragonfly; I am sylph-like in every motion; and numerous young women could testify, if I thought it safe to allow them to do so, of my skill as a disciple of the amatory art. It is, rather, that I am a klutz at long distance. Without being myself affected, everything about me becomes klutzish. The very University itself seems to trip over its own cosmic feet. I suppose if you want to mix languages and combine Greek with Yiddish, I am a 'teleklutz.' "

"How long has this been going on, Menander?" I asked.

"All my life, but, of course, it was only as an adult that I realized this peculiar quality I possess. While still a youth, I simply assumed that what happened to me was the normal state of affairs."

"Have you discussed this with anyone?"

"Of course not, George, old fellow. I would be considered mad. Can you see a psychoanalyst, for instance, confronting the phenomenon of teleklutzism. He would have me in the funny house half way through my first session and write a paper on his discovery of a new psychosis and probably become a millionaire as a result. I'm not going to the booby hatch just to enrich some psychomedical leech. I cannot tell *anyone* this."

"Then why are you telling me this, Menander?"

"Because, on the other hand, it seems to me I must tell someone if I am to remain functional. As it happens, you are the least someone I know."

I did not follow his reasoning there, but I could see that I was about to be subjected once again to the unwanted confidences of my friends. It was the price, I well knew, of the fact that I was proverbial for my understanding, sympathy, and, most of all, for my close-mouthed reticence. No secret placed in my keeping would ever reach the ears of anyone else. —I make an exception in your case, of course, since it is well-known that you have an attention span of five seconds, and a memory-span of rather less.

I signalled for another drink and indicated, by a certain arcane sign that I alone know, that it was to be placed on Menander's tab. A laborer, after all, is worthy of his hire. I said, "Just how does this teleklutzism manifest itself, Menander?"

"In its simplest form, and in the manner that was first brought to my attention, it shows up in the peculiar weather that accompanies my travels. I do not travel very much, and when I do, I go by car, and when I do *that*, it rains. It doesn't matter what the weather forecast is; it doesn't matter how brightly the sun is shining when I start out. The clouds gather, grow darker and it begins to drizzle and then to pour. When my teleklutzism is in particular fettle, the temperature drops and we have an ice-storm.

"Of course, I am careful not to be foolish. I refuse to drive into New

England until March is safely over. Last spring, I drove to Boston on April 6—which promptly had the first April blizzard in the history of the Boston Weather Bureau. I once drove to Williamsburg, Virginia, on March 28, assuming that I might be allowed a fews days of grace considering that I was penetrating Dixie. Hah! Williamsburg had nine inches of snow that day and the natives were trying to rub some of it between their fingers and were asking each other what the white stuff was.

"I have often thought that if we imagined the Universe to be under the personal direction of God, we might picture Gabriel rushing into the divine presence to cry out, 'Holy One, two galaxies are about to collide in an unimaginably enormous catastrophe', and God would answer, 'Don't bother me now, Gabriel; I'm busy making it rain on Menander.' "

I said, "You might make the best of the situation, Menander? Why not sell your services, for fabulous sums, as a drought-breaker?"

"I have thought of that, but the mere thought dries up any rain that might occur during my travels. Besides, if the rain came when it was needed, it would probably produce a flood.

"And it's not only rain, or traffic jams, or the disappearance of landmarks; there are myriads of other things. Expensive objects break spontaneously in my presence, or are dropped by others through no fault attributable to myself. There is an advanced particle accelerator in operation in Batavia, Illinois. One day an enormously important experiment was ruined because of the failure of its vacuum; a completely unexplained failure. Only I knew (the next day, that is, when I read of the incident in the paper) that at the very moment of failure, I happened to be passing the outskirts of Batavia in a bus. It was raining, of course.

"At this very moment, old fellow, some of the fine five-day-old wine in the cellars of this fine establishment, being aged in the plastic, is turning sour. Someone brushing past this table at this moment will, when he arrives home, find that the pipes in his cellar have burst at the precise moment he passed me; except that he won't know that he passed me at that precise moment and that the passage was the cause. And so it will be with myriads of accidents; supposed accidents, that is."

My heart bled for my young friend. And my blood froze at the thought that I was sitting next to him and that at my cozy digs unimaginable catastrophes might be taking place.

I said, "You are, in short, a jinx!"

Menander threw his head back and stared down his nose at me in a most unpleasant way. "Jinx," he said, "is the common term; teleklutz is the scientific one."

"Well, then, jinx or teleklutz, suppose I told you I could perhaps remove this curse from you?"

"Curse is right," Menander said, gloomily. "I have often thought that, at the time of my birth, an ill-natured fairy, irked at not having been invited to the christening— Are you trying to tell me you can cancel curses because you are a good fairy?"

"I am not any kind of fairy," I said severely. "Just suppose I can remove this cur—condition of yours."

"How on Earth could you do that?"

"Not exactly on Earth," I said. "But how about it?"

"What do *you* get out of it?" he asked, suspiciously.

"The heart-warming feeling of having helped save a friend from a horrible life."

Menander thought about it and then shook his head firmly. "That's not enough."

"Of course, if you want to offer me some small sum—"

"No, no. I wouldn't think of insulting you that way. Offer a sum of money to a *friend*? Place a fiscal value on friendship? How could you think that of me, George? What I meant was that removing my teleklutzism isn't enough. You must do more than that."

"How can one do more?"

"Consider! Through my life I have been responsible for anything from inconvenience to catastrophe to perhaps millions of innocent people. Even if I brought no ill-fortune to a single person from this moment on, the evil I have done thus far—even though none of it was voluntary or in any way to be considered my fault—is more than I can bear. I must have something that will cancel it all out."

"Like what?"

"I must be in a position to save humanity."

"Save humanity?"

"What else can possibly balance the immeasureable damage I have done? George, I insist. If you are going to remove my curse, replace it with the ability to save humanity in some great crisis."

"I'm not sure that I can."

"*Try* George. Don't shy away at this crisis. If you're going to do a job, do it well, I always say. Think of humanity, old friend."

"Wait a moment," I said, alarmed, "you're putting this whole thing on my shoulders."

"Of course I am, George," Menander said, warmly. "Broad shoulders! Good shoulders! Made to bear burdens! Go home, George, and arrange to remove this curse from me. A grateful humanity will shower you with blessings except, of course, that they will never hear of it, for I will tell no one. Your good deeds are not to be shamed by exposure, and rely on me, I will never expose them."

There is something wonderful about unselfish friendship that can be duplicated by nothing else on Earth. I rose at once to get to my task and left so quickly that I neglected to pay my half of the dinner bill. Fortunately, Menander did not notice this till I was safely out of the restaurant.

* * *

I had some trouble getting in touch with Azazel and in opening the hyperdimensional gateway between his world and ours. Nor did he seem good-natured about it at all. His two-centimeter-tall body was wrapped in a pinkish glow and, in his piping voice, he said, "Has it occurred to you that I might be showering?"

And indeed there was a very faint smell of ammonia about him.

I said, humbly, "This is a rather enormous emergency, oh Mighty-One-For-Whom-Words-Are-Insufficient."

"Well then, tell me, but mind, don't take all day about it."

"Certainly!" I said, and outlined the matter with admirable conciseness.

"Hmm," said Azazel. "For once you have presented me with an interesting problem."

"I have? Do you mean there is indeed such a thing as teleklutzism."

"Oh, yes. It is common on my world and is usually removed by inoculation during childhood. You see quantum mechanics makes it quite clear that the properties of the Universe depend, to a certain extent, on the observer. Just as the Universe affects the observer, the observer affects the Universe. Some observers affect the Universe adversely, or at least adversely with respect to some other observers. Thus, one observer may accelerate the supernovadom of some star, which would irritate other observers who may find themselves uncomfortably close to that star at the time."

"I see. Well, can you inoculate my friend, Menander, and remove this quantum-observational effect of his?"

"Oh, of course! Simple! It will take ten seconds and then I can return to my shower and to the rite of laskorati I will undertake with two samini of unimaginable loveliness."

"Wait! Wait! That's not enough."

"Don't be silly. Two samini are *quite* enough. Only a lecher would want three."

"I mean removing the teleklutzism isn't enough. Menander also wants to be in a position to save humanity."

For a minute, I thought Azazel was going to forget our long friendship and all I had done for him in the way of supplying him with interesting problems that probably improved his mind and his scientific abilities. I did not understand all he said, for most of the words were in his own language but they sounded very much like saws scraping along rusty nails.

Finally, having cooled down to a dim red-heat, he said, "Now how am I going to do that?"

"Is anything too much for the Apostle-of-Incredibility?"

"You bet! —But let's see!" He thought for a while, and burst out, "But who in the Universe would *want* to save humanity? Where's the worth in doing that? You stink up this whole section— Well, well, I think it can be done."

It didn't take ten seconds. It took half an hour and a very uncomfortable half-hour it was, too, with Azazel groaning part of the time and the rest of the time stopping to wonder if the samini were going to wait for him.

He was done eventually and, of course, it meant I would have to test out the matter on Menander Block.

* * *

When I next saw Menander, I said, "You're cured."

He stared at me hostilely, "Do you know that you stuck me with the dinner check the other night?"

"Surely a minor point compared with the fact that you're cured."

"I don't feel cured."

"Well, come. Let's take a drive together. You take the wheel."

"It looks cloudy already. Some cure!"

"Drive! What have we to lose?"

He backed the car out of his garage. A man passing by on the other side of the street did not trip over an overloaded garbage can.

He drove down the street. The light did not turn red as he approached, and two cars skidding toward each other at the intersection next but one, missed each other by a comfortable margin.

By the time he was at the bridge, the clouds had thinned out and a warm sun was shining down upon the car. It was not in his eyes.

When we finally got home, he was weeping unashamedly, and I parked the car for him. I scraped it slightly, but it was not *I* that had had my teleklutzism cured. At that, it might have been worse. I might have scraped my own car.

For the next few days, he was seeking me out constantly. I was the only one, after all, who could understand the miracle that had taken place.

He would say, "I went to a dance, and not one couple tripped over each other's feet and fell down and broke a collar bone or two. I could dance sylph-like with utter abandon and my partner never got sick to her stomach, even though she had eaten most unwisely."

Or, "At work they were installing a new air-conditioning unit and not once did it fall upon a workman's toes, breaking them permanently."

Or even, "I visited a friend in a hospital, something I once wouldn't have dreamed of doing, and in not one of the rooms that I passed did the intravenous needle pop out of a vein. Nor did a single hypodermic needle miss its appropriate target."

Sometimes, he would ask me, brokenly, "Are you sure that I will have a chance to save humanity?"

"Absolutely," I would say. "That's part of the cure."

But then, one day he came to me and there was a frown on his face. "Listen," he said. "I just went to the bank to ask a question about my bank-balance, which is a little lower than it should be because of the way you manage to get out of restaurants before the bill shows up, and I couldn't get an answer because the computer went down just as I walked in. Everyone was puzzled. —Is the cure wearing off?"

"It can't do that," I said. "Maybe it had nothing to do with you. There might be some other teleklutz around who hasn't been cured. Maybe he happened to walk in just as you did."

But that wasn't it. The bank's computer went down on two other occasions when he tried to check his bank balance. (His nervousness over the paltry sums I had neglected to take care of was quite nauseating in a grown man.) Finally, when the computer at his firm went down when he walked past the room in which it was housed, he came to me in what I can only describe as panic.

"It's back, I tell you. It's back!" he screamed. "I can't take it this time. Now that I'm accustomed to normality, I can't go back to my old life. I'll have to kill myself."

"No, no, Menander. That's going too far."

He seemed to check himself at the edge of another scream and thought over my sensible remark. "You're right," he said. "That *is* going too far. Suppose I kill you, instead. After all, no one will miss you, and it will make me feel a *little* better."

I saw his point, but only to a slight extent. I said, "Before you do anything at all, let me check this out. Be patient, Menander. After all, so far it's only happened with computers, and who cares about computers?"

I left quickly before he could ask me how he was supposed to get his bank balance if computers were always going down at his approach. He was really a monomaniac on the subject.

* * *

So was Azazel, on another subject. It seems that this time he was actually involved in whatever he was doing with the two samini, and he was still turning somersaults when he arrived. To this day, I don't know what the somersaults had to do with it.

I don't think he ever actually cooled down, but he did manage to explain to me what happened and then I was faced with having to explain it to Menander.

I insisted on meeting him in the park. I chose a fairly crowded section since I would have to rely on instant rescue if he should lose his head figuratively, and try to make me lose mine literally.

I said, "Menander, your teleklutzism still works, but only for computers. *Only for computers*. You have my word on that. You are cured for everything else *forever*."

"Well, then, cure me for computers."

"As it happens, Menander, that can't be done. You are not cured for computers, and forever." I rather whispered the last word but he heard me.

"Why? What kind of a hare-brained, idiotic, malapropistic, oniklutzistic rear end of a diseased Bactrian camel are you?"

"You make it sound as though there are many kinds, Menander, which doesn't make sense. Don't you understand that you wanted to save the world, and that's why it happened?"

"No, I don't understand. Explain it to me and take your time. You have fifteen seconds."

"Be reasonable! Humanity is facing a computer-explosion. Computers are going to become rapidly more versatile, more capable and more intelligent. Human being are going to be ever-more dependent upon them. Eventually, a computer will be built that will take over the world and leave humanity with nothing to do. It may then well decide to wipe out humanity as unnecessary. Of course, we tell ourselves smugly that we can always 'pull the plug', but you know we won't be able to do that. A computer smart enough to do the work of the world without us will be able to defend its own plug and, for that matter, find its own electricity.

"It will be unbeatable, and humanity will be doomed. And that, my friend, is where you come in. You will be brought into its presence or perhaps you will only arrange to pass within a few miles of it and it will instantly break down, and humanity will be saved! *Humanity will be saved!* Think of it! Think of it!"

Menander thought of it. He didn't look happy. He said, "But meanwhile, I can't come near computers."

"Well, the computer-klutzism had to be nailed down and made absolutely permanent so that we could be sure that when the time came nothing would go wrong; that the computer would not somehow defend itself against you. It's the price you pay for this great gift of salvation that you yourself asked for and for which you will be honored through all future history."

"Yes?" he said, "and when is this salvation to take place?"

I said, "According to Azaz—my sources, it should take place in sixty years or so. But look at it this way. Now you know that you will live to be at least ninety years old."

"And meanwhile," said Menander, in a loud voice, oblivious to the way people nearby turned to stare at us, "meanwhile, the world will grow more and more computerized and I will be unable to get near more and more places. I'll be unable to do more and more things and will be in a total prison of my own making—"

"But in the end you will save humanity! That's what you wanted!"

Menander shrieked, "To hell with humanity!" rose and hurled himself at me.

I managed to get away but only because there were people about who seized the poor fellow.

Today, Menander is in deep analysis with a Freudian psychiatrist of the most determined description. It will surely cost him a fortune and will, of course, do him no good whatever.

* * *

George, having finished his story, gazed into his pot of beer, for which I knew I would have to pay.

He said, "There's a moral to this story, you know."

"What is it?"

"People just don't have any gratitude!"

# Neither Brute Nor Human

The monthly dinner of the Black Widowers was well under way and Emmanuel Rubin, his fork uplifted, and waving threateningly in the air, temporarily ignored his rack of lamb and said, "Edgar Allan Poe was the first important practitioner of the modern detective story and of the modern science fiction story. I'll give him that."

"Nice of you," murmured James Drake, the host of the occasion, in a low aside.

Rubin ignored him. "He lifted the horror story to new heights, too. Still, he had a morbid and unhealthy preoccupation with death."

"Not at all," said Geoffrey Avalon, in his deep voice, his thick eyebrows lowering into a frown. "Poe was writing in the first half of the nineteenth century, and there was still virtually no protection against infectious disease at the time. Life was short and death was ever-present. He wasn't being morbid; he was being realistic."

Roger Halsted said, "Absolutely! Read any fiction of the nineteenth century. Read Dickens and the death of Little Nell, or Harriet Beecher Stowe and the death of Little Eva. Children frequently died in fiction because they frequently died in real life."

Rubin's eyes, magnified by his thick glasses, took on a stubborn gleam, and his sparse beard seemed to bristle. "It's not death in itself. It's how you treat it. You can deal with it as the doorway to heaven, and treat the dying person as a saint—see the death of Beth in *Little Women*. That can be sickeningly sentimental, but it is meant to be uplifting. Poe, on the other hand, dwells with an unholy glee on the elements of degradation and decay. He makes death worse than it is and—Come on, you all know very well what 'morbid' is."

He returned to his lamb and attacked it with vigor.

Thomas Trumbull growled and said, "Certainly. 'Morbid' is talking about morbidity over what would otherwise be a pleasant dinner."

"I don't see that it makes any difference whether Poe was morbid or not," said Mario Gonzalo, who was neatly dissecting strips of meat off the ribs. "What counts is whether he was a good writer or not, and I suppose no one argues with the fact that he was good."

Avalon said, judiciously, "Even good writers aren't good all the time. James Russell Lowell described Poe as 'three fifths of him genius and two fifths sheer fudge,' and I would say that was pretty accurate."

Halsted said, "My feeling is that a seminal writer has to accept some responsibility for his imitators. There is something about Poe that makes it absolutely necessary for his imitators to be awful. Consider H. P. Lovecraft—"

"No," said Rubin, violently, "we are *not* discussing Lovecraft; we are talking about Poe—"

And oddly enough, Drake's guest, who, until now, had sat mute through the dinner, said suddenly in a loud, almost metallic voice, "*Why* are we talking about Poe?"

His name was Jonathan Dandle; short, plump around the middle, a round face that was now quite flushed, a large bald head with a fringe of white hair about the ears, and round gold-rimmed bifocals. He looked in his early sixties.

He had startled the company into silence, and even Henry, the imperturbable waiter who was the pride of the Black Widowers, allowed an expression of surprise to flit momentarily across his face.

Drake cleared his throat and stubbed out his cigarette. "We talk about anything we please, Jonathan. Poe is as good a subject as any, especially since Manny Rubin writes mysteries so that Poe might be considered his patron saint. Right, Manny?"

Dandle looked about the table from one to the other and some of the redness drained out of his face and left it a normal blue. He lifted his hands in a kind of shrug. "My apologies, gentlemen. It was not my intention to dictate the subject of the conversation."

He looked a trifle unhappy.

Rubin nodded at Dandle in slightly haughty forgiveness, and said, "Actually, if we're talking about the patron saint of mysteries, I could make a good argument in favor of Conan Doyle. The Mystery Writers of America may hand out Edgars, but the archetypical detective, as all of us know—" and, with that, Poe was abandoned.

Dandle listened intently to the further course of the conversation, but said nothing else until Henry had served the coffee, and Gonzalo had produced a quick caricature which he showed the guest.

Dandle regarded it solemnly, then smiled. "It is fortunate, Mr. Gonzalo, that I have no great opinion of my beauty. You make me look like the old-time actor Guy Kibbee. Perhaps you don't remember him."

Gonzalo said, "Certainly, I remember him, and now that you point it out there *is* a resemblance. A clever artist, with a few strokes of the pen, can bare essentials that are not necessarily obvious."

"What a pity, Mario," said Rubin, "that you don't find a clever artist who can teach you to do so."

"And yet," said Gonzalo easily, "you have met any number of clever writers and none has been able to help you."

At which point, Drake rattled his water glass with his spoon. "Grilling time, gentlemen, so that Manny and Mario are requested to shut up.—Jeff, will you do the honors."

* * *

Geoffrey Avalon stirred the melting ice in his half-consumed second Scotch with his middle finger, and said, "Mr Dandle, how do you justify your existence?"

Dandle said, thoughfully, "A good question. Since I had nothing to do with the initiation of my existence in this unfortunate world, I might justifiably deny any need to defend myself. However, I have accepted my existence for over six decades now—after all, I might have killed myself easily enough—so I will defend. How would it be if I told you I am making it easier for people to communicate with each other. Would that serve as grounds for justification?"

"It depends on what they communicate," said Gonzalo. "Now Manny's attempts at—"

"Mario!" said Avalon, sharply, and turned a frowning look in Gonzalo's direction. Then, more gently, he said, "I have the floor and I would rather that we not descend into anarchy this time. —In what way, Mr. Dandle, do you make it easier for people to communicate?"

"I work in fiber optics, Mr. Avalon, and communications by laser light through glass, rather than by electricity through copper, will make for cheaper and thinner cables that would nevertheless carry more messages. I admit that not all the high technology in the world will of itself serve to improve the quality of those messages."

"And yet, sir, if I may be allowed to interject a personal note, you do not yourself show much tendency to communicate, considering that communication is your business. You have said hardly anything at all during cocktails or dinner. Is there a reason for that?"

Dandle looked about him, his face reddening again. It was quite apparent that he flushed easily, and, like almost all people who do, that he was quite aware of it and seemed the more embarrassed— and to redden more—because of it. He mumbled something.

"I beg your pardon, sir," said Avalon. "I didn't hear you."

Drake, who sat next to his guest, and who looked rather

uncomfortable himself, said, "Jonathan, saying, 'I've nothing to say' is no answer."

Dandle said, "It's an answer if that's the answer I choose to give, Jim."

"No," said Drake, peering at his guest out of his wrinkle-nested eyes. "That's not among the permitted choices, Jonathan. I explained the deal on this meeting. You receive a good dinner and good company in exchange for substantive answers. No secrets. No evasions. My own experience is that you've always had plenty to say."

Avalon said, "Let me continue, Jim. —Mr. Dandle, I will accept your answer that you have nothing to say, though I wish you would speak up so that others besides your immediate neighbor might hear you. My next question is this: Why is it that you have nothing to say on this occasion considering that, if we are to believe Jim, such silence is not typical of you?"

Dandle spread out his hands and said loudly enough, "Is a man always accountable for his actions, Mr. Avalon? Does he always know the origins of his moods?"

Avalon said, "Then let me ask you another question. You did, on one occasion, interject a question into the general conversation. You asked why we were talking about Poe, and you did so quite forcibly. I interpreted your remark as indicating that you were offended, perhaps outraged, by the discussion. Is that so? And if it is so, why?"

Dandle shook his head. "No, no. I just asked."

Trumbull stood up and passed one hand over his tightly waved white hair. He said, with exaggerated patience, "Jim, as the host, you must make a decision. We are clearly getting nothing out of our guest, and I think that, under the rules of the club, we might be forced to adjourn the meeting now. In fact, I move you consider adjournment."

Drake waved a hand at him petulantly. "Take it easy, Tom. —Jonathan, you've got to answer honestly. Nothing that is said here will ever be repeated outside these walls. Our waiter, Henry, is a member of the club and he is as closemouthed as we are. More so. I know you well enough to know you haven't committed a crime, or are planning to commit one, but even so, we—"

"You're quite wrong," said Dandle, in a rather more high-pitched voice than before. "I am trying to commit what *I* consider a crime. I'm certainly trying to be dishonest."

Drake said, "You?"

"With what I think is considerable justification, of course."

"After that," said Trumbull, "if Dandle does not care to elaborate, Jim, then we can go no further."

There was silence. Trumbull remained standing. Drake looked at Dandle and said, "Well, Jonathan?"

Dandle said, "You told me, Jim, I would be grilled on the details of my profession. I did not expect this sort of thing."

"It can't be helped. If you had been yourself, none of this would have come up. What's wrong?"

Dandle looked helpless. He clenched his fist, made as though he was going to bring it down on the table, stopped the motion, and said, "It's my sister."

"Your crackp—" began Drake, and stopped suddenly.

"My crackpot sister," said Dandle. "She's dying. Cancer."

There was a sudden silence.

"We've known it for months," said Dandle, "and she may live for months more, but it does produce problems."

The silence continued. Finally, Henry said, "Brandy, gentlemen?"

Avalon said, absently, "Just a small portion, Henry. —What kind of problems, Mr. Dandle?"

"Her will."

"You mean, all this is a matter of money?" said Halsted, with rather more than a shade of disapproval in his voice.

"Not money at all," said Dandle, lifting his eyebrows. "Please understand, gentlemen, that my wife and I are well off. We have a son and daughter, but both are grown and both are reasonably well off. My sister has a house and some money that she inherited from our parents, but this is not something we lust for. At least, not the money. That she can dispose of as she wishes. She can leave it to a farm for homeless cats, if she wishes. It's the house."

He fell into momentary thought. "It was quite clear that she would never marry by the time my parents died. It made sense to leave the family house to her, even though it was unnecessarily large for one person. Still, it's belonged to the family since it was built; I was born there; lived there till I married; I have a profound emotional attachment to it. Now my sister, Rachel," Dandle looked briefly at Drake, "being, as you say, a crackpot, is planning to leave it to a crackpot organization, and I don't want her to. I'd be willing to have it sold to someone respectable. I'd even be willing to have it torn down in a decent way for a decent purpose. But I'm damned if I'm willing to let the—the Cosmic Order of Theognostics infest it."

"The *what*?" said Gonzalo.

Avalon said, "The word comes from the Greek and means 'knowing God.' "

Dandle said, "What they really know are methods for extracting money from fools and nuts."

Avalon said, "I assume they are extracting money from your sister."

"To some extent, yes, but not very much. She is a shrewd woman, financially, and is quite compos mentis outside her obsession. Still, they're angling to get it all when she dies. And they may."

"What is her obsession, sir?"

"I believe it started with her reading of Poe when she was young. I think she read everything he had written; memorized it, just about; and absorbed the unhealthy morbidity that Mr. Rubin mentioned. And she read Lovecraft, too, and grew inclined to believe in horrors from outer space, in elder intelligences, and so on. She lectured me often enough on that stuff. Naturally, she became part of the UFO mania."

"Naturally," muttered Rubin, with a look of distaste.

"She became convinced that intelligent beings from outer space are actually on Earth and have taken over Earth's leaders, and much of the general population. She thinks these aliens are themselves invisible, or can make themselves so, and can live within human beings parasitically. It's all quite mad."

"I suppose," said Avalon, "that if anyone disagrees with her, or tries to argue against her views, she considers it a sign the arguer has been taken over."

"Absolutely. I early on recognized the mistake of trying to oppose her."

Halsted said, "Why haven't the aliens taken over everybody? How does your sister explain that she herself hasn't been taken over?"

"I gather," said Dandle, "that the Cosmic Order of Theognostics fights them with prayer and introspection and meditation and incantation and whatever the devil they claim to do, and they have taught her the same. She has tried to teach me and I've just kept silent and listened. There's a lot of candle burning involved, and the recitation of whole pages of material that has no meaning whatever but I suppose she thinks it keeps me safe—so far."

Drake said, through the smoke of his cigarette, "When I referred to her as a crackpot, Jonathan, I was thinking of the UFO stuff. I didn't know about this alien intelligences bit."

"It's not something I like to talk about, obviously," said Dandle, "and wouldn't be talking about now except under pressure."

Avalon said, "You said you were thinking of committing a crime. Surely, you're not thinking of mayhem against the Theognostics."

"Nothing like that. Just a crime in my own eyes. I've been trying to cheat and deceive my sister, and I'm not really proud of that."

"Would you be willing to explain that, sir?" asked Avalon, stiffly.

"Well, since Rachel was found to have cancer, things are at a crisis. She won't submit to surgery because she is sure that under anesthesia she will be taken over. She is suspicious of radiotherapy, too, since radiation is a weapon of those beings. She is relying entirely on Theognostic ritual, therefore, and you can imagine how effective that is."

Rubin said, "The most ridiculous methods can sometimes help if you believe firmly that they will. The mind is a powerful instrument."

"That may be," said Dandle, "but it isn't helping her. She's going downhill, and, about a month ago, she began to talk of leaving the house and her money to the Theognostics so that they could continue the great fight against the aliens. —So I started a plan of my own." He reddened and stopped.

After a short pause, Avalon said, gently, "Yes, Mr. Dandle?"

"To put it bluntly," said Dandle, "I came to her as an enthusiastic convert. I said she had convinced me and that I was heart and soul with her; that she could leave the money to the Theognostics if she wished, but that she should leave the house to me and I would make it the center of the fight against the aliens. I would allow the Theognostics to use it freely but I merely wanted to keep title to it in honor of our parents. I was hypocritical and obsequious."

"No doubt," said Avalon, "but did it work? People who, like your sister, believe in invisible, untestable dangers would be suspicious of everything."

"I'm afraid so," said Dandle. "She's of two minds about me. She *wants* to believe, but, as you say, she is suspicious. She hesitates to tell me what I'm sure she believes to be the 'higher mysteries', so to speak. I asked for details about the form and attributes of the mysterious aliens, for instance, and she was closemouthed about it—as though she was not sure I was worthy of initiation."

Trumbull said, "Maybe she doesn't know herself."

Rubin said, "She can easily invent anything she wishes and then come to believe it. Such things are very common."

"Last week she said something in a sort of singsong whisper and I thought I was making progress, but then there was nothing more."

"What did she say?"

"Well, they're hermaphroditic and are neither women or men. And they weren't Earthly, of course. They aren't human beings or animals. And when they infest us they live on our spiritual nature rather than on our physical bodies, I gather, for she seized my arm, with a surprisingly strong grip, too, and whispered into my ear, 'They are *worse* than cannibals, and that is not surprising considering where they come from.' "

"Where do they come from?" asked Gonzalo.

"That's what I asked," said Dandle, "but she didn't say. She said that once you achieve a certain enlightenment, you *know* where they come from; that that is the test of enlightenment. It comes over you like a wave of revelation and gives you a certain power against them. *She* knows, and the Theognostics know; but they don't tell anyone because that's their test for the people who are strong against the aliens. It doesn't really make sense, but if I were to try to say that to her, it would mean the end of my chance to save the house. So I just said, earnestly, that I would meditate and try to gain the knowledge." He looked about the table with a grim face. "I'm supposed to be fasting. —She called me this morning."

"Things are coming to a crisis?" asked Avalon.

"Yes. That's why I've been preoccupied this evening, and didn't say much. I was of two minds whether to come here at all, but I didn't want to let Jim Drake down."

"But what was it your sister said to you this morning?"

"She says she wants to make a decision about her will. She feels herself weakening and she knows that she must become one with the Great Divine—which is the Theognostic term for God, apparently —and she wants to make sure she continues the fight from beyond the grave. She can't let me have the house unless she is certain I won't bar the Theognostics from it. And, of course, barring them is *exactly* what I intend to do so I am trying to flimflam her. —It's not exactly admirable of me."

Trumbull said, loudly, "We're on your side, Mr. Dandle. You're fighting a group of pernicious and vicious flimflam operators, and if counter-flimflam is required, so be it."

"Thank you," said Dandle, "but I don't see that I will win out. She wants me to visit her tomorrow at noon and tell her where the aliens come from. If I can't, then she can't rely on me to remain strong against them and the Theognostics will get the house. And, of course, I can't tell her where the aliens come from. They're from outer space, I'm sure. That would fit in with her UFO madness, for they undoubtedly reached Earth by UFO. But where in outer space?"

There was a short silence, then Gonzalo said, "She never gave you any hints?"

Dandle shook his head. "Only the remark about their being worse than cannibals and that that somehow was appropriate, considering where they come from. But what does that mean?"

"Nothing else?"

"Not that I can think of. If she did, it went right past me. —So tomorrow I lose the house."

Avalon said, "You know, sir, that you can contest the will."

"No, not really," said Dandle. "You were introduced to me as a lawyer—"

"A patent lawyer," said Avalon. "I am not knowledgeable on the intricacies of testamentary litigation."

"Well, on the one hand, there is a strong tendency to allow a testator to do as he wishes with his own property. It isn't easy to disallow a religious organization in favor of a relative who is already well off. I doubt that I can prove undue influence, nor would I care to try to make my sister seem to have been of unsound mind, if only out of family considerations. Then, even if I really thought I would win, it would be a long-drawn-out fight in which the legal fees would come to considerably more than I would care to pay. —So I'm going to lose the house."

Avalon said, "We might all of us think about this a bit."

A flicker of hope seemed to enliven Dandle. "Are any of you astronomers?"

"Not professionally," said Halsted, "but we have the usual superficial knowledge of the field that any intelligent and reasonably well-read individuals would have."

"Exactly," said Rubin, "and that means I can make a suggestion. We're looking for something in outer space that has cannibalistic associations. I've read articles recently that in clusters of galaxies, there are occasional collisions and that, in such collisions, the larger member gains stars at the expense of the smaller one. The result is that in some clusters, there is one galaxy that is larger than any of the others, having cannibalized them."

Halsted nodded vigorously. "You are right, Manny. I've read about it, too. There's one outsize galaxy that has five small bright regions within itself that resemble galactic centers. The thought is that it swallowed five small galaxies whole."

Gonzalo said, "Just for the record—what are galaxies?"

Avalon said, "Large conglomerations of stars, Mario. Our own Milky Way Galaxy has a couple of hundred billion stars in it."

Gonzalo said, "Well, then, has that cannibal galaxy—the one that swallowed up its five little sisters—got a name?"

The Black Widowers stared at each other. Finally, Halsted said, "It may, but if it does, it's probably not an ordinary name. Just a particular catalog number like NGC-1111, or something like that."

Gonzalo said, "I don't think Miss Dandle would be impressed by that."

Dandle said, "I don't think so, either. I'm grateful to you for your attempts to help, but if galactic cannibalization is a common phenomenon, which cannibal would be the correct one? And I'm sure my sister knows nothing about modern sophistications in astronomy, anyway. Nor would the Theognostics. Where would they hear of this phenomenon?"

Avalon said, "Does your sister read anything at all in the field of astronomy, Mr. Dandle?"

Dandle said, thoughtfully. "She certainly read everything there is on UFOs and some astronomy—not necessarily correct—is bound to creep in there. She reads up on astrology, of course, which means additional possibly distorted astronomy. And I have seen astronomy popularizations in the house. I haven't actually seen her reading them but I wouldn't be surprised if she did."

"Is she well-read otherwise, sir?"

"Yes. All of Poe as I said, and Lovecraft, and some science fiction. A great deal of general nineteenth-century fiction, I should say, and, of course, she reads the newspapers and a number of magazines thoroughly, if only to find evidence of how far the aliens have taken over the world. I've got to explain to you that there's nothing wrong with her intelligence, outside her—her crackpottery."

"In that case," said Avalon, with a certain sombre satisfaction, "I am quite sure I have the answer." He paused and cast a glance in the direction of the waiter, who was standing at the sideboard, listening with polite but silent attention.

"Henry," said Avalon, "I think that on this occasion we will not need your help."

"Yes, Mr. Avalon," said Henry, quietly.

Avalon cleared his throat. "You see, by far the best-known portion of the Universe, even to astronomers, and *certainly* to the general public, are the planets of our own Solar System. This is especially true for people like Miss Dandle, who are interested in astrology and similar aberrations.

"And of the planets, the one which in recent years has received the most attention and which is, in any case, the most spectacular, is the planet Saturn, with its rings and satellites. The Voyager probes have taken close-up photographs of the Saturnian system and these have made all the newspapers and magazines. Miss Dandle cannot have missed them."

Dandle said, "I'm sure she has not. But what then?"

"Saturn," said Avalon, "is named for an early Roman god of agriculture whom the Romans, with scant justice, equated with the Greek god Kronos. Kronos with his brothers and sisters made up the group of gods called the Titans, and they were the children of Ouranos and Gaea, the god of the sky and the goddess of the Earth, respectively. In a series of most unpleasant myths, the Greeks describe Kronos as castrating his father, Uranus, and taking over the rule of the Universe.

"Since the Fates had decreed that Kronos would, in turn, be replaced as ruler by his own son, the new lord of the Universe took to devouring each child as it was born. His wife, Rhea, managed to save one son by offering Kronos a rock wrapped in the baby's swaddling clothes. The rather stupid Kronos swallowed that without noticing the substitution. The son, still uneaten, was then hidden in Crete, and raised to maturity in secret. Eventually, the son, who was named Zeus (Jupiter, to the Romans), warred upon the Titans, defeated them, released his siblings, who were still alive within Kronos, and took over the Universe. All this Miss Dandle, in her reading, might very well have come across.

"Now, then, Saturn was clearly a cannibal. If there are degrees in such things, devouring one's own children is surely worse than fattening on strangers, so he might well be viewed as worse than an ordinary cannibal. Miss Dandle's statement that the aliens were worse than cannibals and that that was not surprising in view of where they came from would make sense if they came from Saturn."

And Avalon smiled at Dandle with self-conscious triumph.

Dandle said, "You think, then, I had better tell my sister the alien beings come from Saturn?"

"I can't say the matter is certain," said Avalon. "She may, after all, suppose them to have come from some entirely fictitious planet such as Zorkel, the fifth planet of the star Xanadu, in the galaxy of Yaanek. If, however, she has a real astronomical body in mind, then I am virtually certain that it is Saturn. It must be."

"It sounds good to me," said Gonzalo.

"It makes sense," admitted Rubin, looking distressed at having to say so.

Halsted said, "It's worth a try."

Trumbull said, "I can't think of anything better."

Drake said, "It seems unanimous. I'd take the chance, Jonathan."

Dandle began, "Well, since I can't think of anything better, either—"

Gonzalo interrupted. "Wait, Henry hasn't said anything. Henry, what do you think?"

Dandle looked up in astonishment at having the waiter referred to.

When Henry said, "May I ask Mr. Dandle if he shared in his sister's enthusiasm for Poe?" Dandle looked more astonished still.

Drake said, "Please answer, Jonathan. Henry is one of us."

Jonathan said, "No, definitely not. I know 'The Raven'; no one can avoid knowing that; but I know nothing else. I stay away from him."

"In that case," said Henry, "I fear that Mr. Avalon's suggestion, although most ingenious, is not the correct answer."

Avalon looked offended. "Indeed, Henry? Have you anything better to offer?"

Henry said, "Consider, sir, that Miss Dandle was a great devotee of Poe, and that in describing the aliens she said that they were neither female nor male, animal nor human."

"Well?"

"Well, Mr. Avalon, I, unlike Mr. Dandle but like his sister, am an admirer of Poe, though more so of his poetry than of his prose. Among my favorite poems by Poe is 'The Bells,' in the fourth part of which he describes the tolling of the funeral bells. There you have his morbid preoccupation with death, you see, something that is bound to follow his earlier description of sleigh bells, wedding bells, and fire-alarm bells."

"Aha," said Rubin.

"Yes, Mr. Rubin," said Henry, "I suspect you already see what I mean. Part of the description of the funeral bells is—if I may quote:

*"And the people—ah, the poeple—*
*They that dwell up in the steeple,*
*All alone,*
*And who, tolling, tolling, tolling,*
*In that muffled monotone,*
*Feel a glory in so rolling*
*On the human heart a stone—*
*They are neither man nor woman—*
*They are neither brute nor human* "

Henry paused, then said, "Miss Dandle was undoubtedly quoting those last two lines, I think. You stated that she said them in singsong fashion, Mr. Dandle, but not being a Poe enthusiast, you did not recognize them."

Avalon said, "But even so— How does that help?"

Henry said, "It is the next line that counts, as Poe identifies the people who toll the funeral bells."

And he and Rubin quoted simultaneously: " '*They are Ghouls*.' "

Henry said, "Ghouls are creatures of Middle Eastern legend who infest graveyards and feed on dead bodies. That might well strike Miss

Dandle, or anyone, as worse than ordinary cannibalism, just as vultures are worse than hawks in the general estimation."

Avalon said, "I grant that, but I still don't see the point."

"Nor I," said Trumbull.

Henry said, "There is a constellation in the sky named Perseus, named for the Greek hero who cut off the head of Medusa, a creature so dreadful in appearance that anyone looking at it turned to stone. The constellation is pictured as the hero holding the head of Medusa and that head is marked by a second-magnitude star, Beta Persei. I looked it up in the Columbia Encyclopedia during the discussion, to be sure of that fact.

"Because of its position in the constellation, Beta Persei is sometimes called the Demon Star, in consequence. The Arabs, who adopted the Greek view of the sky, named it *Al Ghul*, meaning 'The Ghoul,' their version of something as horrible as Medusa, and our English version of that Arabic name is 'Algol.' That is now the common name of the star.

"Since Miss Dandle quoted that poem to define the aliens, she meant that they were ghouls, and therefore worse than cannibals, and she must have meant that it was not surprising that they were since they came from the star known as 'The Ghoul'—a fact she could surely have picked up from some book on popular astronomy, as I did, originally. I would suggest, then, Mr. Dandle, that you say, when you see your sister tomorrow, that the aliens come from Algol."

Dandel smiled brightly for the first time that evening and broke into applause. "Henry, I will. That *should* be the answer, and I am sure it is."

Henry said, gravely, "Nothing may be completely sure in this case, sir, but it is worth the gamble."

# The Fourth Homonym

"Homonyms!" said Nicholas Brant. He was Thomas Trumbull's guest at the monthly banquet of the Black Widowers. He was rather tall, and had surprisingly prominent bags under his eyes, despite the comparative youthfulness of his appearance otherwise. His face was thin and smooth-shaven, and his brown hair showed, as yet, no signs of gray. "Homonyms," he said.

"What?" said Mario Gonzalo, blankly.

"The words you call 'soundalikes.' The proper name for them is 'homonyms.' "

"That so?" said Gonzalo. "How do you spell it?"

Brant spelled it.

Emmanuel Rubin looked at Brant owlishly through the thick lenses of his glasses. He said, "You'll have to excuse Mario, Mr. Brant. He is a stranger to our language."

Gonzalo brushed some specks of dust from his jacket sleeve and said, "Manny is corroded with envy because I've invented a word-game. He knows the words but he lacks any spark of inventiveness, and that kills him."

"Surely Mr. Rubin does not lack inventiveness," said Brant, soothingly. "I've read some of his books."

"I rest my case," said Gonzalo. "Anyway, I'm willing to call my game 'homonyms' instead of 'soundalikes.' The thing is to make up some short situation which can be described by two words that are soundalikes—that are homonyms. I'll give you an example: If the sky is perfectly clear, it is easy to decide to go on a picnic in the open. If it is raining cats and dogs, it is easy to decide *not* to go on a picnic. But what if it is cloudy, and the forecast is for possible showers, but there seem to be patches of blue here and there, so you can't make up your mind about the picnic. What would you call that?"

"A stupid story," said Trumbull, tartly, passing his hand over his crisply-waved white hair.

"Come on," said Gonzalo, "play the game. The answer is two words that sound alike."

There was a general silence and Gonzalo said, "The answer is 'whether weather.' It's the kind of weather where you wonder whether to go on a picnic or not. 'Whether weather', don't you get it?"

James Drake stubbed out his cigarette and said, "We get it. The question is: How do we get rid of it?"

Roger Halsted said, in his soft voice, "Pay no attention, Mario. It's a reasonable parlor game, except that there don't seem to be many combinations you can use."

Geoffrey Avalon looked down austerely from his 72-inch height and said, "More than you might think. Suppose you owned a castrated ram that was frisky on clear days and miserable on rainy days. If it were merely cloudy, however, you might wonder whether that ram would be frisky or miserable. That would be 'whether wether weather.' "

There came a chorus of outraged "What!"s.

Avalon said, ponderously. "The first word is 'w-h-e-t-h-e-r', meaning 'if.' The last word is 'w-e-a-t-h-e-r', which refers to atmospheric conditions. The middle word is 'w-e-t-h-e-r', meaning 'a castrated ram.' Look it up if you don't believe me."

"Don't bother," said Rubin. "He's right."

"I repeat," growled Trumbull. "This is a stupid game."

"It doesn't have to be a game," said Brant. "Lawyers are but too aware of the ambiguities built in to the language, and homonyms can cause trouble."

The gentle voice of Henry, that waiter-for-all-seasons, made itself heard over the hubbub by some alchemy that worked only for him.

"Gentlemen," he said. "I regret the necessity of interrupting a warm discussion, but dinner is being served."

* * *

"Here's another one," said Gonzalo, over the smoked trout. "Someone has written down all the digits and on all of them but one he has drawn a very clever face. A child watching this is delighted but dissatisfied with the incompleteness of the project. What does he say?"

Halsted, who was spreading the horseradish sauce daintily over his trout, said, "The child says, 'Do that to two, too.' "

Gonzalo said in an aggrieved manner, "Have you heard that somewhere before?"

"No," said Halsted, "but it's a mathematical instance of the game. What's the use of teaching mathematics at junior high school, if I can't solve problems involving the number, two."

Gonzalo frowned. "You're trying to be funny, aren't you, Roger?"

"Who me?"

Trumbull said, "As host of the evening, I would like to recommend that we change the subject."

No one gave any sign of hearing. Avalon said, "Homonyms are usually the result of the accidents of language history. For instance, 'night' by which I mean the opposite of 'day', is cognate to the German, 'Nacht,' while 'knight', by which I mean a warrior of the Table Round, is cognate with the German 'necht'. In English, the vowels changed and the 'k' is invariably silent in an initial 'kn', so you end up with two words pronounced in identical fashion."

"The initial 'kn' does not invariably have a silent 'k'," said Rubin. "There are some words not yet sufficiently Anglicized. I have a Jewish friend, who married a young lady of the Gentile persuasion. Anxious to please her new husband, she bought some ethnic delicacies for him which she displayed proudly. Listing her purchases, she said, finally, 'And I also bought you this nish,' and was quite puzzled when he broke into hysterical laughter."

Drake said, "I don't get it."

Rubin said, with a touch of impatience, "The word is 'knish'—with the 'k' heavily pronounced. It is a ball of dough in whose interior one places spiced mashed potatoes, or possibly some other filling, with the whole then being fried or baked. Any New Yorker should know that."

Trumbull sighed and said, "Well, if you can't lick them, join them. Can anyone give me a group of four homonyms, four words all pronounced alike, with spelling and meaning different in each case? I'll give you five minutes in which I expect blessed silence."

The five minutes passed pleasantly enough, with only the sound of cracking lobster shells impinging upon the ear-drums, and then Trumbull said, "I'll give you one of the words: 'right' meaning 'the opposite of left.' What are the other three?"

Halsted said, his mouth fairly full of lobster claw, "There's 'write' meaning 'to inscribe words,' and 'rite' meaning 'a fixed religious procedure', but I don't think there's a fourth."

Avalon said, "Yes, there is. It's 'wright', 'w-r-i-g-h-t', meaning 'a mechanic.' "

"That's archaic," protested Gonzalo.

"Not entirely," said Avalon, "We still speak of a 'playwright', who would be 'someone who constructs plays.' "

Brant said, "My friend, Tom, mentioned 'right', defining it as 'the opposite of left.' What about 'right' meaning 'the opposite of wrong', and 'right' meaning 'perpendicular'? Would that be a fifth and sixth homonym?"

"No," said Gonzalo, "the spelling has to be different for the words to be homonyms."

Avalon said, "Not always, Mario. Two words can be spelled the same but have different meanings and have different etymological origins; they would count as homonyms. For instance, 'bear' meaning the animal, and 'bear' meaning 'to carry', have the same spelling and pronunciation, but have different origins, so I would call them homonyms; along with 'bare' meaning 'unclothed', of course. The different uses of 'right', however, as in 'right hand', 'right answer', and 'right angle', all stem from the same root with the same meaning, so they would not be homonyms."

* * *

There were fifteen additional minutes before Trumbull felt justified in rattling his spoon against the water glass and bringing the conversation to a halt.

"I have never been so glad," he said, "at any of the banquets of the Black Widowers to put an end to a conversation. If I had absolute power as a host, I would fine Mario five dollars for starting it."

"You took part in it, Tom," said Gonzalo.

"In self-defense—and shut up," said Trumbull. "I would like to present my guest, Nicholas Brant, and Jeff, you seem civilized even if you were more homonymized than anyone else, so would you do the honors and begin the grilling."

Avalon's formidable eyebrows lifted, and he said, "I scarcely think that 'homonymized' is English, Tom." Then, turning to the guest, he said, "Mr. Brant, how do you justify your existence?"

Brant smiled ruefully. "As a lawyer, I don't think I can. You know the old joke, perhaps, of the time God threatened to sue Satan, and Satan answered, 'How can you? I've got all the lawyers.' In my defense, however, I'm not the kind of lawyer who plays tricks in front of a judge and jury. Mostly I sit in my office and try to write documents that actually mean what they are supposed to mean."

Avalon said, "I'm a patent lawyer myself, so I ask the following question without evil intent. Do you ever try to write them so that they *don't* mean what they're supposed to mean? Do you try to build in loopholes?"

Brant said, "Naturally, I try to draw up a document that leaves my client as much freedom of action as possible, and the other side as little freedom of action as possible. However, the other side has a lawyer, too, who is working hard for the reverse, and the usual result is that the contract ends up reasonably iron-bound in both directions."

Avalon paused, then said, "In the earlier discussion on homonyms, you said, if I remember correctly, that homonyms are ambiguities that could cause trouble. Does that mean you ran into a homonym professionally, in your preparation of contracts, that brought about unexpected complications?"

Brant raised both hands. "No, no, nothing like that. What I had in mind when I made that statement was completely irrelevant to the subject now under discussion."

Avalon ran his finger around the rim of his water glass. "You must understand, Mr. Brant, that this is not a legal cross-examination. There is no particular subject under discussion, and nothing is irrelevant. I repeat my question."

Brant remained silent for a moment, then he said, "It's something that took place a little over twenty years ago, and that I have thought about only very occasionally since then. Mr. Gonzalo's game of homonyms brought it mind, but it's—nothing. It doesn't involve any legal problems or any complications whatever. It's just a—puzzle. It's an insoluble matter that isn't worth discussing."

"Is it confidential?" put in Gonzalo. "Because if it is—"

"Nothing confidential about it," said Brant. "Nothing secret, nothing sensitive—and therefore nothing interesting."

Gonzalo said, "Anything that's insoluble is interesting. Don't you agree, Henry?"

Henry, who was filling the brandy glasses, said, "I find it so when there is at least room for speculation, Mr. Gonzalo."

Gonzalo began, "Well, then, if—"

Avalon said, "Mario, let me continue, please. —Mr. Brant, I wonder if you could give us the details of this insoluble puzzle of yours. We would greatly appreciate hearing it."

"You'll be very disappointed."

"That's a chance we will take."

"Well, then," said Brant, "if you'll just give me a chance to think back—"

He rested his face in one hand, thinking, while the six Black Widowers watched him expectantly, and Henry took his usual place by the sideboard.

Brant said, "Let me begin with Alfred Hunzinger. He was a poor boy of an immigrant family, and he had no education worth mentioning. I'm pretty sure he never went to high school. By the time he was fourteen, he was working. Those were the decades before World War I and education was by no means considered one's birthright, or even particularly desirable for what used to be called workingmen.

"Hunzinger wasn't your usual workingman, however. He was incredibly industrious and incredibly intelligent. Intelligence and education don't necessarily go hand in hand, you know."

Rubin said, forcefully, "Indeed, they don't. I've known some very thoroughly educated jackasses."

"Hunzinger was the reverse," said Brant. "He was a very thoroughly uneducated business genius. He had a green thumb, but it was the green of dollar bills. Whatever he touched prospered, and he built a formidable business before he died.

"Nor was this enough for him. He always felt keenly his lack of education, and he embarked on a program of home study. It wasn't continuous, for his business was his first preoccupation and there were periods when he had little time. And it was spotty, for he read promiscuously and without outside guidance. Conversation with him was an exposure to a curious mixture of pedantry and naivete."

Avalon said, "You knew him personally, I take it."

Brant said, "Not really. Not intimately. I did some work for him. Mainly, I prepared his will. This, when properly done, and when there are complex business matters to consider, takes a long time and produces a long document. Periodically, it must be updated or revised, and the wording considered carefully in the light of continually changing tax laws. Believe me, it was virtually a career in itself and I was forced to spend many hours in conference with him and to engage in extensive correspondence, too. However, it was a very limited and specialized relationship. I got to know the nature of his finances rather thoroughly, but to know him, as a person, only superficially."

"Did he have children?" asked Halsted.

"Yes, he did," said Brant. "He married late in life; at the age of 42, if I remember correctly. His wife was considerably younger. The marriage, while not idyllically happy, was a successful one. There was no divorce nor any prospect of one at any time, and Mrs. Hunzinger died only about five years ago. They had four children, three boys and a girl. The girl married well; she's still alive, still married, has children of her own, and is, and has been, very comfortably off. She scarcely figured in the will. Some investments were turned over to her during Hunzinger's lifetime and that was it.

"The business was left on an equal basis one-third each, to the three sons, whose names were Frank, Mark and Luke."

"In that order of age?" asked Drake.

"Yes. The oldest was, to use his legal signature, B. Franklin

Hunzinger. The middle son is Mark David Hunzinger. The youngest son is Luke Lynn Hunzinger. Naturally, I pointed out to Hunzinger that to leave his business in equal shares to his three sons was asking for trouble. The income might be divided equally, but the directing power, the decision-making power, had to be placed in the hands of one.

"He was very stubbornly resistant to that, however. He said he had brought up his sons in accordance with the ideals of the Roman republic; that they were all faithful to him, the paterfamilias—he actually used the term, to my intense surprise—and to each other. There would be no trouble at all, he said.

"I took the liberty of pointing out that they might well be ideal sons while he was alive and with his forceful personality directing affairs. After he was gone, however, hidden rivalries might show up. Never, he insisted, never. I thought him blind, and wondered how anyone so alive to any hint of chicanery in business affairs, so realistic in matters of the world, could be so foolishly romantic where his own family was concerned."

Drake said, "What was the daughter's name?"

"Claudia Jane," said Brant. "I don't remember her married name at the moment. Why do you ask?"

"Just curious. She might have had ambitions, too, mightn't she?"

"I don't think so. At least not with respect to the business. She made it quite clear she neither expected nor wanted any share in it. Her husband was rich—old money—social position—that sort of thing. The last thing she wanted was to be identified with what was—in a manner of speaking—a giant hardware store."

"Well, I see that," said Drake.

"I must admit that the family seemed entirely harmonious," said Brant. "I met the sons at one time or another, singly and together, and they seemed fine young men, much at ease with one another, and obviously fond of their father. What with one thing and another, I reached the stage where it seemed appropriate to invite me to the festivities celebrating the old man's eightieth birthday. It was on that occasion that Hunzinger had the heart attack that carried him off. It was not entirely unexpected. He'd had a heart condition for years, but it was totally unfortunate for it to happen on his birthday.

"The party broke up, of course. He was laid, gently, on the nearest couch and doctors were called in. There was a kind of hushed pandemonium. The confusion was sufficient for me to be able to stay on. It may sound ghoulish, but I conceived myself to have a job to do. He had not yet assigned any son to be the head of the firm. It was too late to have anything in writing; but if he would say something, it might have some force.

"The sons, I suppose, did not know what I had in mind. They were there, of course. Their mother, half in shock, had been led away. No one seemed to notice I was present. I leaned across to the old man's ear and said, 'Which of your sons is to be the head of the firm, Mr. Hunzinger?'

"It was too late. His eyes were closed, his breathing was stertorous. I wondered if he had heard me. A doctor approached and I knew he would stop me, so I tried again quickly. This time, the dying man's eyelids fluttered, and his lips moved as though he were trying to speak. However, only one sound came out. It seemed to be the word 'to'. I heard nothing else. He lingered on for another hour but never said another word, and died, without regaining consciousness, on the couch on which he had been laid. —And that's it."

Gonzalo said, "What happened to the business?"

"Nothing," said Brant, with what seemed the residuum of a vast surprise. "The old man was right. The three sons get along famously. It's a sort of triumvirate. When a decision must be made, they get together and come to one quickly. It's really an amazing thing and if that sort of thing should become infectious, lawyers would all starve to death."

"Then it doesn't matter what the old man said, does it?" said Gonzalo.

"Not in the least, except that for a while it roused my curiosity. What was he trying to say? You see the difficulty, I suppose?"

"Of course," said Drake, fingering his small gray mustache. "You can't do much with the word 'to.' "

"It's worse than that," said Brant. "Which homonym? Was it t-o, or t-o-o, or t-w-o. There are *three* to's in the English language. Incidentally, how so you write that sentence? I've often wondered. You can *say* 'three to's', since all three are pronounced alike, but how do you write it, since each one of the homonyms is spelled differently?"

Avalon said, "I would say, 'There are three words pronounced t-o-o.' The double-o is the most unambiguous way of indicating the pronunciation that all three share and you spell it out."

"Well, in any case, even if I knew which t-o-o it was, it wouldn't help me."

Trumbull said, "Mightn't it not have been a word, Al? Suppose he were saying a longer word such as 'constitution.' That's four syllables and he managed to sound only the third. All you'd have would be t-o-o."

"Maybe," said Brant. "I can't prove that that's not so. Just the same, at the time, I got the impression that it was a word, one of the three t-o-o's, however you want to spell it. I suppose I was desperately trying to read his lips and he might have said 'Headship to so-and-so' and all I got was the 'to'. Which leaves me with nothing. Of course, as I said, it doesn't matter. The sons are doing well. Still—"

Brant shook his head. "I'm a lawyer. It bothers me that I came so close to having it done *right*. Even if he were refusing to choose anyone. Even if he were saying 'Not to anyone', he would have been expressing his last wish and that would have been better than just falling into a situation by default. So for a while I kept wondering, and now you've put it back in my head, and I'll keep on wondering for another while. —And getting nowhere because there's nowhere to be gotten."

A heavy silence descended about the table, one which was finally broken by Gonzalo who said, "At least it's an interesting version of the game of homonyms. Which of the soundalikes was it?"

Trumbull said, "What's the difference? Not one of the three would help us make sense of what the old man was trying to say."

"I told you," said Brant, glumly. "It's an insoluble problem. There just isn't enough information."

"We don't have to *solve* it," said Halsted, "since there's no crisis that has to be eased, or criminal on whom we must visit retribution. All we have to do is point out a reasonable possibility to ease your mind. For instance, suppose he was saying t-w-o."

"Well, suppose he was," said Avalon.

"Then it may be that he was saying something like, 'Give it to son number two.'"

Brank shook his head, and said, "The impression I got was that the t-o I heard was in the middle of the message. His lips moved before and after I heard the t-o."

Rubin said, "I'm not sure you can go by that. His lips were scarcely under control. Some of what appeared to be movement might have been only trembling."

"Which makes it all the worse," said Brant.

"Now wait a while," said Halsted. "My idea works even with the word in the middle of the message. It could have been something like 'Give it to number two son', or 'Number two son gets it.' "

Trumbull growled, "Charlie Chan might say it, but was Hunzinger likely to do so. —Al, did you ever hear this man refer to his children by number."

"No," said Brant. "I don't think I ever did."

"Well, then," said Trumbull, "Why on earth should he start doing so on his death-bed?"

"I wonder," said Rubin. "Consider this. His second son is named Mark, which is also the name of the writer of the second gospel. His third son is named Luke, which is the name of the writer of the third gospel. I'll bet that if he had had a fourth son, that son's name would have been John."

"What's the good of a bet like that?" said Gonzalo. "We can't ever settle it and decide on a winner."

"Why wasn't the first son's name Matthew, then?" asked Avalon.

Rubin said, "Maybe old Hunzinger didn't think of it till after the first son was born. Maybe he simply didn't like 'Matthew'. Anyway, it strikes me that if the word *were* 'two', it would have a double meaning. It would refer to the second son *and* the second gospel and it would mean Mark in either case."

Trumbull said, "There could be a million reasons why the number, two, might point to Mark, but put them all together and they wouldn't be any more likely to get him to refer to 'my number two son' than just one reason would. Why wouldn't he just say 'Mark,' if he meant Mark?"

Brant said, "Well he might have said 'to Mark' at that and all I heard was 'to.' "

Avalon said, "Mr. Brant, I wonder if you at any time noted that old Mr. Hunzinger trusted one of his sons more than another, valued more highly the business acumen of a particular son, loved one more."

Brant bent his head in thought. Then he shook it. "I can't say I did. I have no recollection of anything of the sort. Of course, as I said, my relationship with the family was not a matter of warm personal friendship. It was business, entirely. The old man never confided family matters beyond anything that was relevant to the will."

Gonzalo said, "We keep talking about the sons. How do you know the old man didn't give some thought to his daughter? Suppose he left the business to his three sons, in thirds, but wanted his daughter to make crucial decisions. He might have thought she had the best business sense and should run the show even though she wouldn't want to be connected with the business in any open way."

"What gives you that idea, Mario?" asked Avalon.

"Suppose the word was t-o-o. He might have been saying, 'My daughter,too, should be involved.' Something like that."

"I don't think so," said Brant. "Mr. Hunzinger never mentioned his daughter in connection with the business. Remember, too, that his prejudices are pre-World War I, when women couldn't even vote. In no way was he a feminist. His wife was strictly a homebody and that's the way he liked it. He took care to have his daughter marry a rich man, and as far as he was concerned, that was the limit of his responsibility toward her. At least, I am forced to that conclusion as I think of our various discussions of the will."

Again, there fell a silence around the table, and finally Avalon said, with a rather theatrical sigh, "It doesn't matter what hypotheses we set forward. No matter how clever and ingenious they might be, there's no way in which we can show that they are true. I'm afraid that this once we have to decide that our guest is correct and that the problem, by its very nature, is insoluble."

Gonzalo said, "Not until we ask Henry."

"Henry?" said Brant, in surprise. His voice dropped to a whisper. "Do you mean the waiter?"

Trumbull said, "No need to whisper, Al. He's a member of the club."

"So I'll ask him," said Gonzalo. "Henry, do you have any ideas about this?"

From his place at the sideboard, Henry smiled very slightly and said, "I must admit, Mr. Gonzalo, that I've been wondering what the first name of the eldest son might be."

Gonzalo said, "Frank. Don't you remember?"

"I beg your pardon, Mr. Gonzalo, but I seem to recall the oldest son is B. Franklin Hunzinger. I wondered what the B stood for."

All eyes turned to Brant, who shrugged and said, "He's identified as B. Franklin even in his father's will. That's the legal form of his signature. I always assumed, however, that the B stood for Benjamin."

"It's a natural assumption," said Henry. "Any American named B. Franklin, it would seem, would be bound to be a Benjamin. But did you ever hear any member of the family, or anyone for that matter, address him as Benjamin or Ben."

Slowly, Brank shook his head. "I don't recall any such incident, but it was over twenty years ago and I was not really part of the family circle."

"Or since the death of the elder Hunzinger?"

"Oh, well, I've rarely had any contact with them at all since then, not even with respect to legal matters."

Trumbull said, "What's all this about, Henry?"

"Why, it occurred to me that there are, in a manner of speaking, four homonyms with the sound t-o-o."

Avalon said, in an astonished voice, "Four? You mean that one of the homonyms has two meanings of unrelated derivation as in the case of b-e-a-r?"

"No, Mr. Avalon. I am referring to four homonyms with four different spellings."

Avalon thought briefly, "Impossible, Henry. Manny, can you think of a fourth homonym beyond t-o, t-o-o, and t-w-o."

"No," said Rubin, flatly, "there is no fourth homonym."

Henry said, "I said 'in a manner of speaking.' It all depends on the first name of B. Franklin."

Drake said, "Henry, you're being mysterious and you've got us all confused. Now *explain*."

"Yes, Dr. Drake. Mr. Brant had said that the elder Hunzinger was self-educated, and he had indicated that he was particularly interested in Roman history. He raised his children in what he thought was the Roman tradition. He used terms such as 'paterfamilias' and so on. And he gave his children traditional Roman names. His daughter he named Claudia; one son is Mark, from the Roman Marcus; another is Luke from the Roman Lucius.

"It is possible, in fact, that the original names were indeed Marcus and Lucius, and that the youngsters found Mark and Luke more palatable to their peers. Now what if the eldest had a Roman name also, which had no common Anglicized form. He might not have used it at all, but stayed with Franklin, which becomes the very common and acceptable Frank.

"One common Roman name beginning with B is Brutus, and that has no Anglicized form that is likely to be acceptable."

"Aha," said Rubin.

"Yes, Mr. Rubin," said Henry. "If the elder Mr. Hunzinger had picked up scraps of Latin, undoubtedly Julius Caesar's last words, one of the most famous of all Latin phrases, would be known to him. It contains the word 'tu' which is Latin for the familiar form of 'you,' and is so well known among educated English-speaking people—if only from this phrase—that it might almost rank as a fourth homonym.

"Asked about which of his sons should head the firm, the dying man thought of the oldest, remembered the name he had been given him as a child and may have said something like 'all my sons share, and you, Brutus, will lead.' The phrase 'and you, Brutus' becomes the muttered Caesarian exclamation of 'et tu, Brute', and only the 'tu' was loud enough to hear."

"Good God," muttered Brant, "who could possibly think of something like that?"

"But it's *most* ingenious," said Avalon. "I hope you're right, Henry. I'd hate to see that reasoning wasted. I suppose we could call Hunzinger and try to persuade him to give us his first name."

Gonzalo said, excitedly, "Wait, Jeff, wouldn't it be in *Who's Who in America*? They usually include businessmen."

Avalon said, "They might well have only the legal version of his name—B. Franklin Hunzinger. Of course, they sometimes include the name beyond the period in parentheses to indicate it exists but is not to be used."

"Let's see," said Gonzalo. He took down the first volume of the tome and for a few moments there was the sound of flipping pages. Then it stopped and Gonzalo cried out in triumph, "Brutus Franklin Hunzinger, the r-u-t-u-s in parentheses."

Brant buried his head in his hands, "Twenty years, on and off, this had bothered me, and if I had looked him up in *Who's who*— But why would it occur to me to look him up." He shook his head. "I must tell them. They will have to know."

Henry said, "I don't think that would be wise, Mr. Brant. They get along well as it is, but if they find out that their father had chosen one of them to head the firm—which even as it is we can't be *certain* of—bad feelings might break out. Surely one shouldn't attempt to fix what isn't broken."

# The Eye of the Beholder

George and I were sitting on a bench at the boardwalk and contemplating the broad expanse of the beach and the sparkling sea in the distance. I was immersed in the innocent pleasure of watching the young ladies in their bikinis and wondering what they could get out of the beauties of life that was half as much as they contributed.

Knowing George as I did, I rather suspected his own thoughts to be considerably less nobly esthetic than mine. I was certain that they would deal with the more useful aspects of those same young ladies.

It was with considerable surprise, then, that I heard him say, "Old man, here we sit, drinking in the beauties of nature in the shape of the female form divine—to coin a phrase—and yet surely true beauty is not, and cannot be, so evident. True beauty, after all, is so precious that it must be hidden from the eyes of trivial observers? Have you ever thought that?"

"No," I said, "I've never thought that and, now that you mention it, I still don't. What's more, I don't think that you have ever thought that."

George sighed. "Talking with you, old chap, is like swimming in molasses—very little return for very great effort. I have watched you observing that tall goddess there, the one whose wisps of fine textile do nothing to conceal the few square inches they purport to cover. Surely, you understand that those are mere superficialities that she displays."

"I have never asked for much out of life," I said, in my humble way. "I'll be satisfied with superficialities of that sort."

"Think how much more beautiful a young woman would be—even a woman quite unprepossessing to the untutored eyes of one such as you—if she possessed the eternal glories of goodness, unselfishness, cheerfulness, uncomplaining industry, and concern for others; all the virtues, in short, that shed gold and grace on a woman."

"What I'm thinking, George," I said, "is that you must be drunk. What on earth can you possibly know about virtues such as those?"

"I am totally familiar with them," said George, haughtily, "because I practice them assiduously, and to the full."

"Undoubtedly," I said, "only in the privacy of your own room and in the dark."

*   *   *

Disregarding your crude remark [George said] I must explain that even I did not have personal knowledge of these virtues, I would have learned of them through my acquaintance with a young woman named Melisande Ott, nee Melisande Renn, and known to her loving husband, Octavius Ott, as Maggie. She was known to me as Maggie also, for she was the daughter of a dear friend of mine, now, alas, deceased, and she always considered me her Uncle George.

I must admit that there is a bit of me, that like you, appreciates the subtle qualities of what you call 'superficialities.' —Yes, old boy, I know I used the term first but we will not get anywhere if you are going to interrupt me constantly over trivialities.

Because of this small weakness in myself, I must also admit that when, in an excess of joy at seeing me, she would squeal and throw her arms about me, my delight at the event was not quite as great as it would have been had she been more generously-proportioned. She was quite thin and her bones were painfully prominent. Her nose was large, her chin weak, her hair rather lank and straight and pure mouse in color, and her eyes an undefinable gray-green. Her cheekbones were broad so that she rather resembled a chipmunk that had just completed a fine collection of nuts and seeds. In short, she was not the type of young woman whose arrival on the scene would cause any young man present to begin breathing rapidly and striving to get closer.

But she had a good heart. She bore up, with a wistful smile, at the visible winces that shook the average young man who met her for the first time, without warning. She served as bridesmaid for all her friends in turn with a fresh group of wistful smiles. She served as godmother to innumerable children, and as baby-sitter to others, and was as deft a bottle-feeder as you could see in a long month of Sundays.

She brought hot soup to the deserving poor, and to the undeserving as well, though there were some who said that it was the undeserving who more nearly deserved the visitation. She performed various duties at the local church, several times over—once for herself and once each for those of her friends who preferred the guilty splendor of the movie palaces to selfless service. She taught classes at Sunday school, keeping the children cheerful by making (as they thought) funny faces at them. She also frequently led them all in a reading of the nine commandments. (She left out the one about adultery for experience had taught her that this invariably led to inconvenient questions.) She also served as a volunteer at the local branch of the public library.

Naturally, she lost all hope of getting married somewhere about the age of four. Even the chance of having a casual date with a member of the opposite sex seemed to her to be a rather impossible dream by the time she had reached the age of ten.

Many a time she would say to me, "I am not unhappy, Uncle George. The world of men is sealed to me, yes, always excepting your dear self and the memory of poor pappa, but there is far more true happiness in doing good."

She would then visit the prisoners in the county jail in order to plead for repentance, and for conversion to good works. It was only one or two of the crasser sort who volunteered for solitary confinement on those days on which she was due to arrive.

* * *

But then she met Octavius Ott, a newcomer to the neighborhood, a young electrical engineer with a responsible position at the power company. He was a worthy young man—grave, industrious, persevering, courageous, honest and reverent—but he was not what you or I would call handsome. In fact, not to put too fine a point on it, he was not what anyone in recorded history would have called handsome.

He had a receding hairline—or, more accurately, a receded one—a bulbous forehead, a snub nose, thin lips, ears that stood well away from his head, and a prominent Adam's apple that was never entirely still. What there was of his hair was rather rust-colored, and he had an irregular sprinkling of freckles on his face and arms.

I happened to be with Maggie when she and Octavius met in the street for the first time. Both were equally unprepared and both started like a pair of skittish horses suddenly confronted by a dozen clowns in a dozen fright wigs who were blowing a dozen whistles. For a moment, I expected both Maggie and Octavius to rear and whinny.

The moment passed, however, and each successfully weathered the flash of panic they had experienced. She did nothing more than place her hand on her heart as though to keep it from leaping out of the rib cage in search of a more secure hiding place, while he wiped his brow as though to erase a horrid memory.

I had met Octavius some days before and so I was able to introduce them to each other. Each held out a tentative hand as though not anxious to add the sense of touch to that of vision.

Later that afternoon, Maggie broke a long silence and said to me, "What an odd young man that Mr. Ott seems to be."

I said, with that originality of metaphor which my friends all enjoy, "You mustn't judge a book by its cover, my dear."

"But the cover exists, Uncle George," she said, earnestly, "and we must take that into account. I dare say that the average young woman, frivolous and unfeeling, would have little to do with Mr. Ott. It would be a deed of kindness, therefore, to show him that not all young women are totally heedless, but that one at least does not turn against a young man for nothing more than his unfortunate resemblance to—to—" She paused as no comparable member of the animal kingdom occurred to her, so that she had to end lamely, but warmly, with "whatever it is that he resembles. I must be kind to him."

I do not know whether Octavius had a confidant to whom he could unburden himself in similar fashion. Probably not, for few of us—if any—are blessed with Uncle Georges. Nevertheless, I'm quite certain, judging from later events, that precisely the same thoughts occurred to him—in reverse, of course.

In any case, each labored to be kind to the other, tentatively and hesitantly at first, then warmly, and at last passionately. What began as casual encounters at the library, became visits to the zoo, then an evening at the movies and at dances, until, finally, what took place could only be described—if you'll excuse my language—as trysts.

People began to expect to see one whenever they saw the other, for they had become an indissoluble pair. Some of those in the neighborhood complained bitterly that to get a double dose of Octavius and Maggie was more than the human eye could be expected to endure, and more than one supercilious elitist invested in sunglasses.

I will not say that I was totally lacking in sympathy for these extreme views, but others—more tolerant and, perhaps, more reasonable—pointed out that the features on one were, by some peculiar chance, quite opposite to the corresponding features of the other. Seeing the two together tended to introduce a cancelling effect, so that both together were more endurable than either separately. Or at least, that was what some claimed.

Finally, there came a day when Maggie burst in on me and said, "Uncle George, Octavius is the light and life of my existence. He is staunch, strong, steady, sturdy and stable. He is a lovely man."

"Internally, my dear," I said, "I'm sure he is all of these things. His outward appearance, however, is—"

"Adorable," she said staunchly, strongly, steadily, sturdily, and stably. "Uncle George, he feels about me as I feel about him, and we are going to be married."

"You and Otto?" I said, faintly. An involuntary image of the likely issue of such a marriage swam before my eyes and I turned rather faint.

"Yes," she said. "He has told me that I am the sun of his delight and the moon of his joy. Then he added that I was all the stars of his happiness. He is a very poetic man."

"So it seems," I said, dubiously. "When are you going to be married?"

"As soon as possible," she said.

There was nothing to do but grit my teeth. The announcement was made, the preparations were carried through, the marriage was performed with myself giving away the bride. Everyone in the neighborhood attended out of disbelief. Even the minister allowed a reverent look of astonishment to cross his face.

Nor did anyone seem to gaze gladly at the young couple. All through the ceremony, the audience stared at its various knees. Except the minister. He kept his eyes firmly fixed on the rose window over the front door.

* * *

I left the neighborhood some time after, took up lodgings in another part of the city and rather lost touch with Maggie. Eleven years later, however, I had occasion to return over a matter of an investment in a friend's learned studies of the racing qualities of horses. I seized the opportunity of visiting Maggie, who was, among her other well-hidden beauties, a marvelous cook.

I arrived at lunch time. Octavius was away at work, but that didn't matter. I am not a selfish man and I gladly ate his portion in addition to mine.

I could not help but notice, however, that there was a shade of grief on Maggie's face. I said, over the coffee, "Are you unhappy, Maggie? Is your marriage not going well?"

"Oh, no, Uncle George," she said, vehemently, "our marriage was made in heaven. Although we remain childless, we are so wrapped up in each other that we are barely aware of the loss. We live in a sea of perpetual bliss and have nothing more to ask of the universe."

"I see," I said, my teeth rather on edge, "then why this shade of grief I seem to detect in you?"

She hesitated, and then burst out, "Oh, Uncle George, you are such a sensitive man. There *is* one thing that does interpose a bit of grit in the wheels of delight."

"And that is?"

"My appearance."

"Your appearance? What is wrong—" I swallowed and found myself unable to finish the sentence.

"I am not beautiful," said Maggie, with the air of one imparting a well-hidden secret.

"Ah!" I said.

"And I wish I were—for Octavius' sake. I want to be lovely just for him."

"Does he complain about your appearance?" I asked cautiously.

"Octavius? Certainly not. He bears his suffering in noble silence."

"Then how do you know he is suffering?"

"My woman's heart tells me so."

"But, Maggie, Octavius is himself—well—not beautiful."

"How can you say that?" said Maggie, indignantly. "He's gorgeous."

"But perhaps he things *you're* gorgeous."

"Oh, no," said Maggie, "how could he think that?"

"Well, is he interested in other women?"

"Uncle George!" said Maggie, shocked. "What a base thought. I'm surprised at you. Octavius has no eyes for anyone but me."

"Then what does it matter if you are beautiful or not?"

"It's for *him*," she said. "Oh, Uncle George, I want to be beautiful for *him*."

And, leaping into my lap in a most unexpected and unpleasant way, she moistened the lapel of my jacket with her tears. In fact, it was wringing wet before she was quite through.

I had by then, of course, met Azazel, the two-centimeter extraterrestrial I may have mentioned to you on occa— Now, old man, there is no need for you to mutter 'ad nauseam' in that supercilious manner. Anyone who writes as you do should be embarrassed at bringing up the thought of nausea in any connection whatever.

In any case, I called up Azazel.

* * *

Azazel was asleep when he arrived. He had a bag of some green material covering his tiny head and only the muffled sound of quick soprano squeaking from within gave evidence that he was alive. That, and the fact that every once in a while his little sinewy tail stiffened and vibrated with a tinny hum.

I waited several minutes for him to wake up naturally, and when that did not happen, I gently removed his head-bag with a pair of tweezers. His eyes opened slowly and focussed on me, whereupon he gave an exaggerated start.

He said, "For a moment I thought I was merely having a nightmare. I didn't count on *you*!"

I ignored his childish petulance and said, "I have a task for you to do for me."

"Naturally," said Azazel sourly. "You don't suppose I am expecting you to offer to do a task for me."

"I would, in a moment," I said, suavely, "if my inferior abilities were sufficient to do anything a personage of your stature and power would find of significant use."

"True, true," said Azazel, mollified.

It is truly disgusting, I might add, at the susceptibility of some minds to flattery. I've seen you, for instance, go out of your mind with fatuous joy when someone asks you for an autograph. —But back to my tale—

"I wish you to make a young woman beautiful."

Azazel shuddered. "I'm not sure I could bring myself to do that. The standards of beauty among your bloated and miserable species of life are atrocious."

"But they are ours. I will tell you what to do."

"*You* will tell *me* what to do," he shrieked, vibrating with outrage. "*You* will tell *me* how to stimulate and modify hair follicles, how to strengthen muscles, how to grow or dissolve bone? Indeed? *You* will tell *me* all this."

"Not at all," I said, humbly. "The details of the mechanism that such a deed would require are only to be handled by a being of your magnificent attainments. Allow me, however, to tell you the superficial effects to be achieved."

Azazel was once again mollified, and we went over the matter in detail.

"Remember," I said. "The effects are to be brought to fruition over a period of at least sixty days. A too-sudden change might excite remark."

"Do you mean," said Azazel, "I'm to spend sixty of your days supervising and adjusting and correcting? Is my time worth nothing in your opinion?"

"Ah, but you could then write this up for one of your world's biological journals. It is not a task that many on your world would have the ability or patience to undertake. You will be greatly admired as a result."

Azazel nodded, thoughtfully. "I scorn cheap adulation, of course," he said, "but I suppose I have a duty to hold myself up as a role model for inferior members of my species." He sighed with a shrill, whistling sound. "It is troublesome and embarrassing, but it is my duty."

* * *

I had a duty as well. I felt I ought to remain in the neighborhood during the interval of change. My horse-racing friend put me up in return for my expertise and advice on the results of various experimental runnings, with the result that he lost very little money.

Each day I sought an excuse to see Maggie and the results slowly began to show. Her hair grew fuller-bodied, and developed a graceful wave. Red-gold glints began to appear, lending it a welcome richness.

Little by little, her jawbone grew more prominent, her cheekbones more delicate and higher. Her eyes developed a definite blue that deepened from day to day to what was almost violet. The eyelids developed just the tiniest oriental slant. Her ears grew more shapely and lobes appeared. Her figure rounded and grew almost opulent, bit by bit, and her waist narrowed.

People were puzzled. I heard them myself. "Maggie," they would say. "What have you done to yourself? Your hair looks simply marvelous. You look ten years younger."

"I haven't done *anything*," Maggie would say. She was as puzzled as all the others were. Except me, of course.

She said to me, "Do you notice any change in me, Uncle George?"

I said, "You look delightful, but you have always looked delightful to me, Maggie."

"Maybe so," she said, "but I have never looked delightful to me until recently. I don't understand it. Yesterday, a bold young man turned to look at me. They always used to hurry by, shading their eyes. This one *winked* at me, however. It caught me so by surprise, I actually smiled at him."

A few weeks later, I met her husband, Octavius, at a restaurant, where I was studying the menu in the window. Since he was about to enter it to order a meal, it was the work of the moment for him to invite me to join him and the work of half another moment for me to accept.

"You look unhappy, Octavius," I said.

"I *am* unhappy," he said, "I don't know what's got into Maggie lately. She seems so distracted that she doesn't notice me half the time. She wants to be constantly socializing. And yesterday—" A look of such woebegone misery suffused his face that almost anyone would have been ashamed of laughing at it.

"Yesterday?" I said. "What of yesterday?"

"Yesterday she asked me to call her—Melisande. I can't call Maggie a ridiculous name like Melisande."

"Why not? It's her baptismal name."

"But she's my Maggie. Melisande is some stranger."

"Well, she has changed a bit," I said. "Haven't you noticed that she looks more beautiful these days?"

"Yes," said Octavius, biting off the word.

"Isn't that a good thing?"

"No," he said, more sharply still. "I want my plain, funny-looking Maggie. This new Melisande is always fixing her hair, and putting on different shades of eye-shadow, and trying on new clothes and bigger bras, and hardly ever talking to me."

The lunch ended in a dejected silence on his part.

I thought I had better see Maggie and have a good talk with her.

"Maggie," I said.

"Please call me Melisande," she said.

"Melisande," I said. "It seems to me that Octavius is unhappy."

"Well, so am I," she said, tartly. "Octavius is getting to be such a bore. He won't go out. He won't have fun. He objects to my clothes, my makeup. Who on earth does he think he is?"

"You used to think he was a king among men."

"The more fool, I. He's just an ugly little fellow I'm embarrassed to be seen with."

"You wanted to be beautiful just for him."

"What do you meant *wanted* to be beautiful. I *am* beautiful. I was always beautiful. It was just a matter of developing a good hair-style and knowing how to fix my makeup just right. I can't let Octavius stand in my way."

And she didn't. Half a year later, she and Octavius were divorced and in another half-year Maggie—or Melisande—was married again to a man of superficial good looks and unworthy character. I once dined with him and he hesitated so long at picking up the check, I was afraid I might have to pick it up myself.

I saw Octavius about a year after his divorce. He, of course, had not re-married, for he was as odd-looking as ever and milk still curdled in his presence. We were sitting in his apartment which was filled with photos of Maggie, the old Maggie, each one more atrocious than the next.

"You must still be missing her, Octavius," I said.

"Dreadfully!" he replied. "I can only hope she is happy."

"I understand she isn't," I said. "She may come back to you."

Sadly, he shook his head. "Maggie can never come back to me. A woman named Melisande may wish to come back but I couldn't accept her if she did. She isn't Maggie—my lovely Maggie."

"Melisande," I said, "is more beautiful than Maggie."

He stared at me for a long time. "In whose eyes," he said. "Certainly, not in mine."

It was the last time I saw either.

* * *

I sat for a moment in silence, then I said, "You amaze me, George. I was actually touched."

It was a poor choice of words. George said, "That reminds me, old fellow— Could I touch you for five dollars for about a week. Ten days tops."

I reached for a five-dollar bill, hesitated, then said, "Here! The story is worth it. It's a gift. It's yours." (Why not! All loans to George are gifts *de facto*.)

George took the bill without comment and put it in his well-worn wallet. (It must have been well-worn when he bought it, for he never uses it.) He said, "To get back to the subject. Could I touch you for five dollars for about a week. Ten days tops."

I said, "But you *have* five dollars."

"That is *my* money," said George, "and no business of yours. Do I comment on the state of your finances when you borrow money from me?"

"But I have never—" I began, then sighed and handed over five dollars more.

# The Quiet Place

Emmanuel Rubin, who was host of the Black Widowers banquet that evening, had been at his loudest and most quarrelsome.

He had insisted on the unimportance of algebra to Roger Halsted who taught the subject in a junior high school; denounced the patent system to Geoffrey Avalon, who was a patent lawyer; denied the validity of quantum theory in connection with molecular structure to James Drake, the chemist; pointed out the uselessness of espionage in modern warfare to Thomas Trumbull, the cipher expert; and finally placed the cherry on the sundae by watching Mario Gonzalo, as, with consummate ease and skill, he drew a cartoon of that evening's guest, and telling him he knew nothing at all about caricature.

Trumbull, who, of all the Black Widowers, was least likely to be amused by Rubin in his wilder moments, finally said, "What the devil is wrong with you, Manny? We're used to having you wrong at the top of your voice, and taking on one or another of us with some indefensible point of view, but this time you're tackling us all."

It was Rubin's guest who answered Trumbull in a quiet voice and, at that, it was almost the first time he had spoken that evening. He was a young man, not far gone into his thirties, it would appear, with thin blond hair, light blue eyes, a face that was wide across the cheekbones, and a smile that seemed to come easily and yet had something sad about it. His name was Theodore Jarvik.

"I'm afraid, gentlemen, the fault is mine, if it be a fault to follow professional procedure. I have recently become Manny's editor and I was forced to hand back his latest manuscript with requests for revision."

"For eviscerative revision," muttered Rubin.

"I did offer to cancel out the invitation for this evening," said Jarvik, with his sad smile, "on the supposition that Manny would just as soon not look at me right now."

Gonzalo raised his eyebrows and said, "Manny doesn't mind this sort of thing. We've all heard him say about a thousand times that the true professional writer takes revisions and even rejections in stride. He says that one way you can tell an amateur or a beginner is by noting that he considers his every word sac—"

"Oh, shut up, Mario," said Rubin, clearly chafing. "You don't know the details."

"Actually," said Jarvik, "Manny and I will work it out."

Avalon, from his 74 inches of height said, in his grave baritone, "I'm curious, Manny, have you called Mr. Jarvik a 'young punk' yet?"

"Oh, for God's sake," said Rubin, reddening.

"No, he hasn't, Mr. Avalon," said Jarvik, "but he's *thought* it very loudly."

"That is *not true*," shouted Rubin, at the top of his considerable decibel rating.

"Let's wash out this night," said Drake, in resignation. "You're going to be in such a foul humor, Manny, that—"

"When have I *ever* been in a foul—" began Rubin and then, Henry, the pearl-beyond-price of waiters, interrupted.

"Gentlemen, please be seated," he said. "Dinner is served."

* * *

To due Rubin justice, he did his best to control himself during the dinner. His eyes, behind his thick glasses, flashed; his sparse beard bristled; and he snarled unceasingly; but he managed to say little and leave the conversation to the others.

Gonzalo, who sat next to Jarvik, said to him, "Pardon me, but you keep humming."

Jarvik flushed again, something his fair skin made easy. "I'm sorry, I didn't mean to disturb you."

"It doesn't exactly disturb me. It's just that I don't recognize the tunc."

"I don't know. I'm just improvising, I suppose."

"Is that so?" and Gonzalo was quiet for the remainder of the dinner until the rattle of spoon on glass marked the beginning of the questioning of the guest.

Gonzalo said, "May I volunteer to do the grilling?"

"You can for all of me," growled Rubin, who, as host, had the task of appointing the griller. "Just don't ask him to justify his existence. The editor doesn't live who can do that."

"On the contrary," said Gonzalo, "any editor who has handed back a manuscript of yours has already justified his existence a hundred times over."

Halsted said, "May I suggest we go ahead with grilling our guest and not needling each other?"

Gonzalo brushed some imaginary dust off the sleeve of his loudly checked jacket and said, "Exactly. Mr. Jarvik, during the course of the dinner I asked you what tune you were humming and you said you were improvising. I don't think that's quite right. Once or twice you hummed again after that and it was always the same tune. Now that you are being grilled, you are forced to give full and honest answers, as I hope Manny has explained to you. I therefore repeat: What was the tune you were humming?"

Trumbull intervened. "What kind of stupid question is that?"

Gonzalo turned a haughty face on Trumbull. "As the griller, I am under the impression I can ask any question I choose consistent with human dignity. Host's decision."

"Go ahead, Manny," said Rubin, thus appealed to. "Ask away.—And leave him alone, Tom."

Gonzalo said, "Answer the question, Mr. Jarvik." And when Jarvik still hesitated, Gonzalo said, "I'll help you out. This is the tune," and he hummed a few bars.

Avalon said, at once, "I know what that is. It's 'The Lost Chord.' The music is by Arthur Sullivan of the Gilbert and Sullivan operettas. Except for those operettas, Sullivan is known only for the music to two songs. One is 'Onward, Christian Soldiers' and the other is the aforementioned 'The Lost Chord.' "

"Is that what you were humming, Jarvik?"

"I suppose so. You know how a song gets trapped in your mind and won't get out."

There was a chorus of agreement from the others and Avalon said, sententiously, "It's a universal complaint."

"Well, whenever I'm trapped in some sort of loudness," said Jarvik, "that song keeps going through my head."

Drake chuckled. "If you're going to be dealing with Manny, you'll be humming it till either you or he dies."

Gonzalo said, "Does it have some significance in that connection? What are the words."

"I only know a few words, actually."

"*I* know the words," said Avalon.

"Don't sing them," cried out Trumbull in sudden alarm.

Avalon, whose singing voice was well-known to resemble the sound of an alligator in heat, said, with dignity, "I shall recite them. The words are by a lady named Adelaide Anne Proctor, concerning whom I know nothing, and the poem goes as follows:" (He cleared his throat)

"Seated one day at the organ, I was weary and ill at ease
And my fingers wondered idly over the noisy keys.
I don't know what I was playing, or what I was dreaming then;
But I struck one chord of music, like the sound of a great Amen.
It flooded the crimson twilight, like the close of an angel's psalm,
And it lay on my fevered spirit with a touch of infinite calm.
It quieted pain and sorrow, like love overcoming strife;
It seemed like the harmonious echo from our discordant life.
It linked all perplexed meanings into one perfect peace,
And trembled away into silence as if it were loth to cease.
I have sought, but I seek it vainly, that one lost chord divine,
Which came from the soul of the organ, and entered into mine.
It may be that Death's bright angel will speak in that chord again,
It may be that only in Heaven shall I hear that grand Amen."

There was a short silence and then Halsted said, "You know, I wonder about that. I don't know how many different chords you can strike on a large organ considering all the different stops you can push and pull and the things you do with your feet. I suppose it is a very large number indeed and you're not likely to find a particular chord just by fooling around at random."

Rubin said, testily, "We'll leave it to your mathematical bent to work out the total number of chords, Roger. As for you, Ted Jarvik, we can at least see why you hum that song when things are noisy. All that talk about infinite calm and one perfect peace and trembling away into silence. Naturally, your mind reverts to the song."

"No," said Jarvik quietly, shaking his head, "that's not it."

"Hah," shouted Gonzalo in triumph. "I knew it. I knew it. I have a sixth sense about these things. What is it? What does that song mean to you?"

"Quiet, Mario," said Avalon. "Now, Mr. Jarvik, if Mario has managed to touch a sore point, something about which you do not like to speak, please do so anyway. I assure you nothing you say will ever leave this room."

Jarvik looked about at the assembled Black Widowers in bewilderment, and said, "How did this ever manage to come up? It's a sore point, certainly, but I can talk about it without trouble. It's just something that's totally uninteresting to anyone but me."

"You can never tell," said Gonzalo, grinning.

Henry refilled the brandy glasses, and Jarvik sighed and began:

* * *

I'm a quiet man said Jarvik as perhaps you can tell. I'm told it shows. There's something ironic in the fact that I have to live and work in Manhattan, but a man must earn a living.

Still, I'm a single man; I don't have a wife and children to support—not yet, anyway—and I can indulge myself now and then. So, two or three times a year I take a week off and go to a resort up the Hudson river. It's a large rambling mansion, with a Victorian atmosphere. The clientele is composed largely of people who are middle aged or older and everything about the place is staid and respectable. Even the young people who happen to come there, are impressed, or perhaps *oppressed*, by the atmosphere and behave themselves.

It means that it is quiet to some degree and, at night, particularly, it is very quiet. Soothing. I love it and, naturally, I try to escape even the noise that exists. People will talk after all and since there are hundreds in the house at all times, the talk can mount up. There are also vehicles—trucks, lawn-mowers and so on.

However, the place is set in an estate of thousands of acres of hilly woodland laced by road and pathways, some of which are very rough indeed. It's my particular pleasure to walk those pathways, looking for some place where I can see only trees and huge glacier-brought rocks, seat myself in one of the gazebos that dot the roads and look at the wildness of the scenery and listen to the silence. There are, of course, the calling of the birds, the rustling of the leaves—but that is no bother. Such natural sounds simply punctuate and emphasize the silence.

But no matter where I go, where I sit, sooner or later, usually sooner, I can hear human voices. There are groups, tramping on nearby trails, or following along the one I just took. I always found it irritating and would feel invaded. It's silly, I know. After all, I was only one of hundreds, but I felt I ought to be undisturbed. I would get up and keep on wandering, looking always for a quiet place, a really quiet place—and never finding it.

One time, as I was sitting in one of my favorite gazebos, a man passed, looked at me, hesitated a moment, and said, in half a whisper, "May I join you?"

I nodded. I couldn't refuse, though I resented him at once; and I couldn't rise and immediately leave without being unbearably discourteous.

After we had been there, in utter silence, some five minutes, the inevitable sound of conversation came from up the road, and there was an explosion of feminine laughter. My new-found companion grimaced and said, "Isn't that annoying?"

My heart warmed to him at once. I shook my head. "You can't get away from it."

He said, "In one place you can," then stopped short as though he had been trapped into saying too much. But I waited with an inquiring look on my face, and didn't say anything, and he said, "There's a place I discovered three-four years ago. —Would you like to see it?"

"Quiet?"

"Oh, yes."

"That would be nice."

"Come with me." He rose, and looked about as if he were taking his bearings. It was a beautifully sunny day, clear blue sky, unclouded, not too warm at all, so when he set off, I followed gladly.

I didn't like to speak, but finally, I had to say, "I haven't seen you about."

"I'm usually out on the trails."

"So am I," I said, my heart warming further. "Ted Jarvik is my name," I said, putting out my hand.

He took it and shook it heartily. "Call me Dark Horse," he said.

And at this point, he suddenly walked right into the woods and began scrambling through and around the underbrush. I was glad I had on a pair of slacks. Had it been warmer, I might have been in shorts and I would undoubtedly have been plant-scratched and insect-bitten. As it was, I followed dutifully.

I couldn't make out where he was going. There was no path and we were clambering over boulders as though we were mountain-climbing. Despite the coolness of the day, I was puffing, hot, and sweaty before long. Finally, we stopped for a bit under the hemlocks and my companion said, "I usually stop here to catch my breath. It takes me longer these days."

I panted a bit, welcoming the break, and said, "How do you know where you're going?"

"Landmarks. A tree that looks just so. A rock with a particular pattern of moss. I notice these things automatically and don't forget them. It's just a knack, but I never get lost."

I said, ruefully, "You're lucky. I have no sense of direction at all. I get irretrievably lost in hotel corridors. Maids have to take me by the hand and lead me to my room."

My companion laughed and said, "I'm sure you have many talents. My inability to get lost is the only one I've got."

"You said your name is Dark Horse. You're not an Indian, are you? A Native American?" I was staring at him. He looked as little an Indian as I did.

"Not at all. It's not my name. I just said to call me that. You see I believe if you really want to come out on a vacation, you should shuck all the paraphernalia of your ordinary life. I have to give my real name to the hotel, because I have to make a reservation and I have to use my credit card, but while I'm here, I won't be called by my name. Nor will I talk about my business. I simply won't recognize any part of my ordinary self. Whatever I am, officially, is back in Manhattan. It isn't here."

I was struck by that. "Interesting idea. I ought to do the same. Not that I'm very social when I come up here."

He said, "Rested a bit? Let's go then. We don't have much farther."

I tried to watch where he turned and to observe landmarks, but it was no use. I'm not a noticing man. To me, a tree is a tree and a rock is a rock. —But then we half-slid downward into a hollow and Dark Horse whispered, "This is it."

I looked about. The rocks enclosed us on almost every side. There were trees growing between them here and there. Ferns flourished. It was cool, very cool, welcomingly cool.

Above all else, it was quiet. There was not a sound. A rustle of leaves now and then. A faint insect stridulation. Once a brief bird call. But it was quiet, a healing silence in a world which was one large, long, eternal cacophony of noise.

There was a rocky ledge at a convenient height and my companion indicated it silently. We sat down and I let the silence flow into me. What did the poem say? 'It lay on my fevered spirit with a touch of infinite calm.'

We sat there half an hour and in all that time, I said nothing, and my companion said nothing, and there was not a human sound of any kind. No distant laughter, no crackle of far-off conversation, no vibration of any internal-combustion engine. Nothing. I had never experienced anything like it.

Finally, my companion rose and without saying anything asked the question as to whether we ought to go now. Reluctantly, and without saying anything, I answered that we might.

Out we went. We were a quarter mile away before I dared speak. "How did you find the quiet place?" I asked.

"Accident at first. Since then, I've gone back half a dozen times at least. I love it. It's somewhere out of reach of all the trails and, as far as I know, it's not on any of the hotel maps and it's just a hidden undiscovered nook, known only to me, I think—and now you."

"Thanks for showing me. Really," I said, with infinite gratitude. "You wouldn't think there would be a spot untrodden by human feet in a place like this."

"Why not?" said Dark Horse. "I imagine that all over the world, there are little areas undisturbed by humanity, sometimes in places that are very busy and crowded overall. There are fewer than there used to be, I'm sure, and perhaps someday they'll be all gone—but not yet, not yet."

He led me back to one of the main trails without hesitation. We scrambled over rocks and roots and through the underbrush again and to me it seemed it was uphill both ways—but he got us back. I said good-bye and thanked him again and we shook hands. I went back to the room, got cleaned up and was eventually ready for dinner.

I didn't see him at dinner, though I looked and, in fact, I didn't see him again during the remainder of the stay. To put it baldly, I have never seen him again from that day to this.

The day after he had taken me to the quiet place, I tried to return on my own. I took a book with me and some sandwiches I had begged at the kitchen, and it was my intention to stay there most of the day if the weather held, but of course I never made it. I had no luck at all. I was wrong from the first turning, I believe.

I didn't give up, though. After I returned to the city, I kept dreaming of the quiet place and as soon as I could manage, I returned to the resort, studied the map and marked off the area that I felt must contain it. I could make my way to the gazebo where I met Dark Horse and, from there, I set about a systematic course of exploration.

It did me no good whatever. I could never find the place. No matter how I tried to remember the twists and turns; no matter how I kidded myself into believing I recognized one of those blasted trees or rocks, no matter what bogs I slogged through, what crags I stumbled over, I ended up nowhere. I had bites, and scratches, and bruises, and contusions, and sprains. What I didn't have was the place.

I think it's become an obsession with me. I happened to know that passage of "The Lost Chord" and I suppose I began to hear it go through my head with appropriate changes in words, "I have sought, but I seek it vainly, That one lost place divine, From which came the spirit of silence that entered into me."

And I suppose I hum it when things grow loud and chaotic—

* * *

There was a pronounced pause when Jarvik concluded.

Finally, Halsted said, "I suppose you simply need this fellow who took you there to take you there again so that you can mark off each twist and turn on the map as best you can."

Gonzalo said, hesitantly, "I suppose the fellow really existed. You didn't dream it, did you?"

Jarvik frowned. "Believe me, I didn't dream it. And he wasn't an elf leading me into fairyland, either. It happened exactly as I told you. The problem is that he had a precise sense of direction and I have none at all."

"Then you ought to find him," said Rubin, flatly, "if you're that stuck on being in the middle of nowhere."

"Fine," said Jarvik. "I agree. I ought to find him. Now tell me how. I don't know his room number. I don't know his name. It didn't occur to me to try to identify him at the front desk that evening or the next day."

He shook his head and seemed to debate with himself whether to go on or not. Then he shrugged and said, "I might as well tell you how obsessed I've become. The last time I was at the resort, I spent half the day with the various desk-employees trying to get a list of the people who had been at the hotel the day on which I was taken to the quiet place.

"It took a lot of negotiating and a lot of scurrying through records, and then they were kind enough to make me up an alphabetized list containing two hundred forty-nine names. They did it for me because I was a regular customer and because I spread fifty dollars among them.

"They didn't include addresses because they said that was against policy and if they were caught doing that they would be fired and blacklisted and who knows what else. I had to make do with the list of names. I made one last effort to find the place the next day—and failed, of course, and then spent the remainder of the stay studying the list of names.

"And you know, I've memorized them. Not on purpose, of course. I just memorized them. I can rattle them off in the alphabetical order in which they were arranged. I happen to have one of those memories." He brooded a little, "If my sense of direction were as good as my memory for trivial items on a list; that is, if my sense of observation could give me small variations I could then remember; I suppose I wouldn't be in the fix I am now."

Drake said, frowning through the smoke of his cigarette, "How would the list of names help you?"

Jarvik said, "The first thing that occurred to me was that the false name he used must have some reason behind it. Why would anyone call himself Dark Horse? Possibly because the initials were the same as those of his real name. So I went through the list and there was only one D. H. and the name was Dora Harboard. Well, whatever my friend was, he was not a woman, so that was out.

"Then I thought that perhaps the initials were reversed. So I looked for an H. D. and there was none. Then I looked for unattached males. A great many people were listed as, let us say, Ira and Hortense Abel, to take the first names on the list. It seemed to me I ought to eliminate them, especially if they had children with them. That left me with seventeen unattached males and at first I thought that that was a big advancement.

"But then I realized that Dark Horse gave me no indication that he was unattached. He might well have had a wife and child back in his room, or out attending the mah jong game that was being played in the lounge that afternoon."

Trumbull said, "You could try *force majeure*. Follow up every male name on the list and see if one of them is Dark Horse. Who knows, you might strike it lucky the first name you try. And you know he lives in Manhattan. He said so. Try the phone book to begin with."

Jarvik said, "One of the people listed is S. Smith. I dread the thought of how many Smiths there are in the phone book with S as the first initial. Besides, if I recall correctly, he said that whatever he was officially was back in Manhattan. It seems to me that meant he worked in Manhattan but not necessarily that he lived there. He could live in any of the five boroughs, or in New Jersey, or Connecticut, or Westchester.

"Listen, I've thought of *force majeure*. Just to show you, I thought that I might hire someone at some small nearby airfield to fly me over the resort so that I could see the spot from above, but I know I wouldn't recognize it. Not from above, in a hurried pass. And even if I did, they'd have to land me back at the airport and if I then tried to reach the quiet place from the ground I'd fail again.

"Then I thought that perhaps I could hire a helicopter and if I recognized the spot, I could have myself lowered by some sort of rope while the helicopter hovered over-head. That's ridiculous, though. I wouldn't have the nerve to dangle from a helicopter even if I recognized the place and then, after I left it, what if I still couldn't find my way back. I couldn't very well use a helicopter every time, could I?"

Gonzalo said, "Dark Horse! Isn't that a racing term?"

"Originally, yes," said Avalon. "It refers to some horse of unknown potential that might have an outside chance to win, especially if it enters a race in which all the other horses are known quantities."

"Why *dark* horse, then?" said Halsted.

"I presume," said Avalon, "as an indication of how minimal the information is. After all, most horses are dark in coloring. Besides, 'dark' gives the impression of mystery, of the unknown."

"Well," said Gonzalo, "perhaps this fellow has some connection with the racing game."

Jarvik said, bitterly, "Fine. Suppose he does. How does that help me find him?"

"Besides," said Trumbull. "It seems to me that 'dark horse' has spread out to mean anyone who enters a contest without being a known item. In boxing, tennis; in politics, even."

"And how does *that* help me find him?" said Jarvik.

Avalon sighed heavily and said, "Mr. Jarvik, why don't we look at 'The Lost Chord' from another angle? Roger Halsted pointed out that a complex organ might have many, many varieties of chords and that one chord could be easily lost among the quantity. But that is surely a way of looking at it that is rather too simplistic.

"Any sensation consists of the sensation itself, objectively, and of the person receiving the sensation, subjectively. The same chord is always the same chord if it is measured by an instrument that analyzes its wave function. However, the chord one *hears* may well vary with the mood and immediate circumstances of the listener.

"The person playing the organ in the poem was 'weary and ill at ease.' For that reason, the chord had a particular effect on him. 'It quieted pain and sorrow' which he may have been feeling. From then on, when he sought the chord again, his mood would be one of anxious expectation, of careful attention. Even if he heard the same chord again, the *same* chord precisely, it would not strike him in the same way and he would not consider it to be the same chord. No wonder he sought it vainly. He was seeking to duplicate not only the chord but himself as he had been."

Jarvik said, "You are saying?"

"I am saying, Mr. Jarvik," said Avalon, "that perhaps you ought to attach less importance to the place. You found it on a perfect day. You found it when someone else was guiding you there so that you were, in a sense, carefree. If you find it again a second time, it may be on a less desirable day—when it is hotter, or colder, or cloudier. You yourself will be seeking anxiously, you will not be at ease. The result is that it may not be the same place you remember. You will be bitterly disappointed. Would it not be better to remain with the memory and let it go at that?"

Jarvik's head bent and for a few moments, he seemed lost in thought. Then he said, "Thank you, Mr. Avalon. I think you're right.

If I fail to find the place, I will certainly try to follow your advice and find solace in it. However— I would like, if I can, to find it once more, just to make sure. After all, Dark Horse found it a number of times, and enjoyed it each time."

"Dark Horse knew how to get there," said Avalon. "His own mood was fairly constant, and it might be he always chose days of particularly favorable weather to go there."

"Even so," said Jarvik, stubbornly. "I would like to find it once more, if there were only a way of finding it."

"But apparently there isn't," said Avalon. "You must admit that."

"I don't know," said Mario. "No one has asked Henry."

"In this case," said Avalon, stubbornly, "even Henry can do nothing. There is nothing to seize on."

"What have we to lose?" demanded Mario. "Henry, what can you tell us?"

Jarvik, who had been listening in astonishment, now turned to Rubin and jerking his thumb over his shoulder, mouthed silently: The waiter?

Rubin put a finger to his lips and shook his head slightly.

Henry, who had been listening with absorption, said, "I must say that I agree fully with Mr. Avalon with respect to the subjective nature of the charms of the place and would hate to have Mr. Jarvik spoil an idyllic memory. Nevertheless—"

"Aha," said Gonzalo. "Go on, Henry."

Henry smiled in his avuncular fashion, and said, "Nevertheless, the one thing to seize upon is the phrase 'dark horse', which everyone has been seizing upon, as it happens. May I ask, Mr. Jarvik, if, by any chance, there was anyone on the list named Polk—not a very common name. A James Polk, perhaps."

Jarvik's eyes opened wide. "You're kidding."

"Not at all. May I take it there *was* such a name?"

"There's a J. Polk certainly. It could be James."

"Then perhaps that is your man."

"But why?"

"Mr. Trumbull mentioned I believe that 'dark horse' is used in politics. That, I suspect, is its most common use these days. A dark horse is some politician who is never thought of in connection with nomination by a major party, but who is nevertheless nominated as a way of breaking what otherwise seems an intransigeant deadlock. Nowadays, dark horses rarely show up because the nomination is decided by primary contests. However, as recently as 1940, Wendell Willkie was a dark horse named by the Republican party.

"However, the name is most often used in American history for the very first party nominee who was a dark horse. In 1844, the Democrats were all set to nominate ex-President Martin Van Buren, but he needed a two-thirds majority and intransigeant Southern opposition prevented that. Out of sheer weariness, the convention switched to Tennessee Senator, James Knox Polk, whom no one had thought of in connection with the nomination. He was the first dark-horse candidate, and went on to win the election. He made a pretty good one-term President."

"He's right," said Rubin. "Do you know everything, Henry?"

"No, Mr. Rubin," said Henry, "but I had a dim memory of it and while the discussion was going on, I checked our reference shelf. It may be that the J. Polk on Mr. Jarvik's list is a lineal, or collateral descendant, which is why he took the name of Dark Horse."

"Amazing," muttered Jarvik.

"However," said Henry, "you may still have trouble finding him, Mr. Jarvik, and even if you find him, he may still be the wrong person, and even if he is the right person, you may still end up disappointed in the quiet place. However—may good luck be with you."

# I Love Little Pussy

George and I were sitting on a park bench on a perfect late spring day when a rather ordinary tabby cat wandered into our vicinity. I knew there were feral cats in the park that would be dangerous to approach, but this specimen had the inquisitive look of a tame pussy. Since I am proud of the fact that cats are attracted to me, I held out my hand and sure enough she sniffed at it and allowed me to stroke her head.

I was rather surprised to hear George mutter, "Wretched little beast."

"Don't you like cats, George?" I asked.

"Would you expect me to, in the light of my sad history?" he said, sighing heavily.

"I know your history is sad," I said. "Inevitably so, considering your character, but I didn't know that cats had a role in it."

"That," said George, "is because I never told you of my second cousin, Andromache."

"Andromache?"

* * *

Her father [said George] was a classical scholar, hence the name. He also had a little money, which he left to Cousin Andromache on the occasion of his early death and she, by shrewd investment, considerably increased it.

He did not include me in his bounty. I was a child of five at the time of his death and he could scarcely have left me anything outright, but a more generous soul would have set up a trust fund.

As I grew older, however, I realized that Cousin Andromache, who was 22 years older than I, might well predecease me. It did occur to me—for I was a precocious lad, thoughtful and far-sighted—that, in that case, I might receive a sizable share of the loot.

—Yes, provided, as you say, that I sucked up to her. Please do not try to anticipate my words, however, for that is not the phraseology I intended to use. What I was going to say was that I realized I might inherit a portion of her estate if I gave her the warmth and affection she so richly deserved.

As it happened, Cousin Andromache needed warmth and affection not only richly, but also desperately. When I was still in my teens and she was approaching forty, I realized that she was a dedicated spinster, untouched by human hands. Even at my tender age, I found the situation understandable. She was tall and rawboned, with a long plain face, large teeth, small eyes, limp hair, and no figure worth mentioning.

I said to her once, out of a natural curiosity to determine how unlikely an event might be and yet come to pass, "Cousin Andromache, has any fellow ever asked you to marry him?"

She turned a threatening face on me and said, "Asked me to marry *him*? Hah! I'd like to see some fellow ask to to marry *him*!"

(I rather thought she would indeed like to see it happen, but I had early reached the years of discretion and did not put the thought into words.)

She went on, "If any man ever has the *gall* to ask me to marry *him*, I'll give *him* what for. I'll show *him* a thing or two. I'll teach *him* to approach a respectable woman with any of his lollygagging notions."

I didn't quite see what was lollygagging about a marriage proposal, or what might be in it to offend a respectable woman, but I didn't think it would be wise—or even safe—to ask.

For a few years, I kept hoping that some person, perverse enough to be interested in Cousin Andromache, might indeed make a suggestion or two because I wanted to see what she would do—while I remained at a safe distance, to be sure. There seemed, however, no chance of that. Not even her gathering wealth seemed to suffice to make her an object of marriageability to the male half of the population. One and all, it seemed, weighed the price that would have to be paid, and one and all turned away.

An abstract consideration of the situation showed me that it was exactly what I wanted. A Cousin Andromache without husband and without children would be less apt to dismiss a second cousin as a testamentary possibility. Furthermore, since she was an only child, the vicissitudes of life had left her with no relative closer than I was. That seemed an appropriate situation for me, since it meant I didn't have to work *too* hard at supplying affection. A little bit, now and then, to reinforce my position as the natural heir, would be quite enough.

When she passed that fortieth milestone, however, it must have seemed to her that if no human male wished to dare her wrath with a proposal of marriage, she would make use of a non-human companion, instead.

She disliked dogs, because she had the notion that, one and all, they lusted to bite her. I would have liked to reassure her that no dog, however gaunt, would find her a toothsome morsel, but I had the feeling this would not reassure her, and would cripple me, so I kept silent on the matter.

She also thought that horses were too large for comfort, and hamsters too small, so she finally persuaded herself that what she wanted was a cat.

Thereupon, she obtained a little grey female kitten of nondescript appearance and bestowed every bit of her ungainly affection upon it.

With an appalling lack of even a modicum of wit, she named the kitten "Pussy" and that name was retained by the cat forever after, despite changes in size and temperament.

What's more, she took to cuddling the kitten and saying, in a revoltingly hoarse sing-song:

"I love little pussy, her coat is so warm
And if I don't tease her, she'll do me no harm.
I'll pet her and stroke her, and give her some food,
And pussy will love me because I'm so good."

It was simply nauseating.

I won't conceal from you, old man, that I was quite perturbed at first. Thoughts danced through my mind of besotted old maids who left all their money to their pampered, uncaring pets.

It did occur to me, as to whom would it not, that the kitten could easily be kidnapped and drowned, or taken to the zoo and fed to the lions, but then Cousin Andromache would merely get another.

Besides, she might suspect me of a hand in the felicide. Considering the paranoia peculiar to spinsters, I knew that it was perfectly possible for her to get it into her head that I was primarily after her money and that she could interpret many things in that light and come fearsomely near the truth. In fact, I strongly suspected that she had already gotten it into her head.

It occurred to me, therefore, to invert matters. Why not display a passionate love of the kitten? I took to playing moronic games with it, dangling a piece of string for it to fight with, stroking it (sometimes, a little longingly, in the region of its neck), and feeding it tid-bits — sometimes even (when Cousin Andromache was watching) from my own plate.

I must say it worked. Cousin Andromache softened distinctly. I presume she reasoned that I couldn't possibly be after Pussy's money, for she had none, so she chalked it up to the pure and unalloyed love I had for all of God's creatures. I helped strengthen that notion by telling her, in fervent tones, of how pure my love for them was. It made her accept my love for her with fewer fears concerning any ulterior motives I happened to have.

However, the trouble with a kitten's that eventually it becomes a cat. —Oh, did Ogden Nash say that also? Well, my best bits are constantly being stolen. I'm quite resigned to it.

I don't know, old man, if you have ever owned a cat, but with age, they grow larger, more self-centered, more self-assured, more contemptuous of their owners, more inert, more utterly uninterested in anything but food and sleep. The last thing on their contemptible little minds is the comfort and peace of mind of the person who feeds them.

In addition, Pussy grew rather ill-tempered. It had always seemed to me that tabby cats are comparatively placid and that it is the tomcats who are aggressive. It was clear, however, that Pussy had the disposition of a tomcat, despite her sex,—and an unaltered tomcat at that. What's more, she seemed quite intolerant of me and would deliberately go out of her path in order to pass near me and scratch me surreptitiously. I tell you, old man, I could almost believe the beast could read my mind.

Considering Pussy's disposition, it is not at all surprising that Cousin Andromache went into a small decline. I found her in tears one day, or as close to tears as her tough and scraggy temperament would allow her to be.

"Oh, Cousin George," she said to me, "Pussy doesn't love me."

Pussy was, at the time, sprawled in comfort five feet away and was looking at Cousin Andromache with haughty distaste—its usual expression except when it looked at me, at which time the expression became one of settled hate.

I called the creature to my side, whereupon it favored me with a sneer and a bit of a snarl and stayed where it was. I strode to her and picked her up. She weighed 14 pounds of solid inertia and the task was not an easy one, particularly since she kept adjusting her right forepaw (the most dangerous one) into a position where a rapid swipe could be made.

I clutched both her forepaws to prevent that, whereupon she hung in such a way as to double the pull of gravity upon her. I believe that only cats and truly obnoxious human infants know the secret and I am constantly surprised that scientists do not investigate the phenomenon.

I placed her in Cousin Andromache's lap, pointed at the tableau and said, "See, Cousin Andromache, Pussy loves you."

But I had taken my mind off the malignant devil, so that she had the chance of biting my pointing finger, and promptly did so to the bone. She then got off Cousin Andromache's lap and walked away.

Cousin Andromache wailed, "You see, she doesn't love me!" Characteristically, she said nothing about my massacred finger.

I sucked bitterly at the damage and said, "That's the way cats are. Why not give Pussy to someone you hate and get a new kitten."

"Oh, no," said Cousin Andromache, turning on me one of her censorious looks. "I love little Pussy. Isn't there some way of training a cat to display affection?"

I longed to make some clever comment to the effect that it would be easier to train Cousin Andromache to be pretty, and was able to suppress the longing only because a brilliant idea had illuminated the interior of my skull.

I had recently formed my friendship with Azazel, whom I may have mentioned to you. —Oh, I did? Well, all right. You needn't add "ad nauseum" merely to display your knowledge of Latin.

In any case, why shouldn't I use Azazel's abilities in this respect? What was the use of having a two-centimeter extraterrestrial being of advanced technological abilities on call, so to speak, if one didn't make use of it?

I said, "Cousin Andromache, I believe I could train Pussy to show you affection."

"*You?*" she said, nastily. It was a word, and an intonation, she had used on me before, and I often thought how effectively I would resent it if I were only in a position to do so safely.

But the idea was looking better and better to me as I pictured Cousin Andromache's gratitude to me if I could pull it off.

"Cousin Andromache," I said, earnestly, "let me have Pussy for one day—*one day*. I will then bring back a loving Pussy who will ask for nothing better than to sit in your lap and purr in your ear."

Cousin Andromache hesitated. "Are you sure you will be kind to her while you have her. You know, Pussy is a very sensitive creature, shy and gentle."

Yes, indeed, about as shy and gentle as a particularly irritated grizzly bear.

"I would take very good care of her, Cousin Andromache," I murmured insinuatingly.

And, in the end, Cousin Andromache's longing for an affectionate Pussy overcame her uncertainties and she gave her permission with many an injunction to keep the little thing from being harmed by the cruel, outside world.

Of course, I had to buy a cage first, one with bars as thick as my thumb. This I felt might retain Pussy, if she didn't get too angry, and off we went together.

* * *

Azazel didn't get as angry in those days as he does now when I call him up. He was curious about Earth in those days.

On this occasion, though, what he was, was terrified. He screamed all but ultrasonically. It pierced my eardrums like an icepick.

"What's the matter?" I said, my hands over the affected organs.

"That creature." Azazel's tail pointed to Pussy. "What is it?"

I turned to look at Pussy. It had flattened itself at the bottom of the cage. Its wicked green eyes stared at Azazel with fixed longing. Its tail twitched slowly and then it launched itself at the bars of the cage, which shook and rattled. Azazel screamed again.

"It's just a cat," I said, soothingly. "A little kitten."

"Put me in your pocket," shrieked Azazel. "Put me in your pocket."

On the whole, that seemed a good idea. I plunked him into my shirt-pocket where he trembled like a tuning fork and Pussy, angered and puzzled at his disappearance, spat her displeasure.

Finally, I could make out coherent words from within my pocket.

"Oh, my supple tail," moaned Azazel. "It is just like a drakopathan—just like. They're ferocious beasts that bite and claw and tear, but this cat thing is much bigger and more ferocious by the look of it. Why have you exposed me to this, O Excrescence of a Rubbishy Planet?"

"O Fearless Master of the Universe," I said, "it is precisely in connection with this animal, whose name is Pussy, that I need a demonstration of your matchless might."

"No, no," came his muffled cry.

"It is to make him a better cat. I want Pussy to love my Cousin Andromache who owns the animal. I want Pussy to give my cousin affection and tenderness and sweetness—"

Azazel poked a frightened eye over the top of the pocket and stared at Pussy for a moment. He said, "That creature has no love in it for anything but itself. That is quite obvious from its C-aura."

"Exactly! You must add love for Cousin Andromache."

"What do you mean, add love. Have you never heard of the Law of Conservation of Emotion, you sub-technological dolt. You can't add love. You can only transfer it from one object within a creature's emotional nexus to another."

"Do so," I said. "Take from the superfluity of love Pussy devotes to herself and fashion a strong attachment to Cousin Andromache."

"Taking from the self-love of that super-drakopathan is a task too formidable. I have seen my people strain their intensifiers permanently at lesser tasks."

"Then take the love from elsewhere in Pussy, O Superlative One. Do you wish word to get out that you failed a challenge so small?'

Vanity was, of course, Azazel's besetting fault, and I could see the possibility I had mentioned was gnawing at him.

He said, "Well, I will try. Do you have a likeness of your cousin? A good likeness?"

I certainly had, though I doubt that any photograph of Cousin Andromache could be both a likenss and good at the same time. Putting that philosophical matter to one side, I had a large cabinet photograph of her that I always placed in a prominent position when she came on a visit. I did have to take the fig tree out of the living room on those occasions, though, for the photo had a tendency to wither its leaves.

Azazel looked at the picture dubiously, and sighed. "Very well," he said, "but remember that this is not magic, but science. I can only work within the limits of the Law of Conservation of Emotion."

But what did I care for Azazel's limits of action as long as he did his job?

* * *

The next day I brought Pussy back to Cousin Andromache. Pussy had always been a strong and malevolent cat, but her indifference to others had induced a customary apathy that had kept her evil nature within bounds. Now, apparently, with her sudden wild love for Cousin Andromache frustrated by the absence of her object of affection, she had turned into a demon. She made it quite plain that, were it not for the bars of her cage, which gave dangerously under her pressure, she would tear me into shreds, and I was sure she could do it.

Pussy's mood changed completely, however, when she spied her mistress. The spitting, snarling, slashing devil became at once a panting, purring, picture of delight. She turned on her back, exposing a massively sinewy belly that she clearly wanted scratched.

Cousin Andromache, with a cry of delight, placed a finger through the bars to oblige. I then opened the gate and Pussy went sailing out into Cousin Andromache's waiting arms, purring as loudly as a truck going over a cobbled road, and striving to strop its rasping tongue on my cousin's leathery cheek.

I will draw the curtain over what followed, because it will not bear description. Suffice it to say that, among other things, Cousin Andromache said to the vile cat, "And did you miss your loving Andromache-Womickey?"

It was enough to make me vomicky, let me tell you.

Stolidly, however, I remained, for I was waiting to hear what I wanted to hear and, finally, Cousin Andromache looked up with a pallid glitter in her opaque little eyes and said, "Thank you, Cousin George. I apologize for doubting you, and I promise you I won't forget this to my dying day and will then make you a suitable return."

"It was my pleasure, Cousin Andromache," I said, "and I hope your dying day is far, far in the future."

What was more, if she had at that moment consented to settle a goodly sum on me effective immediately, I believe I would actually have meant what I said. —Within limits.

* * *

I stayed away from Cousin Andromache for a while, not wishing to push my luck, since my presence in her vicinity had, in the past, always seemed to sour her. —I don't know why.

I did phone her every now and then, though, just to make sure all was well, and, to my continuing delight, all *was* well. At least, she would each time trill coyly into my ear, "I love little Pussy", and then cite nauseating details of the cat's affectionate behavior.

Then, about three months after I had brought back Pussy, Cousin Andromache called and asked me to drop in for lunch. Naturally, under the circumstances, Cousin Andromache's wish was my law, so I hurried over at the set time. Since she had sounded cheerful on the phone, I had no apprehensions.

Nor did I have any when I entered her apartment, even though I nearly slipped to destruction on the throw-rug she kept on her polished floor near the entrance for what I could only assume were homicidal reasons. She greeted me with what was intended, I imagine, as a jolly grin.

"Come in, Cousin George," she said. "Say hello to little Pussy."

I looked down at little Pussy and shied in horror. Little Pussy, perhaps because it was so full of love, had grown still farther, and at a rapid pace. She seemed nearly three feet along exclusive of lashing tail and I judged her to weigh, conservatively, twenty-five pounds of whipcord and gristle. Her eyes were flat, her mouth was open in a silent snarl, her eye-teeth gleamed like burnished needles, and her eyes, as they glared at me, were filled with indescribable loathing. She stood between Cousin Andromache and me quite as though guarding the silly woman against any false move on my part.

I dared make no move at all, for who knew what that monstrous creature might consider false.

I tried to be strong, but there was a distinct quaver in my voice as I said, "Is Pussy safe, Cousin Andromache?"

"Perfectly safe," said Cousin Andromache, giggling rather in the same fashion a rusty hinge would, "for she knows you are a relative and mean me well."

"Good," I said, hollowly, wondering if it were possible for Pussy to read my mind. I decided she couldn't or I would not at that moment have been alive, I'm sure.

Cousin Andromache seated herself on the couch and motioned me to take the armchair. However, I waited till Pussy had also jumped on the couch and had placed her head in Cousin Andromache's lap in luxurious abandon, before daring to move sufficiently to sit down myself.

"Of course," said Cousin Andromache, "my loving little Pussy is just a little unreasonable when she thinks someone is trying to harm me. A couple of weeks ago, the newsboy threw the paper just as I was coming out the door. It hit me on the shoulder. It didn't really hurt, but Pussy was after him like a flash. If he hadn't pedalled his bicycle at top speed, I really don't know what would have happened to him. Now the boy won't return and I have to go out every morning and buy the paper at a news-stand. It is comfortable to know, though, that I'm protected from any mugger or burglar."

At the words "mugger or burglar", Little Pussy seemed to be reminded of me, for she turned to look at me and her eyes blazed with the fires of Hell.

It seemed to me I saw what had happened. After all, hate is negative love.

Pussy had had a mild hatred for everything and everyone but herself and, just possibly, Cousin Andromache. To increase Pussy's love for Andromache, Azazel, following the dictates of the Law of Conservation of Emotion, had to withdraw love from all other objects. Since that love was already negative, it grew more negative than ever. And since Azazel had added love with no sparing hand, the other loves grew *much* more negative. In short, Pussy now hated everyone and everything with an extravagant hatred that had strengthened and enlarged her muscles, sharpened her teeth and claws, and turned her into a killing machine.

Cousin Andromache chattered on. "Last week," she said, "Pussy and I were out for a morning stroll and we met Mr. Walsingham with his Doberman-pinscher. I had every intention of avoiding him and crossing the street, but the dog had seen Pussy and snarled at the little innocent creature. Pussy didn't seem to mind, but it frightened me—I don't like dogs at *all*—and I'm afraid I let out a small shriek. That activated dear little Pussy's protective instinct, and she fell on the dog at once. There was no hope of separating them and the dog, I understand, is still at the vet's. Mr. Walsingham is trying to have Pussy declared a dangerous animal, but of course if was the dog that took the initiative and Pussy was merely acting in my defense."

She hugged Pussy and she said that, placing her face in actual contact with the cat's canines, and with no perceptible nervousness. And then she got to the real reason for the invitation to lunch.

She simpered horribly and said, "But I called you here to give you some news I felt I should tell you personally and not on the telephone. —I have a gentleman caller."

"A what!" I jumped slightly, and Pussy at once rose and arched its back. I quickly froze.

I have since thought it out. It seems clear that the sensation of being loved—even if only by a cat out of Golgotha—had softened Cousin Andromache's sinewy heart and made her ready to gaze with eyes of affection on some poor victim. And who knows? Perhaps the consciousness of being loved had changed her inner being to the point of making her seem marginally toothsome to someone particularly dim of vision and particularly lacking in taste.

But that was a later analysis. At the time Cousin Andromache broke the news, my keen mind quickly grasped the vital point—my prosperous relative might possibly have someone else to whom to leave her cash and possessions.

My first impulse was to rise from my seat, seize Cousin Andromache, and shake some sense of family responsibility into her. My second impulse, following a millisecond later, was not to move a muscle. Pussy's hate-filled eye was on me.

"But Cousin Andromache," I said, "you always told me that if any fellow came lollygagging around you, you'd show *him*! Why not let Pussy show him? That will fix him."

"Oh, no, Hendrik is *such* a nice man and he loves cats, too. He stroked Pussy, and Pussy *let* him. That's when I knew he was all right. Pussy is a good judge of character."

I suppose even Pussy would have trouble matching the look of hatred I let *her* have.

"In any case," said Cousin Andromache, "Hendrik is coming over tonight and I believe he will propose that we formalize conditions by getting married. I wanted you to know."

I tried to say something, but couldn't. I tell you I felt as though I had been thoroughly emptied of my internal organs and I was nothing but hollow skin.

She went on, "I want you also to know, Cousin George, that Hendrik is a retired gentleman, who is quite well off. It is understood between us that, if I predecease him, none of my small savings will go to him. They will go to you, dear Cousin George, as the person who turned Pussy into a loving and efficient companion and protector for me."

Someone had turned the sun and the daylight back on again and all my internal organs were in place once more. It occurred to me, in the merest trice, that if Hendrik predeceased Cousin Andromache, his estate would be very likely added to hers, and would also eventually come to me.

I said, ringingly, "Cousin Andromache. Your money does not concern me. Only your love and your future happiness do. Marry Hendrik, be happy, and live forever. That's all I ask."

I said it with such sincerity, old fellow, that I came within this much of convincing myself I meant it.

* * *

And then, that evening—

I wasn't there, of course, but I found out about it later. Hendrik—seventy, if he was a day, a little over five feet tall and pushing a hundred and eighty pounds in weight—came to call.

She opened the door for him, and skipped skittishly away. He threw his arms wide, called out, "My love!", advanced heavily, slipped on the throw-rug, went hurtling forward into Cousin Andromache feet-first, and bowled her over.

That was all Pussy needed. She knew an attack on her mistress when she saw one. By the time the screaming Andromache pulled the screaming Pussy off screaming Hendrik, it was too late for any hope of a romantic marriage proposal that night. It was indeed very nearly too late for anything at all that would involve Hendrik.

Two days later, I visited him at the hospital at Cousin Andromache's hysterical request. He was still bandaged to the eyebrows and a team of doctors were discussing the various possible strategies of skin-grafting.

I introduced myself to Hendrik, who wept copiously, drenched his bandages, and begged me to tell my fair relative that all this was a visitation upon him for being unfaithful to his first wife, Emmeline, dead these seventeen years, and for even dreaming of marrying anyone at all.

"Tell her," he said, "we will always be the dearest of friends, but I dare not ever see her again, for I am but flesh and blood and the sight of her might arouse loving thoughts and I would then once more be attacked by a grizzly bear."

I carried the sad news to Cousin Andromache, who took to her bed at once, crying out that through her doing, the best of men had been permanently maimed—which was undoubtedly true.

The rest, old man, is unalloyed tragedy. I would have sworn that Cousin Andromache was incapable of dying of a broken heart, but a team of specialists maintained that that was exactly what she proceeded to do. That was sad, I suppose, but the unalloyed tragedy I refer to was that she had had time to alter her will.

In the new will, she expressed her great affection for me and her certainty that I was far too noble to concern myself over a few pennies so that she left her entire estate of $300,000, not to me, but to her lost love, Hendrik, hoping it would make up to him for the suffering and the medical bills he had incurred because of her.

All this was expressed in terms so affecting that the lawyer who read the will to me wept uncontrollably and so, as you can well imagine, did I.

However, I was not entirely forgotten. Cousin Andromache stated in her will that she left me something she knew I would value far more than the paltry dross of cash. In short she had left me Pussy.

* * *

George just sat there, staring numbly at nothingness and I couldn't help saying, "Do you still have Pussy?"

He started, focussed on me with an effort, and said, "No, not exactly. The very day I received her, she was trampled by a horse."

"By a horse!"

"Yes. The horse died of its wounds the next day. A shame, for it was an innocent horse. It's fortunate, on the whole, that no one had seen me open Pussy's cage and shake her into the horse's stall."

His eyes glazed over again, and his lips mouthed, silently: Three—hundred—thousand—dollars!

Then he turned to me and said, "So can you lend me a tenner?"

What could I do?